IN THE SHADOW OF TRUTH

(SHADOW SERIES BOOK 3)

J. E. LEAK

CERTIFIABLY CREATIVE LLC

ISBN 978-1-955294-05-8 (eBook Edition)
ISBN 978-1-955294-06-5 (Paperback Edition)
Library of Congress Control Number: 2022918952
First Printing January 2023
Edited by Pam Greer

Published by Certifiably Creative LLC
Ocala, Florida
press@certifiablycreative.com

Printed and bound in the United States of America

To my wife.

CHAPTER ONE

July 1943: Long Island, New York

As a new field agent trainee, Jenny Ryan didn't know what to expect when she arrived at the Office of Strategic Services training center on Long Island. A long gravel drive twisted through neglected grounds, now overgrown with wild blueberry bushes, pines, and oaks. The main house had fallen into disrepair and disuse, as the winds of fortune changed and heirs moved on to smaller dwellings, so the OSS used only a small portion of the mansion's one hundred and ten rooms.

They had built simple wooden structures as classrooms on the expansive grounds, and this is where Jenny spent her time. She'd come a long way from newspaper columnist, writing human interest stories and movie reviews at her uncle's newspaper, to OSS field agent, but this is what she wanted—to do something important. Help win the war.

She was excited, but nervous, knowing this class brought her one step closer to harm's way. As an added complication, her lover, OSS agent Kathryn Hammond, stood six feet away, at the head of the class, looking disarmingly attractive in her olive drab slacks and matching collared shirt, with the top button modestly undone. She was a civilian, so she didn't wear a uniform with insignia, but, mercy, it didn't take away from the hypnotizing effect.

"Any questions?" Kathryn asked, as she swept her eyes across the serious faces of the nine eager recruits in the class. There were ten in all, the tenth recruit less than serious, and, apparently, completely bored with the whole affair.

Kathryn was teaching alternative ways to kill without the traditional instruments of death—the knife and the pistol, both of which were sitting on each recruit's desk. Kathryn had just shown the class how to fold a newspaper into a knife and instructed them on how to stab it into the soft tissue under the chin, effectively dispatching the victim.

Jenny found it fascinating and disturbing, but she noticed the slumping dope in front of her seemed less than impressed.

He raised his hand to Kathryn's query. "Have you ever killed anyone?"

Jenny's eyes snapped to her classmate in disbelief. She considered whapping the jerk on the back of the head with her OSS weapons catalog but thought that might be too obvious. It was clear he had no respect for Kathryn as an agent or as an instructor. She didn't know who he was trying to impress, but most of the women in the group were annoyed by his constant badgering, and the three men, while outwardly more tolerant, were looking to Kathryn to see what she would do about it.

Unfazed, she replied, "Yes, I have."

"With your bare hands?" he asked skeptically.

"Yes, I have," she repeated solemnly.

Jenny recognized the hard set of Kathryn's jaw as an attempt to tamp down the horrific memory, and she swore, if the jackass in front of her pushed the issue any further, she, too, could lay claim to killing someone with her bare hands.

"Hmph," he muttered, tapping his pencil on the back of his

knuckles.

Kathryn crossed her arms. "Do you have something you'd like to say?"

He scratched the side of his head with the eraser end of the pencil and looked her up and down. "I'm just not seeing it."

The class bristled, and Jenny kicked the back of his chair. When he glanced back, she pretended it was an accident as she crossed her legs.

She half smiled. "Sorry."

Kathryn didn't seem to mind the man's attitude, and Jenny imagined he wasn't the first to doubt her abilities.

Kathryn raised her chin and addressed the class. "I can appreciate our friend's skepticism, and so should you. When you were training in D.C. at the Farm, you were taught to question everything and everyone. That hasn't changed. Don't assume anything. Don't assume I have the credentials to teach this class." She looked at the troublemaker. "Don't assume I don't." She sat on the edge of the desk in the front of the room and rolled up the sleeves on her shirt. She casually crossed her legs and tugged at the crease in her matching pants. "Don't assume because of my manner of dress that I'm in the military." She paused. "Don't assume I'm not. Don't assume that because I'm a woman I can't kick your ass—hell, don't even assume I'm a woman." That brought a smattering of laughter. Jenny bit her lip, trying to suppress an involuntary guffaw.

"He is doing what you were all trained to do," Kathryn went on. "This will be the most dangerous job of your life. You are never off duty. Here ... out there ... in your own home. Look. Question. Think. Learn the mindset, because over there, you won't get the luxury of a slipup."

The man looked over his shoulder. "Hear that, you mugs? I'm well trained."

Kathryn grinned and softened her voice to a more personable level. "I fear your attitude has more to do with a caustic personality than a genuine ability to comprehend the skills needed to become a good agent."

Taunting laughter and a few balls of paper came raining down on the man's head.

Kathryn let the students enjoy the moment of levity, but Jenny could see she didn't share in it.

"Killing is serious business," she continued, in a tone that echoed the weight of her words. "I realize that some of you will be unable to perform that task."

Some shifted uncomfortably.

"Look at the person next to you—your fellow agent—your only friend in the field."

The students looked at each other, their connection suddenly dawning on them. They walked into the room individuals proud of their accomplishments and excited to prove that the faith in them was well deserved. But now, face to face, they realized they were a family. They were a special breed, each willing to go above and beyond to win the war. One day, they would turn to each other, or a person just like them, and trust them with their life.

Kathryn let the bond sink in and then prepared them for the cold reality of their future. "Could you kill them in a tough spot?"

No one moved.

"Because you might have to, and believe me, you will be doing them a favor."

Faces that only moments before had registered camaraderie and satisfaction now wore pained expressions of disbelief. Some flinched at the answer they found within themselves.

"If you feel you cannot do that, or you cannot kill yourself should the situation arise, I'm going to ask you to turn in the items on your desk and leave the room."

The students sat motionless for a few seconds more and then gradually shifted their focus to those around them, waiting for someone to admit that taking a life was beyond the scope of their humanity.

"There's no shame in leaving," she assured them, "and no shame in staying. Leaving doesn't mean you're out of the OSS, just out of this course. We'll find another place for you."

A woman in the front row wiped a tear from her face and stood. "I'm sorry. I can't do this."

Kathryn pushed off from the desk and put a hand on her shoulder. "Perfectly understandable." She eyed the rest of the room. "Anyone else?"

Jenny knew she had a mortified but determined look on her face and noticed Kathryn avoided looking at her. Another woman stood, and then, reluctantly, one of the men.

Kathryn nodded. "Thank you for your honesty. Please collect your belongings and report to Building 6, where you will be reassigned."

They rose slowly, their eyes fixed on the floor.

"I meant what I said. There's no shame in your departure. You know your heart ... be proud of that. It will save lives in the long run."

The recruits barely acknowledged the compliment as they returned their weapons and shuffled out of the room in silence.

"Now," Kathryn began, as she stowed the knives and empty pistols in the box in which they came. "Don't assume you're safer or have a better chance of surviving because you have a pistol in your hand."

"Tst," the persistent young man in the front row snorted in disapproval.

Kathryn stared at him for a moment before holding out her hand. "Would you hand me your pistol, please?"

He got up and lackadaisically handed it to her grip first and chuckled. "Am I fired?"

As soon as the grip was in Kathryn's hand, she moved like lightning, shoving the barrel into his midriff.

"BANG! You're dead."

Before he had a chance to catch his breath, she had him turned toward the class, with one arm around his throat and the pistol pointed at his head.

"Or you're a hostage."

He struggled to no avail.

"BANG! You're dead if you try to get away."

He accepted defeat and stopped struggling. She let him go.

"Thank you." She put her arm on his shoulder as she held out his weapon, grip first, just as he had handed it to her. "You okay?"

"Yeah," he grumbled, as he rubbed his neck in embarrassment. He suddenly made a clumsy move to take the pistol and turn it on her as she had done to him. She was too quick again, as the grip was magically in her hand, and she dragged him by the shoulder into another headlock.

"Dang!" he squawked, as best he could, with her arm tightly around his windpipe. "Uncle."

She smiled and let him go. "Good idea ... poor execution." She slapped him on the back. "You'll get better." He sat down. She kept his pistol.

"Never, never give your weapon away ... to anyone. Ever. You never know when it will be used against you."

Kathryn avoided looking at her, and Jenny realized what a big deal it had been for Kathryn to relinquish her gun to her so soon after they had met. She cringed at the memory of Kathryn's arrest because of it and was glad Kathryn had forgiven her for turning the gun over to the police when she suspected she was a murderer.

So much had happened since then, and Jenny was thankful they'd moved beyond misunderstanding and mistrust.

Jenny noticed the trainee in front of her was no longer unruly. Kathryn had picked up a knife, and it was obvious the fellow had no interest in testing her skill with it. Kathryn used herself as the victim this time, pointing out the most vulnerable arteries in the human body and pantomiming how to inflict a mortal wound in each.

The lesson hit home, as Jenny glanced down at her catalog. The page with the small fighting knife came complete with illustrations of a soldier disposing of his German counterpart. On the next page was an anatomical diagram of the arteries that Kathryn was so deftly pretending to sever and a corresponding chart relating the effectiveness of each wound by approximating the number of seconds to unconsciousness and the number of minutes to death after infliction.

Jenny swallowed reflexively as she imagined herself in such a situation. Only moments before, she was convinced she could kill if necessary, but faced with the reality of the act shown on the page before her, she wondered if that was true. Could she really kill someone? Or was she fooling herself for the sake of stubborn pride, or a desire to impress Kathryn?

She stared at the illustration of the German soldier grimacing in pain as the knife was mercilessly thrust into his carotid artery. She imagined the sharp metal blade piercing delicate skin—the sound muted, stealthy, deceptively inane—like a shovel plunged into a soft snow bank. She imagined the muffled scream of pain through a hand over the mouth, and if there was enough time, a desperate moan, as the victim realized it was the last sound he would make. All that accompanied by the sickening gurgle of a life draining away.

She didn't want to imagine how it would feel to have someone's life expire under her hand—by her hand. She closed her eyes and swallowed again as breakfast threatened to make an appearance.

"Any questions?" she heard Kathryn say. She opened her eyes to see Kathryn staring at her, her expression one of detached interest, like the professional she was. Mumbles of *no* and numbly shaken heads surrounded her, and Jenny added hers to the group, which seemed to satisfy Kathryn, who went on to give a quick summary of the rest of the tools and weapons found in the catalog.

Day one was over, and they were dismissed with instructions to become familiar with the catalog and to learn the manual inside and out. Jenny didn't give Kathryn any undue attention as she followed the others out of the room, but she knew Kathryn had felt her doubt and her horror, and she was sure she would be questioned about it later.

"Would you stay, please?" she heard Kathryn say.

Jenny turned, surprised Kathryn singled her out when she had been so careful to appear unbiased while in class. Surprise turned to disappointment when Jenny discovered the invitation was directed at the cocky young man from the seat in front of her. She didn't envy the conversation he was about to have. Come to think of it, she didn't envy the conversation she was going to have later either.

· · ·

Kathryn crossed her arms at the smirking recruit before her. "Why are you here?"

"I wanna kill Krauts," he answered defiantly, mirroring her stance.

"Then you shouldn't have gotten yourself thrown out of the army, Hendricks." She paused while he absorbed the fact that she knew his sordid record. "Killing is not really our main objective here," she went on, "but I suspect you know that."

He was silent and serious for the first time, as he pursed his lips and stared at his shoes.

"Whatever you think you're going to accomplish by being troublesome, it won't bring your sister back."

His eyes snapped up, suddenly filled with anger. "What do you know about it? You and most of this class are part of the problem. Women shouldn't do this kind of work!"

"Your sister volunteered," Kathryn said calmly.

"She was grief stricken after those bastards killed her husband. The government took advantage of her!"

Kathryn let him see that she understood his anger, but everyone handled tragedy differently, or in the case of the Hendricks family, in the same way.

"You're grief stricken," she said. "Is the government taking advantage of you? Should I wash you out right now?"

"Don't you dare."

Kathryn raised her brow and waited until he got her point and reeled in his emotions.

"Everyone in this class has a reason, Sam. Grieve for your sister. Put those emotions into everything you do. Honor her memory. Let it give you the strength you'll need to do the things you're going to have to do."

He nodded solemnly.

"Anger can be useful, or it can be dangerous. Harness it, and it can be invaluable. Let it consume you and ... well ..." She knew she didn't need to finish. "Your choice."

She put her hand on his shoulder and gave him a warning. "Start thinking about the people around you, or you're out."

He looked at the floor and nodded again.

Kathryn patted him on the back and headed for the door. "Don't forget your pistol."

Jenny arrived home and smiled because Kathryn's car was there. Kathryn had said she'd call later and maybe they could squeeze in a late lunch, but surprise appearances were even better. Jenny called out when she entered the house but got no reply. A hopeful glance into the bedroom came up empty, and a peek into the living room yielded the same result.

She turned around and headed toward the kitchen. "Kat?"

No answer.

She worried that she'd find Kathryn sitting solemnly at the kitchen table, arms folded, waiting to have a serious discussion about the reaction she saw in class. All serious discussions took place at the kitchen table. Jenny didn't know why.

Her fear was unfounded, and she smiled as the room came into view. From the cutting board covered with apple cores, grape stems, spent tea bags, and bread crusts, Jenny knew that somewhere lunch awaited. She looked out the kitchen window and saw Kathryn spreading a picnic blanket on the end of the dock. "Mm," she hummed with a grin. "I'm keeping you."

Kathryn looked toward the house and waved as the screened back door closed with a bang. Jenny was smiling—a welcome sight after her shell-shocked demeanor in class. Kathryn feared the first day of special ops training had been a little rough on her, and truth be told, it hadn't exactly been easy on her either. She felt a relaxing lunch on a perfect summer day would go a long way toward balancing her duties as an instructor and her concerns as a friend.

When she arrived, Jenny immediately wrapped herself around her body and stole a badly needed kiss. "Hi."

Kathryn was startled by the open display of affection, but a quick scan of their surroundings showed that between the boathouse on the left and a stand of trees and thick foliage on the right, they were quite secluded. Kathryn relaxed and enjoyed the passionate greeting, knowing it was probably all the passion she had time for this afternoon. She didn't really have time for lunch either, but Jenny was more important than a rehearsal.

"What a surprise," Jenny said with a grin, as they settled onto the blanket.

Kathryn poured a glass of iced tea and handed it to her. "Glad you like it."

"I thought you had a new set to work out at the club?"

Kathryn shrugged as she poured herself a glass and raised it in a toast. "Who wants to be caged in a smoky club all afternoon when I can be here with you? Cheers."

"I couldn't agree more. Cheers."

Lunch hit the spot, and they talked about everything in the world except what had happened in class. Kathryn wound up with her back against a piling, her legs extended and crossed, while Jenny reclined with her head resting on her thigh. Jenny had grown increasingly quiet as she twirled a daisy between her fingers, pretending the act required great concentration.

"Are you all right?" Kathryn finally asked, sensing the day was weighing on her.

Jenny took a deep breath and exhaled. "You haven't mentioned anything about this morning."

"Do you want to talk about it?"

Jenny hesitated. "Are you asking me as my friend or as my evaluating instructor?"

Kathryn smiled and gently guided a wave of blonde hair from Jenny's forehead. "I think they both need to know."

Jenny's lips pressed into a thin line, and the truth came out easily. "The thought of killing someone sickens me."

"As it should."

"But it can't." Jenny looked up. "Not if I want to do this job."

Kathryn wanted to give her every opportunity to back out gracefully, as she suspected pride had a lot to do with her determination. "Do you want to do this job?"

Jenny sat up and twisted her body so that they were face to face. "Yes."

"Why?"

"What do you mean, *Why*? My country has called on me. It's my duty."

"No, your country gave you the opportunity. You decided this is how you wanted to serve her. Why?"

"Because winning this war means that much to me. Freedom means that much to me."

It was an answer, but not the deeply personal, hard-sought answer Kathryn was looking for. She knew Jenny would give it her all —knew that she would probably excel at most tasks—but it took more than that. It took a burning in the soul, an all-consuming fire that hurled one unflinchingly toward danger or death, with equal disregard for both. Kathryn knew Jenny didn't have that. She hoped for her sake she never would.

"Was that the right answer? Did I pass the test?" Jenny joked weakly.

Suddenly, Jenny was a student seeking approval. Kathryn regretted her job's intrusion into their precious personal time, but she realized, with Jenny in training, that would soon be the norm rather than the exception.

"It wasn't a test," Kathryn said with a smile, trying to hide her disappointment. "Just a question."

Jenny nodded and was quiet for a beat. "How do you know? How do you know if you'll be able to kill someone?"

Kathryn was silent. There wasn't an easy answer, and certainly none that would sound reasonable while sitting on a dock in the States, enjoying a lazy, sunny day. "You don't think about it. It's war. It's you or them."

"They're still human beings."

Kathryn looked into Jenny's confused, innocent eyes and

regretted that soon they would no longer hold the same wonder, and they would no longer seek the answers to such questions. The truth was too ugly, and rationalization would soon swallow wonder whole.

"It's different over there." Kathryn paused, trying to figure out how to justify the inhumanity of war to the uninitiated. "It all makes sense somehow when you're there." In truth, nothing made sense. You ceased to feel, you ceased to care, you ceased to think. "The heat of the moment ... the constant fear. It allows you to do things you never thought you could." She looked into the distance. "It's about survival. You do your job and then, hopefully, you come home."

"And then?"

And then it makes even less sense. "And then it's hard to explain to someone who's never been there."

Jenny took her hand. "Sorry."

Kathryn smiled, pushing her memories and the darkness away. "Don't be." She raised her chin and distanced herself from her past deeds. "The urge *not* to kill is more natural than the urge *to* kill. What you're feeling is perfectly normal. As your training goes on, you'll be better able to judge your capabilities."

As will the agency.

"Wait," Jenny said for the third time as she held the phone between her chin and shoulder and rolled down her sleeve. "Ber ... Bernie, slow down. What?"

Kathryn retained the quizzical look on her face as she stood in the foyer lamenting their interrupted goodbye.

"That's impossible. I worked in the same building with him for an entire summer. I think I would know Cal Richards when I saw him."

Kathryn's face went from quizzical to concerned, matching Jenny's expression.

"That doesn't make sense," Jenny continued, as the crease in her brow deepened. "Okay, okay ... let me get this straight. You're telling me that the man they just buried ... your Cal Richards ... is not the Cal Richards I knew from the mailroom?"

Kathryn moved closer and could hear Bernie's answer through the tinny handset speaker. "Correct." Then she swore she heard a sob. "Who did I love? Was it even real?"

Jenny put her hand to her forehead and looked helplessly at Kathryn. "Oh, sweetie, of course it was real."

Another sob. "How will I ever know that?"

Jenny didn't have an answer and grimaced. "I'm so sorry, Bernie. So sorry."

Kathryn backed away to give them privacy, until Bernie's end of the conversation turned into indistinct chatter. Jenny appeared on the verge of breaking down herself. She closed her tear-filled eyes and covered the mouthpiece with her hand to keep it from Bernie. She nodded a few times, shook her head in disbelief, and then got hold of her emotions before she took her hand away and spoke.

"Are you okay? Do you need me to—" He evidently cut her off, and Jenny bowed her head with a dejected, "Okay. I know. Mhmm." She raised her chin, as if he'd changed tack and she had doubts about his next move. "So, what are you going to do? Uh-huh ... yeah ... well, don't do anything stupid ... yes, you. Okay ... mm ... all right. Call me if you ..." *Need me* never came out, so she settled on, "Call me ... I know ... Love you too, sweetie. I'm so sorry."

She hung up the phone and put her hand on her hip, turning to Kathryn in disbelief. "Sergeant Calvin Richards—the Calvin Richards *I* knew from the *Daily Chronicle*—died in a military training accident ... two years ago."

"Two years ago? Then who was—"

"Exactly."

Wild scenarios swam in her head, but Kathryn didn't voice them.

Jenny moved to her side. "Poor Bernie, and there's nothing I can do for him. Why would someone impersonate Calvin Richards? To what end?"

Kathryn took Jenny into her arms to comfort her. Who would orchestrate such a thing? Paul? Forrester? And why indeed?

At the training center the next day, Kathryn sat in a joint meeting between her OSS handler, Colonel Forsythe, and his British Special Operations Executive counterpart, Colonel Holmes, and watched a scowl darken the SOE colonel's face.

"How could she not know he was a different man?" Colonel Holmes asked skeptically, looking up from her report.

Kathryn didn't hide her glare when she retold Jenny's explanation of the mistaken identity. Apparently, she didn't really know the fellow, couldn't even say they were acquaintances. The Calvin Richards she remembered from the *Daily Chronicle* was a skinny redheaded, freckle-faced boy who could have easily grown into the young man who presented himself as Cal Richards four years later.

Holmes accepted the explanation with a less than enthusiastic grunt, but he was intrigued when he learned Jenny felt her uncle had something to do with his arrival and deception.

"Thank you, Kathryn," Colonel Forsythe said, as he sifted through some papers. "You may go. Keep us posted if you learn anything new."

She nodded and rose to leave. Holmes followed her to the exit with his eyes but didn't wait for the door to close before he began rattling off orders in a rapid British staccato.

"Let's start at the *Daily Chronicle*. Get a hold of Paul Ryan. Threaten him with the FBI, the IRS, I don't care. I want answers this time."

Kathryn raised her brow and hoped the OSS would have better luck with Paul than Jenny had. Her uncle had given her a flat-out denial that he knew Cal Richards to be anyone other than who he claimed to be. Things hadn't been right between Jenny and her uncle since before the benefit, and from Jenny's quick accusation, Kathryn could tell not much had changed since then.

It was premature to say Jenny was unraveling, but her personal relationships certainly were. Her truce with Bernie was tenuous, pending his return, and her conversation with her uncle had gone badly, as indictments often do—the part where he called her irrational and paranoid was a highlight in a morning that also included an equally dreadful shouting match with her aunt, who was blindly backing her husband.

Even their relationship was not immune to discord, as the stress of the first week of intensive training took its toll on both of them.

Kathryn was feeling the oppressive weight of their uncertain future. At the end of training was a mission waiting to happen. She could hardly bear to consider it. The thought of Jenny actually in any of the scenarios for which she was training, and the thought that they would probably be separated in a few short weeks, was overwhelming at times. It was getting increasingly harder to hide her feelings about it, and Jenny sensed the change as they both became introspective.

Jenny stopped asking questions about the job when they were alone together. Kathryn didn't mind. The subject had stolen so much from them already. Not even the sanctity of Luc's apartment could save them from themselves. Both were left tiptoeing around each other's sensitivities. Sympathetic smiles and cautious "Are you okay?" questions now dominated their once comfortable space.

Kathryn left Colonel Forsythe's office at the training center and walked across the open courtyard toward the building that housed her classroom. No matter the outcome of Paul's interrogation, she had a feeling all hell was about to break loose, and, somehow, naturally, Jenny was going to be right in the middle of it. She couldn't stop what had been set in motion, but she could bridge the distance that had grown between them. Their time was too short, too short even for their fears.

Kathryn picked up her pace. She had a class to teach and then some tender love and care to administer. Jenny was on edge, especially after the run-in with her family. Her parting words on the telephone that morning about her uncle were ominous, revealing the steely determination of a woman who would not stop until she had the answer.

I know he's lying to me, Kathryn. I know he is.

CHAPTER TWO

Kathryn eyed the expectant faces of her students and braced herself for the first test of their commitment to the cause. Most failed, and she was curious to see how this group would fare.

"At the beginning of the week, I told you to learn your manuals. Is there anyone here who has not done so?" The class stared back confidently. "No one?" She paused, waiting for someone to confess their sin. Saints all, apparently, as the silence continued. "Excellent." She sat on the edge of her desk and pointed at her first victim.

"Hendricks, what's the first line of chapter thirteen?"

Silence ensued as the young man searched the air for the answer.

"Okay," she drew out. "What's the title of chapter thirteen?"

He ran his hand across his razor stubbled chin and shifted uncomfortably.

Kathryn crossed her arms. "You did read the manual, didn't you?"

"Yes, ma'am," he said, as more a question than a statement.

Kathryn smiled curtly. "That's nice."

She slid off her desk and stood over the trainee with her hands clasped behind her back like a drill sergeant.

"Mr. Hendricks," she began pleasantly. "I understand this is a lot to take in. So much to study and learn—new words, new concepts, a change in your lifestyle, how you interact with the world, and on and on. Every day is a new gut check, and you wonder if you're going to make the grade—it's all rather unsettling, really. Isn't it?"

"I suppose," he said cautiously.

"Perhaps I'm being a bit unreasonable to think you could possibly remember such insignificant little details like exact lines of text and numbers of chapters ... things like that, hm?"

Hendricks sat up a little straighter. "Well, yes ma'am, I believe it is. Thank you for your understanding."

"Yes, well, I'm the understanding sort," Kathryn smiled.

She saw Jenny raise her brow in recognition of her disingenuous delivery. Hendricks didn't have a clue.

"After all," she went on, as she paced in front of the class, "it's the gist of the thing that's important, not the silly little details, right, Hendricks?"

"Exactly, ma'am," he said confidently.

"So, we'll dispense with this silliness and you can just give me the gist of chapter thirteen." She turned and stared at him. "Sound fair?"

Hendricks nodded but had no answer.

Kathryn shook her head and exhaled a disappointed breath. "Anyone know the answer?" she asked in a bored tone, expecting a flurry of hands in the air. She was met with a room full of silently shifting trainees. "Any answer?" she asked in disbelief.

Out of the corner of her eye came a movement that caught her attention.

"Rogers, do not even think of opening that manual now. Cheating is not going to save your life out there." She looked back to the rest of the class and raised her voice as she picked up her copy and held it in the air. "I asked you all to *learn* your manuals. I didn't ask you to skim through them or just look at the pretty pictures." She threw the bound paper volume on her desk in disgust. "Did no one do as I asked?"

Jenny looked around timidly before slowly raising the pencil in her hand.

"I did."

Kathryn found it hard not to smile. Of course she did.

"And?" she said sternly, trying to retain her annoyed composure.

"The title of chapter thirteen is Interrogation. The first line is Welcome to hell, you've been captured. The gist is pretty ugly, so don't get captured in the first place."

"Thank you, Ryan." She turned again to the class. "To the rest of you, this is not a fucking game." She let them absorb her anger and disappointment before continuing. "The silly little details in this book could save your life."

Kathryn properly scolded the group, walked back to her desk, and leaned on the corner. "Next week we start field training. That means you are one step closer to deployment. We don't have the luxury of time here, folks. You have to learn, and learn fast, or you're not going to make it."

She looked at the clock above the door. Class was mercifully over.

"That's it for today. I know what you want to do with those manuals ... but please learn them. You're of no use to the war effort if you're dead because you did something stupid out of ignorance. Any questions?"

None.

"Get out of here."

She pushed off her desk and walked to the chalkboard to erase the day's lesson. "Ryan, a moment please?" she called over her shoulder as the class shuffled out.

Jenny looked up in surprise at the stern snap of her last name.

Hendricks nudged her and whispered, "Ass kisser," as he passed by with a wink.

She grinned silently and waited to approach Kathryn until the last trainee exited.

Kathryn turned around, wiping the chalk from her hands. "Lock that, wouldja?" She pointed at the door and then moved to the desk.

Jenny threw the latch and then joined her. "Tough day."

"Yeah. Thanks for knowing your manual."

"It's a hard chapter to forget."

Jenny couldn't have told her anything about any of the other chapters with any certainty, but that one stayed with her because she couldn't help thinking about what Kathryn must have gone through during her interrogation by the enemy. More questions she wouldn't ask.

Kathryn took her hand. "How are you?"

"I'm okay."

It had become an automatic response to the question regardless of whether it was true.

Kathryn brushed her knuckles lightly across her cheek. "We're not doing that anymore, honey. You're not okay, and neither am I."

Jenny deflated beneath Kathryn's touch. The lie fell away, and her strength went with it. She'd been given permission to face the truth, and it was harder than she realized.

"Don't make me cry, Kat. I may not stop."

Kathryn took her in her arms. "Cry if you need to, but we're not hiding from each other any longer."

Jenny held tight but refused to cry. It just felt good to be in Kathryn's arms again. "I love you."

"I love you too. I'm sorry things have gotten so crazy. I just—"

"I know," Jenny said, hearing the words that Kathryn left unspoken. She couldn't bear the thought of what was on the horizon for either of them.

Kathryn pulled back and cupped her face. "Come to the club tonight. I'll pull together some numbers just for you, and then we can go back to my place." She stroked her hair. It may have only been a week, but it seemed like ages since they were intimate. "I've missed you so. I want to feel you again." She kissed her neck. "Make love to you again."

Jenny didn't need to be convinced. In fact, her humming body demanded it, as her head fell back and the kisses followed her pulse line to the base of her neck. "What time?" she whispered, knowing this was not the place to surrender.

The kisses stopped, and "What?" was mumbled into her collarbone.

"Tonight. What time?"

Kathryn released a shaky breath as she reeled in her desire. "Nine."

"I'll be there." Jenny straightened her shirt and gave her a kiss goodbye. "Don't forget where you were."

"Oh, I won't."

Jenny bounded down the wooden steps, and strode across the gravel courtyard, trying to ignore a smirking Lieutenant Branson, who was leaning on the doorway of Building 5, arms crossed, with a cigarette dangling from his disapproving mouth.

CHAPTER THREE

"You can't do this!" Paul Ryan shouted again, as a bright light shone in his face. "Where are we? What do you want from me?"

This wasn't the first time Paul had had government men leaning on him about his brother's work, but like the previous encounters, he would endure anything as long as it meant they stayed away from Jenny.

He heard someone strike a match and then pull on a cigarette in the darkness behind him. A spent match tumbled past his shoulder and onto the table before him. "Relax, Mr. Ryan. We just want you to answer a few questions." A pack of cigarettes breached the cone of light. "Do you want a smoke?"

"I want a lawyer!"

"Do you need a lawyer, Mr. Ryan?" another man asked calmly from the shadows in front of him.

Paul recognized the voice immediately. It belonged to FBI Agent Jake Russo, who commanded the muscle of the government men previously sent to make him talk. He seemed more rogue agent than upstanding citizen, with his gruff demeanor and strongarm tactics, but Paul was ready for him.

"You!" He tried to rise from his seat but was instantly restrained by men to his left and right.

"Take it easy, buddy," the smoking man said, cigarette dangling from his mouth.

"Get off me!" Paul shouted as he struggled.

Jake Russo leaned into the beam of light as he settled into the seat across the table. He was a large man, with an attitude to match. His presence alone was enough to intimidate most, but not Paul. He would die before giving in to Russo and his thugs.

Russo nodded to the two men restraining him and they let him go.

Paul straightened his shirt and glared at the men before turning back to Russo.

"I told you before ... I don't have the information you're looking for."

"Blackmail, murder, killers for hire ... it's a dirty business, isn't it, Mr. Ryan?"

"I don't know what you're talking about."

"Come now," Russo said with a smile. "We now know you hired Vincent LaPaglia to kill your brother."

Paul laughed and sat back in his chair. "That's absurd."

The man to his left shoved him back to the table and into the light.

"We know you hired him. We have the records." Russo held out his hand, and the smoking man retrieved a file from a briefcase. "We just don't know why."

"There are no records."

Russo pinned him with a sneer that disagreed.

"You've got nothing. You can't hold me."

Russo ignored him. "Records are a funny thing, Mr. Ryan." He flipped through the file now spread before him. "You can tell a lot about a man from the records he keeps." He looked up. "Or doesn't keep."

Paul narrowed his eyes, wondering where this was headed.

"These records are from the IRS."

Paul froze for a moment before shifting his worried gaze to the pages on the table.

"It seems you came into a large sum of money once upon a time. You bought the *Daily Chronicle* with it."

"My father gave me that money."

"Your father did no such thing. In fact, you were estranged from your father for most of your life, and he left you nothing when he died." He closed the file and clasped his hands across it. "Business hasn't been very good these past few years, has it? Profits steadily declining, some gambling debt ... you're in quite a bind financially, aren't you?"

Paul was silent.

"We know you owe Marcus Forrester money. You made a gentleman's agreement with deadly consequences should you default."

"You can't prove that."

"We don't need to prove anything, Mr. Ryan. We merely want you to know that we understand the difficult position this puts you in, and we understand why you would be forced to do things you may find unconscionable."

Paul slammed his fist on the table. "I didn't kill my brother!"

"And I suppose you didn't try to have your niece killed for her inheritance."

"*What?*"

"So you could pay off Mr. Forrester and get out from under his thumb."

"You're insane. I love my niece more than my own life. I'd do anything—"

"Even kill to protect her?"

"I didn't kill my brother!"

"Are you saying she needed protection from her father?"

"No!"

"Did you kill Vincent LaPaglia?"

Paul looked around in disbelief. "This is getting ridiculous. Is there anyone you think I didn't kill?"

"Tell us about Calvin Richards."

"I didn't kill him either," Paul said sarcastically.

Russo ominously drummed his fingers on the IRS file. "You would do well to cooperate at this point, Mr. Ryan. Tell us about Calvin Richards."

Paul wiped the sweat from his brow while he considered his answer.

"The kid came back to the *Chronicle* and started hanging around. I asked him to keep an eye on Jenny. That's it. I don't know anything about anything else."

"Keep an eye on her because Forrester was threatening to harm her?"

"Because she's an inquisitive girl with a knack for trouble. I just didn't want her near him."

"Because you owe him money?"

"Because he's dangerous."

"Did he kill your brother?"

"For the last time, no! My brother's death was an accident!"

"So, LaPaglia was only meant to scare him?"

"An accident!" Paul insisted with another fist to the table. "A horrible, tragic twist of fate!"

"It seems like an awfully cozy coincidence that you would owe Mr. Forrester a large sum of money that you can't repay and a known henchman in his employ runs off the road and *accidentally* kills your brother."

"I don't really care what you think. You can't prove anything, and you can't hold me here. This is harassment."

Russo shook his head. "Mr. Ryan ..." He softened his approach. "Paul. We could make these murder charges disappear. This IRS file too. All you need to do is cooperate."

Paul leaned back in his chair and crossed his arms. "Are we through?"

Russo raised his brow at his defiance and passed the folder to his cohort. He rose from the table and disappeared into the darkness of the room. "You're making a mistake."

"I've heard all this bef—"

Before he could finish, Paul found his face smashed into the table by a forearm pressed to the back of his neck. His arms were trapped under his chest, and he was helpless to escape.

Russo stooped to eye level and rested his arm on the table. "It doesn't have to be this way. Would you like to reconsider?"

"Go to hell," Paul ground out through a distorted mouth. "I haven't done anything."

Russo nodded, accepting his choice, and stood. "Your niece is a very lovely girl. I'd hate to see something happen to her."

"You keep her out of this!" Paul shouted, as he moved the large man from his neck with newfound strength. Two men on each arm struggled to hold him back as he lunged for Russo. "Touch her and I'll kill you!"

"Like you killed Vincent LaPaglia for killing your brother?"

"I wasn't anywhere near that bar!"

"No, but Calvin Richards was. You hired him to avenge your brother's death, isn't that so?"

"I hired him to protect Jenny."

"You hired a detective for that, Paul—John Smith—that's no secret. I think, however, that your niece would be very interested in your part in her father's death."

"You stay away from her!"

"That's up to you."

"Stay away from her!"

Russo was unmoved by the demand, and soon Paul's anger turned into pleading.

"Please. She's been through enough. This has nothing to do with her. Please."

"I have no desire to harm your family or your relationship with them, Mr. Ryan." He paused. "You seem to do enough damage on your own. But I'm afraid you leave me no choice." He picked up his briefcase and began to leave.

"Wait!" Paul struggled against the men still restraining him. "What do you want to know?"

Russo returned to the table and nodded to his men. They let him go.

They both sat down, and Russo offered him a cigarette, which he took with a shaky hand.

"I don't care about your finances," Russo began conversationally, as he held his lighter aloft. "I don't care who killed whom or why. I have one singular interest. Tell me what I want to know, and I'll make sure the rest goes away."

"Okay," Paul drew out skeptically.

"What are you giving Marcus Forrester in place of the money you can't pay him?"

Paul clenched his jaw and looked away. "I've told you everything I know."

Russo slid his briefcase off the table. "Wrong answer."

Paul grabbed his wrist. "It's as useless to him as it is to you."

"I'll be the judge of that."

Paul considered his options.

"You promise my family will be safe?"

"You have my word."

Paul doubted Russo's sincerity, but he had no choice. "Information."

"What kind of information?"

"It's random numbers and letters. I don't know. It's encoded, and I don't have the key."

Russo eyed him warily.

"I don't. Neither does Forrester. Only Danny knew. That's why the information is worthless."

"Where is this information?"

"If I tell you where it is, you no longer need me, and I'm sorry, but I won't take your word for my safety once I'm of no use to you. Besides, I can't stop giving it to Forrester, for obvious reasons." He stopped and changed his tact when Russo leaned in menacingly. "But I'll give it to you first, and then I need it back ... quickly. Deal?"

Russo smiled and held out his hand. "Deal."

Paul refused to shake hands. Russo laughed and then stood to leave. "You're going to do this again in a few hours." He buttoned the top button of his shirt and tightened his tie.

Paul looked up in confusion.

"There will be more men, more questions, and more threats. My threats are the only ones you need fear. I promise you that."

"Say, what is this? I told you what you wanted to know."

"Yes, and now your family will be safe. Rejoice, Mr. Ryan, you're a free man. Admit to nothing in your next interrogation, and cooperate only with me, and you'll stay that way. This conversation never happened." He turned to the thugs. "Make sure he gets to his car."

Agent Jake Russo watched his men lead Paul Ryan from the room. He took a seat and leaned back, propping his feet on the table.

"Well, it looks like we broke him," he called out.

Colonel Holmes stepped out from behind a windowed door in the darkened adjacent room and lit a cigarette. "That's one thing you can say about the Ryans ... if you can't buy them, you can break them."

Russo chuckled in agreement. "Now what?"

Holmes took a smug drag on his cigarette and tossed an envelope of money on the table. "Start on the girl."

CHAPTER FOUR

athryn's tune was unusually happy, and she was unusually loose singing it. Love was the theme for the evening, and anyone who didn't believe her when she flashed her dazzling smile and cheerfully sang "The Best Things in Life are Free" didn't have a pulse.

Jenny knew she wore a silly grin on her face as she watched Kathryn from one of the front row tables on the club floor, but after the week she'd had, she felt she deserved a night of unadulterated ogling, and she didn't care how goofy she looked to anyone else.

It felt good to leave her cares outside and just enjoy the beautiful woman on stage—*her* beautiful woman. It seemed so long since she'd seen her perform, she'd almost forgotten she was a singer. Kathryn looked stunning in her shimmering red gown, and genuinely happy. It was an emotion that had been in short supply for both of them lately. Jenny knew Kathryn needed this night as much as she did. Soon, Forrester would be back in town and their relationship would be relegated once more to stolen hours in the afternoons, a thought that Jenny quickly put out of her head.

Dominic leaned in from behind and whispered in her ear, "Did you do this to her?"

Jenny smiled. "I hope so."

"Keep it up. Happy is good, no?"

"Oh, yes."

"That is her own arrangement, did you know?"

Jenny beamed with pride. "No, I didn't."

"She said it was a gift to me, but I think she does not tell the truth."

Jenny smiled, and Dominic straightened, raising his hands in applause as the song ended. Kathryn nodded graciously to her boss and offered a playful wink to Jenny, who gladly returned the gesture.

The band launched immediately into the next song, causing the club owner to pat Jenny on the shoulder and quickly depart, as if staying would be an intrusion. His actions soon made sense when bright horns and smooth clarinets played the intro to "I Know Why (And So Do You)."

Jenny settled back in her chair to enjoy her own personal love letter. Kathryn had promised the last song would be just for her, but she didn't need to tell her that. Jenny could hear it in the intimacy of her voice, see it in the smile that reached her eyes, and feel it in the way she gently caressed the mic stand with the same easy stroke she'd used on the length of her thigh. Jenny was lost in Kathryn's love for her, something that, with all her training and experience in deception, Kathryn couldn't hide.

Jenny bit her lip, as anticipation got the better of her and her silly grin turned into a bad case of I've-gotta-have-her-and-soon. She couldn't wait to get back to Kathryn's apartment. Tonight, they would reconnect. Their lovemaking would be slow and sensual as they explored each other by soft candlelight, and they would lay in each other's arms until the dawn eased them gently into the next day. They would be strong, renewed, and united. Ready to face what lay ahead. They were in love, after all, and what was stronger than that?

Jenny thought back to the first night they'd met. She never could have guessed the path her life was about to take. Now, as she watched the object of her affection onstage, she could only hope the future would be kind to them.

She heard Dominic off to her left snapping his fingers and giving instructions, which she found odd, given the respect he had for his favorite performer. A turn to her right revealed the reason, as Marcus Forrester and an entourage of well-dressed men made their way to the large table on the exclusive upper tier of the club floor.

"Son of a bitch," Jenny muttered and quickly faced forward. She looked at the stage where Kathryn went on with her song, with no change in her demeanor. She wondered if she knew their night was ruined. A slight nod and a smile in Forrester's direction told Jenny she knew, and while she may not be able to hide her love, Kathryn could apparently transfer it, and Marcus Forrester was the lucky recipient.

After the song, Jenny watched Kathryn linger at the piano with her back to the crowd. Jenny tried to be strong. She took a deep breath and straightened as Kathryn prowled off the stage and headed toward her. As she approached, she never looked down. She kept her eyes focused on the table in the third tier. It was just like the night they met, red dress and all. The only thing missing was Cal at the table. She cringed when she thought of him—whoever he was. Thoughts of the impostor led to thoughts of her uncle, and soon the outside world began smothering her.

She stared at Kathryn's hand as she approached, not able to ignore her, and not able to handle what she knew would be indifference on her face. As Kathryn got closer, a small white napkin appeared at her fingertips, and she tucked it into Jenny's numb fingers as she passed.

The acknowledgment alone eased Jenny's discomfort, but not even the warm, soft touch of Kathryn's hand sweeping up her arm and across her bare shoulders as she passed could help the feeling of regret and disappointment at what they'd lost. It didn't take long before resentment set in when she thought of who would be receiving her attention instead.

She imagined Kathryn arriving at Forrester's table, where the grubby bastard would put his hands on her, kiss her lips, and parade her in front of his friends like a trophy. It was almost too much to bear. She gathered her purse and wrap before the mental image made her cry, and still clutching the napkin, she headed for the door. She wound up next to Smitty in the bar as she waited for the valet to hail a cab.

"Tough, isn't it?" he said, as he twisted on his barstool and motioned toward Forrester's table.

Jenny hadn't intended to look, but curiosity got the better of her. She would soon regret it, as Kathryn was practically sitting on Forrester's lap, with one arm intertwined with his and the other arm rubbing his shoulder as they laughed and interacted with the group. Kathryn was good. If you didn't know better, you would swear she was enjoying every minute of it. Jenny quickly looked away in disgust and found Smitty's amused eyes staring at her.

"Yeah," she said, answering his question. "Too tough."

He smiled. "You'll get used to it."

She stared at him. "Like you have?"

His amused grin disappeared, and he looked briefly back to the table. His jaw tensed, and Jenny had her answer. She patted him on the chest in mutual understanding as the valet signaled her taxi had arrived and she headed for the exit.

"Good night, Johnny."

"Yeah. See ya, kid," Smitty mumbled, as he twisted back to the bar and ordered another drink.

Jenny sat in the back seat of the taxi and silently cursed Forrester's name as she headed home alone. He couldn't have planned a more devastating disruption if he tried. Why tonight of all nights? She was angry, and for the briefest of seconds, Kathryn was included in her ire.

Couldn't she just tell Forrester she had plans? Couldn't she put their relationship first for once? Jenny closed her eyes and exhaled her disappointment. Of course she couldn't. Kathryn was doing what she had to do, just like she always did, and rightly so.

Jenny deflated into the seat and looked at her hand. She'd almost forgotten the napkin strangled in her fist. She smoothed out the crushed white paper to find a ragged message scribbled in pencil: *I'm SO sorry,* was underlined. *I WILL see you tonight! My place—please? Counting the minutes—love you.*

Jenny stared at the note, feeling Kathryn's obvious frustration. "I love you too," she whispered. She was angry, and maybe a little jealous, but it wasn't Kathryn's fault. She had to be hurting as well.

"I'm sorry, driver," she called to the front seat. "Jane Street in the Village."

She would go to Kathryn's apartment and wait. Maybe they could salvage something of the evening despite their bad luck.

By the time Jenny got to Kathryn's apartment, she was resigned to the delay in their plans. She kept her emotions in check, which she felt was progress. Kathryn didn't have time to feel sorry for herself, so neither would she.

Jenny was certain Kathryn had gotten the worst end of the deal. As bad as she felt about their ruined evening, Jenny couldn't imagine the disappointment compounded by a night of make-believe with Marcus Forrester. He would put his hands on her, and Kathryn would pretend to like it. The charade would spur him on to more intimate behavior, and then—the thought of it made Jenny's skin crawl. She didn't know how Kathryn put up with it. But she did, and Jenny briefly remembered Kathryn's sordid past as a prostitute, where she must have endured much worse than Forrester. At least she didn't have to sleep with him.

She quickly pushed those thoughts away as she entered Kathryn's apartment. The familiar surroundings welcomed her, and her annoyance lost some of its edge. It was only a matter of time, after all. Kathryn would be home before she knew it, and, in the meantime, she would take comfort in the embrace of her personal space.

She dropped her bag on the couch and inhaled Kathryn's scent, which still hung in the air. For such a complex woman, Kathryn was materialistically simple. There was nothing extravagant about her manner of living, save the beautiful grand piano, which seemed wholly out of place amongst the modest furnishings in the rest of the dwelling. The polished piano bench was tucked neatly under the keyboard as far as it would go, and Jenny leaned on the exposed half with one knee and caressed the keys, wishing Kathryn were there to serenade her with something lovely.

The hours dragged on, and soon it was after midnight—still, no Kathryn. Jenny had exhausted her exploration of the apartment and was amazed at how little it exposed about her lover. On the surface, there was one personal photo in the bedroom—the one of her as a child on her mother's shoulders. There was the small glass bottle collection on her vanity, and a curious group of seashells in a jar of water on the kitchen windowsill. The one bookcase in the living room was surprisingly uninformative, neatly ordered with a nonspecific collection of classic and contemporary novels—no genre favored over another, no hint of any one interest.

The lack of personal information reminded Jenny of her time spent at the Farm, working tirelessly to keep any telling characteristics from her fellow recruits. Surely that training couldn't be that ingrained in Kathryn. Everyone needed a place to be themselves.

There were, however, two items of great interest to Jenny: an oil painting hung on the wall at the foot of the piano and a closed door in the hallway on the way to the kitchen. The oil was of medium size, with a plain wide gold gilded frame in the shape of a perfect square. The warm and inviting palate captured a small child taking a shell from an adult woman's hand. The child reached with both hands, as children often do, and one could almost imagine the moments just after the captured scene as the child brought the treasure greedily to her body with uncoordinated fingers. It was a beautiful moment, filled with wonder and innocence, and Jenny could understand why Kathryn had it in such a prominent place in her home. It was signed E.K. Hammond, and Jenny wondered who in the family was the artist.

The closed room was not only a mystery but a temptation. The door wasn't locked—Jenny had tried it—but she sensed it was shut for a reason, so she didn't venture inside. She was sure Kathryn would share the mystery in her own time.

Directly across the hall was the cellar door that led to the back entry that Smitty and Kathryn used when they wanted to leave the apartment unseen, to avoid Forrester's watchdogs. That door was locked, but the skeleton key waited patiently in the keyhole. Jenny was prone to the creeps, so she decided a dark cellar was of no interest to her on this night.

As another hour passed, she found herself still alone. Cozy had gone from comforting to claustrophobic as the walls closed in. Jenny had too much time on her hands. Too much time to think about what Kathryn was doing with Forrester, too much time to dwell on her damaged personal relationships, and too much time to realize that somewhere along the way, her life had spiraled out of her control. She tossed her third *The Etude* magazine on the coffee table and decided she'd learned enough about the artistic possibilities of good jazz and the string approach to Mozart.

She was annoyed again. This was going to be their night. Kathryn shouldn't have said she could get away. She didn't have that kind of control over her life. Forrester called the shots, and if he wanted her with him, she would stay. And why wouldn't he want her with him?

"Fucker," Jenny grumbled, the curse absolving Kathryn for her wishful thinking.

Jenny decided in her mood, it was probably better that Kathryn wasn't coming home. She thought about leaving but knew Kathryn would be disappointed to come home to an empty apartment—*if* she came home. No need for both of them to be disappointed tonight.

She scribbled a note and took a bath. She was too worked up to sleep, so she grabbed a book and curled up in the lonely bed.

"It was the best of times, it was the worst of times ..."

Forrester covered Kathryn's naked body with his own. She wrapped her legs around his thighs and playfully nibbled at his chest.

"I've missed you," he moaned, as he rocked into her.

Kathryn threw her head back and welcomed the rhythm with a pleasurable exhale. "Missed you too. You should have let me stay in Chicago. Look what we've been missing."

Forrester laughed between concentrated thrusts, and Kathryn tightened her grip on his taut biceps. Moans of encouragement had the man straining to keep up with the demand, until Kathryn pulled him to her and guided him on his back. She straddled him and let her slowly grinding hips drive him crazy.

His cries of pleasure were tainted with the sweet frustration of greedy desire, and he grabbed her hips to take what he wanted— what he needed. She pulled his hands away, in complete control of his gratification, and he surrendered to his sublime torture.

Forrester turned his head and held out his hand. "Would you like to join us?"

Kathryn turned her head and watched for the response with great interest. *Come on,* she mouthed as she held out her hand as well.

Jenny refused.

Kathryn laughed and turned to Forrester. "I told you."

Forrester laughed too.

The laughter grew louder and louder, until the noise was deafening.

Jenny's eyes flew wide open as she gasped awake from the nightmare and sat straight up, her heart beating wildly.

"Son of a bitch!"

She immediately reached for the light and wound up sprawled out on the sheets on all fours. She was in Kathryn's bed, still alone, but thankful she was awake and it was only a dream. She scampered backwards to the headboard and pulled her knees to her chest, her skin crawling.

"Cripes," she exhaled, holding her spinning head.

The time read two thirty-four. "Kat?" she called out hopefully.

No answer.

She tried to shake off the sick feeling in the pit of her stomach. "It was just a dream, Jenny," she told herself. "Just a dream."

It had to be a dream. Kathryn told her she didn't sleep with Forrester. Jenny's mind reeled. Did she say she *didn't* sleep with Forrester or she *hadn't* slept with Forrester? Jenny tried to remember ... she said didn't. She paused again. Did that mean she doesn't, period, or she hadn't yet but may have to one day? And was this the day? The thought of it sent chills up her spine.

"God," she said, as she shut her eyes tight against the possibility. She hugged her knees and rocked to the mantra *it was just a dream ... it was just a dream....*

CHAPTER FIVE

Kathryn wearily pulled herself up the steps leading to her door. It was three a.m. and she was exhausted. She leaned her forehead against the door as she inserted her key and, more or less, fell into her living room as the door gave way.

There was a note on the bookcase next to the door, where she quietly placed her keys. It read: *Stayed up as long as I could—sorry about tonight. You owe me breakfast.* Kathryn smiled. Breakfast and a whole lot more.

An evening that held such promise had quickly turned into a suffocating yoke of guilt and regret. The stage spotlights kept her from seeing Forrester's arrival, but she sensed the wave of movement in the third tier and knew their night was over. She nodded with a smile in his direction as a sickening wave of anger-induced nausea washed over her. She couldn't see Jenny either, but she didn't dare look her way for fear she'd catch a glimpse of her frustration at Forrester's intrusion. She would be angry. Not just at Forrester, but at her too for promising things she couldn't deliver. All this drifted through her mind as she finished her song without conscious effort. The applause brought her back to herself, but her nod of appreciation was halfhearted.

She couldn't let this get to her. Why had this gotten to her? She was a master of adaptation. Regret had no place in her world. Jenny had gotten under her skin. She made her want things. Expect things. Crave things. God, this had to stop. She was Forrester's for the evening. Jenny would have to wait. Jenny would always have to wait. She hated herself for it, and when she slipped the note she'd written on a napkin into Jenny's hand, she didn't look at her. She couldn't. Jenny's body language would telegraph bravery, but her eyes would show ... what? Contempt? Betrayal? Sadness? Sympathy? Whatever it was, it would break her heart, and she couldn't be that weak. Ever. Forrester's doting mistress had a job to do.

She knew Jenny understood, but it had to hurt, no matter how much she tried to hide it or convince herself it was all for the greater good. The worst part was that this wouldn't be the last time. She had to clear those thoughts from her mind. Why were they there to begin with?

She would dissect that later. She stepped out of her shoes and shed her coat along with her persona. She was Jenny's again now and wanted nothing more than to fall into her arms and sleep for a week.

She quietly slipped into the kitchen and took a bottle of milk from the refrigerator. She shut the door and leaned against it, putting the cold bottle against her throbbing cheek. It had been a rough night.

The evening started with drinks at the club and then it was off to a typical cocktail party at the home of one of Forrester's companions. The night continued with more meaningless business discussions, where she played the attentive escort flawlessly. Forrester was the topic of hushed whispers, as his associates marveled at his audacity to flaunt his mistress in public during his divorce. Afterward, they were to meet with some new contacts, which made Forrester jumpy and anxious. Kathryn did her best to calm him, though he continually refused to acknowledge anything was wrong. She'd never met this crowd before, but off to the side, leaning casually on the banister of the grand stairway, was the tango partner who had brazenly swept her into his arms the moment Forester had left the room at a previous gathering. When Forrester sent his goons after him at the conclusion of their dance, she feared for his life, but here he was, alive and well, much to her great relief.

Forrester saw her relieved smile and leaned in, whispering, "I told you I just wanted his name."

"Thank you, Marc."

"Perhaps you shall dance again tonight," he said with a grin.

"Perhaps," she said cordially, as they walked away. That was all she needed ... a lust-struck musician drooling at her backside and a sexually challenged man on her arm egging him on. Her journey toward utter misery was complete—or so she thought.

Forrester made the rounds, trying to be nonchalant when he greeted his new partners in crime. Kathryn feigned ignorance about their true motives and smiled pleasantly as she always did. When the men exhausted their small talk, they excused themselves, one by one, to their private meeting. Kathryn quickly escaped to the balcony before the elusive tango player had any delusions about a chance in hell with her.

Blissfully left in peace, Kathryn stood on the balcony and got lost in her thoughts of Jenny. How disappointed she must be. Forrester's timing couldn't have been worse, and she was sure Jenny was as miserable as she was. She would have to do something special to make it up to her. A delicious grin split her lips as she imagined how wonderful her contrition would be.

She took a deep breath and exhaled an exasperated sigh. The cool stone railing felt good under her hands, but not as good as a cool glass of wine, glowing in the candlelight, with Jenny wrapped in her arms. She enjoyed the image for a moment but soon realized it was wholly out of place.

"What are you doing, Hammond?" she mumbled to herself. Thoughts of Jenny Ryan should have been the last thing on her mind. Of more immediate concern was Forrester. What was he up to? Who were these new men?

She should have been devising a way to get into that meeting, not rejoicing in her exclusion by daydreaming about her lover. She shook her head and felt the loss of her pleasant thoughts immediately. She suddenly noticed her aching feet and tired legs, and she hung her head as she shifted her weight from one leg to the other, stretching out her tight calves with a soft groan.

A pair of hands slowly wrapped themselves around her waist, and she rolled her eyes. The tango dancer was not only persistent but forward. She turned with an annoyed smirk.

"Listen—"

"Expecting someone else?" Forrester cooed.

"Sorry, darling. Of course not," she countered quickly with a tender hand to his cheek. "I didn't expect you back so soon. Everything all right?"

"I told you everything is fine. My associates understand my position, and they will just have to come to terms with it." He took her hand and patted it like a small child. "Why do you worry about such things?"

"I do worry, Marc. You know I do."

She wasn't going to pretend she didn't know what his quick return signified. Short meetings always meant he didn't get what he wanted and, oftentimes, a notice in the obituary column followed in retribution. His standing among his kind had been severely tested after Charles Lawrence's attempted coup, and the fact that these men were not afraid to defy his wishes showed he hadn't regained his throne yet.

Forrester wrapped her arm around his. "No worrying tonight. There's someone I want you to meet."

Finally, Kathryn thought. *Progress.* Forrester was efficient in his dealings. Perhaps he had found an ally after all. She pushed her shoulders back and held her head high, ready to impress and ready to make up for her lack of focus.

A group of four men watched their approach with great interest, and Kathryn wondered which one of them had sold his soul to the man on her arm. They had almost reached the group when the amorous tango dancer intercepted them wearing an arrogant smile.

Oh, for the love of Pete, Kathryn internally grimaced. *Not now.*

"Darling," Forrester began in a sugary tone he reserved for when he wanted to impress, "I don't think we've all been formally introduced. This is Thierry Bouchaule. Thierry," he said, turning, "as promised, Kathryn Hammond, the most beautiful woman in the room."

"Indeed." Bouchaule grinned as he took her hand gently but confidently to his lips. "*Enchanté, mademoiselle.*"

From the knowing looks on the two men, it didn't take long to see that there were no allies in the room and that this was no business introduction. It was about pleasure, and it would be anything but hers.

Kathryn found her wrist crushed in Forrester's grasp as he discreetly manhandled her into an unoccupied room and slammed the door.

"Let go of me!" she protested. "You're hurting me."

He unleashed a backhanded slap that caught her full on the left cheek, causing her head to snap violently to the side.

"Shut up!" he said.

She turned back to him, her free hand holding her stinging face. "You don't pay me enough for that," she said, barely containing her reflex to ball up her fist and hit him back.

His eyes narrowed and he tilted his head, slightly confused. Kathryn knew the comment had been a mistake. Forrester loosened his grasp and she yanked her arm away.

"So that's the way it is," he drew out slowly, as though the nature of their relationship had just become clear to him.

She had to think quickly to save her assignment and eight months of work. She swallowed her pride *and* her anger.

"I'm sorry I said that, Marcus," she said quietly, feigning humility.

In hindsight, she was sorry for a lot of things. When he suggested she sleep with Bouchaule while he watched, she could have said anything other than *I'm flattered, but no, thank you.* Bouchaule, to his credit, took it in stride. In fact, he seemed pleased, but surprised, by the suggestion in the first place. He was a gentleman about it at least, turning Forrester's demand into a request by deferring to the affected party. *If it pleases the lady,* he had said, bowing slightly.

It definitely did not please the lady, but that shouldn't have made a difference. She had rationalized her decision in her head and thought she was appropriately graceful in her refusal, but her rejection couldn't have been a bigger insult to Forrester, which he made abundantly clear as soon as the tango dancer was out of sight. Now she had to grovel, not only to save the evening, but also to save her assignment.

"Treat me like a whore and I can't help but feel like one," she went on in her defense. "I don't appreciate being handed over like this morning's newspaper—for his pleasure, or yours." She rubbed her wrist and looked up, wounded. "I thought I meant more to you than that."

His eyes narrowed again, and she could see him trying to decide whether he would forgive her. She added some tears to help him decide and quickly wiped them away to appear brave. He tugged at the collar of his shirt in annoyance and seemed to disregard any sympathy she may have won.

"You made me look like a fool out there," he said angrily. "We had a deal. You do what I say, when I say."

He was stabbing the air with an accusing finger, and Kathryn was on the lookout for another slap—she hadn't yet decided whether to let him get away with it again.

"There is nothing I asked you to do that you haven't done for me before," he went on as a justification of his request.

"What we do in our home is private," she said, winging it. "I'm glad someone here can tell the difference."

He raised his chin at her sarcasm—a warning.

"Think about it," she continued, hoping her rationalization would make as much sense to him as it did to her at the time. "Our deal was that I make you look good. You want to impress a man? Possess something he cannot have. I made your stock rise out there. Any man can get a whore, Marcus. Now he thinks I'm devoted to you—" She paused, playing the moment perfectly. "Which I am."

He had no comment.

She exhaled her false frustration and went on the offensive. "My God, what were you thinking? Do you want them to think I'm a whore?" She pretended a new thought had just dawned on her. "Is that what *you* think? After all this time, is that all I am to you?" He seemed shocked by the suggestion, and she knew she'd struck a nerve. "I don't need your money or your things, Marc. I can get that anywhere, from anyone."

What started as an angry accusation turned into an emotional declaration of devotion. She allowed her voice to falter, to really sell it. "I only want you, but I can't have that, so I do the best I can. I'm sorry that's not good enough for you." She turned to hide her tears, pretending she was ashamed of them.

He chewed on her words, and if her performance had any impact at all, it didn't last for long.

"I've still got a wife, Kathryn," he finally said sternly. "I don't need your dramatics. Go make yourself a drink. And for God's sake, stop crying." He straightened a cufflink and then his tie. "Clean yourself up. I'll expect you by my side shortly." With that, he left the room.

She closed her eyes with the slamming door and rubbed her stinging cheek.

"Shit."

Kathryn went to the small bar away from the milling guests and was annoyed to find no ice. She went to the empty kitchen, and after retrieving the metal ice tray from the freezer, slammed it down on the counter, forgoing the release lever. She was angry at Forrester for hitting her, but a good share of the anger was directed squarely at herself. It was unthinkable, but she let her personal life interfere with business. She should have said yes. She would have said yes, if not for—

"Hello, Disaster," Bouchaule said with a smile from the doorway, hands in his pockets.

Kathryn returned the smile as a matter of course, acknowledging the name he called her when they first met, and was glad the slapped side of her face was toward the door. "Hello, Thierry. I was just—" She looked up into the cabinets and grabbed a glass. "There was no ice at the bar." She filled the glass with ice, hoping to dissuade him from ambling over.

He was by her side before she knew it and stilled her hands. "Are you really that devoted to him, or are you just afraid?"

"I don't know what you mean," she said coyly, still hiding her face.

Bouchaule let go of her hands and dumped the glass of ice into a dishtowel, carefully folding it into a neat bundle. He turned her head and placed the wrapped cubes gently to her cheek.

"This will help with the swelling."

She looked into his sympathetic eyes and relieved him of the cold compress by replacing his hand with her own. "Thank you."

He smiled weakly. "I apologize."

"For?"

"The arrangement was not my idea."

She stared at him for a moment, wondering if he really thought that made a difference. "You went along with it."

He chuckled sheepishly and blushed. "If you have not noticed, you are a very beautiful woman, and I am only a man."

Kathryn looked him up and down but remained silent. Humility became him.

He moved closer. "I ask you again. Are you really that devoted to him, or are you just afraid?"

He was direct, she'd give him that. "I—"

"And you need not lie to me. I can see the truth in your eyes."

She stopped mid lie and marveled at the man's charisma. Between his physical beauty and suave demeanor, he could have anyone he wanted. She supposed they were a lot alike in that respect.

Still, she didn't know him. To her, he was just a tango dancing musician with good taste in women—caution, as always, was still in play.

"He's under a lot of pressure," she said.

"No man should treat you that way." He moved in closer and gently stroked the good side of her face with the back of his hand. "I would never treat you that way."

She moved away. "I think I've had enough of men for this evening," she replied. "But, thank you."

He nodded in understanding. "Let me give you my card." He held it out.

Kathryn turned her cheek and dropped the icepack to the counter to remind him of who she had to deal with and what he was capable of.

"You can't be serious."

Bouchaule insisted she take his card.

"I am *very* discreet."

She glanced at his offered card and then stood motionless —*Thierry Bouchaule, MD, PhD*—he was a doctor. Was he one of Forrester's new connections? Was he somehow connected to Daniel Ryan's medical research? She wasn't sure, but she wasn't going to dismiss it.

She smiled as she plucked the card from his hand. "You're a pretty good dancer for a doctor."

"I like to think I am a pretty good doctor for a dancer."

They both grinned. He took her hand holding the icepack and placed it back on her cheek.

"Take care of that." He ran his hand down her arm before breaking contact. "I look forward to seeing you soon."

He left her standing alone in the kitchen with a business card pinched dumbly between her fingers.

CHAPTER SIX

athryn carefully crept across her living room, skillfully avoiding the floorboards she knew to creak. She peeked into the bedroom on her way down the hall to the bathroom, and by the glow of a small nightlight, she saw Jenny curled up in her bed. She smiled as she quietly pulled the door shut and then tiptoed down the hallway, glad the day was over.

She looked at her swollen red cheek in the bathroom mirror. Forrester's heavy Masonic pinky ring left a welt just below her cheekbone, and she knew by morning, it would be a bruise. Her eyes swept up to the small scar above her eye from the car accident with Jenny and she shook her head.

"Why don't you just take up boxing?" she mumbled sarcastically.

She unhooked the back of her dress and let if fall to the floor in a heap. She then removed the diamond studded cuff bracelet Forrester had given her as a peace offering for his violent outburst and threw it on top of the dress in disgust. For the first time, she noticed the finger marks around her wrist were already bruising where he had grabbed her arm.

"Bastard."

His apology came as a complete surprise, as he had all but

ignored her after he stormed out of the room. He went on networking to keep up appearances, and she dutifully joined him as commanded. There was only so much she could do to disguise her abused face, but she managed to conceal it with some foundation and a cascading wave of dark hair. Forrester barely acknowledged her presence as they stood side by side, and his indifference made her feel like an outcast—an outcast who had blown her assignment.

She couldn't do anything but play his game and stew over her situation. Was he still angry? She couldn't tell. She looked around for Smitty, but he was nowhere to be found. That wasn't a good sign. She briefly entertained the notion that Forrester might have it in for her. If he was ready to discard her, she knew more than most, and most had been killed for less, but surely that was unreasonable. She knew him better than that—she was more valuable to him than that. On the other hand, she never would have predicted his violent response to her rejection, and she remembered Smitty's comment about arrogance making one careless. Perhaps she should listen to him more often.

When the evening ended, Kathryn asked a passing valet to call a cab. That finally got Forrester's attention, and he told the man to disregard the request.

Kathryn turned in controlled anger, aware of appearances and the other exiting guests. "I'm not going home with you, Marc," she said in a low but firm voice. She didn't know where he was emotionally, but she wasn't spending the night with him, and she wouldn't let him get away with hitting her without comment.

Forrester glanced at his driver, who was holding the backseat door open on the long black car.

"Take a walk."

When the driver complied, Forrester turned back to Kathryn. "Get in."

Kathryn balked. "I did as you asked, Marcus. I fulfilled my obligation to you this evening and I'm taking a cab home—on your dime."

"Get in the car, Kathryn," he said sternly.

"Or what?" she said, just above a whisper. "You'll hit me again?"

Kathryn thought for a moment that he would. Instead, he set his jaw and quickly glanced at the passersby before softening his approach considerably.

"Please, get in the car." She didn't move. "I need to talk to you. Please."

Kathryn looked around for Smitty again before she acquiesced. Forrester had sent him away, but she knew he was out there somewhere—watching.

Forrester followed her into the car, where they sat in tense silence for what seemed like an eternity. If Kathryn felt like an outcast before, she felt like an outcast in a vise now, as uncertainty and anger filled the confined space and pressed in on her.

"I'm listening," she finally said, before the urge to get out of there overwhelmed her.

"I don't know where to begin."

"Then I'm calling a cab." She attempted to slide toward the door to her left.

"No." He grabbed her wrist again, but this time she pulled it away before he had a good hold on it and she sucked the inflicted pain through clenched teeth.

"Damn it, Marc!"

He was immediately remorseful and tried to comfort her, but she slid out of his reach and found her back pressed against the opposite door as she held her aching wrist defensively.

He put his head in his hands and then violently pounded the side panel of his door three times with his fist.

Kathryn was frozen, as she realized the door at her back was locked and she was trapped in the car with an unraveling madman.

He stopped suddenly and clenched both fists in front of him, shaking as he tried to control his rage. He closed his eyes and slowly opened his hands, mumbling something indecipherable.

Kathryn didn't dare move. In fact, for a moment, she wasn't sure that Marcus Forrester was even aware of his surroundings. She knew he could be a brutal man, but she'd never seen him this way before, and she didn't know what to do.

A long exhale seemed to bring him back to the present, and he shifted away from her, toward the window, resting his elbow on the door handle as he pressed his fist into his tight lips.

Kathryn slowly started breathing again, as it appeared his tirade was over.

"I didn't mean to hurt you," he finally said into his knuckles. "I—" He shook his head. "Things are not going well. I—" He shook his head again and waved his hand dismissively, as if he knew anything he said would be a feeble excuse for his actions.

Kathryn remained silent and let him stumble through whatever was coming next.

"I didn't think—" He looked her way with no trace of anger. "I thought you wanted him."

"You were wrong."

He acknowledged the obvious with a pitiful nod and stared into the empty front seat.

"I'm a very powerful man, Kathryn."

"I know that."

"I'm also a very insecure man." He looked her way again. "I think you can understand why."

Kathryn nodded respectfully, all the while marveling at the change in his demeanor.

"That being said," he went on, "you can understand why a man such as myself would have a hard time believing that a beautiful, sensual woman like you would want to be with someone like me."

Kathryn bowed her head and closed her eyes, partly out of relief that her assignment appeared intact, and partly out of loathing for what she was about to do. *Twenty minutes,* she begged herself. *Just play the part for twenty more minutes.*

In twenty minutes, she would be in a cab and on her way home, leaving this miserable night behind.

"Aren't you tired of pretending to be strong, Marc?" she asked out of the blue. "Always looking over your shoulder?"

He delayed his response, but when he finally answered, his tone was that of a father to a naïve child. "I deal with very dangerous men, Kathryn. You know that."

"There's only one dangerous man in this car, and he doesn't have to pretend with me."

Forrester was silent as he looked her up and down. Kathryn watched his bravado disappear before her eyes. Hesitantly, he held out his hand, asking for forgiveness.

Twenty minutes.

She braced herself against his revolting touch and disguised her disgust as relief with a wanton smile. Her hand slid into his clammy palm, and he guided her to his side, where he lifted her hand to his lips and kissed his way down to her damaged wrist.

"I didn't mean to hurt you," he whispered between kisses.

"It was a misunderstanding," she replied with a grimace. She was glad he couldn't see her face. She was finding it harder than expected to endure his puerile attempt at reconciliation. *Come on, just twenty minutes,* she groaned internally. Unfortunately, part of her groan escaped, and Forrester mistook her disgust for desire, causing him to pull her closer, where he buried his head into her neck and kissed her throat on the way to her mouth.

Another groan escaped from deep within as Kathryn felt trapped in his arms. His hot breath on her skin encroached like a noxious fog, and she was repulsed by his lips seeking hers. His hold got tighter. She couldn't move. Her struggle to pretend became a struggle for survival, as she suddenly lost her ability to play her part. She wanted to scream, wanted to fight her way out of his arms, out of the car, out of his life.

Not a moment too soon, he slowed his advances—stopped by his shortcomings—and brought her gently to his chest with a guiding hand on the back of her head. Kathryn closed her eyes and focused on calming her ragged breathing.

"Are you all right?" he asked.

She nodded shyly, using the added time to compose herself. She would blame the stress of the evening for her inability to perform her duty—admitting it was anything else would be an invitation to failure, and she'd come too far for that.

"I'm glad we're okay," she lied, as she ran her hand up his chest. "I was afraid you were through with me."

"Through with you?" he said in a surprised chirp and resettled his arms around her. "Angel, you're the best thing I've got."

Kathryn climbed into the bath, eager to wash the evening, and Forrester, from her memory—there would be time enough to examine that disaster in the morning. She turned her focus instead to the fact that she had a beautiful woman in her bed. A relaxed grin spread across her face as she sank into the warm water. She washed her face and winced, as her swollen cheek protested the action, but no matter, all that was over now. She was home, where she had someone she loved waiting for her.

She quietly entered the bedroom, turned off the nightlight, shed her robe, and carefully slid under the cool sheets. Jenny was sleeping on her side with her back to her, so she leaned over and carefully peeled back the corner of the sheet, revealing a bare shoulder. She gently kissed the warm exposed skin and inhaled the sweet smell that was uniquely Jenny.

She smiled and lay back on her pillow, trying hard to contain a relieved sigh. The darkness leached a universal reverence from all it enveloped, and the stillness drained the tension of the evening away.

"How'd it go?" Jenny said softly.

Kathryn noticed her voice sounded as weary as she felt.

"I'm sorry, honey," she whispered. "I didn't mean to wake you. Go back to sleep."

"How'd it go?" Jenny repeated.

"Same ol', same ol'," Kathryn said on an exhale, as she rolled over and kissed Jenny's shoulder again. "Go back to sleep. We'll talk in the morning."

Jenny was still for a beat. "What does that mean?"

Kathryn put a calming hand on the tense shoulder before her. "That means you close your eyes and—"

Jenny rolled over to face her, and Kathryn was glad the darkness hid her face. Jenny didn't say anything, but she could feel the tension of her silent stare.

Finally, Jenny said, "I was worried about you. I didn't know you were going to be so late."

"I know. I'm sorry. Things just ... well ... things just dragged on and on."

Jenny shook her head. "Don't be sorry. I know it's your job. It's none of my business."

Kathryn propped her head up with one hand as she leaned on her pillow. She reached out and laid a hand across Jenny's abdomen. "You're upset with me."

"No." Jenny raised a hand and let it fall back on the bed.

Kathryn sensed she was sorry she'd said anything.

"I'm not upset with you." The hand went up and down again. "I hate this ... this whole situation. I hate that we can't spend time together. I hate that you have to be at his beck and call. And I *hate* that he touches you."

She covered her face with her hands. "I hate that I'm even bringing this up."

Kathryn tried to formulate the right thing to say, but Jenny, obviously disgusted with herself, suddenly threw the sheets back and slid to the edge of the bed.

"This is certainly not what you needed to come home to." She paused. "I think I'm going to go."

Kathryn stretched out and put a hand on Jenny's hip.

"If you leave this bed, it's because you want to, not because I want you to."

Kathryn felt Jenny relax under her touch.

"I don't know how you put up with me," Jenny said meekly.

Kathryn sat up and slid in behind her. She wrapped her arms around her and buried her face in the cascading waves of blonde hair.

"Likewise, I'm sure."

Jenny leaned into her. "I need to bottle this moment and keep it with me so that I can uncork it whenever I start acting like a spoiled child."

Kathryn leaned back and pulled them down onto the bed. "Does this mean you're staying?"

"For as long as you'll have me."

"Hm. That could be a while. Are you sure you've got the time?"

Jenny exhaled a chuckle and, with it, the last of the tension. "I'm really sorry," she said quietly. "I missed you. It was dark. It was late." She turned her head. "You know how the dark magnifies everything?"

"Mm," Kathryn drew out. "Quite familiar with the dark."

"Anyway," Jenny continued, "I tried to sleep, but I kept wondering what you were doing. I couldn't imagine what you were doing." She paused. "Okay. I *could* imagine what you were doing ... and I can imagine quite a lot."

Kathryn kissed her before easing her mind. "We went to a—"

"Kat," Jenny interrupted with a raised hand. "You don't have to explain."

Kathryn captured the raised hand and kissed it. "We went to a cocktail party, which was typically boring, then there was a meeting of global lowlifes, which is always interesting, and then I came home." She was too tired for the sordid details. She did, however, know what was really bothering Jenny. "I told you I don't have sex with him." It felt good to say it without it being a lie.

Jenny didn't immediately say anything, but Kathryn sensed that wasn't the end of it.

"Can I ask you something?"

"You can ask. I'll answer if I can."

"How do you manage not to sleep with him? I mean, how can you avoid that?"

"I'm just there to make him look good."

"And he doesn't want to have sex with you?"

Kathryn chuckled. "He couldn't have sex with me even if he

wanted to."

"I don't get it."

"He ..." How could she put this? She tried to think of something clever, but she was just too tired. "The bastard's impotent."

A beat of silent astonishment passed, and then Jenny said, "Oh, my God." She covered her mouth, shocked and oddly amused at the same time. "I don't think I needed to know that."

Kathryn smiled. "You asked."

Jenny gently placed the cup of coffee on the nightstand and fanned the steam from the aromatic brew toward Kathryn, who was still sleeping. She looked so childlike, curled up on her side with the covers tucked protectively under her chin. Jenny hated to go, hated even more that she had to wake up early to go to class. Saturdays were for sleeping in, or so it used to be. Lately, she'd found there are no days off in the life of an agent in training.

She begrudgingly finished tucking in her blouse and zipped up her skirt.

"The next sound I hear better be that skirt hitting the floor," Kathryn mumbled, slowly coming to life.

"Morning, baby," Jenny said with a grin, as she leaned over with a kiss. "I'd love to stay, but I've got a date with a code cruncher."

"That's a crying shame," Kathryn said, pulling her arm from its cocoon to wipe the sleep from her eyes. "I was going to make you breakfast."

"I'll take a rain—" Jenny's eyes went round. "Kathryn! What happened to your wrist?"

Kathryn pulled her hand away from Jenny's stunned fingers and quickly tried to cover her bruised wrist. "It's nothing." She got up and turned her face away. "Why didn't you tell me it was so late?" She put on her robe as she tried to sneak past.

Jenny grabbed her sleeve. "Look at me."

Kathryn stopped with an exasperated exhale but didn't turn

around.

Jenny impatiently peered around her, seeking Kathryn's down-turned face. Kathryn reluctantly raised her chin. Jenny anxiously guided her hair out of the way and then gasped.

"Oh, God." She reached for the dark bruise coloring the high cheekbone, but Kathryn moved away. "Kat, what happened?"

"A misunderstanding."

"What kind of misunderstanding puts bruises all over your body? Where else did he hurt you?" She searched for evidence.

"Nowhere else, I promise."

"What happened?"

"We had a difference of opinion. It was nothing."

"Was it a misunderstanding or a difference of opinion?" Jenny asked, irritated at the evasion.

"A little of both," Kathryn said curtly. "Look, can we drop this? It's over." She headed for the hall.

Jenny followed her. "What was it about? Was it about me?"

"What?" Kathryn stopped short and turned. "No, it wasn't about you. It had nothing to do with you."

"Then what was it?"

"Jenny—"

"Jenny, what? Don't keep things from me, Kat. You're not as good a liar as you think you are."

The comment obviously struck a nerve, because Kathryn leaned toward her with fury in her eyes. "You are not privy to everything that goes on in my life."

That brought a familiar sting. It reminded Jenny of the argument they'd had in the French restaurant after she admitted pressing Smitty for details of Kathryn's past.

They'd come too far for a repeat of that scene, and she would stand her ground this time, because she refused to be dismissed so easily. "I'm not privy to things in your personal life. I'm not privy to things in your professional life—" She threw her hands up. "What the hell am I doing here, Kat?

Kathryn bit down on whatever she was about to say and

continued toward the bathroom.

Jenny followed her. "Stop running away from me!"

Kathryn stopped and turned. "I just need a minute to myself, Jenny."

The words felt like a knife plunged into her heart. It was a reminder that she was still an outsider looking in. Maybe she always would be. Jenny turned on her heel with tears in her eyes and started for her jacket. She heard Kathryn's quick stride coming toward her and felt her fingertips claw at her shoulder.

"Jenny, wait. Please. I'm sorry."

Jenny could have gotten away easily, but she stopped and waited, her labored breathing the only sound in a room silenced by the lingering echo of frustration and pain.

Kathryn placed her hands gingerly on her shoulders from behind and exhaled a shaky breath when she didn't step out from under them.

"I'm sorry, Jenny. Sometimes, I just need a minute."

"Keep it up and you'll have all the time in the world."

Kathryn came around to face her. Jenny meant for the retort to sting, but she was unprepared for the fear and regret in Kathryn's eyes when she took her hands in hers.

"And I would deserve it, and more, for hurting you. I'm sorry."

Jenny wanted more than anything to forget the last few minutes and fall into her arms, but she couldn't shake the feeling that Kathryn's disastrous night had something to do with their relationship. "He hit you, Kat, and you're lying about why."

"Jenny—"

"Don't you dare say it was nothing! Have a little more respect for yourself than that."

Kathryn backed off. "I can't afford to!"

They were interrupted by a quick rap on the cellar door, followed by the turning of the key in the lock, and then Smitty, as he stuck his head in. "Say, what's all the noise? I could hear you two yelling all the way down in the—"

"Ugh," Kathryn groaned, as she raised her hand and stormed

toward the bathroom.

"Love you too, doll," Smitty replied sarcastically. He removed his hat and turned to Jenny. "What gives?"

Jenny put her hands on her hips. Maybe Smitty could talk some sense into her. "He hit her last night."

Smitty's eyes narrowed. "That son of a bitch. Kathryn!"

Jenny sat on Kathryn's couch and wiped a tear from her cheek. She could hear Kathryn and Smitty arguing in the bathroom. She wasn't eavesdropping exactly, but it was a small apartment, and shouting didn't lend to a private conversation.

Kathryn was getting it from both barrels this morning, and Jenny regretted her part. Shock had turned her concern to anger, and she realized patience, rather than pushing, would work better with Kathryn, considering the pressure she was under.

Jenny felt terrible. She had promised she could handle the business end of Kathryn's life, and she had broken that promise. She realized it had been naïve to make such a promise in the first place.

The shouting from down the hall eventually stopped and the loud voices became murmurs. Soon, Kathryn emerged with Smitty close behind, hat in hand. He looked sympathetically at her and announced he'd wait in the car. He took the cellar exit, and Kathryn locked the door behind him. She slowly made her way to Jenny's side on the couch, where she collapsed with a weary sigh.

"You heard?"

"Most of it."

Kathryn nodded but had nothing to say. Jenny noticed she'd taken the time to cover the bruise on her face, but she knew the makeup was an illusion and that the bruise remained as a painful reminder of the price of their love.

"You refused because of me."

Kathryn remained silent. It was the same accusation Smitty had leveled, though his was a few decibels louder. Kathryn vehemently defended her decision to him, much as she had to Forrester, she imagined, but there was no denying the truth.

"I made a mistake."

Jenny could see by the firm set of Kathryn's jaw that it was a tough thing to admit, especially when she knew it was unacceptable.

"You can't make mistakes, Kathryn. And I won't let you make one because of me."

"Maybe I have some self-respect after all," she said with a half-hearted grin, trying to put the debacle behind her.

Jenny would have smiled too if the outcome of the evening wasn't so serious. Clearly, Kathryn had literally taken one on the chin for the sake of their relationship. That was noble but not very smart. She took Kathryn's hand and kissed it, acknowledging her sacrifice.

"As you said ... you can't afford to."

Kathryn agreed with a downturned nod, and Jenny knew that doing her job meant compromising something dear to her—the sanctity of their love.

"You knew this would happen. This is why you didn't want to start our relationship."

Kathryn tenderly squeezed her hand but remained silent. She didn't have to say anything. Jenny understood. None of that mattered now. She also understood she would have to do better.

"I let you down, Kathryn. I'm sorry. I told you I could handle it."

Kathryn tugged on her hand and smiled, as if it were nothing. "Well, apparently, I can't handle it very well either, so I won't hold it against you."

Jenny tried to smile, but she knew Kathryn was hurting. She needed comfort, not recrimination, especially from her.

"Are you disappointed in me?"

Kathryn shook her head and stared at their clasped hands. "I'm disappointed in myself, honey. I'm sorry I hurt you—I didn't mean to. I just need to handle myself better in those situations, and that's got nothing to do with you."

"I'm sorry, Kat, but if you're compromising your safety because of our relationship, that certainly does have something to do with me, and I'll not have it. If we're to go on, there is no other choice. You do what you need to do. That's all there is to it."

Kathryn looked up, alarmed. "What do you mean, *if* we're to go on?"

"You need to promise me you'll do whatever it takes."

"Or what?"

Jenny became still and tears filled her eyes. "This is killing me," she said, as she eyed Kathryn's abused cheek and lightly stroked her bruised wrist. "If something happened to you—"

"Jenny—"

"No, Kat," Jenny said firmly, lifting her chin and getting a hold of her emotions. "If something happened to you because of us ... because of your silly romantic notion of fidelity ..." She almost choked on the thought of it. "I couldn't bear it."

Jenny saw Kathryn flinch when she reduced fidelity to a *silly romantic notion*, but considering their situation, she knew she couldn't disagree. She supposed it was disheartening for Kathryn to see her so callous about love, especially when it was her idealistic exuberance that taught her the beauty of it. But things had changed now, and she saw Kathryn buckling under the weight of it.

Jenny steeled her resolve. It was the only thing that would save them. "You're trying to hold on to something we can't have right now."

For the first time, Jenny saw that Kathryn recognized the change in her. The idealistic ingenue was gone, replaced with someone hardened by reality.

"When did you get so wise?"

"I'm not a child."

"No, you're not."

"Promise me."

Kathryn took a deep breath and exhaled in resignation. "I promise."

"Okay."

The room filled with silence again. Jenny checked her anger and wondered if Smitty could do the same the next time he saw Forrester.

"Smitty won't do anything stupid, will he?"

"No. He's too smart for that."

Jenny nodded and hoped for his sake that was true.

Kathryn had nothing more to say. She went from staring blankly at the floor to checking the clock on the bookcase. "You're going to be late."

Her announcement seemed cold and abrupt, and Jenny wondered if things were indeed okay between them. "They can start without me."

"You don't want to fall behind. It's important."

"You can give me private lessons at the penthouse this afternoon." She grinned, hoping Kathryn would too. She didn't. She was deadly serious as she stared at their clasped hands.

"I'm sorry, honey. I can't."

Jenny didn't need to ask, but she did anyway. "Him?"

"We're going away for a few days."

Jenny closed her eyes and swallowed the curse on the tip of her tongue. This was her chance to be strong, and she wouldn't let Kathryn down again.

"Will Smitty go with you?"

"No. Just the two of us."

"Will you be all right?"

Kathryn's eyes met hers, and Jenny saw longing, fear, regret, and love, all woven into a watery gaze, swimming with exhaustion.

"No," she said, as she reached up and tangled her hand in her hair. "I'll miss you like crazy."

Jenny quickly found herself in Kathryn's arms, engaged in a passionate kiss.

"God, I've missed you," Jenny said.

Kathryn's pleasurable moans agreed, as she guided her to a prone position on the couch and unbuttoned her blouse.

"I'm going to be late," Jenny said with a grin.

"I'll write you a note."

"What about Smitty?"

"Smitty can find his own girl."

CHAPTER SEVEN

The gravel crunched beneath Kathryn's feet as she jogged across the Long Island estate's courtyard to her waiting trainees. She was late, and, apparently, so was Hendricks.

"How're you doing today, bub?" Kathryn asked, slapping him on the shoulder as she jogged by.

"Ready to kick some Axis, ma'am."

Kathryn smiled. "I knew you would be."

The greeting was more jovial than she felt, but like the performance she'd put on for Forrester over the weekend, it was a necessity. She couldn't let the disturbing news that greeted her upon her arrival at the training center affect her focus. She had a job to do, and she would have to shelve her concerns for just a little longer.

"Morning, folks. Sorry I'm late," she said, as she stepped behind her desk at the front of the classroom.

Her meeting with the other instructors ran longer than expected, as rumors flew about green trainees being pulled from the ranks for immediate deployment. All the instructors agreed they weren't ready, but, as always, the demand for agents far outweighed the organization's ability to supply them.

Kathryn found it hard to look at her students. Their lives depended on the lessons they learned from their instructors, and she would be unable to prepare some of them properly for what lay ahead. She had a sinking feeling about Jenny. The way things had been going for them, it was practically a given that she'd be one of the trainees called up.

Kathryn busied herself as she spoke and avoided looking at Jenny altogether, for fear she'd see right through her.

"All right," she began, as she made meaningless piles out of the folders on her desk. "We've been through the equipment, and we've been through the procedures. It's time to put what you've learned into action. Welcome to field training."

The class stared at her, anxiously awaiting her words, and she realized she couldn't avoid eye contact forever. They would feed off her confidence in them—she could give them that at least. She took a calming breath and looked up, ready to get down to business.

"Is there anyone here who has not had time to review the mission?"

A young brunette unabashedly raised her hand.

Kathryn gave the room a distracted glance. "Anyone else?"

No one.

"Thank you." She went back to needlessly organizing files and addressed the unprepared woman. "Ericsson, you may go."

"Ma'am?"

Kathryn looked up. "I'm sorry, was I not clear?" She leaned forward. "Get out."

"Now, wait a minute," the woman protested. "I've got—"

"You've got what, Ericsson? A good excuse? Other things to do?"

The class shifted uncomfortably at the ferocious reprimand.

"We've all got things to do, and my list doesn't include wasting my time and energy on someone who doesn't take this class seriously."

"Ma'am—" the woman tried to explain.

"Ericsson!" Kathryn slammed the folders in her hand on the desk. "Maybe the Joe at the guardhouse will be interested in your tale of woe, but, honestly, I don't care what you have to say. Get out of this class and out of my sight. Every second I waste on you is a second I can't give to someone who does give a shit."

The rest of the class sat in stunned silence while the woman collected her things and quickly left the room shaking her head. Some stared at her back as she departed, and some stared at the floor, but Kathryn felt Jenny's eyes trained on her.

Now wasn't the time to send signals of reassurance, so when Kathryn met Jenny's concerned gaze, she offered no more recognition for her than for a stranger on the street.

"I'm going to assume the rest of you are well versed in what we're doing today?"

Silent nods.

"Are there any questions?"

Silence.

Kathryn understood their apprehension after her outburst, but now was not the time to be shy. "Listen, you're not in high school, and this is not the principal's office. I'm sorry you're uncomfortable, but I haven't the time to hold hands. I'm here to teach you what you need to know to survive. I can't help you if you don't help yourselves. Now, do you have any questions?"

Silence.

Kathryn put her hands on her hips. "Are you telling me that on the brink of your first full-on mission sim, no one has any questions?"

One brave trainee in the back raised her hand. "What kind of resistance can we expect?"

"Excellent question. Thank you."

The room relaxed with the return to the learning environment, and question after question was raised and answered with due care and infinite patience.

Jenny asked a question, but Kathryn knew she already knew the answer and asked just to have her look her way. Kathryn answered the question with the same detachment she had answered the others and moved on. She was sure that left Jenny doubly concerned and reflexively hurt, but she would explain her actions later, preferably while lying in each other's arms after a night of lovemaking. She blinked the thought away.

"If you are captured overseas," she went on sternly, responding to another question, "you're to try and hold out for forty-eight hours. This will enable your cell to disperse and go underground."

She noticed the collective discomfort of the class when they realized they were not holding out to be rescued. "You are not in the military. They will not be coming to your rescue. If you are caught, you are—"

"Royally fucked," a voice interrupted from the back of the room. Everyone turned around to see Lieutenant Branson, the eternal thorn in her side, standing in the doorway with his arms crossed. "That's how it's *supposed* to work, isn't it, Hammond?"

Kathryn did her best to keep her face neutral. She would not give him the satisfaction of a reaction. The education of her team was more important than any feud she had with the man. He had been warned about undermining her authority in front of the trainees, but he took every opportunity to needle her without stepping over the line.

Without revealing her personal feelings toward him, she held up her hand to the back of the room. "Ladies and gentlemen, this is Lt. Jeremy Branson. He is our firearms expert. His team will represent the enemy on our mission today."

She gave him a warning look about whatever he was up to, and he smirked back without comment.

"Thanks ever so much for stopping by to introduce yourself, Lieutenant," she said as civilly as she could.

He tipped the bill of his cap with a look that said he wasn't through. "Good luck today, folks. You'll need it." He disappeared out the door into the bright afternoon sun.

Kathryn swore internally and rubbed her head. "Where were we?"

"We were royally fucked," a small woman said from the fourth row.

"Right. Well, let's not get caught today and we won't have to go into the details of being royally fucked. Okay?"

There was no humor in her delivery, but a small murmur of laughter went around the room as the class sought any excuse to lighten the mood.

"If you have any more questions, now is the time to ask. Once that mission clock starts, question time is over. Understand? You do what I say, when I say it."

The class nodded.

"Good. You all know what your jobs are. Watch me for your signals, and we'll all make it out alive."

More nods.

"Sync your time, and I'll see you on the other side."

The class set their watches to the wall clock and filed out.

Jenny was the last one in the shuffling line of recruits heading for the exit. Kathryn came up behind her and tickled the small of her back, whispering, "Excuse me," in her ear as she passed.

She caught Jenny's relieved smile in response and was glad she knew it wasn't personal.

Kathryn shook her head as she watched her student fumble with his tools. Hendricks was running out of time. A misstep had turned their covert mission into an ugly smash and grab. The mission could be salvaged, but not if the recruit couldn't perform his task. The entire team had performed admirably, but now an alarm was blaring, tripped by a careless oversight, and Sam Hendricks cursed the sound of it, as it rendered him unable to think straight. He was poised with the wire snips over the tangle of wires—frozen.

She knew he was thinking *white, red, blue, then green?* Or *red, white, green, then blue?* His inaction showed he couldn't remember. There wasn't a booby-trapped safe in their mission profile, but they had been warned to prepare for anything.

Kathryn hovered nearby, wondering when he would look at his

watch to see how much time he had left to decide. They always looked at their watches. They might as well be noting their time of death. If he began clipping randomly and, by some miracle, got the sequence right, he would barely have time to stop the mock detonation and break into the safe before the guards showed up. Failure was imminent.

Kathryn glanced to the wall through the doorway and watched the time for the detonation clock wind down to zero. She looked back to Hendricks, and, predictably, he had spent the last few seconds of his life looking at his watch.

To his credit, he didn't turn to her in surprise when he saw the device that would cost him his life. He recognized it immediately and processed what he needed to do to eliminate it. He just didn't process it fast enough.

The mission was over. The team had failed, but Kathryn looked on the failure as an opportunity to hone her own rusty skills and to test Research and Development's new, improved plastic explosive.

She tapped Hendricks on the shoulder and let him know he was a dead man before sending him out the door with a quick flick of her head toward the exit.

His "Sorry, ma'am" got lost in the screeching of the alarm as he sprinted away.

Hendricks looked at the mission clock beside the expired detonation clock outside the door and shook his head: three minutes and thirty seconds before the guards would show up. Even his unflappable instructor couldn't crack the safe, grab the contents, and get clear in time.

He ran in a crouch along the stone wall of their mock German outpost and followed it to its end, where he hopped into the ditch beside Jenny.

"Did you do it?" she asked, rifle in hand.

"Negative," he huffed, out of breath. "Killed in action."

"Ugh, Sam," Jenny groaned. "What happened?"

"Safe was booby-trapped. BV-36. Four wire … couldn't remember the sequence."

"White, red, blue, then green," she said. "How hard is that?"

He looked at her with disdain. "Maybe you should run point next time."

Jenny apologized for her criticism with a pat on his shoulder. "Where's our fearless leader?"

"She's—" Hendricks looked at his watch. "Say, that's not right."

"What?"

"Mission clock in there is three minutes off."

"Are you sure?"

"We're synced." He showed her his watch. "She thinks she has time. She's as dead as I am."

Jenny handed him the rifle. "Not if I can help it. Cover me."

"Wha—wait!"

He stared in disbelief as Jenny sprinted toward the stone building, ignoring the caravan of guards coming up the drive.

"She told us to wait!" he said to the air, but Jenny was long out of earshot.

Pure adrenaline muted the blare of the alarm, and Kathryn easily disarmed the detonator attached to the safe. She removed the device and threw open the black canvas bag at her feet. The usual tools of stealthy safe-cracking were haphazardly tossed to the side in favor of the plastic explosives that would blow the safe open. It wouldn't be pretty, but it would get the job done, and just in the nick of time.

She found a certain thrill to her task. Nothing made one feel more alive than the threat of impending doom. It might be just an exercise, but the explosives in her hand were very real, and the faint acidic smell of the clay-like substance reminded her of its destructive power, as she kneaded it between her fingers and then rolled it into shape.

She had to admit, she found an odd comfort in the danger. It was familiar, and the intense focus staved off the sense of dread brought on by the morning's rumors. The constant alarm reminded her that somewhere, guards were double-timing it to her position. She worked quickly and efficiently, as skills long dormant returned without thought. While her hands continued their work, she reflexively glanced around the room for an alternative escape route. She knew there was none, but old habits die hard.

It would be close, but she had time. Her team had taken out the guards in the immediate vicinity, and in sixty seconds, the safe would be open and she would be out the door with its contents. A satisfied grin doubled her determination. The good showing by her squad pleased her, but defeating Branson's team would really make her day.

She had just finished embedding the knotted Primacord fuse into the malleable plastic explosives placed in the appropriate places on the safe door when she thought she heard her name being shouted above the screeching alarm. She made a half-believing glance over her shoulder and did a double take when she saw Jenny motioning frantically for her to leave.

Not sure why she was surprised, Kathryn shouted, "Get out of here!"

She saw Jenny lean back into the hallway, and confident she'd obeyed her command, she set off the percussion cap on the end of the fuse and pushed up from her kneeling position to sprint out the door. She ran headlong into Jenny's midsection as she approached quickly from behind.

Kathryn bowled Jenny over, and they both wound up sprawled in a heap on the floor. Realizing she had no time for anything but a mad scramble for their lives, Kathryn grabbed Jenny by her shirt with both hands and threw her and herself behind the nearest piece of furniture, which, fortunately, was a solid oak desk.

A split second later, the explosion ripped through the room, and Kathryn ducked her head into Jenny's chest as a piece of hinge came flying through the back of the desk and embedded itself in the bookcase just past their heads.

Kathryn stared at the large projectile in disbelief and then looked through the fist-sized hole it left in the kick panel of the desk. She looked down at Jenny.

"Are you all right?" she shouted above the still blaring alarm and the ringing in her ears.

Jenny didn't answer.

"Jenny! Are you all right?"

Jenny nodded mutely, and Kathryn realized the shoulder to her midsection knocked the breath out of her.

Kathryn leaped to her feet, pulling Jenny with her.

"Get out of here, *now!*"

Jenny didn't really have a choice this time, as a shove in the back propelled her toward the exit. Kathryn quickly returned to the smoldering safe and kicked the mangled door from its remaining hinge. She removed the prize—a small black book of codes that was charred around the edges but otherwise still intact—and checked her watch. Close, but well within the safety zone. They'd done well for their first exercise. She nodded with satisfaction and turned for the door.

She looked up to see Branson and two members of his team crowding the doorway with smirks on their faces and Jenny front and center, looking disgusted with her hands on her head. The alarm abruptly stopped, and everyone looked up, as though the silence was by divine order.

Jenny tilted her head regretfully. "I tried to warn you."

Kathryn pinned her with a furious glare before turning to the smirking lieutenant.

"What is this, Branson? We beat the clock."

"Oh, we moved up the guard response time. Didn't you get the memo?"

She realized he had changed the time on the clock in her room. The exercise was doomed from the start.

"Cute, Lieutenant. What's the matter? Can't win without cheating?"

"Expect the unexpected, Hammond," he said gleefully as he shot her with his forefinger. "*Pow!* You're dead." He looked at Jenny. "And your little disciple too."

Kathryn chewed on the defeat and then slapped the book into Branson's chest as she shoved past. She didn't look at Jenny.

"Enjoy the view while you can, boys," Branson said from behind Jenny's back as she exited the outpost. "She won't have that ass for long."

Jenny responded with a middle finger salute over the shoulder as she stiff-armed the door open and let it slam on the laughter swirling behind her.

The rest of the team had already gathered around Kathryn when Jenny joined them in time to hear some instruction to Hendricks, who was lamenting his unfortunate demise.

"In that situation, Hendricks, you have to make a decision," Kathryn explained. "At least give yourself a chance to be right."

"I know. It was the alarm. I couldn't concentrate."

"Yes, well ... the alarm." Kathryn looked at the guilty party. "That was careless, Johnson."

"Didn't see the tripwire, ma'am."

"You weren't looking either."

The trainee couldn't deny it, so he sought solace in the dirt on his shoes.

Jenny was glad that Kathryn didn't seem angry anymore—heat of the moment, she imagined—but she was sure losing to Branson didn't help.

"You folks did some good things out here today." Kathryn went on. "You made some mistakes, but you recovered admirably for the most part. Unfortunately, our mission failed today—"

"It failed because he cheated," Jenny chimed in, thumbing over her shoulder in Branson's direction.

Kathryn turned, and in a flash, the anger was back.

"It failed because you disobeyed orders."

"Wait a minute ... I was trying to warn you."

"Your orders were to stay put. Your disobedience showed a blatant disregard for everyone who tried to make this mission a success."

Jenny put her hands on her hips, finding the description a bit over the top. "I hardly think—"

"*That* is painfully obvious," Kathryn barked. "Once inside, you disobeyed orders again when I told you to leave. Training mission aside, you could have gotten us both seriously injured. What were you thinking?"

Jenny could do nothing but blink for a few moments. Kathryn was furious and then some, but then it dawned on her that Kathryn was in a teaching situation, where she had to illustrate that mistakes were part of the learning curve but outright disobedience was not to be tolerated. Jenny learned her lesson, and for the benefit of the rest of the class, she took her dressing down squarely on the chin and offered a weak excuse, as she softened her stance and put her hands behind her back in submission.

"Sorry. I just wanted to help."

"This is not about what *you* want! The mission is paramount, and your actions compromised it today, and in the end, we paid for it in failure and with our proverbial lives."

Jenny looked up, confused. She wanted to say, *Okay, I get it already*, but she held her tongue in deference to Kathryn's authority and nodded instead.

Kathryn toned down her ire and addressed the rest of the class. "Don't ever go back, people. Shoot the guards, cause a distraction, do whatever you can to give your partner more time to complete their mission, but do not needlessly sacrifice yourself to a losing cause. This is a game of seconds." She turned to Jenny. "And you wasted yours playing hero instead of doing something that actually might have helped the situation."

Jenny suppressed an eye roll and shifted her weight from one leg to the other, anxious to get out from under the dunce cap. She could have helped, she still reasoned, if Branson hadn't cheated.

"Okay," Kathryn said on an exhale. "I think you all get the point. Nice job today. Dismissed."

The team separated and Kathryn began loading equipment into a jeep to return to the supply shed. When Jenny was sure no one was paying any attention to her, she picked up a bag and walked it over to the open-air vehicle.

Kathryn didn't say anything as she tossed the dark canvas packs into the back of the jeep one by one. Jenny eyed her in silence until she couldn't take it anymore.

"Come on, Kat," she whispered. "You can't tell me you wouldn't have done the same."

Kathryn stopped mid-toss and glared at her. "You screwed up, Jenny."

"It was a training mission, Kat," Jenny said casually in her defense.

Kathryn threw the pack down. "What if it wasn't?"

Jenny threw her pack down and put her hands on her hips, tired of being the punching bag. "I'd probably do the same."

"And that is precisely how people get captured, tortured, and killed!"

Jenny could tell by the anguish in Kathryn's eyes that this wasn't about training or making her an example—it was about personal experience.

Kathryn picked up the pack at her feet and hurled it into the jeep with the others. "You're not cut out for this, Jenny."

Jenny could see where this was going and, personal experience or not, she was not going to allow Kathryn to sabotage her chance for fieldwork over one mistake and ghosts of the past.

"Don't you do that, Kathryn," Jenny warned. "I've worked too hard for this."

"I'm not doing anything, Jenny. You're doing it for me."

Jenny moved closer and lowered her voice, aware of the curious stares from their departing team members. "That's not fair. You're letting your personal feelings get in the way of—"

"You're damn right I am!" Kathryn snapped. "You have no earthly idea what it's like over there. I'm telling you ... you don't have what it takes."

"Well, excuse me for caring about my fellow human beings!" Jenny snapped back, at a loss for an effective comeback.

Kathryn pointed at her. "That's the attitude that's going to keep you behind a desk for the duration."

"You'd like that, wouldn't you?"

"Yes!"

The pair was frozen in fury until Kathryn became aware that every eye within earshot was staring at them. She broke eye contact with Jenny and dared them to continue. "Dismissed!"

The collective group of raised eyebrows went about their business, and Kathryn climbed into the jeep.

Jenny grabbed her arm. "This isn't right, Kathryn. I'll go over your head if I have to."

Kathryn ignored the hand on her arm. "You do that."

Jenny released her hold and stepped back as the jeep peeled away. She stood there, watching the cloud of dust in disbelief, and wondered how they'd gotten so far apart and how they could possibly fix it.

She heard footsteps approaching in the gravel from behind, and from the uneven gait, she didn't have to turn around to know who it was.

She put her hands on her hips to show she was in no mood to take any more noise. "Hi, Johnny."

"Hi ya, kid. Trouble in paradise?"

Jenny cut him a disparaging glare, which she was sure made his day, and he eyed the dispersing dusty trail with interest. "What happened?"

"Jerkhole Branson got cute and screwed with our mission clock. We're dead."

"Oh. My condolences. Why's she barking at you?"

"I went back to warn her about the guards, and we sort of got caught."

Smitty chuckled. "Sort of got caught, eh? You mean she told you to amscray but you just had to save her, right?"

Jenny was in no mood to appreciate his sarcasm either, but one look in his eyes told her his biting humor was only a front to hide his own guilt.

"You know the drill," she said.

"Yeah," he exhaled. "When she says go, just go, and don't look back."

"Yeah. I got that."

"Good. You'll do fine then. Don't worry about it. She'll come around."

"I'm afraid it's a little deeper than that, Smitty."

The two turned to the sound of hurried footsteps as Branson came jogging up from behind and slapped Smitty on the back as he passed.

"The more things change, the more they stay the same, eh, Johnny?" He laughed as his voice trailed off. "Your girlfriend's still screwing up."

"Fuck off, asshole," Smitty called after the soldier's back. He looked at Jenny. "Sorry."

"Don't worry about it. Beat me to it. What the hell is his problem anyway?"

"Hell hath no fury like a redneck asshole scorned."

Jenny raised an eyebrow.

"It's a long story," Smitty said, as he waved off the telling of it. "Listen, I'll go straighten things out with Kat for you. She never stays mad for long."

"Thanks, Smitty, but I don't need you to smooth anything over for me. I can take care of myself."

"Okay, just trying to help."

"Yeah, thanks," Jenny mumbled, trudging off toward the equipment shed.

Kathryn downshifted the jeep into second gear as she powered around the corner and cursed herself for losing her temper. Jenny was wrong, but the dressing down in front of the class should have been sufficient. Why did she have to be so damn stubborn?

Kathryn had let her personal feelings interfere with her objective view, but she didn't care anymore. Jenny could ship out any day, and if there was anything she could do to prevent it, she decided she would do it. Jenny was just too impulsive and headstrong to make a good field agent, of that she was certain. Brass had to see that. They had to.

She came to a skidding stop in front of the equipment shed and unloaded the gear.

"Let me help you there," the check-in clerk called as he jogged out of the office.

"Thanks." Kathryn tossed him a pack.

He loaded a few more onto his shoulders and together they slogged inside.

"Did you have a good day, Miss Hammond?"

"I've had better," Kathryn said drolly as she signed the equipment return manifest.

"How'd you like that new RDX?" he asked with a grin, touting the new plastic explosive.

"Packs quite a wallop." She smiled politely as she crossed the t in her first name with a sharp scratch across the clipboard.

"It might give you a headache," he said. "Something about the composition. You absorb it through your skin"

"Yeah, I think I'm feeling that," she said, doubting it was the chemicals making her head pound.

She gave him the remainder of the explosives and began stowing the rest of the equipment in the storage room while he locked up the RDX in the back with the rest of the hazardous materials.

"You don't have to do that, ma'am," he said on his return. "That's my job."

"Tell you what," Kathryn countered, "I need to decompress for a few minutes, so what say you return this to the depot for me and I'll finish up here." She held up the keys to the jeep.

"Deal!" He snatched the keys and headed for the door. "Lock up when you leave if I'm not back."

"You got it."

Kathryn shook her head as the door slammed. Nice fella. Not very security conscious, but at least he locked up the dangerous stuff before he left her alone with the rest of the warehouse.

She took her time returning the equipment to its proper place, using the mindless activity to go over the mission's successes and its failures. Her thoughts always returned to Jenny and their altercation. She could have handled the situation better, she knew, but she couldn't stop herself. She knew they would have to part, and soon, but she thought they had more time. Just a little more time.

She closed her eyes and leaned her forehead on the cool steel shelving. She should have known. Time was never that accommodating, and she was never that lucky. She didn't know how she was going to mend things with Jenny. She only knew she had to.

She heard the outer office door open and cleared her tight throat and got back to her task.

"Wow, you're quick," she called to the clerk, suddenly longing for a distraction.

"Yeah, but not quick enough to escape with our lives," Jenny said, leaning on the doorjamb.

Kathryn was silent for a moment before coming out with a brilliant, "Hey."

"Hey," Jenny said.

She came to Kathryn's side and they wordlessly put the equipment away together. Kathryn was at a total loss for words, so she opted for the stoic professional approach while Jenny, true to form, got right to the heart of the matter.

"You're being unreasonable, Kathryn, and that's not like you. What's going on?"

Kathryn silently accepted the truth and wanted to hug Jenny for being so perceptive and so forgiving. She closed her eyes and turned away, willing herself not to cry.

Jenny placed a concerned hand on her back. "Kat?"

Quietly, and without turning, Kathryn answered. "They're pulling some of the trainees for immediate deployment."

Jenny was stunned. "We're not ready."

The obvious required no response.

"Am I going?" Jenny asked bravely.

Kathryn shifted and then swallowed, as her fear was put into words. She barely got out a strangled, "I don't know."

Jenny put her arms around Kathryn's waist and rested her head between her tense shoulder blades.

"I'm not ready for this," Kathryn whispered. She turned and enveloped Jenny in a desperate embrace. "I'm not ready."

"Nice try, Hammond," Branson smirked as they sat waiting for Colonel Forsythe to return to his office. "You almost made it. That seems to be your lot in life, but why is it you're always taking people down with you?"

"Not today, Jerry," Kathryn exhaled, as she massaged the headache at her temple.

"Okay, sorry," Forsythe said, as he walked in the door carrying a folder with the telltale classified blue paper inside. "Now, where were we?"

"We were just about to point out Miss Hammond's ineptitude."

Forsythe took off his reading glasses. "I think we can do without the cracks, Branson."

Branson shrugged. "Hey, she not only got herself killed, she lost her puppy too."

"Can it, Branson," Forsythe said calmly.

"She disregarded my directive," Kathryn said as an irrelevant excuse.

Forsythe pushed some papers around on his desk. "And I'm sure you've taken care of that."

"Yes, sir, I have."

"Good. Then I think we're done here. Nice job, Kathryn."

"What? Her mission failed."

"You need to get out of my sight, soldier," Forsythe said impatiently.

Kathryn got up to leave with Branson.

"Stay a moment, Kathryn."

Branson shook his head and left the room with a disgruntled "Tst."

Forsythe, in turn, shook his head but made no comment. He leaned back in his chair and took the classified folder with him. "I suppose you've heard the rumors."

Kathryn nodded, as the knot in the pit of her stomach tightened with every passing second. Colonel Forsythe opened the folder and took out a white slip of paper. Kathryn's heart pounded.

"Some of these recruits are from your unit. I thought you'd want to know."

He leaned across the desk and offered four names. Kathryn took it casually, although she wasn't sure she could maintain her cool façade if Jenny's name appeared before her.

Johnson.

Hayes.

Coleman.

Hendricks.

She closed her eyes, her relief profound, but only for a moment, as she gave thought to those chosen. All had great potential, but all were far too green. She nodded and handed the list back to her superior.

"I know it's hard," he replied.

"I suppose it goes without saying, if this weren't absolutely necessary ..."

"We certainly wouldn't do it if it weren't. They'll have a little more training at their destinations, specifics pertaining to their respective missions. You know how it goes."

Kathryn's nod turned into a head shake, knowing it wouldn't be enough for some of them.

"You learned by doing, Kathryn, and without the basics that these kids already have."

"We all know I'm no shining example of that system in action."

He replaced the list and closed the folder. "You're here, and you've given them a good start. It's all we can do."

He handed her a piece of paper from his briefcase. The flimsy onion paper crinkled in her hand as she took it and snapped it to attention so she could read it. It was a carbon copy of Jenny's new assignment in the code room, signed at the bottom by the personnel officer in sweeping blue ink and dated the day before.

"Would you like to tell her, or shall I?" Forsythe asked.

Kathryn returned the page, relieved that Jenny was not going into the field. "Sir, at this point, I think that would go down a little easier coming from you."

Kathryn squinted into the sun as she left Forsythe's office and hadn't gone ten steps before Branson was in her ear to pick up where he left off.

"You know, I wouldn't feel too good about yourself, despite what he says. It's that blind devotion that took your friend down with you today. Kind of like déjà vu all over again, wasn't it?"

"I'm warning you, Jerry. Not today."

"I don't know what the uppers see in you, Hammond, but I've got to hand it to you—you've snowed them all. Although, come to think of it, if I could get somewhere by sleeping with brass, I suppose I would too."

Without skipping a beat, Kathryn flung her elbow up and caught him square in the face. Branson fell to the ground holding his bloody nose and looked back toward Forsythe's office like a child ready to tattle. Forsythe was standing at the window, smiling as he pulled down the shade.

A muffled "You bitch!" echoed across the courtyard.

Kathryn kept walking and didn't look back.

Kathryn held her breath as she opened the front door of her apartment, not sure how she would be received. She could see the living room light on from the street, so she knew Jenny was there. She was sitting at the end of the couch, crying, and made no attempt to make eye contact as she wiped her cheek with a tattered tissue.

She knew Jenny would be upset, but she hoped she would know she had nothing to do with her reassignment. Kathryn slowly closed the door, struggling to find the right thing to say by the time she turned around. Simple seemed best.

"I'm sorry, Jenny."

Jenny looked up, eyes red and filled with tears. "No, you're not."

Kathryn hoped it wouldn't go this way, but she steeled herself for the fight she was sure would follow.

"Okay," she said in frustration, tossing her keys on the bookcase. "I'm not sorry."

She passed by the couch without another glance and went into the bedroom before she said something to exacerbate the situation. This shouldn't be happening. Things would be fine now. Couldn't Jenny see?

She opened her closet but didn't see the contents. All she saw was another fight, in a seemingly endless string of fights that were driving them further apart. She stood frozen with her hand on the open closet door, her eyes closed, and a fist tangled in the sleeve of a blouse.

Just let her vent, she urged herself, *don't lose your temper.* She heard a floorboard creak and forced herself back into motion by wearily yanking the blouse from its hanger.

The hanger flew off the rod and skittered out of the closet and across the floor, coming to rest at Jenny's feet.

Jenny picked it up and hesitantly came to her side, holding the mangled wire out like an olive branch.

"I didn't mean it like that, baby."

Kathryn relaxed and took the hanger, relieved. There was no

anger in Jenny's eyes, only sadness and regret, which matched her own.

"I am sorry, Jenny." Kathryn reached out and stroked her cheek. "I'm sorry you're disappointed, but I want you to know I didn't have—"

"I know," Jenny interrupted, as she sought comfort in her arms.

Kathryn held her tightly. "It's going to be okay now, honey. Everything's going to be okay."

Jenny nodded into Kathryn's chest and then backed off to wipe her tears. Kathryn sensed there was more to her tears than a reassignment.

She cupped her cheek. "What is it?"

"Ugh," Jenny groaned, as she waved off the waterworks and sat on the bed.

Kathryn plucked another tissue from the box on the vanity and held it out as she joined her.

"Thanks." Jenny wiped her nose with it. "I just talked to Bernie. He wants to join up."

"I thought you said he was 4F because he's colorblind."

Jenny nodded and dabbed her eyes with the tissue. "He wants to be a war correspondent, or find a spot in the Signal Corp photography division."

"What brought this on?"

"He said this thing with Cal opened his eyes and he wants to do the same for others—document the war, bring it home. Show people what's really going on."

"He's had a shock. Maybe he'll change his mind."

Jenny shook her head and wiped her nose again. "No, he's already applied, and they'll take him. He's good."

She started crying again, and Kathryn put her arm around her.

"He can't go over there, Kat. He's not built for that."

Kathryn was silent, recognizing their situations were now reversed. The parallel was not lost on Jenny, who looked up sympathetically.

"Now I know how you felt today about me going over there. I'm sorry I was so stubborn."

"Doesn't matter," Kathryn whispered, as she rubbed small circles on her back.

"I can't let him go. I can't."

"Look, if anyone can talk him out of it, you can."

Jenny shook her head. "I tried. He accused me of not supporting him, of deserting him at the *Chronicle*, deserting him as a friend—you name it. He's so twisted up inside. I had no idea, and I have no idea how to get through to him. He's so angry with me."

She deflated into Kathryn's embrace, utterly defeated by the day.

"I haven't been a good friend to him." She sniffled. "On top of that, I got kicked out of field training and I let you down. I feel like such a failure."

Kathryn made sure Jenny was looking her in the eyes. "First, you have never let me down, and you did not get kicked out of field training. You were placed elsewhere, somewhere where you can be better utilized. Code work is important—even more important than your old job at MO. Without it, the agents in the field are blind, and so are we. You are certainly not a failure. And, as for Bernie, he loves you. He's just ... he's hurting right now. He'll come around."

Jenny sniffled again and nodded, burying her face into Kathryn's shoulder. Kathryn could tell she wasn't buying the sunny forecast, and she tilted Jenny's chin up.

"Is Bernie at home?"

Jenny nodded.

"Then go to him."

"He won't see me."

"Hey ..." Kathryn squeezed Jenny's chin. "Who can resist this face?"

That brought a smile.

"Make him see you. I know you can do that. Spend some time with him. Patch things up."

Jenny was unsure, and Kathryn wanted to make sure it wasn't about them.

She wiped a tear from her cheek with her thumb. "Are we okay?"

Jenny smiled and covered the hand on her cheek with hers. "Yes."

"Then go. I'll try to call you later."

"You really think I can fix it?"

"Honey, I think I'm living proof you can fix anything."

Jenny laughed.

"Here." Kathryn held out the mangled hanger. "Fix that while you're at it."

CHAPTER EIGHT

Forrester lit Kathryn's cigarette and she let her hand linger on his as he flipped the lighter closed. There were three other men around the circular table at the private nightclub, including the mysterious Thierry Bouchaule, whose presence inspired Kathryn's exaggerated fondness for her companion. Forrester certainly didn't mind, as he was the envy of the group, sitting proudly like a peacock, with his feathers on display.

The continuing show of affection had the proper effect on its audience. One man shifted nervously as he stared at her cleavage all night, one kept wetting his lips every time he glanced her way, and one, Thierry Bouchaule, seemed amused by it all, as he casually exhaled his cigarette smoke into the sexually-charged space between them.

The conversation was mundane: legitimate business, politics, the war. Kathryn would not be privy to the real reason for their meeting. She never was. Forrester would indicate when she should make her excuses. If the meeting wasn't behind closed doors, it was merely an exchange of information, and he wouldn't need much time. He would complete the business with his partners, and they would go on as if nothing had happened when she returned.

The telltale hand on her knee told her it was time, but she hesitated, as the hand on her knee became a hand on her thigh, and she reflexively stood up before it became anything else.

"Excuse me, gentlemen." She looked to Forrester. "Darling." She smiled and then ran her hand up his arm and across the back of his shoulders as she departed.

She briefly eyed the waiter heading her way, but virtually ignored him as he passed, for fear any acknowledgment would expose him as the plant sent to eavesdrop on her table's conversation.

She was glad to be out from under Forrester's constant attention. He had been stuck to her like glue ever since he slapped her, and she exhaled a sigh of relief as she rounded the corner and headed for her standard refuge, the ladies' room.

The phone inside the empty lounge was her first stop. She needed to hear a friendly voice.

"Hi," Kathryn said with a grin. "How'd it go with Bernie this afternoon?"

"Well, hi! You got away."

"Mm. Just have a minute though. How'd it go?"

"Eh. He was on his way out with Robert. He didn't have time to talk."

Kathryn could hear the weariness in her voice. "I'm sorry, honey."

"He spoke to me at least—who can resist this face, after all?" The joke fell flat, much like her attempt at reconciliation. "It's going to take time, I guess. I'm glad he has Robert to lean on since I failed him so spectacularly as a best friend." She cleared her throat, pushing aside the hurt and disappointment. "So, where are you?"

"*Bella Donna.*"

"Mm, swanky. Are you beautiful?"

Kathryn giggled, knowing Jenny already knew the answer. "Of course."

Jenny exhaled a laugh. "Tell me."

"Low cut, long sleeve green number, obscenely adorned in diamonds, hair up, but casually sexy, and because I'm not wearing any panties, I can't get you out of my mind."

The line was silent.

"Jenny?"

"Mmph," Jenny moaned. "Woman, that was cruel."

Kathryn smiled. "Thought I'd give you something to look forward to."

"I'm looking forward to it all right."

They both chuckled. Their relationship was back on track, and things were getting back to normal for them, or at least as normal as things ever got between them. Their main concerns now were wooing Bernie back to his senses and keeping Marcus Forrester appeased.

"Is he being nice to you?"

"Mm. Too nice. He's taking me along to Chicago next week."

"Bleh. For how long?"

"A few days, I would imagine."

"Will Smitty be there?"

"'Fraid not."

"I don't like that, Kathryn. He's all the protection you've got."

"I think I can manage."

"I'm sorry. I know you can take care of yourself."

"Don't be silly. I'd wonder about you if you didn't worry." She checked her watch. "Listen, I've got to get back."

"'Okay."

"Think of me."

"Baby, I do nothing *but* think of you."

"That's what I like to hear," Kathryn said with a grin. "Can't wait to feel you in my arms again."

"I love you."

"Love you too, honey. See you tomorrow at six."

Kathryn rearranged the fresh flowers in the vase on the piano at Luc's penthouse for the third time and looked at her watch again. Seven thirty. No sign of Jenny. Something wasn't right. She'd worn out the *traffic must be bad* explanation to herself a half hour ago. Even if Jenny had to work past five, even if she had to walk, headquarters wasn't that far away. She should have been at the penthouse by now. She most certainly would have called.

Kathryn nervously parted the translucent drapes and peered at the busy streets below, as if she could see Jenny approaching. She replayed their last phone conversation in her head, looking for any explanation for her absence, and knew if there was a reason, it wasn't personal.

She had the feeling something was terribly wrong. She picked up the phone and dialed the switchboard at headquarters, anxiously waiting while her call trickled through the system to the proper department. She blinked to attention when the secretary finally picked up.

"How may I direct your call?"

"Jenny Ryan, please."

"Thank you."

The phone rang and then rang some more. "Come on," Kathryn mumbled, worry unraveling her.

"Yeah?" a man answered impatiently as he snapped his gum.

Kathryn was stunned for a moment, not expecting a man's voice. "Jenny Ryan, please."

"Nah, this is Matthews. What can I do you for, sweetheart?"

"Isn't this Jenny Ryan's desk?"

"Uh—"

Kathryn imagined him looking around.

"Oh yeah, so it is. Cute blonde, right?"

"Is she there?" Kathryn asked, exasperated.

"Nah. Went home sick around two. Pale as a ghost, poor thing. How can I hel—"

Kathryn slammed the phone down and picked it up again immediately to dial Jenny's house. Why hadn't she called?

The phone rang in its familiar two short, one long pattern. "Come on, honey, answer the phone."

Again, the phone rang and rang, but no answer.

She called her message service and the club to see if anyone had left a message. Nothing.

While she was on the line with the club, she canceled her nightly nine o'clock show, giving her understudy yet another appearance. She was thankful that Dominic was so understanding on such short notice. Next, was getting out of the evening with Forrester. She feigned a convincing migraine and promised to meet him for breakfast in the morning. He was appropriately worried, but she assured him peace and quiet for the evening was all she needed.

With responsibilities out of the way, she dashed from the penthouse and headed over to Jenny's house.

CHAPTER NINE

Traffic was atrocious crossing the city, and Kathryn thought she might go insane as she got behind one slow moving idiot after another. Finally on the fairly deserted Westside Drive, she floored it and found herself the victim of a speeding ticket. She got an earful from the motorcycle cop by way of a lecture about gas rationing, rubber tire shortages, carpooling—the works.

He ripped the ticket from his book and handed it over to her, interrupting her impatient tapping on the steering wheel.

"Here you go, Miss Hammond. Thirty-five," he said as a warning, reiterating the speed limit. "There's a war on, you know."

As he walked away, she muttered, "No shit."

Suddenly, his face was back in her window. "What did you say to me?"

"I said, thank you, Officer Jones, for being such a conscientious public servant and a true patriot." She held the ticket over her heart and blinked unabashedly.

"Hmph," he snorted and gave her a skeptical look before walking away.

She watched him get on his motorcycle and speed off in the opposite direction. She shook her head as she started the engine, released the handbrake, and then jammed the car into gear.

It was dark by the time she got to Jenny's house, and already she could see something was wrong. Jenny must have taken her beloved father's '37 Cord for its monthly drive into town. It was parked haphazardly in the drive, and a closer examination showed she had clipped the brick mailbox column on the way in, bending the chrome bumper into the flared maroon fender.

Kathryn's heart was pounding as she ran up the steps to the front door. It was unlocked. She slowly opened it and stepped into the darkness.

"Jenny?" she called out with a calmness she didn't feel.

No answer.

She fumbled on the wall for the hall light switch and turned it on. The bedroom door was ajar, so she crept silently toward it, in case Jenny was sleeping. She carefully pushed it open, only to find the bed empty. She headed toward the bathroom, where she slowly pushed the door open.

"Jenny?"

Empty.

She walked back into the hallway and called again, this time loudly, as worry turned to panic.

"Jenny?"

Kathryn smelled the distinct odor of scotch coming from the living room. She hit the light switch on the wall and was met with a room in disarray. Paintings were ripped from the wall and strewn about. The large portrait of Jenny's grandfather over the fireplace was torn and crooked. Kathryn got closer and found the painting had been the target of a bottle of scotch, which lay shattered on the mantle and hearth, its contents painting the wall and what was left of the portrait.

"Jenny?" she called again, as she entered the study and turned on the light. Her panic was complete when she saw the hidden gun case open, rounds on the floor, and Jenny's prize automatic missing from its velvet lined box. Kathryn took in the rest of the room and found the contents of her father's desktop strewn about and the music stand from the exquisite Bösendorfer piano torn from its hinges and used as a bat to shatter the photo frames on its once pristine black case.

"My God," Kathryn said, as fear took panic's hand and she ran from the room, her heart in her throat. She passed the dining room, where more disarray caught her eye.

Papers littered the long mahogany dining table, finally spilling onto the floor when they ran out of room. Blue papers. Classified OSS papers. Kathryn approached in disbelief. This couldn't happen. It was impossible. These never left the center. They were never seen by anyone other than the highest-ranking officials. The scene was so absurd that she looked over her shoulder. Where were the men in the big black cars? Surely, they would know these were missing and they'd be coming after the thief. Words like *spy* and *treason* would be tossed around, and the guilty party would pay dearly—usually with their life.

Kathryn's shock turned to horror as she saw her signature on page after page. Reports. Her reports about her assignment to Jenny.

"Oh, no. No, no, no."

Her legs went weak and she collapsed into a chair, her hands shaking as she sifted through the rest of the paperwork.

The papers contained the Ryan file she and Smitty had been shown. Not only did Jenny now know about her assignment and the dubious backgrounds of her father and grandparents, but the additional pages showed that, according to her blood test, Daniel Ryan was not her father.

"What?" Kathryn said, as she quickly rifled through the papers.

She let the papers fall from her hands, as a horrific thought went through her mind. Any one of the revelations in the classified papers would be devastating, but all three simultaneously? Jenny had gone on a suicidal alcoholic bender when her father was killed, and now she had alcohol and a gun in her hand. If the demolished state of the house was any indication of Jenny's current state of mind, she might already be too late. Kathryn stood, knocking the chair backward, and ran frantically through the lower rooms again. She prayed Jenny was just sleeping it off somewhere.

"Jenny!" she screamed as loudly as she could.

Silence.

She took the grand staircase two steps at a time, darting to the left at the top, and then stopping in her tracks as she glimpsed the shimmering lake in the large bay window.

"The dock."

She backed up and peered into the moonlit yard. Squinting to focus on the distant lakeshore, her look of concentration quickly turned to horror as she made out a human form sprawled out on the end of the dock. Kathryn's heart thundered in her chest, as the unthinkable quickly became a very real possibility. She plastered her hands to the window, as if she could reach through and turn back time.

"Jenny," she whispered in desperation. "Please, no."

She was nearly hysterical as she pushed away from the window and flew down the stairs. "Please, please, please, honey, don't do this."

She tried not to focus on the empty gun case in the study as she rushed through the house, but she couldn't stop her imagination from seeing what she feared she would find when she reached the dock. She flung open the back door and leaped from the small stoop without taking the stairs.

It was a perfect night. The air was still, the moon was full, and the stars twinkled joyfully in a cloudless night sky, unmindful of the drama unfolding beneath them. The atmosphere was surreal. The full moon, like a sun in an alternate universe, bathed the trees in its pale light as they cast long shadows on the neatly manicured lawn stretching to the water. Kathryn ran as fast as she could, as fear and exertion caused her lungs to ache. She cursed as she ran through a spider web and cursed again as she slipped and nearly fell on the dew-laden grass. She was running blind, her senses in denial to avoid the quickly approaching truth. Her labored breathing and the thud of her feet on the soft earth cut the still night as she took full strides to her destination.

As she got closer, she could see that it was Jenny lying there, her blonde hair glowing white as it absorbed the moon's rays. In fact, the whole world was bathed in black and white, like a film, and Kathryn wished that it were, so that she could leave the theater, and this nightmare, behind.

"Please," she begged the motionless form and any god that would listen. "Please don't do this, Jenny. Please."

She slowed as she approached the dock, almost afraid to arrive. The longer she stayed back, the longer Jenny would still be alive, if only in her mind. She stopped at the edge of the wooden planks, her chest tight and her heartbeat thudding in her head. She swallowed her gasping breaths and rubbed her hands on her thighs in nervous trepidation as she gingerly made her way onto the dock.

Jenny lay before her, her legs bent at the knees and dangling off the end of the dock. One hand was on her chest, the other lay on the dock, her silver Browning Hi Power glistening in the moonlight as it lay loosely in her open hand. Her eyes were open, but there were no signs of life. Kathryn stopped and tried to make out whether her chest was rising and falling, but in the subdued light, she couldn't tell for sure. Then she saw a large dark spot on the dock's surface, by the side of her head, and her heart sank. She began to cry, unable to stop herself, and she put her hand to her mouth to silence an involuntary sob. Her whole body felt numb. Her soul was detached, waiting to find out if it would live or die. She thought she'd be sick. She closed her eyes and swallowed hard, begging the shadow beside Jenny's head to just be a shadow.

She made her way around the still form until she was standing at Jenny's side. With her breathing short, and her heart breaking, Kathryn slowly kneeled beside her, as if in prayer. She couldn't see for the tears in her eyes, but she reached out to touch Jenny's face, something she'd done so many times before—to give comfort, to send her love—but this time her hand shook in fear. It seemed so impossible that this simple gesture may be the last they would share and that the savior of her heart and soul may already have left her alone.

In a blurred split second, she found her wrist captured by one hand and the gun pointed directly at her face.

"Shit!" Kathryn exclaimed as she fell back, landing on her backside and nearly off the side of the dock. She blinked away tears. "Jenny! Thank God." She tried to move closer, but Jenny wouldn't allow it.

"Why are you here?" Jenny calmly demanded, still pointing the gun at her.

Almost on instinct, and still half crazed with grief and worry, Kathryn's relief quickly turned to anger.

"Get that thing out of my face!"

She could have disarmed her with one swift move, but Jenny had a choice to make, and she had to make it on her own. Jenny lowered the gun and Kathryn resumed breathing, wiping tears from her cheeks.

Jenny relaxed onto her back again and stared up into the stars.

"Why are you here?" she asked again, this time as a defeated question, not a demand.

"You didn't show up at the penthouse. I was worried. I called HQ, they said you went home sick. I wanted to make sure you were all right."

"Are you sure you're not here to finish your assignment?"

"I wanted to make sure you were all right."

Jenny continued to stare into the sky.

"Let's go inside, Jenny."

"What? And waste this beautiful night? Look at those stars ..."

Kathryn looked up briefly as Jenny continued.

"They don't care about us."

Kathryn watched Jenny carefully. She was flicking the safety on her gun back and forth in what seemed to be a game of will she or won't she use it. Kathryn's concern wasn't for herself, but for Jenny, as her mental status was still uncertain.

"Can I have that?" she asked cautiously, pointing to the gun.

"Don't you have one?" Jenny asked, still staring at the sky.

"Not one as pretty as that."

Jenny sat up, with her face etched in anger. "Don't patronize me, Kat."

"Give me the gun, Jenny."

"That wouldn't be very smart of me, would it? Surrendering my gun to the enemy?"

"I'm not your enemy."

"Ha! A comedian too. Will your talents never cease?"

"I want to help you."

Jenny let out a humorless chuckle. "Help me? With friends like you, who needs enemies, right?"

"Look, I'm sorry for all this—believe me, but I can't change what's happened. What I *can* do is try to help you. You're in trouble. They'll be coming soon. Please let me help you."

Jenny looked hard into her eyes, but there was no recognition of their relationship.

"Please let me," Kathryn repeated.

Jenny considered it, and, after a few silent moments, handed over her gun.

Kathryn took it and extended her hand. "Come on, let's go inside."

Jenny got up on her own and brushed past without a sideways glance.

Kathryn's emotions were raw, and she could barely contain them, but as they walked to the house in silence, she couldn't imagine the turmoil Jenny was in. She seemed to be in a state of shock.

As they entered the house, Jenny paused at the dining room. Kathryn righted the chair she'd knocked over and led Jenny to it. She sat carefully, with her hands in her lap, as if her whole body would shatter if she jarred it too suddenly.

Kathryn gathered the papers on the floor first and then picked up a cut crystal glass and the cap to the scotch bottle that had rolled under the table. She noticed the glass was clean, and she eyed Jenny, who stared blankly at the mess before her.

She wasn't drunk, which was good—or maybe it wasn't. They both could use a drink. Kathryn continued to keep an eye on her as she gathered the classified papers and, stack by stack, put them back into the folder.

"Have you looked at all of these?" She held up the latest bunch in her hand.

Jenny finally looked up and nodded faintly, lifting her arms to the table, where she slowly reached out for the nearest piece of blue paper.

Kathryn quickly moved it out of reach and picked it up, sensing that dwelling on what was found there was not a good idea. Jenny didn't protest. In fact, she showed no emotion at all as she got up and left the room.

Kathryn hurriedly gathered the remaining papers and followed her, not about to leave her alone. Jenny wandered aimlessly down the hall, surveying the house as if she'd never seen it before.

"Come on, honey," Kathryn said, as she put her hand on her shoulder. "Let's sit down."

Jenny shrugged off the hand. "Don't touch me."

"Jenny—"

"Jenny, what?" She turned, rage now building in her eyes. "Jenny, it's going to be okay? Isn't that what you said? Everything's going to be okay now?"

Kathryn opened her mouth to speak but found no words to say.

"I've got nothing, Kathryn! Better yet? I never had anything to begin with. It was all a lie. You, my family—" She looked around. "This fucking house. None of it was real."

"That's not true, Jenny. Whatever your family did in the past, they loved—"

"They're not my family!"

"Blood doesn't make a family. Believe me, I know."

"Oh, spare me. You can lay off the sob story, sister. You're off duty."

Jenny stalked into the living room and plopped herself down on the couch, where she ran her hands across the russet leather surface, as if she'd never seen it before, and crossed her legs.

"Is your mother even dead, Kathryn?"

Kathryn's eyes snapped to Jenny in disbelief, the words like a dagger to her heart. Jenny couldn't have cared less.

"Is your name even Kathryn?"

"Now, wait just a minute—"

"Wait, don't tell me," Jenny began sarcastically with a raised hand. "I know this speech. Believe me, darling, I love you," she exaggerated dramatically. "You were just a job at first, but I grew to love you, and now we shall conquer this together. Sound about right?" She laughed. "You know, you *are* good. God. I've got to hand it to you. Whatever they're paying you, it's not enough."

"You know I love you, Jenny. You know it!"

"I don't know anything. And I'll never trust you again."

Car doors slammed outside.

"Ah—" Jenny got up to answer the front door. "My ride to the gallows is here."

"That's not funny."

"Put yourself in my shoes, Hammond. Sure it is."

Jenny entered the foyer and opened the door. She walked away, letting the men make their own way inside.

Two hulking men in dark suits soon filled her doorway.

"Jenny Ryan?"

"Right here," she said, as she plucked her jacket and purse from the hall tree.

"Come with us, please."

Jenny held up her wrists for the cuffs.

"I don't think that will be necessary, ma'am."

She turned to Kathryn with mock glee. "Oh, look, *now* they trust me."

The other man pointed to the folders in Kathryn's hand. "Are those the files?"

She nodded and held out her empty hand, ever mindful of the nature of their business.

"Orders and ID?"

She had Jenny's gun behind her back, tucked into the waistband of her slacks, and she was prepared to use it if the men didn't pan out. She perused the offered documents and, satisfied the men and their papers checked out, handed over the folders.

"You need to report for debrief," the tall man said sternly.

She nodded.

"See?" Jenny held out her hand to the men. "She's so good. Here I am, just willing to follow you goons like a puppy."

"Let's go, Miss Ryan."

The men led her away.

"Jenny—" Kathryn rushed to the doorway and waited for her to turn around. "For what it's worth … I am sorry."

Jenny looked at the two men guiding her to their car and they nodded in understanding, giving the two women the chance for a few private words. Jenny walked back up the steps to the landing until they were face to face.

"It's not worth anything to me, Kathryn. Leave your key on the table when you leave. I don't ever want to see you again."

CHAPTER TEN

The room on the thirty-sixth floor of HQ was filled with cigarette and pipe smoke and the smell of men whose day had long since rendered them clean. Jenny had been there for two hours already, going over the same questions, giving the same answers. There were six British men, including Colonel Holmes and his two aides, Ronald and Brian, who, as usual, sat mutely at his side. Colonel Forsythe, or anyone connected with the OSS, was absent.

Finally, Holmes dismissed the other men, who Jenny assumed were there to intimidate her, and she was alone with Holmes and his aides. Holmes's demeanor changed, and he leaned in like they were coconspirators. It made her uncomfortable.

"Where is Colonel Forsythe?" she asked.

He ignored her.

"Those files were beyond your classification, Miss Ryan."

"Then don't put them in my in-tray!" she said for the umpteenth time.

But there they were, on her desk, when she returned from lunch. She thought it was just another decoding exercise, but her life would never be the same after she opened the oversized yellow ochre envelope and read its contents. She promptly went to the ladies' room and threw up.

With the files stuffed into the waistband of her skirt under her blouse and suit jacket, it wasn't hard to walk them right out of the high-security area, especially looking like death warmed over.

"Where is Colonel Forsythe?" she repeated more forcefully.

"Oh, Miss Ryan, I don't think you want the OSS involved in this."

"You mean *you* don't want the OSS involved in this."

"I am investigating this incident, and you would do well to—"

"Well, that's convenient," she interrupted, "since obviously you're the one who put them in my in-tray."

"Now is not the time for your vivid imagination."

"How did you know those files were missing? How did those men know to come to my house?"

Holmes leaned back and took a drag from his pipe. "Anonymous caller."

Jenny laughed. An *anonymous caller* is what put her on this path to begin with. "You agencies really do need a new playbook. You've about worn that one out."

"I'm getting a little tired of your attitude."

"And I'm getting a little tired of being manipulated." As soon as it was out of her mouth, it reminded her of Kathryn, when she accused her of the same. She completely understood now why it was so easy for Kathryn to feel that way.

"No matter how those files wound up in your in-tray, you carried them out of this building and to your home. I don't think you realize the trouble you're in. You are under my purview now."

"As punishment?" she said sarcastically.

He pursed his lips, and she swore he was going to laugh, but he resumed his holier-than-thou countenance and pointed at her with his pipe.

"You could be prosecuted for taking those files from the premises."

Jenny had had enough of the British colonel's bullying.

"Those files might just be some random case to you, but that is my life in there, and I have a right to know the truth!"

Holmes sat back with a strange smile pulling at his lips. "What are you going to do about it?"

She looked around the table at three sets of expectant eyes. "What?"

Holmes leaned forward. "What are you going to do about this *truth*?"

Good question. One she hadn't really considered until that moment. "Whatever my father—" She stopped and retracted the word. "Whatever Daniel Ryan was doing … I want to stop it."

Holmes sat back with a knowing grin on his face and pressed the button on his intercom.

"Sally, get Miss Ryan's clearance raised two levels, and get us another pot of coffee and some tea, if you would."

He slid a file across the table to her.

"Welcome to your first assignment. Case DR6498. Meet Daniel Ryan."

Jenny perused the file with a surprising lack of sentimentality.

Colonel Holmes emptied the barrel of his pipe with two sharp raps into an ashtray. "I'm afraid your father's research—"

Jenny interrupted him with a glare that said *that man* was not my father.

"Pardon me," Holmes said with a smile. "I'm afraid Daniel Ryan's research is about to be used against us."

"What was he working on?" she asked indifferently. "Biological weapons, like his parents?"

"We don't know for sure, but we suspect."

Jenny didn't see anything useful in the pages she could read, but there were stacks of coded files with corresponding dates and no explanation of their meaning.

"What is this?"

"That is his project."

"How did you get this? What does it say?"

"Let's just say we intercepted them, and our problem is that we don't know what they say."

"Where was this information going?"

Holmes eyed her carefully as he answered. "Marcus Forrester."

Jenny's eyes snapped up immediately. It was all becoming a little clearer. "He has the key?"

"We don't think so."

Confusion knitted her brow. "So, it's worthless."

"Men have been killed for the information in your hands, including its author, so it is worth something to somebody."

Jenny stared at the lines of code as if her heritage could somehow magically transform it into coherent language. Then she remembered there was no magic in her heritage. She had no heritage. The realization hit her and she swallowed her emotions, pretending to concentrate harder on the pages before her.

She looked at the intercept dates. "Wait a minute ... these are recent. Who's passing this information?"

Holmes paused for a moment, and Jenny knew he was letting her come to her own conclusions before offering his own theories. She let him spill his first.

"Paul Ryan? Kathryn Hammond? You?" he said.

Jenny was stunned at the accusation.

"Say, what is this? I'm here to help you. If you honestly think that I—"

Holmes raised his hand with a grin. "Relax, Miss Ryan. Just catching you up on the case."

She calmed down, recognizing her piece in the puzzle. She cleared her throat and moved on.

"Kathryn Hammond." She shook her head. "She's a lot of things, but she's not helping Forrester."

"You're sure?"

Jenny's first reaction was from her heart, and it said *of course I'm sure,* but then she balked, realizing she wasn't really sure of anything anymore. She dismissed the idea of Kathryn's guilt, not because she thought it was improbable, but because she wanted all traces of the woman's memory out of her head.

"Yes. I'm sure."

"Which brings us to Paul Ryan," Holmes said.

"Well, it is a family tradition," Jenny said coldly, as she pored over the pages and pages of code.

Holmes had a satisfied glint in his eye, and Jenny could see his plan to recruit her against her family had worked flawlessly.

"Where would he get this?" Jenny asked, almost to herself.

"We thought you might be able to tell us that."

She wracked her brain, trying to think of where her uncle would get such information, but short of her father giving it to him sometime before his death—something she found highly unlikely—she came up empty.

"I haven't a clue." Then something occurred to her. "How would you like me to handle him?"

Holmes smiled, and she imagined he was quite pleased with her easy betrayal.

"Reveal nothing. You are estranged at the moment, correct?"

Jenny bristled, imagining that information had come from one of Kathryn's reports.

"Yes."

"You have been close in the past though?"

"Yes," she replied quietly, resigned to the fact that they may never be again.

Holmes asked if she could fix things with him, and Jenny was hit with a wave of sadness, as a tender memory pulled at her heart. *You can fix anything.* She wrested Kathryn's soft voice from her head and crushed it beneath the anger she now relied on for strength.

"Yes. I can fix it."

Holmes nodded. "Excellent."

Jenny walked from the interrogation room a free woman. When she asked Colonel Holmes if she was under arrest, he simply replied, "Do I look like a policeman?"

One of the goons was ordered to take her home, but she couldn't bear the thought of entering her dark, empty house, with its memories haunting every room. She briefly entertained staying at the penthouse, but with memories reminding her of what a fool she'd been to believe Kathryn Hammond's lies, she knew she'd find no solace there. She didn't want to be alone, and there was only one other place she could think of to go.

Kathryn heard someone repeatedly saying her name. Then her name came with an accompanying shake of her shoulders.

"Kathryn!"

Her vision cleared, and she found herself staring into Smitty's concerned face.

She was sitting on the floor in the foyer of Jenny's house when she slowly blinked her partner into focus. She glanced past him through the open door. Jenny once stood in that open door. Smitty was out of place.

"What are you doing here?"

He raised his brow. "What am *I* doing here? What are *you* doing here? You're supposed to be with Forrester. I was at the penthouse at seven ... you never left. I called the club, I called—"

"I left early."

He glanced at the disarray in the living room. "What happened here? Where's Jenny?"

"She knows."

He blinked. "She knows what?"

"Everything. That she was my assignment, all about her father, her grandparents—everything."

Smitty eyed her warily. "What have you done?"

Kathryn slowly cut her eyes up to her once trusting friend and blew out a humorless chuckle.

"Thank you, Smitty, for your undying faith in me. I can't tell you how it warms my heart."

He shook off the comment, and she knew he was sorry he'd made it. "What happened? Where's Jenny?"

"She had the case files. All of them."

"She doesn't have access to that information." He looked around again, as if he'd see them stacked in a corner. "Here? She had them here? That's impossible."

"They took her away," Kathryn said quietly.

His posture softened as the ramifications washed over him. He exhaled, as if he'd been holding his breath since the day she'd met Jenny, and then kneeled beside her and placed a comforting hand on her shoulder.

"We destroyed her life, Smitty. She never had a chance." She paused, reflecting on their brief time together. "*We* never had a chance either." She looked up and forced a bittersweet smile. "But you knew that."

The truth stared back at her from his solemn face. In him, she saw a reminder of everything she should have been and wasn't. He never stopped being a professional, never stopped putting the job first. She, on the other hand, had become the epitome of compromise, doing just enough to maintain her status quo on the job without sacrificing her relationship with Jenny.

That was over now.

She tapped Smitty's bum knee. "Get off this." She held out her hand. "Come on. Help me up."

He stood with a wince and a groan and pulled her to her feet. She tried to walk away, but he held fast to her hand and pulled her into an embrace.

"I'm sorry, honey. Are you okay?"

She patted him on the back, more for his comfort than for hers, and pushed away with a hand to his chest.

"It was hardly unexpected."

"That's not what I asked."

Kathryn held up her hand and shook her head, stilling any further conversation as she disappeared into the master bedroom on her way to the bathroom. She didn't want his comfort, or his pity, and she didn't want him to see her break down. Not when he had been right all along.

Kathryn didn't know how long she'd sat on the floor in the foyer mindlessly watching the moths flirting with the lighted wall sconce. In fact, she didn't even remember sliding numbly down the wall. She remembered being loved though, and she was glad, because the memory of it was all she had left.

She didn't watch as Jenny was led away. She promised herself she would never watch her walk away, and she would at least keep that promise. She sat clutching the house key in her hand, oblivious to the metal digging into her palm. She kept telling herself it was time to go, time to walk away from everything she'd come to care about, everything she'd come to live for, but she couldn't move. She couldn't face the truth that it was over.

She leaned on the bathroom sink, trying to maintain her composure. Her legs felt weak and her arms shook under her weight. She closed her eyes as she felt a familiar emptiness consume her spirit from deep within. She felt her demons come back to life, the little fiends leaning forward on one knee, anxiously awaiting her next move.

She looked in the mirror at her pained-wracked face and shaking body and was repulsed.

"Don't you dare cry," she warned herself tersely, as she gripped the sink, trying to derive some strength from its cold, hard surface. "How did you think it would end?"

She had known the answer all along. It was there, just waiting for the moment to reveal itself. She released her hold on the unsympathetic porcelain and straightened to her full height, shedding the weakness of the foolish fantasy she once knew as love. Her demons rejoiced and danced in the air as they dusted off a well-worn cloak of darkness and settled it comfortably around her shoulders.

Welcome home, Kathryn Hammond. We've missed you.

Bernie opened his front door and wiped the sleep from his eyes. "Christmas, Jenny. It's almost two in the morning."

"I need to talk to you. May I come in?"

Bernie scratched his chest through his loose white t-shirt and peered back into the apartment. Jenny knew he wasn't alone, but she didn't care.

"Please, Bernie. It's important."

"Well, isn't that rich?" Bernie said, planting his fist on his hip. "You show up here in the middle of the night and say pretty please, and I'm supposed to let you in. Well, you know what, Jenny? I would have liked that too, but, unfortunately, you were just too damn busy. Well, guess what? I'm kind of busy right now too."

He tried to close the door, but she slammed her shoulder into it until they were face to face.

"I know I hurt you, Bernie, and I'm sorry, but if you shut me out now, I'm afraid we'll never save our friendship." She began to cry. "Please," she begged, coming undone. "I can't lose you too. You're all I've got left."

"Jenny ..." He immediately replaced his anger with concern and cupped her face, searching for her eyes by the light escaping his doorway. "Bug, what is it?"

One look into Bernie's worried face and she couldn't be brave any longer. His forgiveness tore down the first brick in her fragile wall and allowed her anguish to flow freely, until she collapsed into his arms, sobbing uncontrollably. She knew Bernie hadn't seen her like this since the night of her father's death, and he would know this was about more than their strained relationship.

His boyfriend, Robert, made his way into the living room, tucking in his white t-shirt. He helped bring her into the apartment and then stood by helplessly, looking for some instruction. Bernie cocked his head toward the front door, and Robert agreed, as he picked up his jacket from the couch and left without a word.

Jenny was inconsolable as Bernie rocked her gently and let her unburden her pain into his arms. They wound up on the bathroom floor, when Jenny thought she'd be sick again, but the nausea passed, and she eventually exhausted herself. She woke up with her head cradled in Bernie's lap as he sat with his back against the tub.

"I'm sorry," she whispered hoarsely to his knee. She curled up on her side and clutched the bathrobe draped across her shoulders.

"Shhh," he said, as he stroked her head. "None of that."

She sat up and faced him. "I love you, Bernie. You're the best friend I've ever had, and I've been such a shit."

"Oh, sweetie," Bernie said with tears in his eyes. "You're my shit."

They both exhaled a welcome laugh. She hugged him but didn't let go.

"Bug, please don't start crying again. You're going to make me cry, and we both know that's not pretty."

Jenny laughed again and sat back on her heels, wiping her eyes and nose. "Oh, like I am right now?"

"Nonsense." Bernie groaned as he reached his full length to unravel a handful of toilet paper. "You're the most attractive species of raccoon I've ever seen. Here." He handed the paper over and got to his feet, kneading the blood back into his numb buttocks. He extended his hand and helped her up. "Come into the kitchen after you wash your face. I'll make us some coffee."

They sat at his small kitchen table, where Jenny told him everything she could without breaching security. Her parentage wasn't classified, but Colonel Holmes wanted her relationship with her uncle to be as normal as possible, so it was up to her discretion who she told. For security reasons, her employment by the OSS was classified, and the colonel suggested she say she worked for the Office of War Information and leave it at that. She was tired of lying to Bernie, and a sanitized version of the truth was better than no truth at all.

Bernie sat in stunned silence at her tale, not surprised that her relationship with Kathryn didn't work out but utterly shocked that her father wasn't her father and that she was now working some secret government job.

"I suppose you can't talk about it, huh?" he asked about her work.

"No, and for crying out loud, don't tell Uncle Paul. In fact, don't tell anyone anything I've told you tonight."

"He doesn't know the parentage thing?"

"I'm not sure. Dad—I mean Daniel Ryan—just kind of showed up with me. Everyone assumed I was his."

"Jeez, Bug."

She shrugged, not willing to dwell on it. "So, I'd appreciate it if you wouldn't say anything to anyone, and that includes Robert, please."

"Hey, I can keep a secret."

She raised a warning brow. "See that you do."

She shifted in her seat and tiptoed into her next question.

"So," she drew out. "Robert."

Bernie leaned back, dragging his hands across the table like he was ready to mount a defense if he had to. "Yeah?"

Jenny was sorry he saw the need to get his back up. "I'm glad he was here for you."

"I know you don't like him, Bug, but he's really been great."

"He broke your heart, Bernie. I'd have something against anyone who did that." She paused. "Myself included."

Bernie smiled. "That was a long time ago. He and I have both changed since then." He leaned forward again and took her hands. "And as for you, I have not yet begun to think up ways in which you shall make it up to me."

She laughed, happy to have his friendship once more.

He tugged on her fingers. "Do you want to talk about what happened with your girl?"

Jenny shook her head. "I've closed that door, Bernie, and I'm not looking back."

She knew he'd be satisfied with that answer. That's how she'd dealt with her breakup with Marcella, after all, and Kathryn Hammond was no less a villain than she. In fact, she was worse, because she used her from the start just to get information for an assignment.

The scope of the woman's plan and her flawless execution were incredible, and Jenny quickly had to change the subject to avoid feeling the pain of a lost love that never really existed to begin with.

She tugged back on Bernie's fingers. "Listen, about this war correspondent business ..."

"I thought we already had this discussion," he said soberly.

"Yes, but that was when you were being unreasonable and pissy." She smiled, only half kidding. "I was hoping things might have changed."

She watched him carefully to make sure he wasn't offended. He didn't seem to be when he quietly said, "I have to do something, Jenny."

"Bernie, you're documenting the war on the home front and bringing it to the masses. That's important."

He scoffed at her description. "Spoken like someone who has a truly important job with the Office of War Information."

She tightened her grip on his fingers. "You know it's not for you. I can see it in your eyes."

He stared at their hands. "Everyone's afraid, Jenny. I'm no different."

"Will you think about it?"

He looked up. "I've given my notice to the *Chronicle*. I leave in three weeks."

***

Smitty exhaled smoke into the stillness of the night and threw his spent cigarette out the car window as he stared helplessly up at Kathryn's illuminated living room window.

He had led her back to her apartment and then watched in his side view mirror as she got out of her car and approached from behind.

"Wait here, please," she had said tersely, as she put a hand on his car door and made a halfhearted effort to lean into view.

He didn't even have time to respond before she pushed away and strode purposefully toward her apartment. Smitty didn't know what she had in mind, but he had a sneaking suspicion, and all he could do was hope he wasn't right.

There would be time later to contemplate who gave Jenny Ryan the classified files. He didn't need to ask Kathryn who she thought would do such a thing. Colonel Holmes would be at the top of her list. He wouldn't disagree, but what the SOE thought it would gain by exposing Jenny to the truth about her family was a mystery.

Kathryn emerged from her apartment with a small suitcase in hand, which she threw onto the backseat of his car before sliding into the passenger's seat.

"Take me to the estate."

"Kat ..."

"Take me, Smitty, or I'll drive myself." She stared straight ahead with her hand on the door handle, poised to leave if she had to.

Reluctantly, he started the car.

Kathryn crossed her legs and covered her exposed knee with her light overcoat. She pulled a cigarette from her purse, and Smitty reached into his breast pocket and produced a lighter, which Kathryn leaned into.

Cigarette lit, Kathryn inhaled deeply and exhaled a thanks along with the smoke.

It felt good. Calming. Familiar. She sat back in her seat and took another satisfying drag. She had reverted to someone she knew well. In many ways, Jenny had been right. Their relationship had been a lie. A lie that Kathryn knew couldn't last. She felt bad for Jenny. She had become a victim of her own desire and Kathryn's ability to satisfy it. To her credit, Jenny had almost convinced her she could be someone else.

She shook her head. Maybe she *had* been someone else. It was so hard to tell. That was her gift, after all, to become what one expected her to be, what they needed her to be. But who was she, really? She didn't know. It didn't matter now. She knew who she had to be, what she had to do. It was the least she could do for Jenny. Someone had set her up—Holmes, if she had to guess—and she was going to find out why, but first, she would get to the bottom of Forrester's evil little scheme and bring his world crashing down around him. She was good at that, it seemed.

Smitty wished Kathryn would talk to him. Break down. Yell at him. Something. She chain-smoked in silence all the way to their destination, and he wondered if she was making up for lost time or trying to calm her nerves.

He briefly thought of saying "I told you so," just to get a rise out of her and to keep her present, but she was shutting down. She was silently severing all emotional ties to Jenny like a mad gardener clipping her prized roses at their roots.

He understood that this was her way of coping. It was her way of achieving a state of indifference. He'd seen her do it before and couldn't argue with the effectiveness of the technique, only the means by which she would obtain it. He pulled off the road in front of the large wrought iron gates leading to Forrester's drive.

"Please don't do this, Kat," he begged. "Not tonight. It's not too late. I can still take you home. I'll stay with you if you like, but please don't go in there like this."

"Like what?" she asked coldly. "Isn't this what you wanted? For me to get my head back in the game? For me to get back to my old self? Well, I'm not there quite yet, but come morning, I will be. I promise you that. Now, are you going to drive me up, or do I have to walk?"

He gritted his teeth and continued on. When he stopped at the portico, Kathryn exited the car with a terse thanks. Nausea churned in his gut when he watched Forrester answer the door and take her in his arms.

CHAPTER ELEVEN

Kathryn dozed lightly on her side and felt fingertips gently tracing her arm from shoulder to elbow. In her half waking state, she thought it was Jenny, and that the last twenty-four hours had been nothing but a nightmare. She smiled and rolled onto her back, only to be greeted by Forrester's smiling face.

"Good morning, darling."

The real nightmare had begun, or, more accurately, was just sinking in.

It started the moment she entered Forrester's home, just after midnight the evening before. She thought she'd prepared herself for the job ahead, but face to face with her grinning assignment made reverting to form seem like it was going to be harder than expected.

"I thought you were ill, darling," Forrester cooed as he cupped her face upon her arrival.

He had been working late in the study when she called to tell him she was coming over, but now he was dressed in his nightclothes and robe, slippers on his feet, and a drink in hand. He kissed her on the cheek and took her suitcase from her hand, setting it on the floor beside them. Kathryn kicked the door closed with her heel, quickly coming to grips with the fact that she'd already passed the point of no return and had nothing to lose anymore. She smiled and leaned in to his kiss.

"I'm fine now. I woke up and I missed you," she lied, moving closer. "I wanted to be near you."

She gazed seductively at the drink in his hand and borrowed it, taking a significant swallow for courage before returning it to him.

"I wanted you," she whispered, as she leaned in and kissed him on the mouth. She took it slowly at first, not sure what to expect—from either of them. To her surprise, she found it easy, as did he, and he not only accepted her mouth, but he tried to take more.

She pulled away and smiled, as her latent fear of revulsion dissolved with his eager response. She stroked his cheek with a devilish grin. Her control over him was an empowering drug—much like the drink warming her belly.

She pointed at his glass. "You'd better finish that. You're going to need it."

He licked his lips, tasting her sweetness mixed with his expensive scotch, and silently watched as she picked up her case and walked into the main hall and up the grand staircase.

Kathryn smiled as she walked away, thankful she'd found her disconnect switch. Embrace the power, liberate the mind. It was all coming back to her now.

Forrester eventually followed and entered the bedroom slowly, unsure of what to expect. Kathryn was unpacking her makeup and a few items of clothing from her case.

"Darling?" he asked hesitantly. "Are you all right? You look tired."

She turned, telegraphing insult.

"Beautiful," he quickly countered. "But tired."

She straightened and crossed the room, shutting the door behind him before she faced his way and loosened the belt on her overcoat.

"I am tired."

The belt fell to the floor and her coat parted, revealing her naked form to a stunned Marcus Forrester, who looked ridiculous, standing there like a cast iron lawn jockey with a drink in his hand.

Kathryn made no effort to reveal her body further, preferring to let the light fabric hang where it may and her movements dictate her exposure. She wasn't sure her audience appreciated her bold approach, but if his audible swallow was any indication, he would quickly warm to the idea.

She moved into his personal space and removed the drink from his hand, setting it carefully on the nightstand beside him. She thought about downing the contents of the glass, but she was in control now and preferred to stay that way.

"I am tired, Marc," she repeated. "I'm tired of waiting for you to make love to me."

She was impossibly close. She knew he could feel the heat of her skin through his nightshirt. He tried to avert his eyes from her long, naked torso, the intimacy making him uncomfortable. He backed up and stepped to the side, reaching for his drink again.

"What is this, a cruel joke? You know I can't ..."

She was back in his face instantly, with her hand around his and the disputed glass getting an excellent view of her left breast.

"Look at me, Marcus."

He hesitated and turned his face away.

She forced the glass into his chest, sloshing the contents over their hands. "Drink that if you have to. Drink the entire bottle if you have to, but I want you, and you're going to make love to me tonight."

"What is wrong with you?" he snapped, corralling the glass from her grasp, but not its contents, which splashed all over her chest and coat.

Forrester stood like a deer caught in headlights, as the scotch glistened down Kathryn's body and highlighted every lovely peak and valley on her exposed pinup-worthy frame.

"That'll work," she said with a smirk and then licked an errant drop of liquor from the side of her mouth.

"Honestly," Forrester complained, slamming his empty glass down. He pulled a handkerchief from the nightstand drawer and wiped his face before picking up the phone. "If you want sex, all you have to—"

Kathryn moved in and carefully took the phone from his hand, returning it to the cradle. The sledgehammer approach had gotten her this far, but now it was time for some delicate maneuvering.

She ran her hand up his arm, to his neck, and then through his hair. "If I wanted sex with someone else, I certainly wouldn't be standing in your bedroom wearing nothing but an overcoat and your sixty-year-old scotch."

"Kathryn, I can't—"

"Shh." She covered his lips with her fingers. "There's more to sex than that." She moved closer and situated her thigh between his legs as she leaned in. "Let me show you, Marc," she whispered in his ear. "Let me show you how to please me."

She kissed his ear, then his neck. "You want to please me, don't you?" She lingered in his ear. "You want to feel me, don't you?"

Her sensual kisses crackled in his ear and mixed with her warm breath until the sexually stoic Marcus Forrester actually exhaled a pleasurable moan.

"I want you to feel what you do to me," Kathryn went on unmercifully. "I want you inside me when I come, and I want you to know that you did this to me."

His breathing increased. Any other man would have taken her by now, but Forrester's lack of response on her thigh reminded her that this was no ordinary man and that she had her work cut out for her.

She pulled back and looked as aroused as possible. "Touch me, Marc. I want you to. I need you to. Please," she practically begged as she cupped his tense jaw.

She saw that he was buying it, and that he was willing, so she slipped her thumb into his mouth, and he sucked the scotch from it, seeking approval with his questioning eyes.

"That's it," she said, feigning sexual gratification as he licked the remaining alcohol from the rest of her fingers and hand. She slowly parted her coat and curled her fingers under his chin, leading his mouth to her breast. "You missed a spot."

He kissed her breast and chased the trail of liquor like a desperate alcoholic in need of a fix. Kathryn ran her hand through his hair, making erotic sounds of approval as he tasted her nipple for the first time. Her stomach roiled at his touch, and then she was angry at herself for losing focus. This wasn't anything she hadn't done before with many men. She'd promised Smitty she'd get her head in the game, but the game had left her. She silently swore at herself and redoubled her efforts to appear aroused.

He looked up at her reaction and seemed surprised and apprehensive all at once. She imagined he wasn't used to being an instrument of pleasure. She shrugged her coat from her shoulders and guided his head back to her chest before he lost his nerve.

Kathryn didn't know if Forrester's problem was emotional or physical, nor did she care. While his mouth and hands wandered her body, her mind pulled her away from the physical sensations until she felt nothing. She was nothing.

She moaned for effect as she let him explore her, and she showed him how to make love to her with no more thought than she'd proffer a stranger asking directions to the nearest subway. She'd never felt so disconnected from her body. So disconnected from everything. She didn't dare think of what she'd lost in Jenny. She'd break down completely.

Forrester watched in wide wonder her reaction to his efforts, and Kathryn knew he now felt the power of sexual control. Control was something he knew well, and something he relished. He followed her verbal pleasure map, and she escalated her responses until she decided it had gone on long enough. She threw her head back into the pillow with an exaggerated cry and held his hand to her center as she arched her back and faked the best orgasm she was sure he'd never been a part of.

A half hour later, he still had his head on her chest and one leg draped over hers, hugging her like a grateful child.

"You've made me feel like a man again," he said with equal parts appreciation and melancholy.

"You are a man, darling." She tenderly stroked his head—and his ego. "You are a man." Kathryn stared at the ceiling. This was her life now, and she deserved every wretched second of it.

"We're here, hon," the lady cab driver called out as she looked at the snoozing blonde in her rearview mirror.

Jenny groaned as she lifted her head from the back of the seat and rubbed her eyes. Her watch read seven-fifteen in the morning. She'd only gotten three hours' sleep at Bernie's, and the early morning sun was stinging her eyes. After paying the cabbie, she got out and stared dejectedly at her large house, as the events of the previous evening came crashing back. A brick from the demolished mailbox column lay in her path, so she kicked it onto the grass and slowly approached her damaged car.

She put her hands on her hips. Not only had she destroyed the bumper and fender, but the impact had pushed the twisted metal into the left front tire, which was now flat. She'd have to put on the spare and wait until after the war to find another whitewall tire.

"Fucking perfect."

She threw her hands up, finding it the least of her problems, and headed for the front door. She glared at the still burning porch light, which was a testament to Kathryn's thoughtfulness that would go wholly unappreciated.

Once inside, Jenny was struck by the smell of ammonia, and her confused expression quickly turned into a scowl when she realized Kathryn had cleaned up before she left. Defiantly, Jenny kicked over the waste pail full of broken glass and miscellaneous rubbish by the doorway to the living room, sending the wreckage skittering down the hallway.

"Bitch," she said, as she followed the debris field toward the kitchen.

On the kitchen table, Jenny found a letter. Perfectly centered atop the letter was Kathryn's key. She scooped up the letter and the key and opened a drawer below the kitchen counter, where she tossed in the key and took out a box of matches.

She struck a match and held the envelope over the sink, where she lit the corner and watched the flames consume the words *Dearest, please read!* written in Kathryn's sweeping hand. She watched the letter burn, feeling nothing but hate and disgust for its author.

She watched until the letter was nothing but ashes, and to ensure there would be no resurrection, she turned on the faucet until all traces of the lies and the woman who wrote them disappeared down the drain.

Jenny was emotionally wrung out and drained. She stalked into the bedroom and was annoyed to find the nightstand light on—another unwanted courtesy.

Jenny considered extinguishing the lamp with a well-placed pitch of her shoe but thought better of it. It was her favorite lamp, and one of the few items that she had added to the house and not some remnant of a Ryan gone by.

She lifted her heel and removed one shoe, then the other, and tossed them into the open closet instead.

"Leaving lights on," she muttered at Kathryn's offensive kindness. "I think I know my way around my own damn house."

She slammed the closet door and entered the bathroom, mashing the light switch with her open palm before cranking on the hot water in the sink. She pulled the hand towel from the towel ring on the wall and found it damp from Kathryn's final visit. She threw it to the floor in disgust.

"For the last time, get out of my house, get out of my life, get out of my head!" She yanked another hand towel from the shelf next to the sink and snapped it to its full length before tossing it to the counter. She washed her face and dried it, moaning into the clean towel as she pressed it to her tired eyes.

She straightened, and as her haggard face appeared in the mirror from behind the towel, she was struck by the stranger looking back at her. For the first time in her life, she questioned who she was.

She leaned closer, searching her bloodshot eyes for an answer. She blinked. Her eyes—she'd seen them before, and not as a reflection in a mirror. Of all the lies surrounding her, there was one truth that could not be denied, and maybe, just maybe, that truth would hold the answer.

She made her way into the study, barely noticing that everything had been put meticulously back in its place. A neat pile of now frameless photos on top of the damaged piano was her destination. She pushed aside another note from Kathryn, one pointing her to a piano refinisher in town, and this time Kathryn's intrusion was ignored in favor of the only photograph she had of her mother: the one with Daniel Ryan under a sprawling oak tree.

There was no question this woman was her mother. They were almost identical. Jenny reached out and touched her mother's smiling face. She longed for this woman now, as never before. She longed to be a daughter, to feel a blood connection, to have a mother to comfort her and tell her everything was going to be fine. It struck her how alone she was, how the only person she felt would understand was a woman she'd never met. A woman long since dead.

"Who am I?" she whispered, almost believing a mother's love would take pity on her from the grave and provide the answer.

"Who were you?"

She turned over the black and white photo to find a handwritten message she never knew was there.

Your love grows like a beautiful vine of yellow roses, tucking and weaving its way through the latticework of my life, until I no longer know if the lattice holds up the vine or the vine holds up the lattice. In the end, it matters not. For the rose will continue to bloom and grow, bloom and grow ...

We did it, Danny! Soon we'll be together—love you till the end of time. Bess

Jenny peered at the smudged date. It was dated one month before she was born. One month before her mother's death. She turned the photo back over and looked at the smiling faces. With his arms wrapped around her, Daniel Ryan was obviously in love, and from the message, so was her mother. What had they done? Why were they not together? If Daniel Ryan was not her father, who was?

Jenny realized she knew next to nothing about her mother except her maiden name from her birth certificate. Other than that, the woman, and her life, was a mystery. She searched the photograph for clues. There was a plain stone building in the background with three tall chimney stacks. Not much to go on. Her quest for answers had led her to more questions, but the questions replaced her anger and gave her something to focus on, something she gladly embraced, rather than face the events of the last twenty-four hours.

Only one person could help her in her new quest, and it coincided with her new assignment. She picked up the phone and swallowed any trace of pride.

"Hi, Uncle Paul. What are the chances there's still a desk for me at the *Daily Chronicle?*"

CHAPTER TWELVE

athryn's sex partner groaned when she got out of bed and padded across the hotel room to her purse.

"Where are you going?" the man said, as he reached in vain for her retreating naked body.

Kathryn eventually turned and threw a condom package onto his bare chest.

"What is this?"

"You're a doctor," she said with a smirk. "Figure it out."

Thierry Bouchaule laughed uncomfortably. "Well, I know what it is ... I just thought that you would—"

"I would what?"

"Well ... take care of things."

Kathryn stood at the foot of the bed and raised an eyebrow. "That's what I'm doing."

He looked at the condom in his hand and balked at it like a child offered spinach.

"You big baby," Kathryn said. She crawled onto the bed and slid the length of his body before settling into the crook of his shoulder.

Bouchaule turned the condom over in his fingers and glared at it with disdain.

Kathryn rolled her eyes and snatched the packet from his hand. Shifting to support herself on one elbow, she said, "As much as I find you wildly attractive, darling, I have no intentions of being the mother of your children." She held up the offending item. "We do this my way, or we don't do it at all. Understood?"

He offered a crooked smile but was still hesitant to agree.

"I've got another hour," Kathryn said matter-of-factly and then offered a not-so-subtle glance at his diminishing erection. "You, however, seem to have a limited window of opportunity."

He blushed and tried to urge his manhood back into service with his hand. "I hate those things."

Kathryn smiled seductively and opened the condom packet with her teeth. "I promise to make it worth your while." She grinned and ran her hand across his smooth chest and down his abdomen, to his working hand, where she took over.

Bouchaule smiled in approval and put his hands behind his head, as if he had no doubt that she would be true to her word.

Kathryn came out of the bathroom covering her dripping torso with an oversized towel. Clad in nothing but his cotton briefs, Thierry Bouchaule lingered at the window, his tall, well-built frame silhouetted by the late afternoon sun, as he parted the drape to peer down on the street below.

She crossed the room to stand at his back, where she embraced him from behind and pressed her cheek to his shoulder.

"Something interesting out there?"

"Do you trust him?"

She lifted her cheek and pulled back the drape to see the top of Smitty's hat as he tried to be inconspicuous while getting a shoeshine from a boy across the street. Kathryn let the drape fall and gave Bouchaule a conciliatory pat on the back.

"I trust him with my life. In fact, right now, he's the only man I trust."

Bouchaule turned to face her with disappointment evident in his pursed lips. "I hope that changes very soon."

Kathryn smiled and looked deeply into his eyes as she caressed his face with her hand. "I'd like that."

He kissed her hand and turned his back on the window to pluck a cigarette from the gold case on the nightstand. He lit it, exhaling as he spoke. "Your friend does not like me."

"My friend doesn't want me to get hurt."

"I would never hurt you, Kathryn. Your heart is safe with me."

Kathryn looked at him sideways and took the cigarette from his hand with an amused grin. "I don't think he's worried about my heart."

Bouchaule's casual mood suddenly turned serious. "Is it so impossible that you would care for me?"

Kathryn exhaled a drag and frowned in confusion at his mood swing. "Why would you say that?"

He hesitated, but then raised his chin. "I could fall in love with you."

Kathryn chuckled as she pulled a bit of tobacco from her tongue. "I bet you say that to all your women."

He moved closer. "I have never met a woman like you before."

"Yes," Kathryn said with a smirk, doubting his sincerity. "I'm unique. Just like everyone else."

He cupped her face in his hand. "I am serious."

His eyes told her it was the truth. "What gives? I come up here for some recreational fun, and, suddenly, you're all hearts and flowers. You don't even know me, Thierry."

"I know that I want to spend the rest of my life learning you." He kissed the length of her arm, ending with her hand.

Kathryn's casual mood shifted to impatience as she tried to move away. "I have to go."

Strong arms held her tight about the waist.

"I said I have to go."

"I heard you."

"Then let me go." She gave him a warning look, and he reluctantly loosened his grasp but held fast to her trailing hand.

"Why must you leave?"

"I've got a rehearsal."

He smiled, brimming with charm and bravado, and pulled her to him. He wrapped his arms around her waist again and kissed her neck. "You have no need for rehearsals ... you are magnificent. Stay with me, just a little longer."

Kathryn pushed away from his grasp and clung to her slipping towel.

"I've got to go, Thierry."

He raised his chin, his mood clouding again.

"It is because of him, is it not?"

"Who?"

"Forrester."

"Of course not. What's it got to do with him?"

Bouchaule moved closer and gently took her hand. "You need not be afraid of him. I will not let him hurt you."

"Who says I'm afraid?"

"My brave darling," Bouchaule said with a condescending tone reserved for a wilting wallflower. "You do not have to make believe. Fear is nothing to be ashamed of." He kissed her hand. "I told you ... I will not let him harm you."

"Please," Kathryn said quietly. "I've got to go."

Bouchaule straightened, as his gentle demeanor fell away. "I do not like that he controls you so."

Kathryn looked up with anger in her eyes. "No one controls me." She wrenched her hand from his. "Not Marcus Forrester, and not you!"

"Wait—" He tried in vain to interrupt.

"And when I say I've got to go, I've got to go. I'm not going to stand here and defend my actions or justify everything I do. If that's too much for your ego to take, then we may as well call it quits right now."

Bouchaule ignored her tirade and boldly wrapped himself

around her from behind as she tried to walk away. "I have upset you, my darling. Forgive me."

Kathryn struggled for the appropriate few moments and then relaxed her tense body into his embrace. The tug between make believe and genuine anger gave her pause, and she closed her eyes, cursing the agent in her who still hadn't shed her useless self-respect. She reached up to hold the cheek resting on her bare shoulder and silently exhaled a slow, centering breath. "I'm sorry, Thierry. It was a beautiful afternoon. I just ..."

Bouchaule tightened his embrace and rocked her gently. "The pleasure was mine, and if I want you to stay, it is not because I want to control you. It is because I do not want to be without you."

"I know." She patted his cheek and let her head fall back on his chest. She was in control again.

"Do you really have a rehearsal?"

Kathryn exhaled to the ceiling. "No. I've got to meet Marc at the office."

"You do not have to deceive me, Kathryn."

"Maybe I don't like going from your arms to his. It makes me feel—"

Bouchaule turned her in his arms and didn't let her finish. "We will do what we have to do for now."

"For now?"

"I am not a complicated man, darling. I mean what I say."

Kathryn tilted her head and smiled. "Are you going to save me, Thierry?"

"Do you need saving?"

Kathryn gazed longingly into his eyes and parted her lips as she leaned closer. "Very much."

Bouchaule was more than willing to oblige, and he covered her mouth with his in a passionate kiss.

Kathryn entertained his passion but then pulled away, licking her lower lip, as if she may never taste him again.

"What is it?" he asked.

Kathryn turned away. "I know what you're doing."

He smiled "Yes. I am going to make love to—"

"No." She extricated herself from his arms. "You're just using me to get to Forrester."

"What?"

Kathryn smiled at his act and casually went to the bar and poured a drink.

"It's all right, Thierry. It comes with the territory."

Bouchaule moved to her back and put his hands tenderly on her shoulders. "It is also not entirely true."

She moved from under his touch and handed him the drink she'd just made. "But part of it *is* true?"

He took a sip and eyed her warily as she walked away. "If you think I am just using you, then why are you here?"

Kathryn sat in the low-slung chair in the corner and crossed her legs, exposing her flesh to the hip. "Because part of me hopes it's not true, and the rest of me would be happy to bring Forrester down. If you care, then I trust you will protect me from him when that happens. Do you care that much, Thierry?"

He crossed the room and stood before her. "I do."

"Will you protect me?"

He knelt at her feet. "Yes."

"Can I trust you?"

He slid his hand up her shapely leg and under her towel, causing her to uncross her legs at his advances. He leaned into her body and captured her lips with a whispered promise. "Yes."

***

Kathryn emerged from the hotel later than expected, and Smitty could tell from the faint whisker burn on her cheek that she had slept with the suave Dr. Bouchaule. He kept his thoughts to himself until they got into the car, where he could no longer hold his tongue.

"You didn't have to do that, Kat."

She lit a cigarette and blew the smoke out her open window. "He's an attractive man. Why not?"

Smitty glared at her. "Because punishing yourself for what happened to Jenny will not change anything."

Kathryn chuckled, as if the notion were absurd. "Sleeping with Thierry Bouchaule is hardly what I consider punishment."

He glared at her again. He knew Kathryn sensed his jealousy, and she had the grace to apologize. "Sorry."

Smitty took the apology, thankful at least for some kind of exchange. It was a departure from the wordless treks down the busy halls of headquarters, the silent rides in elevators, and the all too familiar awkward silences in the car as they drove to this place and that. That is how it had been between them since Kathryn's relationship with Jenny ended a month ago. He knew better than to bring her up, but something had to be said. Kathryn now rarely spoke unless spoken to, saving what little personality she exposed for her award-worthy playacting with Forrester and now, apparently, her role with Bouchaule.

"Was it worth it?"

"I know what I'm doing, Smitty, and for your information, it was worth it." She looked out the window. "It's all going to be worth it."

Smitty wasn't sure he agreed, no matter what she'd found out. The personal toll the assignment and Jenny's departure were taking on her was becoming more and more evident, and now she was taking on more. He wasn't so sure it was merely work related.

"Things can't go on like this, Kat."

"It'll go on for as long as it has to go on."

"Okay, *you* can't go on like this."

Kathryn turned to him, and he could see anger in her eyes. "And what exactly would you have me do, Smitty?"

She had him there. He was in no position to say how she should handle Jenny's loss or, more immediately, living with Forrester day in and day out. He couldn't even begin to comprehend what it was like for her—to have the man's hands on her, in her, to have to pretend it was pleasing. Just thinking about it sickened him, and he didn't even want to know about her relationship with the good doctor.

Both Forrester *and* the OSS wanted information on Thierry

Bouchaule, and she was right where she needed to be—between them. But it was slowly killing her, and he wasn't going to stand by and watch it happen.

"You need to start taking care of yourself, Kathryn. Sleep, for instance. This few hours here, few hours there, is not healthy."

She exhaled wearily and let her head drop to the back of the seat. "I'm fine."

"Bull. And I'm not the only one who's noticed."

"Forrester has no complaints, and neither does brass."

"No, but Dominic does."

Kathryn snapped her head up. He knew questioning her professionalism at the club would not be dismissed.

"Nicky? Why? What did he say?"

"What do you think he said? You're sleepwalking through your performances, no pun intended, you're not taking care of your voice … and don't look at me like you don't know what I'm talking about."

She furrowed her brow, as if she didn't know what he was talking about, but then turned away, and he knew she recognized the hollow feeling that must have shown in her work. She closed her eyes and rubbed her forehead. Letting Dominic down was inexcusable. Music had always come naturally to her. It was the one thing that never failed to move her, but her performances now seemed empty and flat. She was talented enough to take her vocal gift for granted and just expected it to carry her through, but he also knew she felt Dominic deserved better. Much better.

"I'll talk to him."

"He's concerned, Kathryn."

"I know."

"I'm concerned."

She put her hand on his knee to reassure him. "I know."

CHAPTER THIRTEEN

$\mathcal{D}$usk had fallen by the time Jenny pulled up to the industrial park that housed her uncle's storage unit. She learned of it while snooping through the outgoing mail on his desk at the paper, where she had returned to the staff part time.

The *Daily Chronicle* had its own storage and archive facilities, but this address was not it. Ever on the lookout for something out of the ordinary, this remote area across town immediately caught her attention. A little steam and a steady hand with a letter opener produced an outgoing cash payment to a storage company for a bill addressed to someone other than her uncle, a name she didn't recognize. It might be a long shot, but it was the only thing she had found out of the ordinary in her uncle's business or personal life.

Jenny didn't want to make a fool of herself in front of her superiors by sending them on a wild goose chase over nothing, so she took it upon herself to do a little investigating on her own before reporting her findings. Now, she sat outside the mystery unit in her idling car, bracing herself for what she might find inside.

The industrial park was a ghost town on this rainy Sunday night. The Cord's headlights illuminated the dingy gray metal slats of the roll-up bay door, and Jenny quickly turned them off to avoid any undue attention. She was sure she was alone but couldn't tame the paranoia that comes with being someplace one shouldn't. The bulb above the storage unit's number was out, just like all the lights above the park's units. In fact, the entire place looked abandoned, and, for the moment, that suited Jenny just fine. She pulled her car around to the side of the building and stepped out into the fine drizzle, flashlight in hand and lock picks at the ready.

It took her fifteen minutes to get inside the unit, but she chose to blame that on the rusty padlock and the miserable weather, rather than her lack of expertise with a lock pick. Once inside, she lowered the bay door behind her and quieted its clanging pulley chain. It was pitch-black inside. There were no windows, no lights, and it smelled stale and musty. She turned on the flashlight and did a quick scan of the small room.

Haphazardly stacked boxes, and what she assumed was covered furniture, filled the space. The layer of dust blanketing every object in the room made Jenny feel that her overactive imagination had led her astray and she'd done nothing but disturb someone's long forgotten tomb.

She felt foolish, standing in the dark, holding her flashlight like a rain-soaked Nancy Drew wannabe, but just when she accepted that she had stumbled upon a dead end, she saw them—footprints in the dust-covered floor, leading into the center of the nondescript piles of boxes and dingy sheets.

The discovery sent a chill up her spine, and she suddenly felt like she wasn't alone. The darkness behind her felt corporeal, like it would reach out and grab her at any moment. She spun the flashlight around to her perceived foe, and finding nothing but the cement block wall behind her, she backed up to it to gather herself. The wall was cold and unwelcoming and did nothing to ease her discomfort. She exhaled a steadying breath and focused her attention and the light on the well-traveled path through the dust on the smooth concrete floor. The footprints were large—a man's to be sure—and she wondered when they had last left their mark.

She trained her light on the stack of boxes straight ahead and tried, unsuccessfully, to shake the feeling she wasn't alone. She took a step and swore she heard something other than her movement and the steady rain on the corrugated tin roof. Her heartbeat quickened and her eyes darted to the dark corners beyond her flashlight's reach. If someone else was in there, she was a sitting duck. There was nowhere she could go. She'd never get away, and after she was caught, no one would hear her scream.

She swallowed hard. When would she learn? An idea that seemed so brilliant in her head once again unraveled under her shortsighted enthusiasm and left her exposed to possible danger. She heard panicked breathing but soon realized it was her own. She held her breath for a few seconds, to listen for signs of company, and hearing none, concluded that her opponent was probably doing the same. It was always like that in the movies—the dead calm before the fatal attack.

Hoping her attacker had never seen such a movie, she slowly put her hand in her pocket, and in the sternest voice she could muster, said, "Come on out of there, nice and slow ... I've got a gun."

She supposed it would have been more impressive had the flashlight in her hand not been shaking with dread, but after a few nerve-racking moments, logic took over and she reasoned that anyone with intent to harm her would have attacked before now. Her bravado was rewarded with continued silence, and she let out a relieved chuckle in honor of her vivid imagination.

She shook her head when reality finally set in. "Jenny, there's only one way in, and the door was locked from the outside. You're an idiot."

She chuckled out loud and wiped the rain from her brow as she shone her light into the room with renewed confidence.

"Okay," she exhaled as she moved in to examine the scene closely. "What have we got here?"

Kathryn exhaled the final drag on her cigarette and smashed the spent butt into the full ashtray under her hand. She listened indifferently as Colonel Forsythe commended her work.

She was fully immersed in Forrester's world now, and her assignment had become a way of life. It was a coping mechanism—anything to keep her mind off Jenny—and hardly something she thought should be commended.

Her aggressive stance with Forrester had opened new avenues for their investigation, and Kathryn lamented the fact that she had not taken it sooner. She wasn't prepared to say the time she'd spent with Jenny was not time well spent, but in the big scheme of things, she shuddered to think what her delay may have cost the war effort.

Thierry Bouchaule was the prize for her efforts. Yesterday had been their first intimate encounter, but not their first clandestine meeting—those had started weeks ago, in Chicago, when the doctor boldly approached her and confessed he couldn't get her out of his mind. Thus, began weeks of teasing and flirting over the phone once Kathryn returned home.

Bouchaule was on her turf for the latest round of dealings with Forrester, and, true to his word, he had been discreet, demonstrating a healthy respect for Marcus Forrester's possessive nature and Kathryn's safety.

He'd been nothing but a gentleman, letting Kathryn dictate how far their physical relationship would go. Kathryn supposed Smitty was right. She could have strung the man along without surrendering her body to him and still gotten the information they sought, but she had already given herself to Forrester, and having learned long ago how to mentally anesthetize herself to the physical intrusion, giving herself to Bouchaule was no more or less a burden than anything else she'd done in her life to meet an end.

She felt no shame in her actions. She sensed it was almost expected of her. Colonel Forsythe was the exception—he was like the kindly father, blind to his daughter's disreputable ways.

"What else can you tell us about Bouchaule's interest in Forrester's negotiations with the Chicago syndicate?" he asked.

"Not much more than is in my report."

Thierry Bouchaule lacked the paranoia of a man in Forrester's position and thought nothing of voicing his displeasure at the industrialist's shortsighted obstruction to his project.

"He is a greedy little man, with no vision beyond his bank account," the doctor had complained. He made it clear that nothing and no one would stand in the way of his work. Kathryn saw an unexpected intensity and determination in his eyes that made her realize Forrester had woefully underestimated his opponent, and perhaps she had as well.

He was a shrewd man when it came to his business dealings. He made no secret of the fact that the Chicago connection afforded him leverage in his negotiations—a power he would not possess otherwise.

"I am a doctor, darling, not a thug," he explained. "I care not for Marc Forrester's turf war, or any other war, for that matter. My work is bigger than that—something these fools would never understand, but I will remove anyone who stands in my way."

It was becoming apparent that the doctors and researchers surrounding Forrester were frantically trying to play catch-up to decipher Daniel Ryan's project, while Bouchaule exuded the calm and confidence of a man already well versed in its secrets.

Kathryn would have taken the Frenchman's attitude as a reflection of his arrogant suave sophistication, but she sensed a legitimacy to his claim that would soon be borne out by his unsolicited declaration.

"It is mine, by rights," he claimed cryptically. Bouchaule never mentioned names, so whether he was involved with the Ryan project wasn't clear, but Kathryn felt his possessive attitude spoke for itself.

The doctor's self-assurance threatened Forrester, who was uncharacteristically out of his element and grasping at straws to keep the upper hand. Bouchaule let Forrester play his power games, but Kathryn sensed he was merely waiting for his chance to strike—like a lion stalking its prey.

If Colonel Forsythe had information on Bouchaule's past and his connection to Daniel Ryan, he did not divulge it, which did not surprise her, but Holmes was another matter. He had already broken the OSS's standard protocol when he showed the Ryan file to Smitty and her. She didn't know what to expect from the man, and she was not alone in her uncertainty, as all eyes turned to Colonel Holmes, who was uncharacteristically silent as he devoured her latest report like a self-absorbed child opening gifts on Christmas morning.

Sensing the sudden attention, he looked up.

"Your interaction with Bouchaule has brought us valuable insight, and it seems you have become quite indispensable to Mr. Forrester."

"It seems."

He nodded. "Very good. Very good. About time."

Kathryn glared at him for his comment, but his attitude was hardly out of the ordinary.

The colonel rubbed his forehead and frowned as he looked over her report on Thierry Bouchaule. "I'd like you to approach some of the others."

"I'm afraid that's not how it works, Colonel. Forrester and Bouchaule approached me."

"Make yourself available and appear interested," he said impatiently. "I shouldn't think it difficult for you, Miss Hammond."

Smitty bristled at the officer's attitude. "She's not your whore, Holmes."

The colonel glanced at the papers before him and then looked up. "Clearly, Mr. Smith, she is."

Smitty stood in defense of his friend. "Now see here—"

"Enough!" Forsythe slammed his palm on the table. "Sit down, John. Holmes, you're out of line."

Kathryn lit another cigarette and took a disinterested drag, staring at the men like a bored spectator at a chess match.

Holmes corrected himself with a patronizing grin. "What I mean to say is that, clearly, Miss Hammond has graciously dedicated herself to our objective."

Kathryn returned the patronizing grin. "While it is true that I'm dedicated to your objective, Colonel Holmes, those men approached *me*. It doesn't work the other way around without raising suspicions." She spread the photos before her. Typically, these other men would brag about their conquest. It would hardly be discreet, and I'm of no use to you dead."

The colonel caught her drift, but not her logic. "What of Bouchaule? He is not your typical man?"

"A man that attractive has no need to boast. He takes a woman because he can, not because he needs to impress."

Holmes stared at her for a moment and then reluctantly backed down. "I defer to your expertise in the matter."

Kathryn peered at him through the smoke she just exhaled and waited for it to clear before she spoke.

"That's why you chose me, Colonel," she said, sending notice that his insults were powerless.

He held her steely gaze and smiled curtly. "Indeed." He closed Kathryn's report and opened one of the blue classified folders beneath his hands. "Thierry Bouchaule was deported from the United States in late June of '40. How is it that he is back in this country?"

Kathryn stared at him, wondering why on earth he would ask her.

"I don't know, Colonel. Immigration officer is not on my resume. My guess would be that people like you let him in so that people like me can extract information from him."

Holmes gave her a disparaging look and went back to the classified report in his hands. He flipped a few pages and went back to Kathryn's report with a frown, as if something was incongruent.

"You intimate here that Daniel Ryan terminated his project sometime before his death. Is this a fact or your opinion?"

"In my opinion, Colonel—"

"We're not interested in opinions, Miss Hammond, we need—"

"On the contrary," Forsythe broke in. He silenced Holmes with a warning look and shifted to face his agent. "Please continue, Kathryn."

Kathryn motioned to the thick folder of Daniel Ryan's coded documents in the center of the table.

"May I?"

"Please." Forsythe pulled them closer.

Kathryn straightened and removed the top sheet from the disheveled pile. "See this short series?" She pointed to a line of text containing eleven characters, a mixture of letters and numbers. "This represents a date." She studied it briefly. It was a simple code, unlike the complex string of numbers in the rest of the document. Any first-year agent could decipher it easily. It was meant as an annoyance, not a deterrent.

"Twenty April 1937." She paused and looked up at the interested group. "By the way, I'm sure you've noted that this is the European way to write the date ... day first, not the month first, like an American would."

They nodded.

She turned the page over to observe the Received By date stamped on the back and thumbed through the others to do the same. The pages were in order, the top sheet being the latest received but older in origin than the one before it. She went through the stack and pointed out how the coded dates were in descending order, in contrast to their interception dates.

"The most recent documents you have are from July 1940, nothing after. Keep in mind, Bouchaule was deported a month earlier. He is no longer working with Daniel Ryan. This is where it gets interesting: The documents you're intercepting now are going backward. There is nothing from the year preceding Daniel Ryan's death, which makes me believe he either terminated the project or couldn't continue without help from—"

"Bouchaule," Forsythe uttered in astonishment.

"Perhaps," Kathryn agreed. "But my point is, he went through a lot of trouble to keep this information under wraps."

"He used the U.S. government to subsidize his work and turned around and sold it to the Germans," Holmes said.

"Daniel Ryan didn't need money, Colonel. You're missing my point. I don't think he was passing anything to anyone."

"I think you underestimate man's propensity for greed."

"I think you've underestimated Daniel Ryan. I think he wanted this project stopped and the information safeguarded—from everyone. Including the U.S. government."

"I think you have an overactive imagination, Miss Hammond."

"I assure you, Colonel Holmes, that is one thing I do not have."

Jenny Ryan did, however, and Kathryn struggled to keep her memory from her thoughts as she defended the woman's father. She picked up a pile of the coded documents and waved them in the colonel's direction.

"This is not about greed. Not for Daniel Ryan anyway. No one goes through the trouble of covering their tracks like he did without—"

"If you're right," Forsythe interrupted. "Why didn't he destroy the documents?"

Kathryn reached for her cigarette, flicking the ash into the ashtray. "I don't know."

"Does Forrester know what's in here?" Holmes asked impatiently, as he stabbed his finger into the documents on the table.

"Forrester brokers information, Colonel. He doesn't care what it's about, only that there's a demand, which he exploits for a handsome fee. This time is different, however."

"Then he must know what it is."

"He knows it's valuable, and he knows the lengths to which these men will go to get it. The *what* is irrelevant. At this point—"

"That's absurd," Holmes interrupted. "Why would a man go to such lengths to acquire something he knows nothing about?"

Kathryn stared at the man, amazed he didn't see the parallel. "Same reason you do, Colonel."

Holmes chewed on her words as she continued.

"As I was saying ... at this point, Forrester is in trouble. Without the key, he's basically brokered useless information. He's dancing as fast as he can, but I don't know how much longer he can stall. Without Daniel Ryan to point us in the right direction, deciphering these documents is nearly impossible, and finding that key is like looking for a needle in a haystack."

The group was silent as they absorbed the well-known truth. Holmes gathered his papers, and Forsythe officially ended the briefing.

"Thank you, Kathryn. Is there anything else?"

"Bouchaule has asked me to get the key to the code if I can. Should I tell him Forrester doesn't have it?"

Holmes and Forsythe exchanged looks. Forsythe deferred to his British counterpart.

"Tell him he doesn't have it."

"And Forrester?"

They exchanged looks again. Holmes nodded to Forsythe, who replied, "Let him fall."

Kathryn nodded, and the meeting was adjourned.

Kathryn and Smitty walked toward the elevators in silence. Smitty regretted the end of their briefing, for it meant another wordless day on the job. He absentmindedly counted the solid click of Kathryn's heels on the hard polished floor with each long stride and, to his surprise, was interrupted when she had something to say after all.

"Thanks for coming to my defense in there."

"He was out of line, honey."

Kathryn smiled. "Skip it, Smitty. He's not worth the trouble."

"You shouldn't let that prig talk to you like that, Kat." He looked at her for her reaction and cut her off before she began. "And if you say anything other than, 'You're right, Smitty' ..."

She bowed her head with a broad smile and acquiesced to his unwavering support. "You're right, Smitty."

"Damn straight."

Jenny stood in the center of the crowded elevator at OSS headquarters and waited for the doors to open to her floor. When the heavy panels parted, she took a step forward with the rest of the group and then froze in her tracks, causing the large man behind her to run into her back.

"In or out, doll," he muttered, as he shouldered past.

Jenny was oblivious. The sight of Kathryn and Smitty coming toward her from the busy hallway paralyzed her.

She thought she'd prepared herself for this eventual chance meeting. She'd gone over every possible scenario and how she would react to it. If they were alone together, she would ignore her. If they were in a professional setting, she would acknowledge her with a cool "Hammond," letting her know she'd accepted their relationship for the game that it was and that she was no longer the naïve child who had fallen for her ruse.

In the past month, she'd tried not to feel anything for or about her. Kathryn Hammond was paid to do a job, and she did it brilliantly, which is why they chose her. She wasn't worth anger or resentment—or so Jenny had convinced herself—that is, until she saw her.

Kathryn's face was downturned. She was smiling, almost laughing, and Jenny was immediately seized with hatred. She hated her for being so beautiful, hated her for taking her breath away, hated her for laughing and smiling when she had so callously destroyed her life. What right did this heartless creature have to be happy?

The crowds jostled in and out of the elevator, and Jenny could do nothing but seethe and stare as Kathryn and Smitty turned right and headed for the neighboring bay of elevators. Soon they were out of view and the elevator doors were closing. Jenny quickly stepped into the hallway and didn't dare look to the side. She walked purposefully down the corridor toward her meeting with Colonel Holmes and put thoughts of Kathryn behind her. She had more important things to focus on.

She increased her stride and passed a stern-looking Colonel Forsythe, who didn't notice her, as he fumbled with a file in his hands. It was her day to be invisible, she supposed, but she wouldn't be invisible much longer. She would have Holmes's undivided attention, and she was sure he was going to be pleased with her discovery.

The colonel was in his outer office giving instructions to his secretary when Jenny entered the room.

Holmes grinned and extended his hand in welcome. "Ah, Miss Ryan. Good to see you. Come in."

Kathryn watched the elevator doors close on Jenny's back as she walked down the hall and away from the elevator bays. She briefly shut her eyes, invoking her promise never to watch her walk away, and suppressed the urge to run after her. Smitty saw her, too, but showed no sign of it until he snuck a glance at her halfway through their descent.

Kathryn stared straight ahead, her face a stone mask. They left the building and got into the car with the silence as strained as ever.

Memories of happier days with Jenny inundated her, and she involuntarily shook her head, as renewed disbelief at the outcome of their affair wrapped itself around her heart.

It seemed like an eternity had passed since the dubious security breach that sent her world into a tailspin. She was sure it was no accident. Holmes and his aides were her first and only suspects. Files like that didn't accidentally wind up out of the classified loop.

She never liked Holmes and was suspicious of him from the start. She thought it was a reflection of her bad attitude after their previous interactions overseas, but she felt vindicated when he revealed the Ryan files to her and Smitty, against Colonel Forsythe's better judgment. They never should have seen those files. Assignments are strictly compartmentalized. Only a handful of officials are privy to the full picture, and she and Smitty were certainly nowhere near that chain of information. It was clear to Kathryn that the whole thing had been carefully planned from the beginning. She was a pawn, and she played her part above and beyond their expectations.

She gave Colonel Forsythe the benefit of the doubt in her conspiracy theory. It didn't seem like his style—if there was a style to espionage. Her suspicions didn't change anything, however. What was done was done. She had another part to play now, and a life to endure without Jenny Ryan.

———

They arrived at the club for the afternoon rehearsal, and Kathryn immediately sought out her boss to make amends for her poor work ethic. She found him in his office, where he was pleased to see her, as always. Dominic accepted her apology, all the while denying the need for it.

"Technically, your work is flawless, Kathryn. That is why I said nothing. But I know you. I know your gift. Your song resonates from your soul." He smiled but then shook his head. "You are empty here." He tapped his chest. "I worry for your broken heart."

She let her easy grin cover the pain of the truth. "My heart will survive, Nicky."

"It may survive, but when will it sing again?"

"It will sing tonight, I promise."

He leaned closer and put his hand over hers. "Pretend all you like on the outside, *mia amica*, but when will it really sing again?"

It was a question she couldn't answer, so she remained silent. The way she felt at that moment, her heart might never sing again.

Dominic leaned back in his chair and clasped his hands thoughtfully across his belly. "What of your friend? Is there no hope?"

"I'm afraid that's over."

"Over for her. Not for you."

"Unfortunately, the result is the same."

Dominic nodded regretfully. "I am sorry for the both of you."

"So am I."

With nothing else to say about the subject, and their business concluded, Kathryn got up and promised that, from now on, her work would please him.

Dominic rose and took her hand. "Do not do it for me, Kathryn. Do it for yourself—because you love it. Because it moves you."

Easier said than done, she thought to herself, as she left his office and headed to her dressing room. It *should* move her, and she didn't have to wonder when it stopped, only marvel that she hadn't noticed.

Kathryn sat at her vanity and reached for her powder. She glanced at herself in the mirror and did a double take. For weeks, she had been looking but not seeing. She hadn't seen the dark circles under her lower lids, or her sallow skin, or the way her tired eyes narrowed in protest under even the softest light.

She closed the windows to her soul, not wanting to see the emptiness she knew she'd find there. She didn't want to see who she'd become or acknowledge what she had lost.

Smitty was right. Something had to change. She had tried to lose herself in her assignments. It had worked in the past. She would embrace her character, become the product of her lies. It was a well-worn pattern, almost automatic.

She tried convincing herself that that's what she had done with Jenny—played a role, as ordered. It just hurt less. But she knew that wasn't true. She had been in love. Really in love. The truth made losing Jenny that much harder, made her assignments that much more repulsive. Instead of embracing her considerable power over Forrester and Bouchaule, she found herself torn, desperately trying to hold on to the woman Jenny saw and loved while, at the same time, denying that woman ever existed.

Kathryn put her elbows on the vanity counter and rubbed her temples, trying to stave off the wave of conflicting emotions.

She allowed herself some anger toward Jenny for showing her how to love and then leaving her to flounder without it. But the worst part was that Jenny didn't believe in them. She didn't believe in her.

The pain of it twisted around her heart and threatened to spiral her anger into grief. There was no place in her life for the anger or the grief. *Breathe. Just breathe.* She let the emotion flow through her like the wind blowing through an empty house and then let it go. It wasn't Jenny's fault, and she forgave her for leaving. Her lack of trust was understandable, and while she was in the forgiving mood, she forgave herself, admitting there was nothing she could have done differently.

This time when she looked in the mirror, she didn't flinch at her reflection. No more would she use Jenny's love to punish herself. Instead, she would embrace it, use it to give her strength. A burden lifted, and a warmth she'd thought she'd lost filled her heart. She shed tears finally, not because she'd lost Jenny, but because she'd found something good in herself through their love.

Smitty knocked on the door and entered, uninvited.

Kathryn wiped a tear from her cheek as he appeared behind her in the mirror.

He put a comforting hand on her shoulder. "It's about time," he said of her tears.

She smiled at his reflection and pressed her cheek to his hand.

"I'm sorry, Smitty. I've been horrid."

"Skip it. Are you okay?"

She looked up into his concerned eyes as a reassuring peace settled about her. "I'm going to be."

Smitty squeezed her shoulder. "That's right, honey."

He seemed as relieved as she was, but she wondered if he really understood.

"I really loved her, you know."

"I know you do."

Kathryn turned and looked up in appreciation.

Smitty offered her a tight-lipped smile. "I know you miss her."

Kathryn nodded and turned to the mirror again. She did miss her, but the tears were for having found her again, and this time she would keep her with her always.

The sounds of the band tuning their instruments drifted up from the club below, and Kathryn earnestly wiped the tears away to prepare for rehearsal. She didn't feel joy for her music just then, but she knew she would again, and soon, and that was enough.

After Smitty left, she warmed up properly for the first time in weeks and then went downstairs, where she would let music soothe her ravaged soul.

Jenny smiled curtly at the secretary in the outer office and then slammed the door behind her as she left her meeting and entered the hallway.

"Arrogant son of a bitch," she said under her breath. To be threatened with removal from the Ryan case was not what she had expected when she had entered Colonel Holmes's office.

"I am very disappointed in you, Miss Ryan," he had said, his clipped British accent telegraphing his annoyance. "You should have come to us with this information immediately, not taken it upon yourself to investigate. You could have blown your cover, gotten caught, tipped our hand—myriad things could have gone wrong, all spelling disaster for our case." He shook his head in disgust. "I think your involvement has been a mistake."

Jenny stood up, astonished at his lack of gratitude. "Now see here, Colonel! You've been crawling up my uncle's behind for how long? And what did it get you—nothing. I practically walk in off the street and I bring you the biggest break you've gotten so far."

She leaned in on the desk to show him she meant business. "You need me, Colonel, because I can see things your people can't. This is my fam—" She stopped herself, having banished the word from her vocabulary when speaking of the Ryans. "I know these people. No one you have knows them better." She sat down and raised her chin in confidence. "You'll keep me on this case because you're closer to the truth with me than without me."

She watched Colonel Holmes weigh her outburst against the truth of her words. "You're a high-spirited young woman, Miss Ryan. But don't think for one moment you are indispensable. Insubordination will not be tolerated, do you understand?"

Jenny swallowed her pride. "Yes, sir."

"You will not visit that warehouse again. Is that understood?"

She wanted to point out that the warehouse was not under his jurisdiction, and more than that, it not only contained information he sought, but also information about the Ryan family that would fill in the blank spaces she didn't even know existed. She bit down on her objection and repeated a meek "Yes, sir" instead.

If Colonel Holmes was pleased with her find, he didn't show it. Jenny thought it was grand though, smiling proudly as she handed over the film from her small agency-issued Minox camera.

At first, she thought the warehouse had been a bust. What she assumed was furniture turned out to be printing presses and various items used in the print business. Stacked neatly were boxes and boxes of blank envelopes and reams of paper. Several boxes contained copies of Daniel Ryan's three medical journals. She was reminded that she had given Kathryn a set that she had never returned—another reason to dislike the woman.

Jenny was confused for a moment as to who owned the contents of the unit. More searching revealed personal Ryan family keepsakes. There were old photos, college sporting trophies for the two brothers, etching plates from her grandmother's artwork—all forgotten traces of lives left behind. The warehouse was a Ryan family catchall, it seemed.

It was all very interesting but not what she came for. A large locked desk was the pot of gold at the end of the footprints in the dusty floor.

She made quick work of the lock and tugged on the old oak desk's center drawer, releasing the locking mechanism for the file drawers to each side. To her surprise, instead of files, the deep drawers contained money—lots of it. Cash, in hundred-dollar bills, in neatly banded piles. She couldn't even fathom a guess at how much lay before her, and because of the weakening batteries in her flashlight, she didn't have time to count it.

She opened the large center drawer and found a ledger book. It tracked cash transactions dating back years. To her shock, the handwriting was Daniel Ryan's. She turned to the most recent entries and found Calvin Richards' name prevalent, but in Paul's hand. The amounts to him weren't significant, and she cringed, as it appeared he had been paying him to woo her. She followed the entries back a year and found a gap in the dates—several months of inactivity after Daniel Ryan's death. The entries then started again, with Paul Ryan the new accountant. Jenny didn't recognize any of the other names on the pages. Some were common between the two men, others recent additions to Paul's regime. She found the entries to Calvin Richards calming. Somehow, she found a modicum of relief in the fact that Paul knew the man as Cal Richards and not some imposter bent on treachery. But still, the redheaded man remained a mystery.

She pulled out her miniature camera and took photos of the ledger, starting with the most recent entries and going back for as long as her film and the batteries in her flashlight held out. When her light began to fade, she made sure she put everything back exactly the way she found it. Her light had almost gone, but she couldn't resist opening one last box to take a peek.

She blinked when she was met with pictures of herself. She held her fading light closer and realized they were pictures of her mother. The rest of the room faded away as she reverently reached into the box, gently parting the contents to see every precious item inside. She found pictures, letters, small books of poetry, and weaving its way through the woman's history was a brightly colored silk scarf. From the unique pattern, Jenny recognized it from the picture in the study. She gently removed the scarf from the box and touched it to her cheek. She smelled it, hoping against hope her mother's scent would still be there. The scarf revealed nothing of its owner, and Jenny wilted in disappointment. She closed her eyes and clutched the smooth fabric to her heart. It was the only tangible piece of her mother's existence, and it was all she could do not to take it with her.

She was angry at Daniel Ryan for keeping these things from her. He'd reduced her mother to a picture on an expensive piano and relegated her life to a few memories in a musty box.

Jenny opened her eyes to find her flashlight almost extinguished. She shook the heavy metal cylinder in her hand, begging it to give her a few more moments of light, but beyond a brief flickering, she could coax no such grace from it.

She reluctantly closed the lid on the only family she had but vowed to return—and next time, she would be prepared with fresh batteries and more film.

As Jenny stormed down the busy halls of headquarters with a reprimand ringing in her ears, she could barely contain her anger. Colonel Holmes couldn't possibly understand how important the contents of that box were to her. To hell with the Ryan family and their dirty little secrets. The OSS could have them, and good riddance. She had to spend the rest of the day at the *Daily Chronicle*, but no one was going to keep her from learning about her mother.

"Stay away from that warehouse my ass," she muttered.

The shocks on Jenny's car groaned with every dip into the minefield of potholes on the dimly lit road to the industrial district. She was glad she'd had the fender repaired or she would've blown another tire. As she crept along, she wished she were in her first car—an old Ford coupe. It would have been a little less conspicuous than her relatively rare Cord, and a lot less expensive to repair should all the jarring shake the wheels off.

She'd driven by the entrance to the warehouse section several times, and, to her dismay, found the area quite active for nine o'clock on a Monday night. She was afraid she'd never get to the storage unit unseen, so she devised a new plan.

She parked in a fairly populated portion of the district so that her car wouldn't stand out, and pockets weighed down with fresh batteries and plenty of film, she made her way through a break in the chain-link fence behind the warehouse she sought and waited patiently in the shadows until the coast was clear.

Her lock picks at the ready, she snuck around the building and kneeled before the large padlock. She picked the lock quickly this time and allowed herself a proud chuckle as she set the defeated lock aside and lifted the large bay door. She quickly ducked inside and pulled the door down behind her.

She rubbed her hands together in anticipation. "Okay, Momma, here I come."

She felt as though she were meeting the woman for the first time, and her heart swelled as she pulled the flashlight from the back of her waistband and turned on the switch. She aimed her light at the center of the room and stood in stunned disbelief as she stared into an empty shell.

"No," she breathed.

"What the—" She rushed forward and focused her light into each corner. There was nothing left. No trace of the contents that filled the room the night before—even the floor had been swept.

"This isn't happening."

She panicked and hoped, all at the same time, that she'd broken into the wrong unit. She quickly ducked outside and trained her light on the number under the unit's smashed lightbulb. It was the right place. She shook off her disbelief and closed the door and replaced the lock.

She ran to her car, hopped in, and drove until her heart stopped pounding out of her chest. She pulled to the side of the road and tried to process what had just happened. She certainly couldn't confront Colonel Holmes. He would know she disobeyed his direct orders. What would happen when Uncle Paul found out?

"Damn it!" She pounded the steering wheel in frustration.

The OSS could have the rest, but that one box—her mother's box —belonged to her. She looked at the road sign in front of her car. If she turned left, it would take her home. If she turned right, it would take her to Kathryn's apartment. She would know what to do. She might even know where they would take the contents of the storage unit, and if she didn't, maybe Smitty would, or could find out.

Turning to Kathryn for help was almost too much to swallow, and it made Jenny a little sick to even consider it, but then she reasoned, turnabout was fair play. Kathryn had used her to get information, why couldn't she do the same? If Kathryn truly cared about her, as she claimed, it would be easy to get back into her good graces. Once there, she could easily convince her to help, and once she got what she wanted, Kathryn would get a taste of her own medicine.

Jenny stared at the road sign, weighing her decision. She looked in the rearview mirror and angled it until she could see her face. She closed her eyes and exhaled. Kathryn wouldn't hesitate to do such a thing. That's what made her a great agent. Jenny wanted to be a great agent.

She centered the Cord's back window in the rearview mirror and then turned left, toward home.

Kathryn mingled in the main lobby of the hotel while she waited for Marcus Forrester to arrive. He had made a day trip out of a community award ceremony and had yet to return to town. Kathryn marveled at the public's perception of the man. His industrial endeavors courted favor with the communities they supported, and all the while his dark pursuits ran swiftly under the surface, like the sewers beneath their feet, contaminating the unsuspecting sea with its silent poison.

Kathryn recognized the usual offenders. They appeared anxious as they looked at their watches and nervously scanned the crowd. Negotiations were coming to a head, and anything out of the ordinary set everyone on edge. Kathryn looked at her watch. Forrester was late.

A busboy approached and handed her a note. It was not the explanation she expected. It was an invitation to one of the rooms upstairs. She gave a final glance around the crowded hall and quietly slipped away.

"Thierry, this is outrageous," she said, shouldering past the Frenchman and into his room. "Marc will arrive at any moment, and I've got to—"

She was interrupted by a passionate kiss, to which she momentarily surrendered with the expected moan before pushing away.

"Are you mad?" she said, pretending she was flustered.

Bouchaule smiled and went to the bar, where he poured two glasses of champagne. "Apparently as mad as you, because you are here." He held out a glass. "I have it on good authority that Mr. Forrester has been delayed." He looked at his watch. "For forty-five minutes, at least."

Kathryn ignored the glass and feigned trepidation. "Then he'll call, and I've got to—"

She was interrupted by the ringing phone.

"I believe that is for you."

Bouchaule smirked and turned down the soft music in the background. Evidently, he'd instructed the concierge to forward Forrester's call.

Kathryn picked up the phone with an incredulous glance to her host.

"Hello? Yes, darling." She cradled the phone like she cared. "Yes, the fog was dreadful here too. When will you arrive?"

Bouchaule smiled on cue when he heard Forrester's voice through the receiver say, "In forty-five minutes." Kathryn shook her head at his conceit.

"Yes, Marc. Please be careful. I'll see you soon."

She hung up the phone with a capitulating grin and, this time, took the offered glass of champagne.

"I suppose you arranged the weather too."

He raised his glass. "You would be surprised by what I can arrange."

"Mm. You are full of surprises."

He smiled and turned up the music, then he took the glasses and placed them on the serving cart beside the ice bucket and held out his hands. "Shall we dance?"

Kathryn swept into his embrace, where their bodies molded perfectly as they swayed to the rhythm of the mellow swing song.

"This is not discreet, Thierry."

He leaned in for a kiss, which was given, and then held her tightly against his hip. "I promise you it is."

Kathryn stiffly played along.

"Relax, darling," he whispered in her ear. "You are perfectly safe."

"Someone could have seen you come in."

"No one saw me arrive, and no one will see me leave. I just wanted to be near you again." He ran his hand up the length of her spine. "It has been a long day without you."

Bouchaule's movements were smooth and confident as he kissed her bare shoulder and started to unzip her dress.

Kathryn smirked at his impatience and his growing desire pressing on her hip. "Are we going to dance, or are we going to make love?"

"What is the difference?"

"Depends on how good you are."

"You already know how good I am ... at both."

He eased one spaghetti strap off her shoulder and then the other, gently kissing the spots they once occupied. The closeness of their bodies was the only thing holding up her dress, and still they danced. She playfully untied his perfect bowtie and backed off enough to begin freeing the buttons on his shirt. She slid her hand into his shirt and caressed a nipple. That finally disrupted their dance, as she swore her partner got weak in the knees.

Kathryn smiled into his chest and knew it was time. She kissed her way up his neck to his mouth, and he allowed her dress to fall to her waist as he ran his hands up her torso to her breasts.

He attempted to capture her waiting mouth, but she pulled away with a wicked smile.

"I have something for you." She seductively eyed his lips. "Something you want."

"Yes, you do," he exhaled hungrily and tried again for her mouth.

She stopped his advance with a hand on his chest. "Information."

Bouchaule's passion turned to purpose, as all desire was forgotten and he grabbed Kathryn by the shoulders. "Tell me."

.   .   .

Forty minutes later, Kathryn greeted Marcus Forrester in the lobby with a kiss on the cheek. Fifteen minutes after that, Thierry Bouchaule walked through the front door as if he'd never been there before.

"Very smooth," Forrester said before sipping his champagne.

"Very," Kathryn agreed, smiling to someone across the room.

"Can he give me what I want?"

"No."

"You're sure?"

She smiled. "He wants me to steal it from you. He's got nothing."

In truth, Bouchaule seemed to have gotten what he needed, and his concern was that Forrester not have the same access to it.

Forrester's eyes narrowed at Bouchaule's back. "Lying bastard. He'll pay for that."

Kathryn smiled internally. Bouchaule had said the same about him.

Forrester stewed over the man's betrayal and took an agitated tug at his tight collar.

"Did you have sex with him?"

"No," Kathryn lied into her glass.

Forrester gave her a doubtful glance, wrapped in a flash of anger.

She raised her brow. "Once you give him what he wants, he no longer wants it."

Forrester returned to his champagne, clearly relieved. "What a fool."

"A man like that wants a conquest, Marc, not a girlfriend."

Forrester looked at her with wonder. "Have I told you lately that I adore you?"

Kathryn smiled sweetly and entwined her arm with his. The turn of events would make for interesting final negotiations in Chicago the following weekend.

Jenny sat at her desk at the *Daily Chronicle* and rubbed her tired eyes. Staring at code all morning and working at the paper all afternoon was taking its toll. She was thankful it was Friday and that she'd managed to get the weekend off from both jobs.

She'd had no more meetings with brass, nor had she made any progress in locating her mother's belongings. She stared at the mockup of the *Entertainment* section on her desk and was met with a side column ad for The Grotto. Her feelings for Kathryn had turned sympathetic when faced with the catch twenty-two of her own situation with brass. Even through her anger, she had entertained the thought that Kathryn had actually cared for her. The realization that she may have thrown it all away because of her stupid pride and unforgiving temper hit her like a brick.

Jenny stared at the number for The Grotto and reached for her phone. She didn't know what she would say to the woman, but she had to know for sure. She looked at Paul in his office, and the betrayal all came flooding back. She took her hand off the receiver and focused on the layout for the weekend edition.

A commotion in Paul's office made her look up. He was screaming something into the phone and then angrily hurled it against the wall. All heads turned to the office, as Paul grabbed his jacket and stormed out the door.

Jenny didn't have to wonder what it was about. "Uncle Paul?" she ventured weakly as he brushed past her desk.

He didn't respond, and he nearly ran over the newswire boy rushing down the aisle from the opposite direction.

"Stop the presses!" the boy shouted, waving a piece of ticker tape.

"No one orders that but me!" Paul said, ripping the tape from the courier's hand.

He read the ticker and let his arms fall limply to his sides.

"Jesus, Mary, and Joseph," he said in disbelief, as he dropped the message for any and all takers and bolted to the pressroom.

There was a mad scramble for the tape, but the boy broke the news first.

"Marcus Forrester is dead!"

Jenny snatched the tape from the nearest hand. "What?"

The workers in the newsroom stood in stunned silence for all of about three seconds before all hell broke loose and everyone scrambled for their phones and a notebook.

Jenny stood in numb silence as she let the tape drift to her feet.

Chicago STOP Forrester plane down STOP All onboard killed STOP Six men one woman STOP More details to follow STOP.

Jenny's hand shook as she pressed the phone to her ear and struggled to keep her emotions in check.

"Please," she begged the secretary on the other end of the line. "Your airline has to have a passenger manifest."

She put her head in her hand as the woman responded and quietly hung up the phone. She had gotten the same answer from everyone she'd spoken to at the airport: no passenger manifest on the private charter, and no one could give her a description of the woman.

She felt lightheaded and sick to her stomach. She'd called everyone she could think of, including headquarters, which was a fruitless exercise that led her to secretaries who couldn't say whether Kathryn was on the plane. Smitty was nowhere to be found—she hoped he wasn't on the plane. The club was no help either, as Bobby informed her that Kathryn was off for the week.

The wire room finally told her to stop calling. They would let her know as soon as the names were confirmed. It was assumed the woman was Kathryn Hammond. Jenny even saw it in one reporter's notes. She took issue with the man, only to apologize when he acknowledged her friendship with Kathryn and offered his condolences. It all felt so surreal, so déjà vu. It was like her father had died all over again. Everyone had the same patronizing tone, the same look of pity. She had to get out of there. Kathryn wasn't dead. She couldn't be dead.

Jenny took refuge in an empty office and locked the door. She was overwhelmed by the realization she'd been wrong about Kathryn. She replayed every tender moment they'd shared, every tear they'd shed, every longing look and loving touch. No one was that good. Not even Kathryn Hammond.

She was gripped with a frigid wave of remorse, and she hugged herself to stop her body from shaking. She slid down the wall and sobbed. Why did she burn the letter? Why didn't she listen when Kathryn tried to explain? These were the things she would have to live with. Just like the fight with her father—regret would haunt her, with no chance of a pardon. Despite her vow to the contrary, history had repeated itself.

CHAPTER FOURTEEN

Kathryn basked in a serene calmness she'd never felt before. The setting sun bathed the empty beach with a subtle orange hue, and she smiled as she buried her feet in the sand, still warm from the heat of the day. She sat on the shore, mesmerized by the ceaseless rhythm of the incoming surf, and couldn't help but wish she'd come to this place sooner. She laughed at her wish when she acknowledged life has a way of knowing the perfect time for the perfect place. Her mind was clear, her responsibilities lifted, and like the waves finding their way to shore without her help, the lives of those she tried so meticulously to control would now be left up to fate's fickle desire.

She didn't know what, but she knew something big was about to happen, and things would never be the same.

Thierry Bouchaule had called her the night before at the club and warned her not to go to Chicago. When pressed for a reason, he merely claimed he was fulfilling his promise to protect her. He didn't reveal his plan, but he did say Forrester would not be pleased, and he wanted to make sure she was nowhere near the man when he executed his plan.

She informed her superiors of the warning, and they agreed she should avoid making the trip and should stay out of sight for the duration. Dominic had offered his isolated getaway before, but Kathryn was always afraid to face the solitude of such a place. Today she relished it. She was unafraid of her future, was momentarily at peace with her past, and marveled at the simple pleasure of a mind at rest.

She knew Jenny would be proud of her—contentment was a real achievement—and she wished she were with her to share the moment. She smiled when she realized she was—now and always. She imagined Jenny calling her name above the din of the restless sea, and she closed her eyes and let the memory of her voice fill her heart.

Paul Ryan put a forearm across Agent Jake Russo's chest and slammed him up against his car. "What have you done with it?" he shouted amid the swirling dirt devils in the dusty open field.

Russo pulled the gun from his shoulder holster and pressed it to Paul's ribs. "I suggest you calm down, Mr. Ryan."

Paul eased off, and Russo slowly put the gun away. He straightened his tie and settled his jacket on his shoulders. "I don't know what you're talking about."

"You people can't do this. That warehouse is my property."

"File a report with the police."

Paul knew he wasn't going to win. They had the contents of the storage unit. They no longer needed him to supply documents, but he needed them.

"What do you want for its return?" he asked, anxious to make a deal.

"I'm not sure you have anything that interests us, Mr. Ryan."

"I need that money," Paul said, not hiding the desperation in his voice. "You got what you wanted. I have responsibilities. I need that money back!"

"You seem rather desperate, Paul."

"Take the rest. Just return the money. Please!"

Russo lit a cigarette, and Paul knew he was just giving the illusion of considering the plea. "If we already have what we want, as you say, why would we give you anything?"

"Because it's the right thing to do!"

Russo almost spat out his cigarette in laughter. "Why, that's mighty rich, coming from you, sir. Lordy—" He held his side, still laughing. "I think I hurt myself."

"This isn't a fucking—"

Paul's second angry lunge was stopped by Russo's hand on his gun.

"Now, now," the agent said. "Tell me again what you have that is so valuable to us?"

"I've got information."

Russo raised an interested brow. "A certain key to a certain code perhaps?"

"No. I haven't got that."

The agent shook his head dismissively and holstered his gun as he turned to leave. "We're through here, Ryan. Don't contact me again."

Paul grabbed the stocky man's jacket and didn't let go, even when the gun was presented as a warning. "Damn it, Russo! Don't you have a family? People you love?"

The agent looked at him with cold, dark eyes and a sinister smile. "No." He looked at Paul's fist, buried in his lapel. "You're wrinkling my jacket."

Paul backed down. "I can tell you things."

"What kind of things?"

"About the experiments."

Russo laughed doubtfully. "You're a newspaperman, Ryan. What the hell would you know about experiments?"

"He was my brother, moron. We weren't always estranged. Besides, I know about the experiments. Don't you think that means something?"

The agent took a moment to deliberate.

Paul thought he would help the man along. "You give me the money back, I give you the information. It's simple, ape."

The word ape was barely out of Paul's mouth before Agent Russo's fist was buried into his stomach. The punch brought him to his knees and stole his breath.

Russo hiked up his pants at the thigh and squatted beside him as he wheezed to catch his breath. "How many people have died because of you? How many lives destroyed? You wouldn't give us this information when we asked nicely, but now you'll give it up for money?" He rose to his full height and dropped his cigarette at Paul's knees. "You're pathetic."

Russo got into his car and leaned out the window. "You'll be hearing from us." He started the engine and peeled away.

Paul held up a hand to protect his face from the flying dirt and debris and slumped onto his heels, as his tie flapped and twisted in the swirling wind like a broken bird with no one to put it out of its misery.

Jenny couldn't control her tears as she boarded a crowded southbound train heading to the Jersey shore. She'd just met with Dominic, who had given her the news she was hoping for: Kathryn was not on the plane. She was safe and sound and taking some much needed time off at a private location only he was privy to. He had heard of her frantic call for information and tracked her down to tell her the news. He met her at a busy local diner, knowing his place was bugged, and after some initial grilling about her intentions, gave her Kathryn's location.

After crying in relief for an hour of the ride, Jenny gathered her emotions and focused on what she would say to set things right. Kathryn loved her, of that she was sure, and because of that, Kathryn would accept her apology and forgive her. She hoped. Love would make that possible. Love makes anything possible. Kathryn would understand the shock of the situation and welcome her back into her arms. They would start over, and this time they'd get it right. Forrester was dead—nothing stood in their way now.

A middle-aged man wearing work overalls and carrying his hat in his hands approached her as she exited the mainland train station.

"Miss Ryan?"

"Yes."

"Mr. Vignelli has asked that I see you safely to your destination." He thumbed over his shoulder at a well-kept, but well-used, green Chevrolet pickup truck with the name of a seafood company on its door.

Thanks to her OSS training, Jenny's first instinct was suspicion, but Dominic told her not to worry about transportation to and from the island, so Jenny dutifully followed the man to his truck.

"No suitcase, ma'am?"

Jenny shook her head. "Traveling light." She hadn't even thought of packing anything. She went right from the meeting with Dominic to the ticket window at Penn Station.

As they drove past guardsmen posted along the causeway to the island, Jenny was reminded that the war wasn't far away. German U-boats stalked the shoreline looking for prey, and she didn't even want to think about where Kathryn might be sent, now that her assignment to Forrester was over.

The warm smell of salty sea air mixed with the tang of decaying marshland welcomed her onto a sparsely populated strip of sand inhabited by thickets of bayberry bushes, holly trees, and willowy cattails. As they headed south down the ribbon of road stretching the length of the island, simple shiplap cottages mingled with sprawling summer resorts. The resorts looked relatively empty for what was supposed to be high season.

"Where is everyone?" Jenny asked.

"The gas rationing is killing us here. We don't have the public transportation of the larger seaside destinations, so people aren't making the trip down here. I know it's hard on the community financially, but I can't say I miss the crowds."

Jenny nodded, and they rode the rest of the way in silence. To her surprise, she was dropped off at a dock on the tip of the island, where a boat was waiting to take her across the inlet to another island that looked like nothing more than an endless strip of dunes.

After the boatman ferried her over, he dropped her off at the jutting bulkhead on the bayside beach, where a small boat was moored. He asked if she wanted him to wait, but Jenny glanced at the overgrown path leading to the small wooden cottage at the top of the sea grass laden dunes and said no.

She was determined to revive at least her friendship before she left the island, and no matter the welcome she got, time was all she would need to set things right.

The boatman shoved off, and Jenny took off her shoes, ready to slog through the sand. She looped her shoulder bag across her body and made her way to the cottage, with her stomach in her throat and her heart on her sleeve. The anticipation of interacting with Kathryn for the first time since their breakup was wreaking havoc on her nerves. Silly, she thought. They had been lovers and had shared the most intimate moments—that had to count for something. She ignored the fact that she was the one who had thrown all that away and focused instead on her belief that Kathryn was a reasonable woman. The notion calmed her, but it was quickly shattered by the memories of times when Kathryn had not been reasonable and her temper had gone off like a percussion cap on the end of a fuse.

With every step toward her destination, Jenny's confidence sank like her bare feet in the shifting sand of the pathway. She feared that the shock of the plane crash had tainted her logic and that her first reaction to the news of Kathryn's assignment had been the right one —it was just another job, expertly carried out by a professional.

It had been a month since their breakup. If Kathryn was as smitten as she claimed, why hadn't she attempted to contact her and set things right? Jenny stopped in her tracks and shook her head clear of such thoughts. She could drive herself crazy with second guesses, so she tried to keep an open mind and hoped Kathryn would do the same.

She knocked on the door but got no answer. She hesitantly tried the handle and found it unlocked. She thought about entering but settled for a peek through the wavy, handblown window glass. It was a small, one-room cottage. Kathryn's suitcase was still packed and on the bed, and a bag of groceries and a box of supplies sat on the rustic kitchen table. A small wood burning stove to cook and heat was surrounded by cedar paneled walls adorned with odd nautical treasures, most of which looked like they had been rescued from the beach.

A pair of binoculars lay on the outer window ledge, and Jenny leaned on the deck railing and used them to scan the beach as far as she could see in both directions. In the distance, she could see a figure sitting at the edge of the shore. No doubt, it was Kathryn. Her dark hair stood out against the stark white of her shirt and the never-ending expanse of billowy sand. The cottage and bulkhead were the only structures in sight. The rest of the beach was deserted.

As Jenny trekked down the ocean side of the dunes, she wondered if Kathryn knew anything about the plane crash in advance. After being Forrester's constant companion for the past few weeks, it seemed like an odd coincidence that she would leave his side at the most opportune moment, as it turned out, and disappear.

Perhaps it was an OSS plot. She wouldn't put it past them. Not that she mourned the loss of a man like Forrester and his ilk, but she was constantly amazed at the depths they would go to achieve their objectives.

All is fair in love and war. She would get to test that theory sooner rather than later, as she came within shouting distance of her estranged friend.

Kathryn sat just out of reach of the water line, her arms crossed atop her bent knees, and her chin resting on her forearms. Her eyes were closed, and she wore a peaceful grin. Jenny had called out twice, not wanting to startle her, but her voice was lost in the constant roar of the incoming surf.

She knelt beside her and slowly put her hand on her shoulder. "Kat?"

Kathryn opened her eyes with a start. "Jenny!"

She hopped to her feet and quickly scanned the beach over Jenny's shoulder. "How did you—"

When Kathryn didn't finish her sentence, Jenny knew she saw the boatman in the distance and knew Dominic must have had something to do with it. According to the boatman, no one was ferried over without his permission.

Kathryn recovered from her initial surprise and revised her question.

"What are you doing here?" she asked coolly.

"I had to see you."

Jenny had traveled hours for this moment, and the sight of Kathryn, alive and well, windblown with a touch of sunburn and more beautiful than ever, was quickly reducing her to tears again. She fought them back as best she could for the moment, but she couldn't stop herself from hugging Kathryn in relief.

Kathryn didn't shy away from the physical greeting, but she didn't reciprocate either.

"I thought I'd lost you," Jenny finally cried into Kathryn's shoulder.

Kathryn gently eased her away and held her at arm's length. "Okay, I'm a little confused here."

Jenny pulled the latest newspaper from her bag and unfolded the front page. "Forrester's dead."

Kathryn's eyes widened at the headline, and she stared in stunned disbelief as the news sank in.

Jenny could see that it came as a shock. Kathryn slowly came out of it and took the paper from her hands.

"There was a woman onboard. I was afraid it was you. I was frantic. I realized how much I love you, and I—"

Kathryn folded up the paper and brushed past as if she hadn't heard a word she'd said.

"Hey!"

Kathryn kept walking as if she had no intention of slowing down.

Kathryn could hardly conceive that Forrester was dead, let alone conceive that Jenny was standing before her, professing her love.

She had let her guard down. This was the last place on earth she expected to see Jenny, and her appearance twisted her fragile resolve. She had prepared for a life without her. She had not prepared to let her back in.

"I've got to go to the mainland to call in," she shouted over her shoulder. "Stay or come, it's up to you."

"I'm not leaving here until we talk, Kathryn," Jenny called back.

Kathryn had a feeling that was coming. Jenny was a constant in that way.

"Suit yourself."

She took longer strides toward the cottage, and Jenny followed three steps behind, struggling in the soft sand. Once at the cottage, Kathryn gathered her jacket and shoes and headed for the door. Jenny grabbed her arm as she brushed past.

"You *are* coming back, right?"

Kathryn turned, holding on to indignation as a shield while she escaped. "Look, if you don't trust me to do as I say—" She stopped and softened her demeanor when she saw the desperation in Jenny's eyes. Clearly, she had something she needed to say, and Kathryn knew she did as well, but, as usual, she was running, and Jenny was forcing the issue.

She donned her jacket and fastened the two bottom buttons while she checked her temper and emotional maelstrom.

"I should be back within the hour. If I'm not back in two, I've been ordered back to the city."

She reached into an old ceramic bowl on the table next to the door and handed Jenny a box of matches.

"If that happens, light the lantern in the kitchen window. That'll signal the boatman. When he responds with three flashes from the shore, extinguish the lamp. He'll be here soon to ferry you back over. If you're too tired to make your way home, please stay the night."

She pulled a small green flag from the table drawer and instructed Jenny to raise it on the pole outside in the morning to signal the boatman in the daylight, then she left without further discussion.

As Jenny watched Kathryn trudge down the path to the bulkhead, she realized reconciliation was going to be harder than she thought. She was sure Kathryn loved her now, though. She would have been indifferent toward her, not angry, if she didn't. At least that was a start.

Kathryn sat on the dock of the lighthouse across from Dominic's island and stared at the desolate strip of shoreline. Her mind was as turbulent as the inlet that separated her from Jenny. Her call to headquarters did nothing to restore her equilibrium. It was as cryptic and shocking as the rest of her day.

"Don't tell me where you are," Colonel Forsythe had said.

"What's going on?"

"Just lay low for a while. Check in daily until we have all this straightened out."

The mistrust and uncertainty in his tone made her nervous. Thankfully, none of it was directed at her. She had her own theories as to who could have arranged the plane crash, and her current assignment was at the top of the list.

"Listen, I think Bouchaule is behind this."

"Bouchaule was on the plane. He's dead."

Kathryn held the phone in dumb silence.

"Just lay low. Check in tomorrow."

She didn't remember saying goodbye, only the dial tone in her ear and the intermittent "Don't forget to buy war bonds" message on an endless loop.

She hung up the receiver and then sat on the dock, trying to make sense of the past few hours. Bouchaule was dead. Forrester was dead. The words almost had no meaning. Away from the city and away from that life, they were so out of context. Also out of context was Jenny. Jenny who loved her. What once would have mattered now just made everything harder.

Dusk was falling quickly, and she had to leave soon or risk getting lost in the darkness. She knew how to operate a boat, but she was no navigator, not in the swift twisting currents of the inlet. She looked at her watch and thought about letting the two-hour time frame expire. It was easier than facing Jenny, easier than breaking her heart.

Jenny made a fire between the dunes on the bayside of the island, where the bulkhead was located, and sat anxiously, waiting for Kathryn's return. Night had fallen, and she should have been back by now—if she was coming back. Jenny stubbornly refused to believe she wasn't right about Kathryn's feelings toward her, but as time ticked by, she feared she would spend the night alone and the rest of her days trying to convince Kathryn that they belong together.

She got up and walked to the water's edge to peer into the darkness of the inlet once again and cursed the blackout restrictions, which rendered the majestic lighthouse dormant for the duration of the war and gave her no hope of sighting Kathryn in the dark void. Her senses heightened when the clouds parted briefly and the full moon glistened off the churning water like tiny diamonds thrown across a piece of rumpled black velvet. She quickly scanned the sea, but it offered nothing but its cool, salty breath in her face. Kathryn was out there somewhere, and Jenny sent out a silent prayer that she'd come back to her—to give her a chance to make things right again.

. . .

Kathryn sat a few yards away in the shadow of a dune and watched Jenny pace at the shoreline, just as she had done for the last hour.

It may have been cruel to make her wait, but Kathryn needed to be sure she was strong enough to do what she needed to do. Jenny was a romantic, not a realist, and as much as she longed to pick up where they left off, something integral had been broken, and wishes and stars wouldn't be enough to make them whole again.

Kathryn felt confident in her resolve and allowed a few moments of selfish reflection. How beautiful Jenny looked bathed in the firelight. How brave she was to come so far and bare her soul, not knowing how she would be received. Kathryn smiled. No wonder she had fallen for her. No wonder she had left her with so much.

Kathryn shed a tear for what was, for what could have been, and quickly put the emotions away, as Jenny returned to the fire.

She was getting increasingly restless, muttering to herself and shaking her head. When she sat down and started to cry, Kathryn decided they'd both waited long enough. She approached from the shore, not wanting to sneak up from behind, and stood motionless on the other side of the fire until Jenny looked up.

"Shit!" Jenny spat in surprise, as she jumped up and quickly wiped the tears from her face. "I've been worried about you."

Kathryn came around the fire and stood beside her. "Sorry."

They both stood in awkward silence for a moment and then sat down in unison.

Kathryn picked up a stick and poked at the burning driftwood. "Thanks for the fire. It made finding the beach easier."

In truth, she probably would have been carried into the open sea by the current without it. She had waited a little too long to make use of the available light of the fading day and had no landmark in which to orient the bow of her small skiff.

Jenny didn't vocally reply to her gratitude, so Kathryn turned her head to find Jenny staring intently at her, on the verge of stating her case.

"I wanted to make sure you'd find your way home."

The double entendre was not lost on Kathryn, who looked away and stared into the flames. "Seems you were sure I'd come back."

"You love me, Kathryn. You're not going to run from that, and if you try, I'm not going to let you."

Kathryn resisted the urge to smile. Jenny hadn't lost any of her tenacity.

A long silence ensued, broken only by the impatient waves lapping at the sand and the popping of the fire.

"Everything okay ashore?"

"Mm. I'm to stay put for the time being."

Jenny nodded, followed by more silence. Kathryn knew that wouldn't last long, and right on cue—

"I know you love me, Kathryn. Don't you dare deny it."

"I won't." Jenny deserved to take that with her at least.

Jenny blinked in pleasant surprise, and Kathryn saw her insecurity for the first time. Jenny *had* been counting on wishes and stars, and her devotion had brought her the truth. Little did she know it wouldn't matter.

Jenny beamed, unaware, and shifted closer.

"It's going to be okay then."

Kathryn shook her head and exhaled. "Jenny ..."

"You love me, Kathryn, and I love you."

Kathryn held her tongue and studied her feet before focusing her attention on the rolling froth of the incoming waves.

Jenny moved even closer. "I love you."

"That's not enough," Kathryn whispered to the sea. "Love's not enough," she said louder, turning to find determined green eyes. "Not in the world we live in."

"Of course it is. It's everything."

"It wasn't everything last month when you didn't want to see me again."

Jenny backed off her aggressive stance. "It was childish of me."

"No, it was a perfectly normal reaction to a devastating revelation."

"I didn't mean it, Kat. I'm here. I just needed time. It was a shock."

"I'm not reprimanding you. Anyone would have done the same, and most wouldn't have come back, which is my point. The only reason you're here is because of the plane crash. Who's to say what would have happened otherwise?" She knew they wouldn't be sitting on a beach having a conversation about it.

"I wanted to call," Jenny said quietly.

"But you didn't."

"I just ... I didn't know what to say."

"Love doesn't change the fact that we have the same problem we had before. You don't trust me."

"Kat—"

"It's true, Jenny," she snapped, not willing to listen to false protests to the contrary. "Saying you love me won't erase the doubt in your mind. It will always be there. You'll always wonder what I know. Wonder what I'm keeping from you. Every day, you'll have to deal with that." She paused. "And so will I."

Jenny was silent for a change, and Kathryn was thankful that at least she wasn't lying to herself.

"No matter how much I love you, you know I can't tell you anything about what I've learned about your family. Can you live with that? Can you love me with that?"

"In my heart I can."

"And in your head?"

Jenny was silent again for a moment, but the need to know shone in her eyes.

"Do you know something?"

Kathryn raised her hand in disbelief and then looked away, disappointed. Of course she wouldn't be able to let it go. It was her family. Jenny would be relentless in her quest for information.

"Not that I want—think you can tell me," Jenny quickly clarified. "Just so I know how I would feel about it. It's the not knowing. I don't know where to put that."

That was understandable, Kathryn reasoned, but it didn't change what she could and couldn't tell her.

"Your father wasn't my assignment."

"I was."

"Yes."

"To find out if I knew what he was doing, or where to find it if I didn't."

"Yes."

"I gave you Dr. Stevens, and then your assignment was over."

"Yes."

She watched Jenny process it all, and could see the moment when the truth erased all her doubts.

"You stuck around."

Their myopic dome of firelight gave Kathryn the courage to speak her heart. "I couldn't let you go."

"Then why can't we—"

"Because you've lost your faith in me, Jenny," Kathryn snapped. She pinned her with the ugly truth for a beat and then turned once more to the black sea, saddened. "And I've lost my faith in us."

Jenny grabbed her arm. "Don't say that, Kathryn."

"It's true. I thought it could work. I told you how it would be ... warned you. You said you could handle it, that you would stick by me."

"That's not fair. You knew what was going on. I had no idea—couldn't even conceive that it would be so personal. Imagine the shock of learning something that would change your entire life, shatter everything you are, everything you thought you were. Have you any idea what that's like?"

Kathryn turned in disbelief. How could Jenny not remember how her father's lie had shattered her childhood?

Jenny realized her mistake and released her arm. "Sorry. Of course you do."

Kathryn exhaled and rubbed her forehead. It all seemed so hopeless.

"I'm here now. Doesn't that count for something?"

It should have, but Kathryn had to be strong.

"I'm not saying I don't understand why you turned away, or that I blame you. I was a fool. I knew better. I—" She wrung her hands and forced out the truth. "I just wanted you so damn much."

"You're saying we don't have a chance."

Kathryn didn't protest. Instead, she stared blindly into the fire. Jenny must have felt her slipping away, because she ran a hand up her arm until she settled it on her bicep.

"Please don't give up on me."

Kathryn closed her eyes to hide her impending tears.

Jenny grabbed her arm with both hands. "Please."

Kathryn finally turned to face her, eyes filled with emotion, as the moment of truth came closer. "I'll never give up on you, Jenny." She would be with her always, and would only want the best for her.

Jenny melted with relief. "Thank you."

There was no thanks needed, but Kathryn took it anyway. Before they parted, Jenny deserved to know what was in her heart, deserved a confession straight from her soul.

"I am so hopelessly in love with you," Kathryn admitted past a tight throat. Her voice had no measure of control and sounded as if it was coming directly from the pit of her stomach.

Evidently, that was enough for Jenny. She slid closer. "Kat—"

"Please let me finish," Kathryn interrupted, her voice now steady. "I don't want to hurt you, and I don't want to lose you, but I would rather let you go right now than let you break my heart."

Jenny frowned in confusion.

"I could do that," Kathryn went on. "Let you go." She pinned her with a serious stare before looking away in shame. "I know that's selfish."

"I don't understand."

Kathryn knew it was hard, but Jenny had to see it would be for the best. "I've been sitting here all day, missing you, longing for you, loving you ... remembering you, because I was sure I wouldn't see you again, and you know what I discovered?"

"That you can't live without me?" Jenny said with a grin, obviously trying to use humor to derail the uneasy feeling in her gut.

"I found I could do that," Kathryn continued. "Live with the love you've given me, even if I couldn't have you."

The crease in Jenny's brow deepened.

"If you come back to me, Jenny, I'm lost. I will fall into you and drown forever, and I want to. God help me, I love you. I need you. If I surrender to that and you leave me again—" She looked away, trying to hide how unbearable the thought was. "I don't think I can go through that." She paused for a moment as her voice broke and stared at the constantly churning sea, a parallel to her emotions. "The longer I live with you, the more I don't want to be without you."

Jenny squeezed her arm. "You don't have to be without me. That's why I'm here—to set things right."

"It's not that simple."

"Why?"

Kathryn was silent before reluctantly admitting her weakness. "I'm afraid."

"It's not like you to be afraid."

"Then you don't know anything about me," Kathryn said, as she felt herself wanting to give in. "But you proved that when you turned your back on me."

Jenny was stunned for a moment, but then was encouraged by the outburst. "Okay, let's have it."

Kathryn turned in fury, using the hurt and anger she'd channeled for the past month as her last defense against surrendering her heart.

"How could you not know that I loved you? I understand the shock of finding out about your family and my assignment, but after I poured my heart out to you in that letter, how could you walk away from us as if what we had meant nothing? That my feelings mean nothing? Why am I afraid? Because I don't trust you with my heart."

Jenny had nothing to say, which Kathryn had expected. How could anyone say they would never hurt the other? They couldn't, and Kathryn wasn't prepared to open herself to the possibility. She just couldn't.

"Thank you for worrying about me and coming all this way to find me, but I can't give you what you want."

Kathryn stood up before one more declaration of love from Jenny changed her mind.

"Put out that fire," she threw over her shoulder as she walked away. "It's against blackout regulations."

Jenny let her go and eyed her path to the cottage until the fire's light no longer illuminated Kathryn's tall figure. The soft glow of a candle soon filtered through the cottage windows before the dark shades were drawn, and Jenny gave Kathryn some time alone before attempting to save her from herself.

She turned back to the flames and shook her head. They were on the bayside of the island, hidden from the open sea, so the fire had nothing to do with German U-boats using the light as an illuminated backdrop for their torpedo attacks. Jenny put it out anyway, determined not to let it represent the dousing of their relationship, as Kathryn had.

She knew Kathryn loved her, but she had no idea of the depth of her devotion. She took a long, hard look at her own feelings, and she knew what she had to do.

As she traversed the deck outside the cottage, she heard a wooden chair scoot across the floor inside. When she entered, Kathryn was putting away groceries from a bag set on the chair. Kathryn made a cursory acknowledgment of her presence as she finished what she was doing and then went to the kitchen sink, where she immediately started rattling off instructions.

"I think you should stay on the mainland tonight," she began, reaching for the lantern in the kitchen window. "There's an inn up the main road a mile or so ... you probably saw it on the way in. The boatman will drive you there. Nice place, you can—"

Jenny quickly moved in and stilled the hand about to light the match that would signal the boatman. Kathryn immediately tensed as Jenny pulled her away from the sink and took her other hand.

Kathryn tried to back away. "Please don't do this, Jenny."

Jenny held fast to her hands but left the distance between them. "I never read your letter."

Kathryn looked up in surprise.

"I burned it. I never read it."

Kathryn froze for a moment, but then relaxed and exhaled a chuckle. "How fitting."

Jenny moved closer. "I had no idea, Kat."

Kathryn freed her hands and slipped by, heading for the box of supplies. "That's not your fault. It's mine. You shouldn't have needed a letter. I just don't know how to have a relationship."

"That's not what I meant."

"I have my silly songs and awkward attempts at romance, but obviously there's more to—"

"Stop." Jenny moved between Kathryn and the table and took her hands again. She waited until her agitation subsided.

"I knew you loved me. I tried to deny it because ... well, because I'm an idiot and I couldn't believe someone as incredible as you—"

Kathryn shook her head in protest and tried to pull away, but Jenny pulled her back and forced her to listen.

"Someone as incredible as you could possibly have fallen for me."

Kathryn wanted to give in to everything Jenny's love promised, but that would mean falling, and falling hard. The war loomed over them like the sword of Damocles, and she could feel their eventual breakup like a cleaver to her chest. She'd worked so hard to let Jenny go, but seeing her again erased any progress she'd made. She closed her eyes and tried to shut out their doomed future—and their broken hearts.

Jenny squeezed her hands. "Look at me."

Kathryn couldn't help but obey.

"You're beautiful, and smart, and there is nothing silly or awkward about you or your love. No one has ever loved me the way you do. No one. Forrester is dead now, and the rest we will deal with, just like we always have."

"Forrester was never our problem."

"No, I walked away from us. That was our problem. Well, that's not going to happen again. If you need a commitment from me, then I'm yours, and I promise you, I will never doubt your love again."

It would be so easy, Kathryn thought. One step, and into the abyss. She closed her eyes again, struggling against her fear. She couldn't shake the feeling it would be a mistake.

"Please, Kat," Jenny whispered, as she held tightly to her suddenly trembling hands. "Give us a chance." She brought her hands to her lips in prayer and kissed them. "Please. I won't let you down."

Kathryn opened her tear-filled eyes and cupped Jenny's face. It was all right there at her fingertips. In the short time since she'd left the beach, she'd already felt the pangs of regret eating away at her for turning her back on the opportunity to try again. Jenny was under her skin, a part of her soul. Living without her was a half-life at best. She looked into the face of love and couldn't fight it any longer. She let her protective skin drift into the void of the unknown future and let the strength of Jenny's faith in them ground her. She wanted to say *please don't hurt me*, but in the end, she could only ask, "Are you sure?"

"Yes."

She pulled Jenny in and held her tightly, like she was a buoy in the churning inlet outside. "Please be sure," she pleaded softly into cascading blonde hair, not caring whether she was heard.

"I'm sure, honey," Jenny whispered. "I promise."

Stepping back after Kathryn released her, Jenny was met with worried eyes that brimmed with tears. She took her hands again. "I love you. I know you're afraid of what's to come. I am too, but not of this. Not of us."

Kathryn bowed her head. "I didn't used to be afraid of anything. Then I met you and, suddenly, I was afraid of everything. Of hurting you, of losing you, of leaving you." She exhaled ruefully.

Jenny was unsure of what Kathryn was saying. "When you put it that way, it sounds like I ruined your life."

Kathryn kissed her hand. "No. You've made my life worth living. You've brought me joy and hope. Things I thought I'd never feel again. But while those feelings are wonderful, they come with a price."

Her words made Jenny wary, but Kathryn reached out and caressed her face, reassuring her.

"I love you so much, it frightens me. I'm ... out of control. My thoughts, my emotions, my body ... God, when you're near me, I long to touch you, to feel you touching me, loving me. Being apart from you was like cutting out the best part of myself and leaving it behind. I don't ever want to do that again. I don't think I can."

The depth of Kathryn's love brought her to the verge of tears, and Jenny moved closer. "Oh, Kat."

Kathryn kissed her. It wasn't passionate. It was gentle, and kind ... a woman coming home. Jenny welcomed her gladly, and soon the room was filled with their soft moans as the kiss deepened.

Breathless, Kathryn pulled back and pressed her forehead to Jenny's, as if she were having second thoughts. Before Jenny could say a word, Kathryn led her by the hand to the bed, where she slowly shed her clothes and stood naked before her.

Symbolism noted, Jenny removed her own clothes while Kathryn watched intently, as if she'd never seen her naked before.

No words were spoken. They didn't need them. Jenny sat on the bed and held out her hand. Kathryn settled beside her and lightly traced her skin with her fingertips, starting at her collar bone, and down to her breasts, until she cradled one in her hand and took it into her mouth. Jenny felt her body surrender to a familiar longing, and Kathryn pulled them onto the mattress, where they lay side-by-side, staring at each other.

Behind the dark desire in Kathryn's eyes, Jenny discovered a vulnerability she'd never seen before. The caresses and kisses stopped, as if Kathryn had forgotten how to make love to her. She was on the verge of tears again. There was love in her eyes, but not trust. Not yet.

Jenny slid closer, slipping her thigh between Kathryn's legs, until there was no space between them and they were wrapped in each other's arms. "Do you want to talk about it?" She asked quietly, although she wasn't sure anything she could say would restore Kathryn's faith in her.

"No," came Kathryn's whispered reply, as she tangled her fingers in her hair. "I'm yours now." An apologetic smile followed, as if to say *poor you*, and Jenny was ready to prove she never wanted her more.

"You've always been mine. I'm going to make you see that."

She gently eased Kathryn onto her back with a hand to her chest and looked deeply into her eyes as she traced a delicate path around her breasts and teased hardening nipples to gasps of approval. She leaned in and kissed her slowly, until Kathryn's body writhed beneath her. She slid her hand to Kathryn's lower abdomen and stopped. Insistent moans filled the air through their kiss, and she knew Kathryn longed for her touch, but she waited instead of slipping her hand between her legs. Kathryn opened her thighs in anticipation, and Jenny knew she'd find her hot, wet, and ready for her. The heady scent of her arousal made her wet too. She broke their kiss and caught her breath. "I'm going to show you that you're mine."

Kathryn invited her in with breathy desperation. "Yes. Show me. Fucking *own* me."

Jenny had only heard Kathryn use her favorite curse word once before, and to hear it now, in this context, caused a rush of hot adrenaline to all her sensitive parts. She wanted to take Kathryn, rough and hard. Mark her body with reminders of her love, and, yes, her ownership.

She stared into Kathryn's eyes, her own breathing betraying the spike in her desire and determination. Raw energy crackled between them, fueled by lust, promise, and something Jenny couldn't place. Something heavy and serious. Kathryn arched into her hand, begging her to take her.

"Please. I need you to touch me."

Jenny didn't move.

"Please, Jenny."

This wasn't the usual playful, but desperate, pleading of old. This was lifesaving, life affirming pleading from someone teetering on the edge of a cataclysmic shift. She no longer wanted to take her roughly. This moment was everything, and she would make sure her love was seared into Kathryn's soul forever.

Kathryn threw her head back into the pillow and stifled a groan as she ground against the hand on her abdomen. "God, Jenny ... please, please, please." *Save me*, she wanted to scream. Now was not the time for teasing. She needed Jenny to possess her. It had nothing to do with sex. She didn't know how to verbally explain what she needed or how important this was. All she could do was beg and hope Jenny would understand her.

Jenny kissed her softly, not roughly like she expected, and when she finally slid her fingers through her wetness, she gasped into Jenny's open mouth. "Yes. God, yes."

Instead of plunging inside, Jenny lightly circled her entrance. "You're mine."

"Yes. Please. Take me."

Kathryn raised her knees, opening herself fully, and Jenny pressed into her with a two-fingered thrust that was slow and deep. Kathryn's voiceless exhale turned into a low, pleasurable growl by the time she readied herself for the next thrust. But it didn't come. Jenny didn't move.

"You're mine."

It was a demand, and Kathryn had never heard such a possessive tone from Jenny before. She looked into her eyes.

"Yes."

Jenny slowly slipped deeper, her knuckles pressing against her swollen center.

She gasped and grabbed Jenny's shoulder, panting through the mind-numbing sensation.

"Mine."

She swore there was malevolence in Jenny's eyes—a hunter, and she was the very willing prey. "Yes!"

She waited for her to move, to release her from the sudden bloom of ecstasy, but Jenny held fast, as a steady wave of pleasure kept swelling. She panted out unintelligible cries as she tightened her grip on Jenny's shoulder and fisted her other hand in the sheets. The surge of pressure built until she thought she might explode.

"Mine."

"Yes, yes! A thousand times, yes! Fuck!"

Jenny eased back, and before Kathryn could even take a breath, she entered her again, pressing deeply and staying there while she moaned her approval. When Jenny curled her fingers up against that hallowed spot that drove her wild, her drawn out cry turned into a panting whine as her body arched in rigid pleasure.

Jenny was relentless and bore down. "Mine."

"God!" The sustained pressure was driving her mad. She needed relief, release, anything! "Fuck me. I need you to fuck me!"

The pressure remained.

"Please. Jenny. I need—"

"You're mine."

"Y-yes! Fuck—"

Jenny fucked her slowly at first and then increased her pace. She didn't know whether Jenny's voice was in her head or in her ears when she heard *mine ... mine ... mine ...* with every rhythmic thrust, but she didn't want her to stop.

"Yes ... yes ... yes ..." She was reaching her peak, about to tumble over, when she began breaking apart. Her insistent *yes* turned into a desperate "I need you, I need you, I need you." She couldn't stop saying it, breathing it, living it, and then she was coming, and crying, and Jenny's arms were around her, comforting her. But she couldn't stop saying it. And then she was clinging and sobbing. "I need you, I need you."

"You have me. Shh ... you have me. I've got you."

She held on as the waves of her orgasm and her emotional breakdown rolled over her. She was surrounded by love and at home in the safest place in the world—Jenny's arms.

. . .

The frantic beating of Kathryn's heart under her ear had slowed to a calmer rhythm as Jenny rested her head on her chest. Kathryn's arms were around her, and she lazily combed her fingers through her hair as their breathing returned to normal.

Jenny took her hand and kissed it. "That was intense. Are you okay?"

"More than okay. I've never experienced anything like that. It was ... fuck," Kathryn said on an exhale.

Jenny huffed out a laugh. "I love hearing that word coming out of your gorgeous mouth."

"Sometimes, no other word will do."

Jenny rolled onto her side and draped a thigh over Kathryn's midriff. "I'm so proud of you right now. I'll have you swearing up a storm in no time."

Kathryn laughed and kissed her on the forehead. "Seems I am yours after all."

Jenny smiled but then became serious. "Are you?"

The answer came without hesitation. "For the first time in a long time, I'm free. Free to give myself to you, and only you. So, yes. I'm yours."

Jenny kissed her hand again. "You're going to make me cry, because I love the sentiment, but I'm not sure you can promise me that. We've still got a war to win."

Kathryn propped herself up on her elbow. "I'm not doing that anymore for them. I don't have to surrender my body to get what I want. It's lazy, and it's self-destructive. I'm not doing it again."

Jenny frowned. "Because of me? Because of us?"

"Because I'm better than that."

A slow grin formed on Jenny's lips. "God, I love you. I *have* ruined you, and I'm not sorry."

Kathryn gathered her in her arms and pulled her on top of her. "I love you too. You've saved me in every way."

CHAPTER FIFTEEN

Kathryn pulled the sheet up over her bare shoulder and rolled over with a satisfied grin. She had the most wonderful dream. She slowly opened her eyes to find a seashell placed regally on the pillow beside her. She smiled. It wasn't a dream.

She reached for the small mound-shaped slipper shell and turned it over in her fingers. She pressed it to the heel of her palm, where the empty flat shell attached itself. She got Jenny's message and grinned.

She squinted at her watch on the nightstand and sat up in disbelief. She'd slept most of the morning away. She donned her white blouse and padded to the cast iron wood stove, where she moved the coffee pot over the heat.

It was a misty, overcast morning, and from the kitchen window, she could see Jenny on the beach below, leaning against a large log as she nursed her cup of coffee. She watched her for a few quiet moments, reveling in their beautiful night together and getting used to the idea that they really were together again.

She stepped into a pair of linen pants, and, coffee in hand, joined Jenny to listen to the choir of waves and foghorns blaring in the distance.

"Why didn't you wake me?" she asked, leaning down for a kiss.

"You looked like you could use the sleep."

"Mm." She settled in beside her. "It was glorious. When did you get up?"

"Early. I couldn't sleep. I walked around the island."

"That's three miles."

"It was nice." She stared at the incoming surf, magically appearing out of the fog. "Gave me a chance to think—clear my head."

Kathryn gave her a sideways glance at her tone. She couldn't possibly have changed her mind about them. Not after last night. She nervously shifted her gaze away and took a sip of coffee to prepare for the inevitable letdown. Her heart was beating double-time, and she swallowed, audibly searching for something to fill the ominous silence before Jenny dropped the bad news she knew was coming.

"You know, there used to be a Coast Guard life station on the other side of the island," she began, "but a terrible Nor'easter blew through here in '31 and took most of the north end with it. They relocated it nearer to the lighthouse." She pointed across the inlet, into the fog, where it would be. "The deck on the cottage is made from the salvaged timbers. In fact, that's actually the third incarnation of the cottage. Mother Nature tends to be hard on these barrier islands. The shorelines are constantly shifting. This used to be the tip of a peninsula until 1840. Dominic says—"

Jenny turned and blinked at her in confusion, and Kathryn knew her random babbling had revealed her insecurity.

Jenny took her hand, silencing her. "Kat, I'm not having second thoughts. Didn't you get my message?"

Kathryn took a breath and relaxed with a smile before retrieving the small shell from her pocket. "I did."

Jenny smiled. "I'm going to be stuck to you like that little mollusk to the bottom of a ship."

The creature usually lived on the bottom of scallops and horse-shoe crabs, but the point was well taken.

"Sorry," Kathryn said with a shrug. "I guess I still can't believe you're here."

Jenny put her hand on Kathryn's cheek and gently guided her mouth to hers, unleashing a slow, sensual kiss to remind her of their night together. She pulled back only to speak.

"Does that help?"

"Mm," Kathryn moaned, as she indulged in another kiss and made sure Jenny knew she would not doubt her again.

The call of a persistent gull roused Jenny from her brief, contented slumber. She opened her eyes to find herself surrounded by Kathryn, who was pressed beside her, propped up on one elbow, with her other arm resting across her hip. Kathryn gazed down at her, her eyes still half-lidded from the bliss of their morning lovemaking, and Jenny smiled. She had never made love on a beach before, and the pervasive fog helped make it an ethereal experience. What a way to start the day.

She reached up and touched Kathryn's face to make sure she wasn't an apparition conjured up out of the thick mist. Kathryn turned her head and kissed her palm and then her wrist.

Kathryn had never looked at her this way before. Gone was the maelstrom of emotions dominated by the fear she always saw lurking behind her longing and lust. She looked ... content. In love. Unafraid. And as she said, free.

It was what she always wanted for her, and she'd give anything to have her look at her that way forever. "I love you."

"I love you too. More than I could ever say."

Jenny smiled and tilted her head. "Well, that's sad. Maybe you should start now and we just might—"

A ship's horn blared in the distance, pulling Kathryn's attention to the wall of fog enfolding the inlet. Her peaceful countenance vanished, replaced by a pensive look that she tried to hide when she leaned in for a languid kiss.

Their kiss deepened, and Jenny felt the pressure building in her core as her body caught fire. She opened her eyes to witness Kathryn's surrender and found herself staring into the familiar face of masked concern.

"What is it?"

Kathryn offered a dismissive half smile and a shrug. "It's nothing."

Jenny tugged on her hand. "Hey, if it's about us, tell me."

There would be enough they couldn't tell each other once they returned to the city and got back to work. She was going to make sure personal feelings weren't one of them. As if Kathryn could read her mind, she nodded and guided a lock of blonde hair from her face.

"I wish I could have kept you out of all this."

"Well, you couldn't."

Kathryn nodded, but Jenny could tell it didn't make her feel any better.

"They were my family, Kat. I was in it up to my eyeballs, whether I knew it or not. Even if I'm late to the game, I'd rather be in it than not … no matter what I find."

"So, how are you handling that?"

Jenny thought for a moment. "I don't think I am, really. I've been so busy … so angry. I—"

She shook her head. Without Kathryn in her life, she'd had no one to talk to about what had happened. No one to understand what she'd lost, how much it hurt. She buried herself in work and ran from the pain. It was easy to see why Kathryn made it her coping mechanism of choice. Jenny looked up into well-traveled, sympathetic blue eyes and squeezed her hand.

"I've missed you. I'm sorry I hurt you."

Kathryn brought her hand to her lips and kissed it. "We were in a tough spot, Jenny—both of us." She kissed her hand again, absolving them both. "That's all in the past. Let's focus on the future from now on."

"You'll get no complaints from me," Jenny said, as she slid her hand behind Kathryn's neck and welcomed the new mandate with a kiss that set them both on fire.

The women had a leisurely morning on the beach, using the rare break in their busy lives to get reacquainted and solidify their renewed relationship. They watched the distant shore appear with growing regret as the sun broke through the clouds and burned off the foggy veil protecting them from the rest of the world.

The time had come for Kathryn to go ashore and check in and for Jenny to begin the first leg in her trek back to the city.

Brass instructed Kathryn to stay put for a few days, until Forrester's funeral, but Jenny, reluctantly, had to leave. She'd left too much undone at home because of her frantic search for information after the plane crash, and she had to get it all done before Monday morning.

As they crossed the boardwalk beneath the red and white light-house, they passed tourists and soldiers on leave enjoying the beautiful afternoon and dodged small children gathering clamshells dropped from above by seagulls seeking access to lunch.

They walked to the end of the pier, where they stood shoulder to shoulder, and leaned on the weather-beaten wooden railing overlooking the sparkling sea. Just being on the populated side of the inlet changed their demeanor. Their responsibilities were now tugging on them like the pulley weights used to turn the great lens in the towering lighthouse behind them.

Kathryn had seen a well-dressed man with a white carnation in his lapel, and it reminded her of Forrester and then of the elegant Bouchaule. Both were dead now. She gave no thought to the loss of the brutal Marcus Forrester, but she felt a strange pang of sadness for the loss of the Frenchman. She didn't know enough about his work or his personal life to say whether he was a good man, but, superficially, she found herself moved by the loss of his beauty and grace. With both assignments terminated at once, she gazed down at the heaving tide and wondered what was next for her at the OSS.

. . .

Jenny gazed up at a large silver blimp sporting U.S. NAVY on its side as it lazily drifted along, escorting two smaller airships out to sea on antisubmarine patrol. Seeing a photographer behind the Plexiglas skin of the blimp's gondola reminded her that Bernie was overseas somewhere. She couldn't help thinking he was over there because of Cal Richards, and Cal Richards was in his life because of her.

So much of her life had changed in one month, as had so many of the lives around her—or maybe it was only her perception of the lives around her that had changed. Her feelings toward her family weighed heavily on her, but Kathryn had helped her see that no matter what they'd done, and no matter what her lineage, they were her family, and they did love her. Blood does not make a family, Kathryn had reiterated, and Jenny knew it to be true—another denial falling away as she accepted the pain of her family's subversive past.

Her uncle came to mind as she wondered what the fallout would be from the disappearing contents of the storage unit. She seemed at a dead end. She couldn't confront Holmes or her uncle, and that left only Kathryn as her best hope to find out the truth, but mining her for information about her family was off limits. She closed her eyes, pretending to absorb the warmth of the sun on her face, until she felt Kathryn's hand seek hers in concern.

"What are you thinking?" she asked.

Jenny turned to her and smiled. Her answer would be her first lie of omission in their renewed relationship, and it settled uncomfortably around her shoulders as she offered a glance at the blimp above. "The photographer reminded me of Bernie."

Kathryn looked up at the airship and squeezed her hand. Jenny sensed she was not fooled or offended by the lie. "And how is Bernie?"

"He's ... serving his country, which ... is what he wanted." She wanted to say *which is my fault*, but she reigned in her guilt about his decision. He lied on his signup form about being colorblind and memorized the test so he would pass. It almost made her laugh when he told her, because it sounded like something *she* would do. He was in, and just like that, Cal's death kept reverberating through their lives. She wondered if they'd ever learn the truth about who the man really was and why he had ingratiated himself into their lives.

She could feel Kathryn's concerned stare on her cheek and returned to the question.

"He's fine. I got a letter from him last week. He's in the Signal Corps, where he'll be photographing the action, which terrifies me." She shook her head, trying not to dwell on it. "How about you? What are you thinking?"

Kathryn couldn't tell Jenny the details of her assignments, but, as her lover, keeping the intimacies of them a secret seemed unfair, at the very least, and a slight she was afraid would come back to haunt her. The men were dead and her affairs over, but she wasn't going to have a repeat of secrets exposed without warning, so she would offer Jenny what she could—all cards on the table.

"What is it, Kat?"

Kathryn pondered for a moment while deciding on her tact.

"There will be times when we won't be able to share what we're thinking and feeling." She turned and looked Jenny in the eyes. "I think we both understand that and know it has nothing to do with how much we love each other or trust each other."

Jenny looked down, and Kathryn sensed she was embarrassed by her failed attempt at deception. Kathryn squeezed her hand to let her know it was okay.

She squinted at the horizon and focused on a lone ship silhouetted against the white backdrop of the edge of the earth. She admired the vessel's bravery, sailing without a convoy escort in the dangerous Atlantic. She was tempted to liken her confession to such a foolhardy endeavor, but after making such an eloquent statement about love and trust, she knew that she, like that ship, had no other choice, and the risk was as inconsequential as the thought of failure.

"I couldn't tell you about my assignment to you."

"I know, honey, we've been over this."

"There are things I can't tell you about what came after," she quickly continued while her nerve still held.

Thankfully, Jenny kept silent.

"I did things while we were apart." She looked down and shifted her weight to one leg as she lifted her foot to the lowest rung of the railing. "At the time, I convinced myself it was a necessity, but if I were honest with myself, I'd have to say I did it out of hurt and anger." She fidgeted, not sure whether the admission was hurting or helping her cause. "Either way, it's just an excuse."

She could tell by Jenny's silence and vacant stare out to sea that she had a pretty good idea of what she was talking about.

"I don't expect you to say anything. I don't know that there's anything *to* say, but I felt it fair you should know."

Jenny nodded slightly and continued her silent stare.

Kathryn turned her attention to the horizon once more and felt a flash of panic as her courageous ship had disappeared from view. Her eyes darted along the junction of earth and sky, refusing to believe the risk had been too great to overcome. She finally spotted the vessel, far south of its original position, and she breathed an inaudible sigh of relief. Now, if only Jenny could find it in her heart to bravely push on.

Jenny let the confession sink in. Kathryn didn't have to tell her anything. They weren't a couple at the time—she owed her nothing —yet here she was, trying to be as open as possible, and Jenny only loved her more for it.

"These things you did ..." Jenny began hesitantly, preparing herself for the answer. "Have you set a precedent that has to continue once you return home?"

"No. My past actions are of no consequence to us any longer."

Whatever it was must have involved Forrester, Jenny surmised, which conjured up nothing but sympathy for Kathryn. She turned and smiled, trying not to look too relieved it was over. She would have handled whatever was thrown her way, but she was glad she didn't have to, for her sake and for Kathryn's.

"Then let's not worry about it," she said confidently. "We're looking forward from now on, right?"

Kathryn smiled and squeezed her hand. "Right. Thank you."

"I once told you to do what you had to do, and you promised me you would. Nothing's changed."

Nothing had changed and everything had changed, but Kathryn nodded, and Jenny was glad that was out of the way.

The time had come for them to part, and neither was prepared to let the other go, even if it was only for a few days. They both stared at the pitching sea below, as their awkward silence was filled by the waves crashing over the jetties and the ever-present cry of the gulls.

"It's going to be okay, Kat," Jenny finally said, wondering if Kathryn was making a mental checklist of the hurdles like she was. "We're going to make this work."

"I know."

They had to make it work.

Kathryn pressed her shoulder closer to Jenny's and took a more intimate grasp on her hand.

"You should go. You've got a long trip home and a lot to do before morning."

Jenny closed her eyes and enjoyed the soft hand in hers. She bathed in the memory of it on her body, of it finding her most intimate places and lingering there, its only ambition her pleasure. She held on tight and longed for one last passionate kiss before they parted.

"Where's a ladies' room when you need it?" Kathryn joked, seeing the telltale flush of Jenny's neck.

Jenny smiled and looked around, on the off chance there happened to be one. There wasn't, of course, and they would have to settle for a public goodbye.

"This morning was beautiful," Jenny whispered. "And last night ... God ..." She put her hand on her warm chest.

She had to get out of there before she changed her mind about leaving, which she couldn't afford to do. She gave the hand in hers one final squeeze before pushing away from the railing. She gave Kathryn a restrained hug and whispered, "I miss you already."

"I'll see you soon," Kathryn said with a brave grin as they broke apart.

Jenny filled her heart with Kathryn's beautiful sun-drenched image as she backed away slowly and then finally turned to leave.

Kathryn looked away immediately and returned to the rail, where she watched the sun glisten off the surface of the ever-changing sea. Jenny had come back to her. They would be together now. No demons scoffed at her optimism. No ghosts of the past threatened to undermine her future.

She closed her eyes as she inhaled the warm, salty air and then exhaled slowly, whispering, "Thank you," to the gentle wind that would carry her appreciation to whatever force in the universe had extended such grace.

CHAPTER SIXTEEN

Kathryn slipped a handkerchief under the black netting of her veil and wiped a crocodile tear from her cheek as the priest said his final amen. Smitty was at her side, supporting her elbow, and she was the picture of grief as she stood among the grandiose tombstones of the nineteenth century rural cemetery and blended in with the swarms of mourners and curious onlookers. It was an overcast day, gray and dramatic, like her performance.

They'd traveled three hours from Manhattan to attend services in Forrester's upstate hometown. The important and the wealthy filled the English country Gothic-style stone church, and sufficiently sated with tales of Marcus Forrester's good deeds and God's blessing, they walked the few hundred yards across the manicured lawn to his final resting place, between an old Civil War general and the city's ancient founder.

Kathryn lingered respectfully off to the side, while Forrester's widow sat front and center before the industrialist's calla lily-draped black coffin.

Alice Forrester was without emotion as she stared at the spray of dozens of white lilies before her. The priest closed his book and stepped forward to offer his condolences as the crowd dispersed. The robed clergyman patted her hand as he tendered his words of comfort, and she nodded and lowered her eyes, looking like she wanted it all to be over.

A line of well-wishers passed between the widow and the coffin, but Kathryn didn't move from her spot. She loved the spiritual solitude of cemeteries, but she hadn't attended a funeral in one since her mother's, thirteen years ago. It was a day much like this one, with the sun showing its respect by refusing to shine.

She became lost in the memory of the lanky girl of fourteen, standing motionless as her father, overcome with grief, threw himself across his beloved wife's casket and sobbed uncontrollably. Her brother, Clayton, dropped her hand and helped friends physically drag their distraught father from the service to their waiting car.

She was left alone by her mother's side, too numb to comfort her father, and too dazed to comprehend that a pretty box adorned with flowers would be the last she would see of her mother. She plucked a red rose from the spray on the lid, her mother's favorite, and slowly stepped back as six burly groundskeepers, three on each side, picked up the thick straps at their feet and, hand under hand, lowered the casket slowly into the ground. She instinctively reached out as the coffin descended, but she was hesitant to touch the cold, hard surface, afraid to forever associate it with the body inside. The coffin reached its final resting place, and the gravedigger passed her a handful of dirt.

"Go on, honey," he said with a compassionate smile. He looked at the flower in one hand and the handful of dirt in the other and motioned toward the hole in the ground. "Pay your last respects to your momma."

Kathryn looked at him like he was crazy. She pulled the flower protectively to her chest. It was hers to treasure always. She'd be damned if she was going to help bury her mother. She put the dirt in the pocket of her best Sunday coat and walked silently to the family car. The dirt had since disappeared, spread lovingly into her mother's prized rose garden in the backyard, but the flower she still had on her bookshelf at home, pressed into her mother's large volume of Shakespeare's plays.

Smitty kept a close eye on her as he watched real tears paint her cheeks. She clutched the white handkerchief in her black-gloved hand and pressed it against her quivering lower lip. He knew she didn't weep for Forrester, but the tears obviously afforded her some kind of cleansing, so he let her go on, her eyes staring blindly ahead, her head at an aimless tilt.

Duty soon called, however, and Smitty tightened his grasp on her elbow to bring her out of it. Kathryn blinked herself back to the present to find Alice Forrester standing before her with a white calla lily held reverently in her hand.

"Miss Hammond."

Kathryn was stunned for a moment, positive that Emily Post had never set a precedent for such an awkward confrontation, and merely stammered, "Mrs. Forrester. I'm … I'm very sorry for your loss."

The small, middle-aged woman smiled in appreciation of the sentiment, but said, "Marc and I had separate lives for many years. It is I who am sorry for your loss. He spoke fondly of you."

Kathryn hardly knew what to say. It certainly wasn't the confrontation she would have expected. In fact, it was no confrontation at all.

"Thank you. He spoke fondly of you as well."

The widow left no time for an uncomfortable silence. She touched Kathryn's gloved hand and handed her the lily with a bittersweet smile. She acknowledged Smitty with a nod and quickly turned and walked away, taking the arm of a somber-looking distinguished gentleman they knew to be her companion.

Kathryn and Smitty stood silent for a moment and then looked at each other in curious bewilderment.

Kathryn turned to the flower in her hand, and Smitty raised his brow and shook his head.

"Are you all right?" he asked.

Kathryn took one last look at Forrester's casket and put her memories away. "Yeah," she replied as she wiped her cheek. "Let's get out of here."

As they walked toward the car, parked on the gravel access road, a young clergyman approached from behind, calling Smitty's name.

"Mr. Smith?"

He turned. "Yes?"

"There's an urgent phone call for you, sir." He pointed over his shoulder at the back of the church on the hill. "You can take the call in the rectory. First door on your left as you pass through the loggia."

Smitty thanked him and scanned the surroundings suspiciously.

"Go on," Kathryn said. "I'll be all right from here to the car."

Smitty weighed the danger, no less paranoid for Forrester's passing, and before he could render his decision, the priest had offered his arm to Kathryn for support.

"I'll escort the lady to her car, sir."

Kathryn smiled and sent Smitty on his way with a cock of her head.

"I'll have the driver meet you in front of the church."

Smitty threw a wave over his shoulder as he launched into a wounded jog up the knoll to the old stone building.

Kathryn folded herself into the back of the large black sedan as her young escort went on his way. She instructed the driver to follow the lake road to the front of the church.

Mourners were slowly filtering to their cars, but her driver didn't move. He focused on one man in particular, walking a few yards ahead on the opposite side of the road.

"Is there a problem?" Kathryn asked, eager to get out of there.

The driver waited until the short man he was watching got into his car. He then turned and passed a small blank envelope over his shoulder.

Kathryn eyed him warily and opened it. Inside was a handwritten note in a familiar hand—Thierry Bouchaule's.

My dearest Kathryn,

As always, you look stunning in black.

Kathryn looked up to where the driver's curious mourner was pulling away in his large black car.

"Did he give you this?"

The driver nodded.

"Follow him."

"I'm sorry, ma'am—"

"Follow him!" she commanded.

"I can't!"

The driver lifted his hands and pointed to the empty ignition switch, from which his keys had been taken at gunpoint.

With an exasperated exhale, Kathryn exploded out of the car, with the note still clutched in her hand, and pulled the black netting of her hat away from her face to get a good view of the license plate, at least. The car drove away and made a U-turn onto the tree-lined road parallel to theirs. The sedan was heading in her direction, but all Kathryn could do was stare across the roof of her car, as time stretched into measured moments of clarity and she saw Bouchaule's face in the backseat, above the blur of headstones, as he passed. She reached out to him in vain and mouthed his name, and he responded with a regretful hand pressed to the window glass, like the closing scene of some tragic love story.

Bouchaule's car disappeared into the distance, and Kathryn's eyes narrowed as she quickly scanned the churchyard for Smitty. He was nowhere in sight, just as Bouchaule had planned. She looked around for another car to commandeer, but they were alone on the side of the hill. She slammed her fist onto the roof in frustration.

"Damn it!"

She looked at the rumpled note in her hand and read the remainder of the message. She shifted her focus to the empty road at the top of the hill and leaned on the roof with her elbow as she covered her eyes with her hand.

"Damn it," she said again—for so many reasons.

CHAPTER SEVENTEEN

I pray the tears you shed are for me and now know they need not fall at all. You gave me your trust, now I give you mine. We are bound by our secrets.

Were it another place and time, I would have you by my side. My work takes me far from you now, and that is my only regret. You are free. Live well, my darling. I will never forget you.

Thierry

Kathryn sat in Colonel Holmes's office and watched him place the note she'd received at Forrester's funeral on his desk before sitting back in his chair. The SOE colonel glared at her, obviously annoyed at her indifference.

"You didn't get a license plate." It was an accusation.

"No, sir."

He turned to Smitty. "And you were fooled by a man pretending to be a priest."

Smitty shifted in his chair and swallowed his embarrassment in silence.

Holmes stared at him expectantly, but then pushed his irritation aside. He opened a classified blue folder and addressed Kathryn again.

"When he comes 'round again, see that you—"

"He's done with me, Colonel."

He looked at her, still in her mourning attire, and eyed her up and down, as if he agreed with Bouchaule that she looked stunning in black. He raised his brow and promptly disagreed with her.

"He's not going to leave without you."

"He already has."

"How do you know that?"

Kathryn exhaled a disbelieving chuckle. "Read the note, Colonel. He's gone. This man is obsessed with his work. He killed seven people to get out of this country unnoticed. I was an attractive means to an end—nothing more. He can service his libido anywhere, believe me. It's over."

The colonel burst from his chair and slammed his fist on the oak desktop before her. "The devil it's over!" he shouted. "A year of work! We had it in our grasp!"

Kathryn calmly absorbed the officer's frustration, a frustration she secretly shared, but there was nothing to be done about Bouchaule now.

The door to the office suddenly flew open, and Colonel Forsythe rushed in with a handful of wire telegrams.

"Sorry I'm late." He sifted through the communiqués, pulling one out. "The plane went down just outside of Chicago. Eyewitnesses say it was struck by lightning. Bouchaule was ID'd by luggage found in the wreckage—obviously a plant. We've since confirmed that man's identity—one of the Chicago syndicate. The woman was his wife."

"An act of God, Hammond," Holmes said. "Bouchaule will be back, and when he contacts you—"

"You'll be the first to know, Colonel Holmes."

Her sarcasm wasn't lost on anyone but her intended target, as

Holmes merely nodded absentmindedly, as if she actually meant it. The Englishman packed up his briefcase, conferred with Colonel Forsythe on the side for a moment, and thanks to Kathryn's news, left a little worse for wear.

Colonel Forsythe pulled up a chair and exhaled a heavy sigh. Smitty took no time in offering his apology.

"I'm sorry, sir. The guy was dressed as a priest, for crying out loud."

"I know, John. There was nothing you could have done anyway. Thank you for coming in. You may go. New assignments have come down, so Janie has some papers for you on the way out." Smitty nodded and left the room.

Kathryn leaned back in her chair and crossed her legs, relaxing, now that it was just the two of them.

"Holmes is coming a bit undone, sir," she commented dryly, arranging her gloves across her knee.

"We've all worked very hard, Kathryn, for a very long time," Forsythe said sternly.

Kathryn regretted her tone. "I know. I'm sorry things worked out this way."

Forsythe nodded and pulled out Kathryn's file.

"We've closed the Forrester case. We'll leave Bouchaule's open for now, but as far as you're concerned, I feel it's safe to say that you've completed your assignment."

Kathryn nodded.

Forsythe was about to go on when he looked up in admiration. "Thank you, Kathryn. You went above and beyond what was expected. Bouchaule may be a dead end, but we have more information than we could have hoped for, and a lot of it is thanks to you."

Kathryn all but shrugged off the compliment. "We all worked very hard, sir, as you said."

He smiled at her typical answer and moved on, taking out a request form. "You asked for an assignment in the field overseas some time ago ..."

Kathryn froze at the mention of her long forgotten application.

Forsythe's face came into sharp focus as her heartbeat quickened and a myriad of things rushed through her mind. She was being sent overseas. She should have seen it coming. If they were shipping out green recruits, things had to be desperate. It only made sense that she would go.

She knew it was her obligation and duty to go, but she couldn't help the rising panic when she thought of what it meant to her relationship with Jenny. They had just found each other again. Jenny had made a commitment to her. It couldn't be over so soon.

She paused, mid-panic, shocked by her selfish hesitation. She couldn't refuse. Winning the war was more important than her wants and needs, and, as for Jenny, she would be the first to agree. Kathryn swallowed hard and braced herself for the blow. If she was needed over there, they need only ask, and she would comply. As it should be.

"While I feel you've proved yourself more than ready," the colonel went on, "I feel you are more valuable to us here at the training center."

Kathryn blinked in disbelief, reflexively offended.

"Sir, you can't, in good conscience, send partially-trained kids over there and leave someone with experience behind."

"I can, and I will. Your experience is needed here, Kathryn. Someone has to train these recruits."

"You've got a whole center full of instructors, sir."

"They haven't field experience, and that's what we need right now. Those recruits are better off half trained by someone with experience than fully trained by someone who has no earthly idea what it's like out there."

He smiled gently, recognizing the hurt in her protest. "It's a compliment, Kathryn, not a slight."

Conflict played across Kathryn's face and held her mute in the face of his logic. He was right, but it felt so wrong. The young recruits had so much to live for, and she had so much to make up for—her self-flagellation was interrupted by thoughts of Jenny: the best thing that had ever happened to her.

Kathryn exhaled and closed her eyes against the selfish relief of being left at home to continue with her relatively comfortable life.

"I know how you feel, Kathryn," the colonel assured her. "Do you think I want to be stuck here behind a desk pushing papers while my friends are overseas in the thick of it?"

She opened her eyes. He didn't understand. A few months ago that may have been the reason, but now he didn't understand at all, and she was too ashamed of her relief to explain it to him.

"You do more than push papers, sir."

"And you do more than just train new recruits. You're an inspiration to us here, Kathryn. Ask anyone."

Kathryn shifted uncomfortably, trying to escape the undeserved flattery.

"You've been in the den of the devil, and you're still here fighting."

She had no choice but to fight. Without it, her life was merely stolen moments of undeserved breaths. The colonel's accolades were wholly misplaced, and Kathryn suddenly felt the walls closing in. Guilt, and the weight of her accountability, crawled under her skin like restless vipers, until she couldn't stand it. She abruptly got up and paced the room.

"Stop it. There's a trail of death and destruction in my wake that negates anything positive I've ever done or ever will do."

The colonel leaned back in his chair and regarded her skeptically.

"If you really believe that, then what's the point?"

"Sometimes I don't know."

He hid a smile under his bowed head and leaned forward, crossing his arms on his desk.

"I think you do," he replied calmly.

She rubbed her forehead and then threw her hand up at her lame excuse. "I'm sorry, sir. It's been a long day."

"Yes, it has."

Kathryn sat, resigned to her conflicting emotions.

"We take our victories where we can find them, Kathryn. Day by day. That's our motto."

Kathryn agreed, but one day at a time wasn't enough to satisfy her unsated remorse. She had to be sure every option was open. "If you need me over there, don't hesitate to assign me, sir. I mean it."

"I know you do."

Confident she wasn't shirking her duty, she nodded.

The colonel put away his papers and clasped his hands across her folder.

"Enjoy the next few days off, and we'll see you at the center on Monday, Kathryn."

Kathryn joined Smitty in the outer office, and together they walked down the hallway to the elevators.

"Too bad we have to wait so long to leave, eh?" he commented cheerfully.

Kathryn turned. "Leave?"

"Overseas. The training camps." He held up his papers.

Kathryn slowed her pace and eventually stopped, realizing her silence about Jenny had brought about an unexpected consequence. "I don't have an assignment overseas."

Smitty's commitment to the contrary was evident in his deflated posture.

A few more quiet moments went by before Kathryn finally spoke. "I'm sorry if you took that because you thought I was going."

"No, I—" He cut himself off, obviously thinking better of lying to her. "I thought you wanted to get out of here. You know, to forget about ... things."

"Yeah," she drew out, "about that ..." She started walking again, hoping to soften the blow of her reasoning. She hadn't told him about Jenny yet. She was just getting used to the idea herself, and she didn't want to face her partner's misgivings about the possible conflict of interests.

Her admission went over as expected. Smitty didn't understand how she could have spent all day traveling with him and not told him about Jenny, but she pointed to his disgruntled attitude as the prime reason for her reticence.

He apologized, realizing how his desire to protect her had pushed her away, and he acknowledged how hard the loss of her relationship with Jenny had been. By the time they got to the car, he managed to wish her well, albeit reservedly.

"You know I want you to be happy, Kathryn. You deserve it."

She held up her hand before he could utter the obligatory *but*—

Smitty swallowed the word and the warning to follow. Kathryn was glad he could see that her relationship with Jenny had moved far beyond the reach of protestations from him.

The rest of the ride to her apartment was spent in introverted contemplation. They would have two months before they would part —two months to get used to being without each other for the first time since they were children.

Kathryn's mood was solemn as the car turned down her street. Smitty was leaving, her assignment to Forrester had been a failure in her eyes, and Bouchaule had gotten away. She couldn't even tell her superiors what he had gotten away *with*, but, clearly, he had gotten what he came for.

She didn't buy the "act of God" theory about the plane crash. She almost laughed out loud when Forsythe said there were eyewitnesses —eyewitnesses to a lightning strike on an aircraft—what were the odds? Apparently pretty high in a world where payoffs defined the truth.

Kathryn debated whether to tell Jenny about her relationship with Bouchaule. He was alive out there somewhere, and even though she knew the chances of him showing up again were slim to none, her promise that he would be of no consequence to them seemed almost like an untruth. She tried to ignore the feeling. After all, if he did show up, Jenny would just say *You do what you have to do*. What else was there to say?

Kathryn always did what she needed to do, and she'd brooded long enough about her history to know that looking back never changed the past. It only made the future more difficult to embrace.

She certainly didn't need any help making things difficult, and she wasn't going to muck up what she had now by dwelling on Bouchaule.

Her disposition changed immediately when she looked up and saw the living room light on in her apartment. Jenny was there. So many days in the last month she'd wished for such a sight, and faced with it now, she couldn't suppress a grin.

Her expression wasn't lost on Smitty, who brought the car to a halt at the curb and forced a grin of his own. "Say hi to the kid for me."

Kathryn took in the sight of him before getting out of the car. His arm was casually thrown over the back of the seat, his hat pushed back off his forehead, and his expressive brown eyes said more than his words dared.

She loved him too and understood everything he wasn't saying. She leaned in and kissed him on the cheek, lingering before his face as she smoothed the lipstick away with her thumb.

His jaw tensed under her hand, and he couldn't meet her eyes.

Kathryn wasn't sure if he found her actions cruel or simply overwhelming. Either way, it had been a long day for them both, and too much to say resulted in nothing to say. Kathryn offered her regrets in her pursed lips and tendered her love through the hand still cupping his face.

He took her hand and kissed it and then quickly faced forward, putting both hands on the steering wheel in a symbolic effort to control his fragile emotions. "Go on, get out of here."

She squeezed his thick shoulder and ducked out of the car without another word.

Kathryn blew out the tension of her day as she climbed the steps to her apartment. It could only get better now—Jenny was waiting for her. It would be their first time together since their day at the beach.

She reached for the door, only to have it opened for her.

"Hi, baby," Jenny beamed.

A broad grin split Kathryn's lips. "I've missed that."

· · ·

Jenny put a hand behind Kathryn's neck and pulled her into the apartment, where she greeted her with a proper kiss.

"Mm," Kathryn hummed, as she kicked the door closed behind her. "I've missed that too."

Jenny backed down off her tiptoes, smiling as she took the black clutch and gloves from Kathryn's hands.

"Thanks for leaving the key," she called over her shoulder as she crossed the living room.

"You're welcome." Kathryn smiled as she slipped out of her shoes. "Keep it this time. I don't want to find it in my mailbox again."

Jenny stopped and turned. "Sorry."

Kathryn caught up with her and kissed her on the head before moving on to the bedroom. "Don't be."

Jenny followed and leaned on the doorjamb, realizing it was probably the first of many sensitive reminders of their past life that would sporadically rise to the surface.

"How'd it go today?"

"Ugh, exhausting." Kathryn shed her black fitted jacket and stepped out of her matching skirt.

Jenny folded the gloves in her hand and put them and the purse on the nightstand at her hip. She crossed her arms, enjoying the view, as Kathryn's black slip fell to the floor.

"Bath?"

"Mm. Please. I'm dying to get off my feet."

"Coming right up."

Jenny drew a hot bath and took great pleasure in slowly washing every inch of Kathryn's body. She wasn't surprised or disappointed when she found herself pulled playfully into the tub, clothes and all. It seemed like forever since either of them had laughed, and their squeals echoing off the porcelain caused them both to pause and stare at each other, as the water sloshed over the sides of the tub and onto the floor.

They dissolved into a fit of giggles as they accidentally splashed some more water onto the floor and realized they really didn't care.

They eventually wound up in robes on the couch. Kathryn rested her head in Jenny's lap and stretched out her legs, crossing her feet on the far arm of the sofa. They shared a bottle of wine and listened to swing music playing softly on the radio in the background as they relished the simple pleasure of being in each other's company again. Soon, their easy conversation faded into contented silence.

Jenny looked down and saw that Kathryn had fallen asleep. She smiled, glad that she was getting some rest. She looked tired when she came home, and Jenny knew it was more than just physical. She also knew Kathryn wouldn't talk about it, either because she couldn't, or she wouldn't, trying to preserve the illusion of a carefree evening.

Neither was carefree, of course, Jenny least of all. So many changes—personally and professionally—but she had one constant back in her life, and she was grateful for that. She took in Kathryn's face, so relaxed in sleep, and she hoped her mind was free of the troubles of the waking world, if only for these few peaceful moments.

Jenny was not so lucky. Her mind was filled with turmoil. Since discovering the storage unit, her superiors had all but ignored her, virtually cutting her out of the Ryan case loop. Holmes had done away with their weekly update meetings—her part in them, anyway —and had done everything except pat her on the head when he thanked her for her service and sent her on her way. She knew it was irrational. She had done her duty for the good of her country, not personal accolades, but she couldn't help feeling used. She had more right than anyone to know what was going on.

Every day that she went to work at the *Daily Chronicle*, she could see her uncle paying the price for her actions. He was in a constant state of upset, downing antacid tablets and headache powders with alarming frequency.

The triumph of her discovery had turned to guilt when she heard her aunt tell of the decline of their marriage, "due to the stresses of his job," as she put it. She'd had enough of Paul's erratic behavior and was on the verge of divorce.

Jenny closed her eyes, fighting against the remorse she felt. This isn't what she wanted. She just wanted to get to the bottom of her family's secrets and get access to what belonged to her—the box of her mother's personal effects.

Kathryn's breathing became slow and steady as she drifted deeper into her slumber, and Jenny marveled at her ability to keep everything inside.

She would love nothing more than to seek Kathryn's counsel on her troubles, but it was all assignment-related, and she felt she had to bite her tongue to keep from breaking protocol.

She wondered if Kathryn struggled so, or had she gotten so used to the self-imposed silence and the isolation it wrought that she'd forgotten what it was like to be at liberty to share her thoughts and fears?

Jenny reached out to touch Kathryn's face, admiring her strength, but drew back, not wanting to wake her. Jenny thought back on the woman's tragic childhood and her life until now, and her heart overflowed with love for her. She wished she could take it all away and give her peace. Empathy overwhelmed her, and tears filled her eyes. She quickly wiped them away before she ruined their evening.

Kathryn stirred, and with a quick intake of breath, she opened her eyes.

Jenny knew she was caught, but she smiled bravely and chirped "Hi" anyway, hoping against hope that, in her sleep-induced stupor, Kathryn wouldn't notice she was crying.

"Hey ..." Kathryn craned her head up. She wasn't fooled, and she swung her long legs to the floor and had Jenny's hands in hers in an instant.

"What is it?"

Jenny tried to dismiss her tears by blaming the wine and a long day, but Kathryn wasn't buying it. Jenny finally had to admit that the past few weeks were taking their toll on her, and once the tears started, she couldn't stop them. The truth about her family, their breakup, and all that spiraled after, rushed to get out all at once.

Kathryn held her while she cried it out. It didn't take long. Her emotions escaped like a held breath, and the release left her relieved.

As the last tear fell, Jenny sat up straight and wiped her face with the sleeve of her robe.

"I'm sorry I'm such a baby," she sniffed.

Kathryn lifted Jenny's chin. "This is tough stuff, Jenny. You've handled yourself so well. If you need to cry, I'm here. If you need to talk—" She paused, realizing that for some issues, she was not an option. There were vague sympathetic answers to the vague problems her work presented, but none that would ease the burden. Still—

"Your superiors are there to help you," she went on. "You can tell them your concerns. If you don't feel comfortable with them, there are professionals in the organization that are there for that purpose ... to listen and help you through this."

Jenny waited a moment, and then a slow grin formed on her lips. "Did that work for you?"

"We're not talking about me."

Kathryn tried to remain serious, but Jenny's widening grin forced a chagrined chuckle.

Jenny playfully leaned into Kathryn's shoulder. "You're full of it, but thank you for the pep talk."

They both leaned back, side by side, and rested their heads on the back of the couch. Kathryn took Jenny's hand.

"I'm sorry it's so hard, honey."

Jenny shrugged and squeezed her hand. "I don't know how you do it, Kat. You're so strong all the time."

"Tst. Hardly." She leaned forward and retrieved her glass of wine from the coffee table. The uncomfortable feeling from Forsythe's office was returning, and she took a drink, hoping the subject would change by the time she leaned back.

"Seriously," Jenny went on predictably. "I mean, tonight, for instance, you had an upsetting day."

Kathryn looked at her as if she were clairvoyant.

Jenny smiled as she placed a comforting hand on her knee. "I can tell, yet you don't say anything about it, and you find someplace to put it all."

"Not well enough, apparently," Kathryn half-joked as she took another sip of wine.

"Where do you put it?"

Kathryn stared at her distorted reflection in the wine. At that moment, she wanted to put it all at the bottom of her glass. She would drown her guilt, escape the memories and the pain, and with it her responsibilities and obligations. It would be so easy—a few glasses, a bottle perhaps—but easy wasn't allowed. She forfeited easy when her cowardice cost the lives of the six men overseas.

"Sometimes I don't put it anywhere," she said with a shrug. "I cried like a baby at the funeral today. I couldn't help it. It was like I was fourteen all over again and it was my mother they were putting into the ground."

"Oh, Kat."

"And sometimes I just push it out of my mind and tell myself I'll think about it later."

That was all she planned to say about the matter, but Jenny stared at her with expectant eyes, and Kathryn knew she would wait as long as it took for her to reveal what was on her mind.

"Smitty has been assigned overseas."

Jenny's eyes widened and she slowly sat up. "Kat ... are you ...?"

"No, honey. I'm staying on at the training center."

Jenny physically slumped in relief. "I'm sorry about Smitty."

Kathryn tried to hide her trepidation over Smitty's departure, but Jenny saw right through her.

"How are you with that?"

Kathryn took another sip of wine and let it settle in her stomach before she answered. "He'll be fine. He's good at what he does, and I know he'll be careful."

"That's not what I asked."

Kathryn looked at her, wishing for the moment that she were a little less tenacious.

"I'll miss him."

It was a simple statement, filled with love and adoration, and purposely absent any hint of sadness. She stared into her glass, imagining the hazards of the European theater reflected in the deep burgundy of the merlot, and she closed her eyes briefly to shut out her memories and her fears about it.

"I don't want to think about it," she said quietly before taking another drink.

Jenny knitted her brow. "Are you sorry you're not going?"

Kathryn saw apprehension in her eyes and knew she had to admit the truth. "No. I'm not sorry."

Jenny breathed a sigh of relief. "Me either."

"But I'm not glad," Kathryn quickly added defensively.

"I understand."

"Do you?"

Kathryn didn't know how she possibly could. She didn't know what she'd done—the debt she owed. She only knew of the repercussions, and even then, it was from Smitty's stilted point of view.

Jenny was looking at her with renewed concern, and Kathryn knew her reaction had been a little strong.

"Sorry."

"It's okay, baby," Jenny assured her. "If I had been ordered overseas, I would have gone, but I don't think I would have said I was *glad* about it. It's terrifying, exciting ... it's what we were trained for. But I'd also be leaving you, and that's never a happy occasion," she said with a smile. "In the same vein, I know you must be torn about staying home when the action's over there."

Close enough, Kathryn relented. "Well, plenty of action around here lately, hm?"

Jenny took her hand with a squeeze of support, and she returned the squeeze with an appreciative smile.

"Thanks. Tough day."

"Are you all right about the funeral this morning?"

Kathryn nodded, happy to leave the guilt over her home front assignment behind. "It took me by surprise. So raw, like it was yesterday." She rubbed her forehead. "Not that you'd ever forget."

But she had forgotten. Especially the part about her overwrought father. How could she have forgotten that? Seeing the scene through adult eyes, she realized his pain was as great and as real as hers. He'd lost the woman he adored, but he also had to live with the horrible truth that it was his fault.

After all their years estranged, they finally had something in common. The circumstances were different, but the results were the same. They both had blood on their hands and guilt as their constant companion. Like father, like daughter. The epiphany was disturbing for a moment, but it soon twisted into a comforting irony.

She stared quizzically into her glass. The wine was starting to go to her head. It must be. She was starting to feel sympathy toward her father.

Jenny must have seen the bewilderment in her eyes and knew the wine had overstayed its welcome. "I'm going to wash my face. Do you want some water?"

Kathryn pushed the glass away. "Please."

Jenny collected the glasses and left the room.

Kathryn stood and rubbed her temples, begging her mind to clear. Memories so long hidden and a future she chose to ignore wrestled for the upper hand in her head.

The future lost out to the physical reminders of the past, as she lovingly caressed her mother's piano and followed the case's swooping curve to its end. She stood face to face with the small painting of her mother's hand, passing a seashell to her very young, innocent self. Memories washed over her and brought a bittersweet smile to her face.

"Always tell the truth, Kathy," her mother was fond of saying. "You may have to suffer the consequences, but you'll be thankful in the end."

"And why is that again, Mom?" she would ask.

"Because your soul will be free," was always the cryptic response.

The answer made no sense to the young girl who thought she was smart enough to get away with anything, but the woman she had become understood perfectly.

It was advice she couldn't follow, and before she knew it, the path behind her was littered with lies, death, and deception. Her soul was anything but free, and the young girl they called Kathy had been lost forever.

Kathryn closed her eyes and reached for the painting. *What ifs* taunted her. Who would she be had her mother lived? Where would she be? Would she have found Jenny? The last question gave her pause, but then she smiled. Jenny would have found her. She was sure of it.

"Beautiful hands," Jenny commented as she returned, holding out a glass of water.

Kathryn took it and smiled, as she stopped absentmindedly tracing the outline of the hands in the painting. "Yes, they were."

Jenny raised her glass in a toast. "Hers too."

Kathryn laughed and accepted the compliment on her mother's behalf. Her demeanor changed from one of introspection to relieved distraction.

Not surprisingly, Jenny noticed.

"Are you okay?"

Kathryn smiled. "Mm."

She was indeed okay. She had once told Smitty that Jenny soothed her soul. It was never truer than when she was in her presence, and one look or kind word made her feel alive and worthy of grace. She knew her soul would never be free, but she'd found the closest thing to it in the woman by her side.

"I love you, you know."

Jenny smiled. "I know."

Kathryn laughed at the self-assured reply and glanced back to the painting, certain her mother would have liked this girl.

Jenny pointed at the small signature in the corner of the canvas.

"Who's E.K. Hammond?"

"That's me."

Jenny almost choked on her water. "You painted that?"

"Mm-hm."

"You're an artist too?"

Kathryn laughed at Jenny's surprised expression. "Used to be."

"You never stop being an artist," Jenny stated with some authority. "You merely misplace your muse."

"Oh, is that what happens?"

"Yes, it is. Don't you think?"

Kathryn looked at the painting, feeling the guilt of wasted talent. "I suppose you're right."

"Of course I'm right." She put a hand on her hip and sized up the painting like a promoter planning a campaign. "We need to find you a muse, because you are too gifted not to be doing this every day."

While Jenny focused on the painting, Kathryn tried hard not to cast her eyes toward the closed door in the hallway, next to her bedroom. She had a muse. It just wasn't very pretty, and the resulting art wasn't much to look at. She'd given up painting entirely and turned her back on her studio and a talent that perpetuated more pain than pleasure.

Jenny was oblivious to her reaction, mesmerized instead by the depth of the meticulous layers of colored glazing.

"Kathryn, this is so beautiful."

Kathryn uttered a quiet "Thanks" as her eyes drifted self-consciously to the floor.

Jenny peered closer at the signature. "What does the E stand for?"

"Ethelyn"

Jenny looked her up and down, trying the name on for size. "Oh, my."

Kathryn laughed. "Yes, well. Mother had a curious sense of humor and a very dear aunt to appease. My father didn't feel it his place to argue after twenty-two hours of labor, so they compromised and, mercifully, addressed me by my middle name."

Jenny raised her brow and glass in thanks. "Here's to compromise."

"I agree."

"An artist." Jenny shook her head. "What else haven't you told me about yourself?"

Kathryn stared at Jenny's smiling face. The lighthearted question was a sober reminder of her complicated life and the secrets she tended.

She'd told Jenny many things—more than anyone else—but not everything. Some things she couldn't tell her, other things she just wouldn't, but some things were so integral to who she'd become that she felt compelled to reveal her darkest truths. *You'll be thankful in the end* echoed through her mind. She set her water glass down on the coffee table and took Jenny's hand.

"Come with me."

CHAPTER EIGHTEEN

*P*aul indignantly signed his name to the bottom of his statement and slammed the fountain pen on the table.

"Easy there, boy-o, that's my pen," Russo complained as he retrieved his green striated fountain pen and secured the cap.

"Where's my money?" Paul asked impatiently.

Russo calmly picked up the document and blew on the wet ink. "You're a broken record, Paul."

"I've told you everything I know, now give me my money."

"How much do you need?"

"What do you mean, how much? All of it!"

It was apparent to Paul from Russo's widening smirk that the rules had changed. He lunged for the document, only to have it predictably snatched away.

He pounded the table in frustration. "We had a deal!"

"Yes. You give us information. We will give you money. Just think of us as your new financial institution."

Paul peered into the dim corners of the room, knowing the agent's boss was behind the darkened windows somewhere. "You can't do this."

Russo leaned in, causing the hanging light to throw menacing shadows upon his face. "You will tell us who the money is going to and why, and we'll make sure you get what you need."

Paul raised his chin in futile defiance. "I'm not going to be part of your rat squad."

Russo leaned back and held up the signed papers. "You already are, Ryan."

The smoke from Colonel Holmes's cigarette curled loose spirals into the still air of the empty interrogation room. He had taken a drag to light it but quickly abandoned it to the ashtray in favor of Paul's incredible story, which he held tightly in his hands.

His mind was racing as he drank in the words. He devoured page after page of the document like it was a mystery novel he couldn't put down. It validated everything he already knew but hesitated to believe, and it proved that now, more than ever, Bouchaule was needed to make sense of the senseless.

Holmes didn't need the papers in his hand to brand Daniel Ryan a traitor. Selling secrets to the enemy through Forrester was enough. He was disappointed that Kathryn Hammond's assignment to the man hadn't yielded actionable proof, but both men were dead now, so it was a moot point. Kathryn Hammond did lead them to Bouchaule, however, and he knew her particular set of skills would prove invaluable. She might not think Bouchaule would come back, but he would make sure that he did.

How long Daniel Ryan had been passing information and how much of the weapon project had been compromised was unknown. They only knew a dangerous virus sample was unaccounted for and vital archived research records had gone missing.

The government had lost control of their man and the work they'd commissioned. Holmes regarded it as damn irresponsible and the reason he didn't trust the United States to retrieve and contain what they had let slip away. Outwardly, Holmes's superiors gave their American ally the benefit of the doubt, but, covertly, they gave their man carte blanche to get the job done—*whatever it takes*, they had told him—and Holmes took the directive literally and liberally. This was war. No one would be spared.

The more Holmes learned about how Daniel Ryan had deceived his own government, the more infuriated he became. He could only shake his head at the thought of the project in German hands. Such incompetence with something as dangerous as a biological weapon was unforgivable. Madness!

Typical of the Americans, he stewed. It was not their country a mere channel of water away from invasion. It was not their country's population that would be the first wiped out by the deadly infectious disease outlined in the Ryan files.

Over a year had passed since the FBI learned of Daniel Ryan's betrayal, and the SOE had tasked Holmes with infiltrating the German project to uncover the extent of the damage and neutralize it at all costs.

It appeared the Germans were stalled, lacking the final piece of the puzzle to bring their diabolical scheme to fruition. They lacked a vaccine that would spare their troops and civilians the devastation that would befall the unfortunate victims of the weapon. The Americans were suffering the same dilemma, and, for this, Holmes both thanked and cursed Daniel Ryan, who had left everyone in the dark.

Ryan had been the head of a Department of War research team charged with developing a vaccine for the deadly virus they had cultivated in their labs. A rumor circulated that he had succeeded, and because of it, Daniel Ryan's indeterminate mortality had met its measure.

The vaccine rumor delighted his superiors and stunned the tight-knit scientific community within the department. If it was true, the angel of death had been unleashed. No one dared use the weapon without a vaccine. The memory of bodies piled up like cord wood in the streets during the horrific influenza pandemic of 1918 was a sobering reminder of nature's indiscriminate destruction. But if a vaccine was available, the virus would quickly become a viable means of warfare. The invading army could win the war without firing another shot.

Paul's story substantiated the rumor that his brother had found a suitable reservoir for the lethal virus, where it would be innocuous until released. If true, antibodies from this reservoir would be used for a vaccine. *Preposterous*, claimed those closest to the science involved. It had only been a decade since advances in technology allowed the scientists to isolate the influenza virus used to create the weapon, and, in that time, no one had even come close to solving its ever-mutating riddle—the only thing standing in the way of success.

The initial reaction to the rumor was that it was black propaganda started by the Office of War Information, aimed at shaking German confidence. The charge was denied, of course, and with no evidence to show success, and Daniel Ryan himself claiming none, the rumor was dismissed as wishful thinking designed to boost morale.

A suspicious lab accident changed all that. The three top men on the Ryan project team were exposed to their own deadly virus. Two would die horrible, agonizing deaths within hours. The other, Daniel Ryan himself, appeared to be immune. The vaccine rumor resurfaced and became the stuff of legend. The hunt for the truth had begun.

With the lone survivor of that accident now dead, both sides were in a race to discover the key to the coded research documents Paul had been supplying to Forrester. Only then could they replicate the scientific breakthrough that Daniel Ryan had apparently taken to his grave.

Fear that the Germans were close to the answer led to desperate actions by otherwise rational and methodical government agencies. Holmes, with his unrelenting dedication, was the perfect candidate to allay that fear. He vowed to break the traitorous flow of information to the Germans and uncover the truth of Daniel Ryan's elusive vaccine before the whole world paid the price.

The contents of Paul Ryan's storage unit held some interesting items, and Holmes picked up just such an item as he waited for Agent Russo to return. It was a black and white photograph of five men in white lab coats, posing in their laboratory, with champagne glasses held high in celebration. He focused on two men in particular: a twentysomething Daniel Ryan and his proud father.

Holmes turned the photograph over. Written on the back in pencil was *February 1914 Leipzig*. The setting was a university in Germany, a few months before the outbreak of World War I.

Holmes wondered what they were celebrating. The officer was well aware of man's propensity for mutual annihilation, and ever since he first saw the photo, Holmes privately held the notion that these men were somehow responsible for creating one of the most lethal biological weapons ever known to man. He found it too much of a coincidence that four years later, as the war ground into a stalemate, the world would be ravaged by one of the deadliest pandemics ever.

True or not, he'd lost a sister and a brother to the influenza pandemic, and he remembered vividly their pain-wracked deaths, marked by hemorrhagic eyes, ears, and lungs, and the horror after, as their lifeless bodies lay in their own beds, covered in bloody sheets because the hospitals and morgues were too full to take them. He would not see history repeated—by either side.

He had no pity for Daniel Ryan, whom he viewed as the bringer of devastation. His death by Forrester's henchman, Vincent LaPaglia, was fitting retribution for the evil he tried to unleash onto the world and, frankly, saved him the trouble. It didn't make sense that Forrester would turn on his prized scientist, and he suspected LaPaglia was hired by someone else—perhaps Thierry Bouchaule, trying to wrest back control of the project? He didn't know, but Ryan was dead, and as far as he was concerned, the lot of them could rot in hell. Bouchaule's time would come. He would see to it.

Holmes reached into another folder and picked up a recent photo of Kathryn Hammond dancing with Bouchaule. He studied it purposefully and reminded himself that sacrifices in war have to be made. It justified the next phase of his plan, and he could only smile at his sinister brilliance.

The graceful plume of smoke lazily wafting from his cigarette was interrupted when the unattended butt burned itself out and fell onto the table. Holmes was oblivious, lost in his narcissistic haze, until he heard footsteps in the hallway. He put his photographs away and picked up Paul's story again.

Jake Russo returned from conducting his business and sat in the chair opposite his boss.

Holmes was indifferent as he perused Paul's story. "Everything in order?"

"He cooperated, just like you said he would, sir."

"Excellent."

Russo scoffed at the document in Holmes's hands. The connections in the ledger could come in handy, but the fantasy Paul had spun in his statement belonged in a dime store pulp fiction novel, as far as the agent was concerned.

"Some tall tale there, eh boss?"

Holmes lifted his eyes. "You read it?"

"Yeah, what a crock. That guy'll say anything for his dough."

"Desperate men do desperate things, Mr. Russo."

The agent shook his head and laughed as he lit a cigarette. "And how, brother."

Jake Russo didn't feel the bullet that took his life. A single shot between the eyes guaranteed his silence and his eternal devotion to the cause.

His final cigarette rolled from his lifeless lips as his body slumped to the table. Colonel Holmes leaned forward to rescue it before it tumbled to the floor. He set his Webley revolver on the table and sat back, taking a long drag on Russo's smoke as his eyes narrowed and he contemplated his next move.

His plan now set, he exhaled in satisfaction and smiled, saying, "Very desperate things."

CHAPTER NINETEEN

Paul tossed the leather case filled with cash onto the passenger seat as he ducked into his car. He smirked as he turned the engine over and revved it to life. The motor was racing like his heart. He had pulled it off. He had deceived Russo and, evident by the cash beside him, his superiors as well. Now it was finally over. The government was satisfied he'd revealed all he knew about his brother's work, and thanks to a fortuitous twist of fate, Forrester was out of his life. Daniel could rest in peace. His secrets were safe.

Paul blew out a relieved breath as he gripped the wheel. He was sure he was in trouble when Russo set their meeting in an isolated building on the wrong side of town and tossed a pen and paper under his nose, demanding full disclosure. He thought they had miraculously broken his brother's code and discovered the secret that had cost so many so much.

It seemed so long ago that his brother had come to him in desperation. It was the summer before the U.S. officially entered the war. To most, in 1941, the conflict was still something that was going on *over there*, but Paul Ryan suddenly found the war deposited solidly at his doorstep.

"I need your help," Daniel had said.

"Well, well, well," Paul had replied. "What brings the golden child to kneel at my feet?"

He was only half kidding and normally would have received a retort in the same vein, but not this time.

"I'm in serious trouble, Paulie," Daniel had said as he pushed inside and closed the door.

His childhood name, not heard in years, sobered Paul and took him back to the innocent days of tree house forts and endless summers, when *cross your heart and hope to die* forged a trust that would not be broken.

Daniel peered past his brother's shoulder. "Where's Bets?"

"She's out back in the garden."

He nodded and seemed relieved they were alone. "I'm going to do something, Paul, and there's a good chance it may get me killed."

"Then don't do it," was Paul's immediate response, still not certain his brother was serious.

"I don't have a choice. They'll come after Jenny."

Paul was stunned for a moment as he processed the absurdity of the statement. "Jenny? What has she got to do with it? What have you done, Danny?"

Daniel faltered and looked away. Paul could tell from his pained expression that something was tearing him up inside, but he remained silent.

Paul grabbed him by the shoulders. "Dan!"

Reluctantly, Daniel raised his eyes. He made vague references to a Department of War project, but balked when pushed for details.

Paul reminded his brother that he knew his general area of expertise and that it wasn't hard to put two and two together and realize the project was some sort of biological weapon. What he couldn't understand was how his niece became involved.

"What about Jenny?"

Daniel knew his weak spot. He need only mention a danger to Jenny and Paul would move heaven and earth to protect her. Daniel claimed she was safe for the moment, but it would only be a matter of time before desperation would bring about drastic measures and his daughter's safety would be used as a bargaining chip. Classified military secrets aside, Daniel knew Paul needed to know what he was up against.

"When I'm gone, the government may come to you looking for answers."

"Gone? Government?"

"They may get rough, threaten you, push you around. But stand firm. I'm going to give you what you need to appease them."

"Appease? Danny, what the Sam Hill are you talking about?"

Daniel shook his head in frustration. "Trust me when I tell you, they'll come for you, Paul."

Paul straightened and then relaxed, skeptical. "Surely, you're overreacting. My God, this isn't Nazi Germany. Our government doesn't go around—"

Daniel stabbed his finger into Paul's chest in a sudden burst of anger. "Do *not* underestimate our government's capacity for treachery!" He held fast to his rage to punctuate his warning and then backed off, fighting to control his emotions. "You have no idea, Paul."

Paul held up his hands in surrender. "Okay, Danny, okay. Take it easy."

There was a long, uncomfortable silence as Daniel backed off to compose himself.

Paul didn't know this man before him. His brother was always in control, always confident and quick with a plan. There was nothing he couldn't do. He need only set his mind to it. Seeing Daniel writhing under the weight of desperation, driven by fear—Paul wondered how he could have fallen so far.

With the utmost respect, he put his hand on his brother's shoulder and quietly asked, "What have you done, Danny?"

Daniel closed his eyes. His weary exhale told Paul his confession was a last resort, so he squeezed his shoulder and let him reveal it in his own time.

"I've been working with some men on a project."

"What men?"

"Germans."

"Why would the government—" Paul realized the government had nothing to do with it. He blinked in disbelief and released his brother's shoulder in reflexive disgust.

Daniel held up a hand. "It's not what you think."

"You're giving information to the Nazis behind our government's back, Dan. There aren't many ways to take that."

"I said Germans. Not Nazis."

"What's the difference?"

"Don't be so narrow-minded, Paul. These men were my friends. Brilliant men of science—"

"Are you mad?" Paul interrupted. "No German is your friend. They are hell bent on world domination, and you're giving them the keys to the kingdom! You're betraying your—"

Daniel grabbed his brother by the biceps. "Would you please shut up and listen to me!"

Paul was undaunted. "They're Germans!"

"They're dead!" Daniel shouted. "My friends are dead!"

Silence absorbed the echoing anger of their voices and Daniel released his hold. Paul was ready to listen.

"They're dead for refusing to work for the Nazis. They raided their labs after they killed them, and now I fear the worst."

Paul considered his brother carefully. He was not a foolish man, nor was he naïve. He certainly wasn't a traitor. If he trusted those men, they were worthy of it.

Underestimating the Nazis seemed to be a universal epidemic. His brother and his friends were just more victims, crushed under the relentless columns of hobnailed boots as they marched over Europe.

"The Nazis have your research."

Daniel nodded solemnly. "I fear so."

"How bad is it?"

"If it's true? Catastrophic."

"What do you mean, *if it's true?*"

"It's complicated."

Of course it was. Everything about Daniel was complicated. It always had been, and this was no different. If he was going to help his brother and keep Jenny safe, he demanded to know the details. Either his brother trusted him or he didn't. Daniel relented, albeit guardedly. It wasn't a matter of trust, he claimed, but a matter of safety. The less Paul knew, the less he could tell under duress. He told his brother only what he wanted known, only what, with a little searching, could be easily exposed.

As Paul listened to scientific medical jargon he had no hope of understanding, he saw glimpses of the passion and precision that made his brother so successful in his field. He felt the weight of his brother's sense of betrayal, as a lifetime's worth of work devoted to saving lives was turned in on itself, in an attempt to create a viable weapon that would alter the balance of power and assure the U.S. a victory as they were drawn inexorably into the escalating war.

Daniel explained the government's desire for such a weapon, the need, and, eventually, as casualties built up, the desperation that would force such a drastic measure—by either side. But this was not the way. It could never be the way. Even with a vaccine, such a weapon would never be safe. Mutation, the bane of his scientific existence, would soon render any vaccine obsolete. His own government acknowledged this yet ordered him to press on. It was then that he realized the extent of their determination and the folly of their logic.

Victory at all costs.

A moment of arrogant satisfaction followed by devastation, as mankind drowned in a cesspool of death and disease, wasn't a victory worth savoring.

"Anyone with the most rudimentary knowledge of virology knows that outcome is assured," Daniel went on, frustrated. "The Nazi scientists know this. But do they care? Do we?"

Paul didn't know the first thing about virology, but he suspected the questions were rhetorical. As Daniel unfolded his story, he remained silent. Complicated was an understatement and catastrophic was kind.

His brother and a group of his like-minded scientific brethren had spent their lives dedicated to the etiology of the virus. The war separated them, but their work went on. It had to go on. They knew what was at stake, which is why they all agreed that should a vaccine ever be found, they would keep it between themselves until it was needed toward its intended purpose—to stop the threat of another pandemic if the virus appeared again.

But now the Nazis had access to their research, their triumphs, and their failures. It could be the end of everything, but Paul sensed they didn't have everything, a notion upheld by his brother's silence. Daniel had a secret.

"What aren't you telling me, Dan?"

"It's not important," he insisted dismissively.

"I doubt that."

"It's not important to you or why I've come to you."

For the moment, Paul allowed it to be unimportant and focused on his brother's immediate plight. If he was astounded by the machinations that brought his brother to such an impossible situation, he was doubly astounded by his solution.

Daniel saw no other way to keep the reins on his project than by offering to ally with the Nazis. He would share misleading information to draw out his counterpart in the Nazi project. Promises of collaboration and rumors that he had successfully created the elusive vaccine would do it. He could then be on the inside to continue confounding researchers and keeping them from the truth, just as he had done at home. There was only one man he knew who could discreetly organize such an unholy alliance, and when his older brother heard the name Marcus Forrester, he was livid.

"You're in league with the devil!"

Daniel chuckled humorlessly. "You mean Forrester or the Nazis?"

"How could you get involved with that man? You know what he can do."

"As did you."

"What's that crack supposed to mean?"

"I know you've had dealings with Marc Forrester."

"I don't know what you're talking about."

"I know how you bought the paper."

Paul was silent for a moment and then raised his chin, trying to salvage some modicum of dignity as his pride fell to his feet. "What of it?"

"You should have come to me, Paulie. I'd have given you the money."

"Well, that would have defeated the purpose, don't you think?"

The two men stared at each other, as the ensuing silence magnified all the years of sibling rivalry, all the years of condescension, all the years of estrangement, all the years—all the wasted years. They had been stripped of the trappings of their egos and conceit and were faced with the naked truth of their fragile mortality.

Paul refused to accept that they had run out of time.

"This is absurd, Dan. Forrester is bad enough, but the Nazis?" He shook his head. "I won't let you do it."

Daniel pulled a small leather-bound journal from his jacket pocket. "Not your decision. Now—"

"I'm not helping you commit what amounts to suicide."

Ignoring Paul's protests, Daniel held out the journal. "If something should happen to me, this is for Jenny."

Paul pushed it away along with the suggestion. "Nothing's going to happen to you, Dan."

"Guard it. Keep it someplace safe. One day she'll have questions. You'll know when, and she'll know what to do with the answers."

"Danny ..."

"Paul." He grasped his brother's arm and sent all his concern and urgency through his tightening fingers. "It's important. It's everything —all I can give her now."

Paul stopped objecting and watched tears well up in his brother's eyes. Confirmation of lost hope was the last thing he wanted to see. He had never seen Dan so undone. He was like a condemned man on his last hour, desperate to justify his life, his choices—to be understood and forgiven.

Paul realized he may well lose his brother and tried to push away the thought of it, unable to conceive such a loss.

"Dan, this is ridiculous. There's got to be something we can do. Hide you, fake your death—something. We'll go to Dominic. His people can make you disappear. You can start a new life."

Daniel said it was tempting, but he had turned a blind eye to the questionable moral and ethical decisions of his superiors during the 1918 pandemic crisis. He did what he could, but it wasn't nearly enough to ease the haunting guilt of his silence.

Now the Nazis had hold of the project. He was well aware that morals and ethics were silent hostages to their brutal experiments, and he would not allow history to repeat itself. He had a voice now, and the power, and he would not fail to exact it, no matter the cost.

He pushed the journal into his brother's midsection. "Just take care of this, Paulie. Please. I'm counting on you."

Paul refused to take it. "I won't help you do this."

Daniel's eyes grew dark and cold. "Then they'll come after Jenny in retribution! Is that what you want? To lose us both?"

As the hopelessness of the situation sank in, Paul knew there was no need to reply or question. He was sure his brother had thought of every possible alternative. The situation had moved far beyond the point of protest. He solemnly took the small journal.

"There's no way out for me, Paul. I can't tell our government the truth, and when they find out what I've done, I'll be executed for treason. You can imagine what the Nazis will do when they find out I've deceived them, and I assure you, they will find out. And Forrester ... well, he's the least of my worries. Ours is just a business transaction."

"What does he get?"

Daniel hesitated.

"What does he get, Dan?"

"A piece of the action when the vaccine is produced."

"But ... there won't be a vaccine."

Daniel's indifferent look reiterated his resignation and his prophetic demise. "No, there won't."

Paul exhaled any hope he'd been holding and stared at the book in his hands: his brother's abridged life, trapped between ruled lines and cloaked in misdirection as a memento to his beloved daughter. It wasn't at all fitting. Not at all.

"Tell me what I need to know."

Daniel gently placed a comforting hand on his arm, acknowledging the dark shroud they now both shared.

Paul tried to close his heart and mind to the powerful emotions he felt flowing from his brother's touch. It was overwhelming. Daniel's guilt, grief, loss, and regret joined with his own to brand his soul, and the pain spread through his body like a wildfire until he thought his knees would buckle.

His brother's hand fell away, its energy sapped, and Paul looked for any distraction to regain his composure. He opened the stiff cover of the journal in his numb hands to find a personal inscription to Jenny on the facing page. He quickly passed over it, disallowing thoughts of her imminent grief, and thumbed blindly through the pages until he reached the end. He offered a final glance at his brother's history fanned out before him and noticed the handwritten text within appeared to be gibberish. He looked up, hurt.

"Coded? You don't trust me."

Daniel vehemently disagreed. "I'm trusting you with that and Jenny's life. There's no one I trust more."

Paul held up the journal. "And the key?"

"We'll get to that. For now, it's best you know as little as possible." He pulled an envelope from his back pocket and handed it over. "This is for when they come to you. It's the story you'll tell them. They'll be satisfied it's all you know, and it will all be over. Draw it out for as long as you safely can. Play hard to get, but not too hard. I want them to focus on you. Keep Jenny out of this. She needn't know anything about it." He paused and suddenly looked lost. "It'll be hard enough on her when—" His voice trailed off, his regret for his daughter's heartbreak left unsaid.

Paul nodded numbly. The scene was so surreal. Here was his spirited brother, plotting the course of his affairs like a terminally ill man arranging his funeral.

"And this is for you," Daniel said softly as he handed over another envelope. "Everything I never said and should have." His words were barely a whisper, and he swallowed his rising emotions as he made a feeble attempt at a smile. "Life seems dreadfully brief all of a sudden."

"Dan …" Paul was beyond protest, beyond disbelief. He had no words, only the tears now welling in his own eyes.

They embraced, reluctant to let go. The tangle of strong arms made them one man, united by death, the great leveler. Years would have to be lived in a few disconsolate moments. Time was no longer a luxury. They had work to do.

Their relationship would be the first victim of the plan. They would keep their distance and feign contempt for each other in public when at all possible. Everyone was aware of their rivalry, so no one would question they'd had a falling out. Hopefully then, his apparently estranged brother would be the last person they'd look to for answers when the carefully planned betrayal could no longer be suppressed.

His work was too important to destroy, and too dangerous in the wrong hands, so it was carefully coded and hidden in plain sight. In his letter, Daniel had given Paul the basics of his research and just enough extra detail to make the information seem like a legitimate breakthrough. If worse came to worst, Paul would recount it and the government's curiosity would be sated.

As for Jenny, she was young and innocent. Daniel knew she was only useful as leverage while he was alive. Once something happened to him, he was reasonably certain she would be safe. Paul understood the danger and would see to her safety, above all else.

The brothers played their parts perfectly. A year went by uneventfully, and Paul thought Daniel was just being paranoid.

Everything changed as 1942 arrived. Daniel's worst nightmare had begun. Someone was becoming frantic for a solution, and the first act of desperation left two of his top researchers dead.

Paul remembered Daniel was far too calm the last time he talked to him.

"It's time to give them what they want," he had said.

Paul shut his eyes against the memory. He could still hear the hollow desolation of the crackling phone line, as neither man knew how to let the other go.

Finally, a shaky voice said, "I don't know how to say goodbye, Paul."

"Then let's not."

The cold silence grew exponentially with each passing second, until Daniel put them both out of their misery and disconnected the call. Twenty-four hours later, he was dead.

The engine in Paul's Cadillac purred softly in the background as he blinked away a tear and wiped his nose with the handkerchief from his breast pocket. He sniffed away his emotions and put the car into drive.

"It's done, Danny."

If only he had been right.

CHAPTER TWENTY

*J*enny watched as Kathryn paused with one hand pressed against the closed door to her spare room and the other on the doorknob. She closed her eyes and bowed her head slightly, as if asking permission from some unknown source before she dared enter.

Kathryn had offered a preamble of sorts before she led Jenny to the door—a warning about what she would find behind it and the chance to back out. Jenny found it a ridiculous offer. No matter what lay inside, she was not going to turn away from Kathryn's past. Besides, she was not the one gripped by apprehension.

She put her hand on the small of Kathryn's back. "You don't have to do this."

Kathryn opened her eyes and turned. "No. I want to."

The statement was an obvious lie, and Jenny sympathetically tilted her head.

Kathryn relented. "I need to. I just—" She looked up at the door and rubbed its white painted surface as if pleading with the memories beyond it for kindness. She gave the solid wood surface a final pat and exhaled. "I just need to."

She opened the door and turned on the light.

Jenny was immediately struck by the faint smell of oil paints and varnish, a familiar scent that reminded her of her grandmother's studio.

Kathryn scooped up some wayward brushes and dusted off her painter's stool, the only seat in the room. "Sorry. It's been a while."

Jenny waved off the apology, and the place to sit, anxious to discover another facet of her complicated lover.

Jenny didn't know where to start. The room was overflowing with neatly stacked canvases leaning against the bare wall like dominos with no place to fall, and there was a huge canvas on an oversized easel in the middle of the small space, draped with a white sheet. A wooden table beside it held a small canvas smeared with leftover palette paints of vibrant reds and rich browns, surrounded by dabs of bright yellow and orange.

Kathryn looked a little lost, like she was unsure where to look or what to say. In the end, she found the floor an intriguing place to stare and sat on the stool before the covered canvas and worked the stiffened bristles of the brushes in her hand.

"May I?" Jenny asked, motioning to the cork bulletin board on the wall to her immediate left. It was bursting with photographs and scrap pieces of paper covered with loose sketches in pencil and charcoal.

"Please," Kathryn said, finally looking up. "Feel free to look at anything. If you have any questions—" She paused, as if just realizing who she was talking to and how funny that was. "Well ... I'll do my best."

Jenny smiled and laid a comforting hand on her knee before turning to the board. It was the most disorganized thing in the room, with the items haphazardly tacked up like the storyboard to a schizophrenic's dream. She clasped her hands respectfully behind her back as she leaned in to process the array of obvious reference materials.

Kathryn had explained that painting had been part of her therapy when she returned from overseas, and the sketches and photos on the board certainly bore that out. There were many photographs that appeared to be of the same six men, but some were enlarged to such an absurd degree that the details were no longer recognizable.

Jenny didn't have to ask if these were the men killed during her captivity. It was hard to conceive the brutal deaths of the cheerful group before her, so she purposely shut out the horror of it, knowing it would undo her.

She moved on to an eight by ten group shot of twenty or so men. Leaning a little closer, she was surprised to see a familiar face.

"Is this Lieutenant Branson from the training center?"

Kathryn continued staring at the brushes in her hand. "It is."

"He helped rescue you?"

Kathryn chuckled. "No, he did not." She turned and deposited the brushes in a jar off to the side. "Branson was the unofficial leader of a group of hometown fellas left over from the International Brigade during the civil war in Spain. When that war was over, they drifted around until Germany invaded France and they took up arms again."

"Small world."

"Mm."

"He didn't try to save you with the others?"

"He gave strict orders against it."

"God, he was an asshole even then."

"No," Kathryn said. "He was right. The others ignored his orders, and everything just snowballed after that. When it was all over, Branson took the brunt of the blame for how things went down."

"And he blames you for it."

"Something like that."

Jenny looked back to the picture and shook her head. "He's still an asshole."

Kathryn smiled. "His personality may leave a lot to be desired, but Branson is the kind of soldier the military strives for. He'll do as he's told without question, no matter how dirty the job. He simply got caught up in an incident where he made an unpopular decision, even though it was the right one. For morale's sake, someone had to pay, and unfortunately ..." She shrugged.

"Hmph," Jenny said. "Asshole."

She turned away from the sketches of crumpled bodies, thankful the drawings lacked detail. It wasn't the images of death that bothered her. She'd seen that and more when she'd cataloged newsreels. The sketches before her were Kathryn's experiences. She knew those men, and their deaths were a cross that Kathryn, for some misguided reason, chose to bear. Jenny felt the pain of every line drawn, as if they were carved into Kathryn's soul with a jagged knife.

Navigating around the room, the large covered canvas was too obvious to ignore, and though she had permission to look at anything, Jenny still sought Kathryn's consent with questioning eyes. Kathryn nodded and promptly moved off the stool, deciding the far corner of the room was a safe place to stand.

Jenny pulled the sheet back and tried not to flinch at the image. Glassy eyes stared out from the canvas, and Jenny didn't need the pool of blood surrounding the prone face to tell her the subject was dead. Her eyes drifted to the montage in the upper part of the painting, where the same man was seen laughing and smiling, his soul reaching out from behind his bright eyes. Kathryn had a gift all right. Her subjects came alive on the canvas—even when they were dead.

"That's Joshua Grayson," Kathryn commented softly from the back of the room. "His mother—"

"Came to the club. I remember."

Kathryn nodded, still avoiding the painting.

"This is incredible, Kat."

"Incredibly morbid," Kathryn mumbled under her breath.

The painting must have been Kathryn's last memory of the young man, and Jenny imagined she had consigned him to canvas, hoping to purge the horrific scene from her memory. If the room hadn't been used for some time, Jenny wondered where Kathryn put her painful past now?

She gently replaced the sheet over the canvas. "Why don't you paint anymore?"

"I thought that would be obvious."

"What's obvious to me is that you are incredibly talented and have something to say."

Kathryn crossed her arms and leaned casually against the wall. "Nobody wants to see what I have to show them."

"Art isn't about what the audience wants to see … it's about what the artist is compelled to share."

"I'm not interested in sharing."

"What I mean is, art is for you, not for someone else."

Kathryn smiled gently "I know what you mean. I don't want to be in that place anymore."

"Where do you put those feelings now?"

Kathryn pushed away from the wall and met Jenny before the easel. She put her arms around her and kissed her tenderly on the lips.

"I put them in their place, which is one hundred yards behind my sprinting body at all times."

Jenny vaguely shook her head and placed a comforting hand on Kathryn's chest before turning back to the stacks of stretched canvas. Kathryn couldn't run forever, and locking all the memories and emotions in a room couldn't contain the horror forever. Jenny could only vow to be there when the walls crumbled, as they always do.

A large slotted bin on the far wall contained smaller finished canvases, and Jenny was drawn to them, wondering if she'd find any trace of the woman who had painted the gentle portrait above the piano.

The first two paintings were smaller versions of some of the details in the large canvas on the easel, and Jenny realized the bin contained intimate studies of the larger works that were leaning against the wall.

The next painting was a pleasant surprise, and Jenny smiled to find the same warm palette and gentle emotion that graced the painting in the living room. This painting was of a beautiful woman, with her head thrown back in laughter. She had long dark flowing hair and striking features—strong, like her outgoing personality, which rolled off the canvas in the form of her brightly colored dress and bold red lipstick. She reminded her of Kathryn and wondered if she could be a relative.

"Who is this woman, Kat?"

Kathryn didn't look up, which led Jenny to believe there was only one woman portrayed in the canvases.

"Juliette Fournier. She was the head of our resistance cell in Paris. Very good. Very charismatic."

"Very beautiful," Jenny added, taking in the woman's dark, exotic features.

Kathryn exhaled softly and looked up. "She was also my lover."

Intense green eyes quickly met blue but just as quickly looked away, not sure how to respond. Jenny carefully returned the canvas to its rack and reached for the next, needing a distraction from her racing thoughts. She couldn't help imagining them as a couple, arm in arm, so elegant and confident. Juliette seemed Kathryn's equal in every way, her mentor perhaps. It would be silly to say she was jealous of the woman, but Juliette Fournier's painting was disarmingly beautiful and was a testament to the obvious love with which it was painted.

As the next canvas cleared the rack, Jenny physically drew back with a gasp, repulsed. It was the same woman but barely recognizable. She was stripped of her dress and lay crumpled at the base of a bullet-riddled, blood-stained wall. Her face was beaten, her beautiful hair haphazardly shorn and strewn in wispy tufts about her lifeless body.

"Oh, God," was all Jenny could muster. The guilt of her jealousy shamed her, and she was humbled by Kathryn's loss. "I'm so sorry, Kat."

Kathryn looked away again and didn't respond.

It was a horrifying painting, meticulously imbued with the same attention to detail as the portrait but having the opposite effect. Jenny quickly returned it to its place—for her emotional sake as well as Kathryn's. The Germans had brutally murdered Kathryn's lover. Jenny couldn't imagine. What if it was Kathryn lying there? She felt sick, her imagination filling her with the raw emotions of the scene. She pushed it away for another time and with it the empathy that was just as debilitating. Words seemed so inadequate, but the injustice required some acknowledgment.

"Is there no end to their brutality?" she complained, as the canvas hit the back of the bin. "Bastards."

Kathryn slowly looked up. "The Germans didn't do that. The partisans did."

"But—" They were the good guys.

"My mission had been compromised. Juliette was the only possible source. When they were waiting for O'Brien and me, her duplicity was obvious."

Jenny stood motionless, trying to comprehend such a personal betrayal.

Kathryn filled in the uncomfortable silence with the details.

"She didn't deny it. She *couldn't* deny it. The partisans beat her, dragged her through the streets, cut off her hair with a straight razor, and threw her at the base of the wall. They handed me a gun and said that as the lone survivor of her treachery, it was my right to execute her."

Jenny stared with wide expectant eyes, wondering if Kathryn had killed her. When the answer wasn't forthcoming, she uttered a barely audible, "And?"

"She pleaded for her life," Kathryn replied with the hollow candor of a bad memory relived. "Said she had no choice. The Germans had her children. If I killed her, I would be killing her children as well."

Kathryn remembered staring at her battered lover as she crawled, sobbing, to her feet. She once idolized the woman. Fiercely independent and highly respected by her peers for her part in organizing their resistance cell, Fournier had befriended her during the lean, early days in Paris. She took her in, showed her the ropes of her world of high-priced escorts and their ilk, and when the war came, she took advantage of lonely, loose-lipped German officers in the throes of passion or drink. They were easy marks for the beautiful women, and they spilled their secrets effortlessly. It was almost a game, and Juliette was the best.

They'd been lovers from the outset. The Frenchwoman's seduction was irresistible, and she was the last person on earth Kathryn would have doubted. In hindsight, the woman's position was perfect. She was able to transfer information with ease from client to rebel and back.

Her trust betrayed, Kathryn felt neither anger nor pity as the gun in her indifferent hand hovered over Juliette's bloodied skull like an executioner's axe waiting for its cue to fall.

She didn't fire. After her experience at the hands of her captors, she had no stomach for execution. Juliette's life was not hers to take. There were others around her more incensed, for whom the killing would actually have some meaning. She passed the gun to the man beside her and stepped back, leaving the sobbing condemned woman to proffer her misplaced gratitude when she thought she'd been spared.

Kathryn looked up to find Jenny still waiting for the rest of the story.

"I believed her. She begged for her life and I left her to it ... such as it was."

The crowd was not so lenient, nor so naïve. Kathryn watched the man with the gun shove the groveling traitor into the muddy ground with a boot between her bare shoulder blades and shoot her in the back of the head to a chorus of cheering onlookers.

After seeing the painting, Jenny didn't ask the outcome. Instead, she closed her eyes with a pained expression on her face. "The children?"

Kathryn exhaled an unsettling chuckle. "There were no children. Juliette was having an affair with a German officer. She'd been feeding him information the entire time."

A quiet beat of disbelief passed before Jenny found her voice. "How could she have done that to you?"

It seemed like a silly question to Kathryn, especially from someone in the spy trade.

"You do what you have to do to win. What she did is no different from what I do. She just got caught."

Jenny's eyes grew round with indignation. "You are nothing like that woman!"

Kathryn bowed her head to hide her smile, not surprised that Jenny would come to her defense.

"You're not," Jenny insisted.

Kathryn nodded and allowed Jenny her biased opinion, turning her amused grin to one of gratitude.

Jenny turned once again to the bulletin board of photographs, and Kathryn imagined she'd had enough of the horrors portrayed in the canvases. She leaned closer to O'Brien's photograph, and before Jenny could ask for that story, Kathryn filled her in.

"Smartest man I've ever known. He was a code man sent by the SOE. A charming Irishman with an infectious smile." She couldn't help the grin that curled her lips at his memory, but the warm thought quickly turned to ash in her mouth.

Her job had been to slip away during an extravagant dinner party given by a besotted high-ranking German officer and simply unlock a door. O'Brien would have access to a German communications room in a château in the French countryside, complete his job, and sneak out. Simple.

"The mission went horribly wrong."

"They were waiting for you."

Kathryn nodded. "We tried to escape, but they were everywhere. We knew we weren't going to make it, but still you run, you know? You have to try."

She saw Jenny swallow as she nodded. "Of course."

"We were on a walled estate and trapped on the grounds. We took refuge in the stables, where we found ourselves cornered in the tack room." She shook her head. "Stupid. There was no way out, but you're desperate to get out of the hunt."

The soldiers would find them soon enough, but the reprieve would give them time to do what they knew they had to do. She paused in her story, as her everlasting shame and regret rose to the surface. Many times, she wished she'd been shot in the back as she ran away rather than endure all that followed, but the Germans would do her no such favor. They were not interested in killing. They wanted to capture, and O'Brien was the perfect prize. His knowledge of the SOE code system would be invaluable.

He wasted no time preparing himself. Neither of them had an L pill, the lethal cyanide capsule given to agents who found themselves in such a situation, so O'Brien pulled back the slide of his Browning automatic, loaded a round into the chamber, and handed it to Kathryn before pulling out a photograph of his wife and son from his shirt pocket. It was a personal item that he shouldn't have had with him, but Kathryn imagined it gave him great comfort now. He scribbled a goodbye message on the back and kissed it, hoping the Germans had the common decency to see that it got to where it belonged. He offered the pencil to Kathryn, but she declined, realizing she had no one.

She looked at the Browning resting in her open palm and pressed the cold metal slide to her perspiring forehead, begging it to do its job quickly.

"You okay over there, lass?" O'Brien asked with unnerving calm as he removed a revolver from his waistband and pulled back the hammer.

Kathryn could only nod, her wide eyes revealing her fear.

He smiled. "We're going to do this together. Won't hurt a bit. Promise."

She nodded once more, taking a deep breath to steady her shaking hands. She watched O'Brien cross himself and kiss the medallion of a saint that dangled on a gold chain around his neck.

Kathryn wondered why he bothered. It was obvious his saint and his god had failed him miserably.

"Forgive me, Father," he whispered. He put the gun barrel to his temple and held out his hand. "Ready?"

Kathryn took the offered comfort and awkwardly raised her weapon to her head. She inhaled deeply and held her last breath as she waited for him to count to three.

"Been a pleasure," he said with an easy grin, as if parting from a casual luncheon date.

Kathryn flinched at the memory of the deafening percussion of his discharging gun as it resounded off the stone block walls of the tiny room.

O'Brien's body fell away from her and she stared at his lifeless form, paralyzed, with her numb finger wrapped around her trigger. Her arms felt heavy and the gun wound up in her lap. Everything seemed in slow motion—the sounds of the approaching soldiers, her breathing, her thoughts.

She paused in her recollection. "I couldn't do it. I couldn't pull the trigger. This man—" She held out her hand to the imaginary body on the floor. "This man had everything to live for. A wife, a beautiful baby boy ... God." She wiped away an angry tear. She had nothing and no one to live for, and she hesitated. She couldn't take her life.

The sounds of the soldiers got louder, shaking her out of her ineffectual haze. She knew codes that couldn't be exposed and members of her cell that had to be protected. She could not be taken alive. The door to the stable was kicked in, and she knew there was no choice. She put the gun to her temple and closed her eyes.

She looked up at Jenny, whose face was etched with foreboding.

"It jammed."

Jenny closed her eyes. "God. The aversion to automatics."

Discarding her worthless firearm, Kathryn tried to pry O'Brien's gun from his dead hand, but it was too late. The soldiers poured into the room, and she was met with a rifle butt to the head. Captured.

Kathryn bowed her head and rubbed her forehead. The rest of her life was defined by her inaction. "I should have died that day. Maybe I did."

Jenny wasn't going to pretend she shared Kathryn's regret about the jammed automatic. She couldn't imagine a life without her, and though she would never voice it, selfish tendencies were not exclusively Kathryn's.

"Seems to me it was the day you decided to live," she countered tentatively.

"It was the wrong decision. I knew what the protocol was. You know it too. I failed in my duty because I was too selfish to do the right thing."

"You were scared. Anyone would be. My God—"

"There's a difference between scared and irresponsible!"

Jenny threw her hand in the air. It was clear Kathryn expected recrimination, but Jenny had none to give. She was irritated by how Kathryn clung so desperately to her guilt-ridden path when, clearly, so many things had led to the tragedy. If only Juliette hadn't betrayed her. If only the gun hadn't jammed. If only Smitty hadn't led those men to attempt a rescue.

That Kathryn would rather have died than have to live with her past reflexively stung, but it spoke volumes about her implacable grief.

Jenny knew she couldn't lift Kathryn's burden any more than she could change the past, but like a change in light alters the appearance of the landscape, so might a change in perspective.

"In the end, you did the right thing. You protected the code."

Anger flashed in bloodshot blue eyes. "At what cost? Those men lost their lives because of me!" She pointed over Jenny's shoulder. "Look at them!"

Jenny gave a halfhearted glance behind her, but she purposely didn't absorb the images. The true weight of Kathryn's guilt was already choking her like phantom hands around her throat. She swallowed hard. This was no time to falter.

Kathryn went on with her tirade, taking responsibility for things only a mind reader could have prevented, and Jenny had heard enough. Kathryn's anger was fueled by her ever-present guilt, and Jenny understood that, but the woman was only human, and while what happened was horrific, she wasn't going to let Kathryn sink even deeper into the mire of self-pity.

"Stop it, Kathryn. If you let this destroy your life, they win."

"I've got news for you. They already have."

"If they have, it's because you've let them."

Kathryn looked like she'd been stabbed in the back. "Go to hell, Jenny. You don't know what the fuck you're talking about!"

"There's no room in hell, Kat. They put up the no vacancy sign when you took up residence there."

Both women stared at each other, their hearts racing with the unexpected confrontation. Jenny was poised to defend herself and kept her guard up to deflect any spear thrown in the heat of the moment, but she saw Kathryn's anger quickly dissipate with a tension-breaking sigh. "I'm sorry. That was an ugly thing to say." She held out her hand. "Please forgive me. I just ... I try every day not to let them win."

Jenny readily accepted her hand and sealed the apology with a soft kiss on her knuckles. "I know. I'm sorry I said that."

Kathryn exhaled and looked around the room. Jenny wondered what she was thinking. "Why did you let me in here?"

"Maybe I wanted you to convince me it wasn't my fault."

Jenny didn't think it was her fault, but in the end, it didn't matter what she thought. "I can't give you that peace."

Kathryn nodded. "I know."

Jenny pulled her into her arms and hoped she knew she'd always be there for her.

Kathryn was awakened by the shrill ring of her telephone. Her heart pounded as she untangled herself from Jenny's protective embrace and lunged for the black handset before she was even conscious of moving. Phone calls in the middle of the night were never good news.

"Kat!" a man's voice boomed over the line. Wherever he was, it was noisy, and the shouting could almost be excused as a necessity. She turned on the light and squinted at the small carriage clock on her nightstand. It was four a.m.

"Who is this?"

"Tommy!"

Jenny lifted her head with a furrowed brow, squinting against the light and the intrusion.

Kathryn put her hand over the receiver. "Tommy Wallace."

"I heard," Jenny groaned under her breath and then mouthed, *What time is it?*

Kathryn held up four fingers, eliciting an eye roll and another groan.

"We're in L.A.! We're a hit!" the trumpeter gleefully shouted, causing Kathryn to back the receiver away from her ear. "Aw, baby, it was swell," he went on. "I wish you could have been here! You hear that?" The background noise and music got louder, and she could almost see him holding the handset up to the room. "That's all for us! They love us out here, and I love them! And I love you for setting this in motion for me. We're a hit!" he repeated, his voice peaking to a boyish squeak.

Kathryn laughed. "Of course you are. Was there ever any doubt?"

"You gave me the brass ones to go for broke, gal, and I'll love you forever for it! Woo!" he yelped in delight. "Three encores, and it's all your fault!"

Kathryn laughed and rubbed her eyes, her groggy voice warm and low as it stirred the early morning calm. "That's great, man."

Jenny was delighted to see Kathryn smiling and laughing, despite the hour. It had been an emotional night for her, and while there was no breakdown like at the club, there were unchecked tears as she stood before the photos of the fallen and, for the first time, honored the men instead of just mourning their fates.

"You should be here, Kat!" Tommy beamed, oblivious. "This is the town for you. This is where the action is."

"Hey, T?"

"Yo."

"Do you know what time it is here?"

She sensed Tommy glancing at his watch.

"Aw, nuts," he drew out through his laughter. "Time difference. I forgot. Sorry! And tell that gorgeous little blonde flopped over your thigh that I'm sorry too."

Jenny raised her head. "Flopped?" She leaned closer to the phone. "I'll have you know, that gorgeous little blonde is deliciously *draped* over that thigh, thank you very much. Salaciously *slung*," she went on. "Nefariously *naked*—"

Kathryn playfully put her hand over the receiver and whispered, "Nefariously?"

Jenny looked her straight in the eyes and deadpanned. "It's four in the morning."

Tommy's laughter escaped through the tinny handset speaker.

"I'm sorry, doll!" he yelled to Jenny.

"Congratulations, Tommy," she yelled back. She settled her head back onto Kathryn's shoulder with a grin, content to be one of the gang.

"Hey, Kat!"

"Right here, man," Kathryn said, wincing at the volume.

"Oh, sorry. Listen, angel." His voice took on a more serious tone and the background noise fell away. "Thank you. Really. You saved my life. I needed this."

"You were born to make music, Tommy."

"So were you. You sure I can't—"

"No, but thank you. I'm flattered."

Tommy laughed. "Don't be flattered, just accept."

It suddenly got noisy again.

"Nuts. The boys just came to drag me back out there."

"Blow them away, man, blow them away."

"I love you, lady! I mean it!"

"Love you too, Tommy. Be—" The line disconnected. "Careful." Kathryn looked at the handset and shook her head with a chuckle.

As she hung up the phone and turned out the light, she felt a sublime sense of accomplishment. Tommy had made it. He had worked hard to make his dream come true, and though their goals were different, the satisfaction was the same. She settled back into Jenny's loving arms and drifted off into contented slumber. She had made it too.

CHAPTER TWENTY-ONE

Kathryn crossed the stage at The Grotto and leaned over the piano to point to a troubling measure on the sheet music. She made a suggestion, and the band leader agreed, penciling in the changes. She had just straightened for the run through when the swinging front double doors of the club caught her eye.

Jenny emerged with a wave, followed by Smitty. Kathryn raised her chin and smiled to the pair as she prepared to add her vocals to the reworked passage. They'd been at it all afternoon, and Jenny's smiling face was just what she needed.

She woke up mid-morning to that smiling face, only to learn Jenny had been watching her sleep for hours. When asked what she had been thinking, Jenny simply replied, "How I love you more and more every day."

Kathryn pulled her into her arms and made love to her until their responsibilities beckoned them to get on with their day.

When rehearsal was over, Kathryn sauntered over to the bar and greeted Smitty with a peck on the cheek. She offered Jenny a warm smile and a brief squeeze of her hand. Just the sight of her sent her body humming with arousal, and she had to fight against the urge to take her in her arms again, to feel her body pressed against hers, to taste her lips and surrender to the sensual return of her touch. Fighting against all that, she merely grinned instead and said, "Hi, you."

She hoped Jenny had a clear calendar for the afternoon, because in about thirty seconds, she was going to spirit the woman away to her dressing room and show her a proper greeting, where clothes would definitely be optional.

"Hi yourself," Jenny replied, trying to hide her disappointment. She realized they were in a very public place—Kathryn's workplace, no less—but after their incredible morning, how could Kathryn be so aloof? Even Smitty rated a peck on the cheek.

"What's your afternoon look like?" Kathryn asked casually.

"Well, I—" Smitty began before an elbow to his ribs silenced him.

Kathryn addressed Jenny with a smoldering look. "You."

That was encouraging. "I'm free for the rest of—"

The swinging double doors caught Kathryn's eye again, and suddenly she was no longer paying attention to Jenny's answer. She was looking past her shoulder at a broad shouldered man in an Army Air Force uniform, silhouetted against the bright light from outside.

"Oh, my God," she exhaled in delighted wonder.

The soldier slid his hat from atop his head and put his hands on his hips, surveying the room like Superman, on top of the world.

"Well, I'll be," Smitty muttered.

Jenny wished someone would tell her what was going on.

"Luc," Kathryn whispered as she rushed to the entrance.

Jenny looked closer, and sure enough, it was Dominic's incredibly handsome son, scooping Kathryn off her feet and into his arms, where she kissed him on the lips and held tightly to his neck, as they spun around until he gently placed her feet on the ground.

"God, it's so good to see you," Kathryn beamed, cupping his face in her hands. "Are you okay?" She stepped back and looked him up and down for an injury that might have sent him home. "Does your dad know you're here?"

He gave a glance toward the empty office. "No, I wanted to surprise him."

"I think he's downstairs."

"Say, is that her?" Luc asked, motioning over Kathryn's shoulder.

She couldn't hide her proud grin and took his hand, eager to introduce them. "Come on."

Jenny straightened as the pair arrived, securing the odd mood Kathryn's enthusiastic greeting had wrought.

"Luc." She offered her hand with a sweet smile. "I've heard so—"

She was swept off her feet into a gentle bear hug, and it seemed the gregarious man had no intention of letting her go.

"You've made her so happy," he whispered in her ear. "Thank you so much."

Jenny returned the hug, instantly charmed. "It's my pleasure, believe me."

Luc chuckled and set her down. "I can imagine," he said with a wink.

He turned to the bar and held out his hand. "Smitty."

"Welcome home, Luc."

"Thanks. I've only a few days, but there's nowhere I'd rather be." He smiled at Kathryn, who continued to beam in his presence.

Jenny noticed the greeting between the two men was strained and imagined she and Smitty were silently sharing custody of a strange little creature called jealousy. It was ridiculous, she knew, but she had never seen Kathryn so effervescent. On the one hand, it was a sight to behold—Kathryn's laughter, her broad smile, the light in her eyes—but on the other hand, it was at the sight of Luc, not her, and as much as it pained her to admit, it took her by surprise and offended her, as if she had exclusive rights to the woman's happiness.

Kathryn put her hand on Luc's chest. "Let's go find your dad."

Everyone smiled and nodded. Kathryn offered a parting grin at

Jenny before gleefully taking the soldier's arm and heading for the wine cellar.

"I'm so happy to see you," Jenny could hear her saying as she curled her hand around his bulging bicep.

She shook her head and chastised herself for being so childish. She wanted Kathryn to be happy, and obviously Luc held a special place in her heart. She could see why. She'd only just met the man, but already his engaging presence had drawn her in.

Jenny turned on her bar stool toward Smitty, who was pouring a whisky, with a chaser of envy.

He cut his eyes to her. "Amazing together, aren't they?"

"They're good friends."

"Yeah." Smitty lifted his glass and toasted their backs. "Good friends."

Jenny watched him down the whisky with disdain.

"What does that mean?"

Smitty must have recognized the turmoil in her eyes and kept his thoughts to himself.

"Nothing, kid. They're good friends is all."

He poured another drink, and Jenny looked at him sideways.

"Bit early for that, isn't it?"

Smitty chuckled, dismissing her holier-than-thou posturing. He pulled a bottle of scotch from under the bar and held it up. "Drink?"

She stared blankly at him and then slowly smiled at her reluctant partner in misery. "Please."

Kathryn still had a smile on her face as she drove home from the impromptu welcome home party. The look on Dominic's face when he saw his son for the first time in over a year—

"Luciano!" he gasped, and promptly dropped a bottle of expensive wine at his feet.

"Papa," Luc said grinning, as he held out his arms and the two men embraced.

Kathryn left them to their reunion and was honored when she and Jenny were included in the family get together after her show. Smitty was invited but made his excuses, which wasn't surprising. The two men merely tolerated each other out of respect for their mutual love for her.

Jenny and Luc got along well, which pleased Kathryn to no end. She sensed a little apprehension on Jenny's part at first, but Luc could melt a glacier with his smile alone, and Jenny wasn't nearly that tough a sell. The two of them were laughing and joking in no time, and Kathryn tendered her appreciation by holding her hand under the table all through dinner.

"So, how did you two meet?" Jenny had asked with genuine curiosity.

The mood turned serious and the table went silent.

Luc wiped his mouth with his napkin and gazed upon Kathryn with adoration. "She swooped down on me like an angel out of the darkness and saved my life."

"Honestly, Luc," Kathryn disagreed, as she leaned back in her seat to escape his misinterpretation of the truth. "You practically landed in my lap. What else could I do?"

Luc raised a challenging brow. "Did you save my life?"

Kathryn crossed her arms, unable to deny it.

"Like I said—" He turned to Jenny, the only one at the table who didn't know the story. "We met in London in '40. It was—"

"Wait a minute," Kathryn interrupted. She leaned over and put her arm around his shoulder. "Ask him what he was doing in London."

"What were you doing in London?" Jenny dutifully inquired.

Luc smirked at Kathryn. "I was getting pissed in a pub."

She punched him playfully in the arm for downplaying the reason. "This darling boy was so anxious to get into the war that he dropped out of Cambridge and joined the RAF."

Dominic made a grunting sound at his son's decision, but he couldn't hide the pride in his eyes.

Jenny raised her brow, impressed.

"Anyway," Luc drew out, dismissing his short stint in service to the King. "It was the beginning of the Blitz. The air raid sirens started screaming, so off to the Tube I go—the Underground, you know?"

Jenny nodded.

"I had just exited the lift down to the platform stairway when *boom!*" He snapped his fingers. "Lights out."

A German bomb had made a direct hit on the station. The explosion funneled down the elevator shaft like a train unleashed from hell, pulling the walls down in its wake.

"I woke up in the dark, cradled in someone's arms. I felt like my head had been split in half." He looked back to Kathryn. "She saved my life."

Kathryn lowered her eyes. The truth was a little less noble. If she allowed herself, she could still remember the ringing in her ears, the taste of the gritty slurry of airborne debris in her mouth, and the acrid smell of smoke and explosives poisoning her lungs. She wasn't a hero, and she wasn't brave. She was trapped in unnerving blackness with a bleeding stranger, and the whole world had evaporated around her. She was terrified and on the verge of hysterics. If she could have escaped from the man thrown on top of her as she hit the bottom of the stairs, she would have, but she was pinned down by his dead weight, and she couldn't move.

Between the foul air and the warm mass on her chest, she could hardly breathe. She panicked and struggled to free herself as fear devoured whatever courage she had left. She cried out for help, but there was none to be had. In the black void, tactile reminders of her plight were within reach on all sides: hard, soft, sharp, dead. The sound of bombs and falling debris continued sporadically, and she wondered if the next sound of shifting rubble would mean her demise.

The wounded stranger lay across her like a spent lover, and she could feel the sticky warmth of his life seeping onto her chest from a wound to his head.

She was in a tomb of the dead and the dying, and she had to escape. She was not one of them. She was very much alive, and though battered, relatively unharmed. She pushed with all her might to move her unwelcome load but made no progress. Realizing no one was that heavy, she reached around the stranger's muscular shoulders and found a large slab of concrete across his back that was trapping them both. She continued to struggle out of sheer stubbornness, but the futility of the situation finally reduced her to tears. Giving up, she closed her eyes and wept.

With her eyes closed, the darkness made sense. She had shut out the incomprehensible void and replaced it with one of her own making. It calmed her immediately. She had wrested a small measure of control from the unknown and restored her equilibrium. Soon, fear and despair turned to anger, and she cried out in frustration, giving the universe fair warning.

"I am not going to die here!"

"Neither am I," a weak voice mumbled into her chest.

That was her introduction to Luciano Vignelli.

Amid the death and destruction, she had found a purpose. Saving his life became her focus. Maybe it was the guilt of thinking only of herself in the first disorienting minutes of the nightmare, or maybe she didn't want to die having not made a difference to someone—anyone, or maybe she just didn't want to die alone. In any case, her reasoning was secondary to her resolve. Her last day would not be spent cowering in a hole in the ground, defeated by the German war machine. She was going to do everything in her power to save this man and herself.

She used Luc's necktie as a makeshift bandage for his head, and together, they managed to slide out from under the gentle arch of a ten-foot section of stairway ceiling that was intact and supported on one side by the steel handrail.

They dragged themselves along an open path that led them to the far wall, where Kathryn propped herself up and held Luc protectively in her arms, his weight now a comfort.

The wall seemed to be breathing above their heads, as warm wisps of air, filled with the smells of the main tunnel below—the electric rail, the huddled masses—promised to spare them suffocation for the time being. They were the only survivors in their stairway section of the station, and they would spend eighteen hours trapped in the pitch black void of their concrete crypt, relying on each other for company and sanity.

In their sight-deprived isolation, touch became their anchor and words became their lifeline when the oppressive nothingness seemed too much like death itself. They confessed sins, great and small, and found darkness an impartial judge.

Eventually, their occasional rapping on a pipe running up the wall beside them was answered, and they knew it would only be a matter of time before the beleaguered rescuers would reach them.

By the end of their ordeal, the level of comfort and familiarity made it hard to believe they hadn't known each other their entire lives. Their friendship continued, as they spent the next few weeks convalescing in the English countryside, far away from the war, at the ancestral estate of Luc's lover.

If there was such a thing as halcyon days during a war, those would have been it. She would recall them fondly as the last true carefree days she'd spend before she resumed the original purpose for her trip to London: a meeting with a British SOE operative set up by Juliette to prepare for her special mission. The betrayal had already been set in motion, and her experience in the Underground would soon seem like a picnic on the Thames compared to what was to come.

Kathryn vaguely heard Luc finishing up their rescue story as she looked over to see Jenny smiling proudly at her. Dominic's son had a flair for the dramatic, and only he could make a necktie around the head and a game of sit tight and wait sound like a heroic feat. Kathryn chuckled and shook her head at him.

"Let's just say we saved each other and call it even, shall we?"

He shrugged. "Suit yourself, but we all know you, so why don't we let your modesty speak for itself, hm?"

Kathryn waved a dismissive hand at the table of knowingly nodding heads and left them to their illusions.

It was a good evening—the closest thing to a family get together she'd had in ages—and she considered herself lucky to be so loved and in such fine company. It was all the more special because Jenny was included and their relationship was silently, but respectfully, accepted.

As she drove, Kathryn got so lost in her thoughts and memories that she realized they were halfway home and Jenny hadn't said a word.

"Hey—" Kathryn tugged on her hand. "Everything all right?"

"Mm-hm." Jenny smiled.

Kathryn eyed her suspiciously. "Sure?"

Jenny nodded. "Nice evening."

Something was amiss, Kathryn could tell, and to her mind, it could only be one thing. "I'm sorry about tonight. I know we had plans, and I didn't really even ask—"

"Oh, Kat, no." Jenny halted the apology with a raised hand. "I'm thrilled to finally meet Luc. He's a swell fella. I like him a lot."

Kathryn had three favorite people in her life, and two of them were going to get along famously. She was delighted. "I'm glad."

Jenny smiled but still stared blindly ahead.

"You sure you're all right?"

Jenny nodded, but Kathryn saw her clasping her hands tightly in her lap, as if she was willing herself not to say what was on her mind. She knew the silence wouldn't last much longer.

"Does he know everything?" Jenny asked tentatively. "About you? Who you work for? What happened over there?"

As Kathryn suspected, all was not fine. Jenny's insecurity surprised her. After all they had shared, how could Jenny be jealous? How could she not know the depth of her love for her and how everything and everyone else paled in comparison?

She was the one staring at the road ahead instead of answering, and she used the brief pause to come to grips with her failure to communicate to the one person she thought she had given her all.

The situation could have been amusing if it weren't so confounding. Luc knew nothing of her life, really. He knew what she wanted him to know, and her lies of omission began the day they met. As they waited in the dark for any sign that they might be rescued, he tried to stay conscious by reminiscing about his childhood. When it was her turn, Kathryn painted her young life as a happy one, for that is how she wished it in the end. The truth at that moment was unimportant. She had long ago learned to create a life she never had, to live in a world of her own design, and to become someone other than who she was. It was liberating, and she embraced it fully.

Once they were convalescing, she admitted her less than honest recollection of her youth and apologized without going into detail about the tragic truth.

He simply shrugged and said, "Sometimes we just have to make life what we need it to be at any given moment."

He didn't question her need to be less than straightforward, and it was never mentioned again. That was Luc and the nature of their relationship: deep and shallow, all at the same time. For all she knew, his secrets were as dark as hers. They were what they needed to be for each other, and that was more than enough.

Her relationship with Jenny was so much more than that. She had to know that. She had to.

"No. Luc doesn't know. He knows something traumatic happened, but he doesn't press it. He knows I'm not just a singer at a club, but he doesn't press that either."

"Unlike me, who makes you relive every horrific detail."

Kathryn pulled off to the side of the road. Things were worse than she thought.

"Hey," she said, reaching over to cup Jenny's face. "What gives?"

Jenny tried to look away.

"Hey," Kathryn said again sternly. "Say what's on your mind." She waited on the nonexistent reply and then realized her anxiety might be misconstrued as anger. "Please."

Jenny chewed on her words, and Kathryn imagined only their bitter taste forced her to spit them out. "It's just that I—we had to work so hard for us. It's like this man just—exists, and he's got your heart."

Kathryn dropped her hand. Jenny didn't understand her at all. The one person she cherished more than anyone hadn't a clue. She vacillated between anger and disappointment, mostly at herself for actually thinking she'd done pretty well at this relationship business.

"It's not Luc," Jenny went on. "I adore him. I understand the attraction completely. I just—" She shook her head, unable to justify her emotions, even to herself. "I'm sorry. I don't know what's wrong with me. I—" She gave up trying to explain and buried her face in her hands, thoroughly ashamed.

Kathryn slid across the front seat of the car and took Jenny's hands in hers. "Oh, Jenny. Luc lets me be who I *want* to be ... just an average girl who grew up to sing in a fancy nightclub. It's such a relief—"

"As opposed to being with me, which is—"

Kathryn squeezed the hands in hers. "Stop." She found repentant green eyes and made sure they held her gaze. "You let me be who I *am*. That gives me such peace."

That someone could know her truth—all of it—and still find her worthy of love seemed so inconceivable, yet before her was the living proof of her good fortune. Her heart swelled with admiration and gratitude, and the unexpected rush of appreciation made her place her hand on her chest to contain it. She was overwhelmed by the intensity of feelings so foreign that she felt suddenly possessed by another person. Tears filled her eyes as she gave in to the avalanche of emotions, and she wished she were a poet, armed with grace and insight and the skills required to speak eloquently from the soul. But Jenny didn't fall in love with a poet, and Kathryn could only hope Jenny could see the depth of her adoration in her eyes.

"I don't have the words to express what that means to me."

Jenny squeezed her hand back, as her tears bravely fell where Kathryn's feared to tread.

"Ignore me. I'm being utterly ridiculous."

Kathryn brushed a tear from her cheek. "I know it's been hard, and for that I'm sorry. I can't even promise it will get easier—"

Jenny put a finger to Kathryn's lips, silencing her, and then followed it with a gentle kiss. "I told you I'll never doubt your love for me."

Kathryn chuckled, more out of relief than humor. "Can I have that in writing?"

Jenny drew a heart on Kathryn's chest and sandwiched it between their initials.

Luc's leather bag sat packed and waiting beside the front door of his apartment. Kathryn carefully draped his short uniform jacket atop it and rejoined him on the couch, settling back into the crook of his outstretched arm to await their inevitable separation.

"It's almost cruel that you come back to us for such a short time."

He smiled. "That's what Dad said."

She put her head on his chest and relished the steady beat of his heart—constant, like his friendship, no matter the distance or time spent apart. Dominic would arrive shortly to accompany him to his train, so she closed her eyes and savored their last few minutes together.

"Please be careful, Luc."

He lifted her chin and smiled into her concerned eyes. "We're going to grow old together, you and I. When we met, it was fate. No silly little war *dare* interfere with that."

She smiled as best she could. Fate hadn't been particularly kind to her. She laid her head back on his chest and closed her eyes again, knowing every heartbeat measured the dwindling moments until his departure.

"I'm not going to see you off."

He tightened his hold around her shoulders. "I know."

There was nothing more to say about parting. War was a merciless mistress who took without warning or design, and they were too schooled in her wanton ways to pretend she had no interest in them.

Luc refused to succumb to silent melancholy. "I'm so happy you found Jenny."

Kathryn smiled. She imagined he was relieved to see her happy. When he last saw her, she was departing London on her way back to America to rebuild her life, and she was a shell of the vibrant woman he had met months earlier.

"She's something, isn't she?"

"She's definitely done something to you. I'll love her forever for that."

Kathryn smiled wistfully. "Me too."

"She seems to have gotten past her jealousy."

Kathryn lifted her head.

Luc laughed at the expression on her face and eased her head back onto his shoulder. "Yes, it was that obvious."

"She's a passionate woman," Kathryn offered by way of an excuse, but then she shook her head. "You're a gay man. You're no threat to her. She knows that." And while she was on the subject of jealous friends— "You're no threat to Smitty either, for that matter."

"Ugh, Smitty," Luc groaned. "He hasn't changed."

"Now, now." She patted Luc's chest in Smitty's defense. "He's a good man."

Luc must have sensed something in the restraint of her reply. "But?"

Kathryn sat up slowly and shook her head. "Smitty's in love with me. He always has been."

"I'm in love with you," Luc countered softly, taking her hand.

His adoring eyes mirrored his words, and Kathryn cupped his handsome face in silent reciprocation.

"But I'm not your life. Smitty—" She exhaled, mildly exasperated. "You know I love him dearly—more than he'll ever know—but to let him in would be to encourage him, and that would be cruel. I can't give him what he longs for. He's invested so much of his life in me, and I can't be responsible for his happiness. I'll only make him miserable. He needs to let go and move on."

"And what are you doing about that?"

"I'm working on it."

Luc raised his brow, and Kathryn knew he couldn't fathom how she would sort that out. She couldn't either. She only knew it was something she had to do.

Just like reassuring Jenny that she means everything to her was something she needed to do. She admitted to Luc that she was confounded by her jealousy, and he laughed.

"Everyone wants to feel special. You're a pretty low-key gal. I'm sure she was just surprised to see you so—" He paused, evidently unsure how to describe her exuberance.

"Happy?"

"Okay, happy."

It was the second time in as many days that the depth of her devotion had been called into question.

"See, that's not right. She makes me happy ... happier than I've ever been. When I'm with her, all this madness melts away. She means so much to me. And try as I might, I don't seem to be able to impart that to her. I'm not sure what to do."

Luc's crooked smile told her he loved her in love, happy at last.

Kathryn playfully slapped him on the arm. "Stop grinning at me like an idiot and help me."

His reply was simple. "Do what you do best."

She looked at him as if the meaning to life had just fallen out of his mouth. Wheels in her head turned, and she knew exactly what to do.

"Thank you. I will."

CHAPTER TWENTY-TWO

*J*enny looked at the clock on the mantle and paced nervously past the burning candles on the coffee table in front of her large leather couch. Kathryn was late. In her defense, she had called and said she'd gotten hung up unexpectedly on an errand, but that was an hour ago. Surely she would have called again if she was going to be later than that. Dinner was already beyond edible, and now worry was superseding any annoyance she may have had.

She was blowing out the spent candles when she heard the car door slam. She ran to the door, with her long house robe brushing against her velveteen slacks as she made the sharp turn into the foyer. She flung open the door and stood in the doorway, as Kathryn grabbed her oversized handbag and rushed up the steps, with a hand already in the air in apologetic surrender.

Jenny put her hands on her hips in annoyance, once worry was vanquished. "You'd better have dinner in that bag, because ours is in the garbage."

"I'm sorry, honey." Kathryn gave her a peck on the lips and handed over a bottle of wine as she stepped over the threshold and then quickly slipped out of her shoes. "I hear PB and J goes well with that," she joked.

"Kat, where have you—" She looked at the Bordeaux in her hand and then up at Kathryn's retreating back as she passed through the foyer on her way to the bedroom. "Where the hell did you get a Haut-Brion?"

Kathryn smirked diabolically over her shoulder and then disappeared from view. "Connections."

Jenny shook her head and shut the front door. If Kathryn thought she was going to be bought with a fancy bottle of wine ... "Where have you been, Kat? I've been worried sick. Dinner is—"

Jenny found her lips suddenly occupied as Kathryn appeared again, sans dress, and captured her mouth in an intimate plea for forgiveness.

Jenny reflexively ran her hand up Kathryn's slip-encased hip and melted into her sensuous kiss with a pleasurable moan.

Kathryn pulled back with a confident smile, but within seconds, she found she'd underestimated her powers of persuasion, when Jenny regained control of her weakened knees and picked up where she'd left off.

"Dinner is ruined, Kathryn. You promised you wouldn't be long."

"I'm really sorry, honey." She produced a large flat envelope from behind her back—a peace offering. "I made you a gift." Her eyes twinkled and her voice lifted with the promise of something worthwhile.

Jenny slumped in exasperation, finding it hard to be angry. "I don't need gifts. Just get home for dinner on time, please."

Kathryn pulled back the envelope with overexaggerated disappointment. "You don't want the gift?"

Jenny deliberated, albeit halfheartedly.

"You *made* me a gift?"

"Sort of."

Jenny exhaled her impatience.

Kathryn smiled and kissed her on the forehead. "You think about it. I have *got* to shower. I've been in a room filled with ... well ... you'll see. Give me five minutes."

She darted into the bedroom, gift in tow, and left Jenny alone in the hallway to contemplate her failed disciplinary skills.

Jenny let her unspoken protest dissipate into the sound of the running water and weighed the extravagant bottle of wine in her hand. She shook her head and savored the taste of Kathryn on her lips. "God, I love that woman."

Kathryn soon emerged from the bedroom wrapped in her sleek burgundy full-length robe as she twisted her damp hair off her shoulders with one hand and pinned it up with the other.

Jenny sat back on the couch and crossed her legs, marveling at Kathryn's feminine elegance. Kathryn pulled the large envelope from under her arm and sat opposite her on the coffee table. Jenny noticed her playful mood had been replaced with one more reflective, and she wondered what could have happened in the last few minutes to instigate such a dramatic shift.

She leaned forward. "What is it?"

Kathryn set the thick envelope beside her and took her hand. "First, I'm truly sorry about dinner."

"I'm not really mad."

"Second, I know I'm not the most demonstrative person in the world when it comes to expressing how I feel to the people I care about."

"Wait a minute," Jenny interrupted. "If this is about the other night, I told you, it's not you, it's—"

"So,"—Kathryn cut her off as she presented the large beige envelope—"I made this for you, and if ever you need a reminder of how I feel and how much you mean to me ..." She pushed the envelope closer, until Jenny reluctantly accepted it.

"This isn't necessary, baby. I know how you feel."

"You don't want?" Kathryn playfully tugged the gift back toward her.

Jenny smiled, glad to see the humor return. "Of course I want."

She opened the flap and peered inside, and then gazed at Kathryn in befuddled adoration as she slid the twelve-inch black disc from its sleeve. "It's a record."

The record sported a red, white, and blue label, with V Disc written in bold letters and a disclaimer from the War Department of the United States claiming ownership of all content. Jenny held it up. "Roosevelt's fireside chats?"

"No, silly." Kathryn grinned as she took the record and stood. "I recorded a song for you. Two, actually."

Jenny swiveled in her seat as her eyes followed Kathryn to the phonograph console behind the couch. "But there's a ban on recording music because of the strike."

"Well," Kathryn drew out as she held up the 78, "you see this label?" She pointed at the V Disc logo. "A friend of mine is heading up a new project that will send new music to the boys overseas. The AFM has given special clearance to the War Department to allow the sessions and distribute these recordings." She lifted the cherry veneer cabinet lid and slid the record onto the turntable spindle. "So, I volunteered to provide backup vocals on occasion ... that's why I was late, sorry again ... and, in exchange, he let me borrow the band and some studio time."

She switched on the player and carefully set the needle on the edge of the spinning disc. After a few audible pops, the needle found its groove, and violins swelled like a wave of lilting flowers, creating the perfect introduction to a song of love and devotion.

Kathryn slid in behind her on the couch and pulled her close, wrapping her long arms around her. Jenny relaxed into her welcoming embrace, and her body hummed with approval as the warmth of Kathryn's tall form pressed against her and made them one.

"Close your eyes," Kathryn whispered in her ear. Jenny dutifully complied and leaned in to the kiss planted below her ear. Her bliss was tempered by a niggling thread of guilt that her irrational insecurity had manifested itself as doubt in Kathryn's mind. She didn't doubt Kathryn's love; on the contrary, she saw it every day, in every stolen look, every intimate touch, every confession of the soul. Jenny couldn't explain her jealousy about Luc. It came from a place deep within, vicious and unbidden. Somewhere in the dark recesses of her psyche lurked a spoiled little creature, pissing in a corner to bolster her floundering ego.

Kathryn mercifully pardoned her weakness, maybe even appreciated the voracity of it. Such passion could not exist without love, after all ... that is what she told herself to make herself feel better.

Enveloped in Kathryn's arms, Jenny had never felt safer, more loved, or more in the right place, with the right person. They complemented each other perfectly.

If she needed any further proof that their love was here to stay, she need only get lost in the most intimate gift she'd ever been given. Kathryn's love song was like a mirror held up to her soul. The tune was unfamiliar, but the words could have been written by her own heart.

Ever since their reunion on the island, where Kathryn bravely revealed the depth of her love, Jenny's own feelings had blossomed. Kathryn's confession had given her heart permission to soar.

Before that, Kathryn had been a fantasy, a waking dream, something to believe in because she wanted it so badly that she couldn't bear not to. But in the back of her mind, she knew that what made Kathryn so special also made her dangerous. She was an exquisite woman who could have anyone simply because she wished it. Perfect strangers would fall under her spell armed with nothing more than a fantasy of their own and a devilish twinkle from those endless blue eyes.

It wasn't that Jenny consciously waited for the day Kathryn would turn her affections elsewhere, but fantasies are just that, and reality has a way of exposing dreams that are too good to be true. When their affair had ended, Jenny thought reality had caught up with her and chastised her in the most spiteful way for ignoring it.

Only after, when she'd so readily accepted that she'd merely been used, did she realize she'd been waiting for the inevitable end. She had loved with abandon each day like it was the last, and when she'd thought it was over, she could only shake her head and tell herself *I told you so.* It was comforting. She didn't have to mourn what was never real.

But it was real, and the fantasy paled in comparison to reality. One of the great, wonderful mysteries of life was that Kathryn Hammond had lost her heart to her. More and more, Jenny gave herself over to a love she'd only imagined possible in her dreams. With each passing day, that love grew, but this time it was not with the frantic urgency of a castle built on shifting sands but, rather, to a deep, profound need to surrender to a force greater than her own will.

She had an insatiable desire to be everything to Kathryn: her rock, her shelter, her last. Anything less would be an injustice to the devotion that had invaded her soul and taken over her reason. Kathryn's song echoed the same, and though Jenny sensed that love every day, the physical manifestation of it, in the divine magic of melodic strings and the luscious timbre of Kathryn's delivery, held her spellbound in a wave of sensations that pulled her closer than ever to the woman she loved. Kathryn's voice, one she thought she knew so well, took on an intimate clarity she had never heard before. Jenny could have attributed it to the studio setting or the tonal warmth of the tube-driven phonograph console, but she preferred to think it was because their souls were singing as one. At that moment, they were physically and spiritually closer than they had ever been, and she never wanted it to end.

Kathryn hoped her gift was enough. It wasn't much, just a song, but it said everything she felt in her heart and was somehow unable to articulate. In the studio, she had the luxury of multiple takes, but she chose the first one, as it seemed the truest to her heart. She had to admit, she'd never sounded better.

The flawless strings swelled to the finale, and Kathryn sealed the ensuing silence with one more kiss to the nape of Jenny's neck before reaching to save the phonograph needle from label groove purgatory.

Jenny held her fast as they listened to the needle grind until it was mercifully silenced by the automatic record arm disengaging the turntable. Kathryn took her immobility as a good sign, and she smiled and pressed her head against Jenny's in relief.

"Do you know?" she whispered.

Jenny reached back and laid an affirming hand on her cheek. "I love you so much right now."

It was just what Kathryn wanted to hear. In an uncertain world, no matter how strong the bond, a physical reminder could bridge the gap between the mind and the heart when even the principles didn't realize there was a space.

"Promise me something," Kathryn began.

"Anything."

"Remember this moment ... whatever happens ... remember this moment and how much I love you."

Jenny twisted in her arms, concern knitting her brow. "What do you mean *whatever happens*? Kat, what's—"

Kathryn silenced her with a reassuring kiss. "It doesn't mean anything. Just remember that you're a part of me, and I will love you always. Promise?"

Jenny turned fully and returned the kiss, cupping Kathryn's face in her hands. She pulled back and looked into her eyes. "Of course I promise."

Kathryn smiled. "Thank you."

Jenny chuckled and shook her head, sliding down in Kathryn's lap to rest her head on her chest. "That's a silly thing to thank me for. I couldn't forget this feeling if I tried. Not that I would want to."

Kathryn tightened her embrace. Mission accomplished. "Good."

They lay in contented bliss for a few glorious minutes, until Jenny lifted her head. "What's on the other side?"

Kathryn momentarily thought it was a commentary on the mutual feeling that they could both die right then and there and be perfectly happy, but she realized it was about the other side of the record.

"Ah. I recorded "Clair de Lune" on the piano, for those nights when I'm not here. You can put on the record and I'll serenade you to sleep in absentia."

Jenny smiled and tangled her fingers in Kathryn's talented digits. "I love listening to you play." She was silent for a moment and then blurted out, "What do you think about moving in here?"

Kathryn froze except for her eyes, which were darting around the room like she'd never seen it before. It was one of those questions like, *"Do you love me?"* It required an immediate response, and paralyzed indecision was not one of the better choices. It wasn't that she was indecisive—she would love nothing more than to live with the woman she cherished—but there were other considerations. She had no assignment at the moment, but one could come up at any time, and it might require that she live at her own apartment. She fully expected Jenny to be offended by her silence, maybe even hurt, but she could only manage to utter "Uh ..." in reply.

To her relief, Jenny laughed into her chest.

Trying to gracefully recover, Kathryn merely stated the truth. "I can't give up my place."

Jenny calmly shrugged and looked up. "I'm not asking you to give up your place. Just live here while you can. It wouldn't be much different than our arrangement now, except we'd be less nomadic, and there'd actually be food in the fridge."

Kathryn wanted to, and her widening grin gave Jenny hope.

"Come on, Kat. I think we can find some room in this big ol' mansion for a shoebox filled with personal possessions and a few white shirts."

Kathryn threw her head back in laughter and then playfully tickled the giggling woman in her lap.

"Is that what you think of me? A shoebox worth of stuff and some white shirts? I'll have you know, I have an extensive hat and shoe collection too!"

Jenny grinned and patted Kathryn patronizingly on the hand. "I'll clear off a *whole* shelf in the closet."

"In that case ..." Kathryn softened her demeanor and tenderly kissed her new roommate on the forehead. "I'd love to."

Jenny smothered her in a hug. "Thank you for saying yes." She pulled back and gazed into Kathryn's smiling blue eyes. "And thank you for my beautiful gift. I promise to make you a really grand house-warming gift when you bring over your shoebox."

Kathryn guided a lock of blonde hair behind Jenny's ear. "You are my beautiful gift."

"Mm." Jenny leaned in and kissed her. "You are deliciously romantic."

Kathryn chuckled. "Shock."

"Stop. You made me a record." She retrieved the thick cardboard sleeve from the coffee table to moon over it.

"Oh, one thing." Kathryn pointed to the envelope and cleared her throat to officially announce, "I am required to inform you that disc belongs to the U.S. government. At war's end, it is to be turned in for immediate destruction."

Jenny snorted at the thought of it. "The hell you say. Just let them try to take it back." She settled into the safety of her snickering lover's arms, pleased with her dissention.

The record represented so much more than just a song. It was the gift of love, mysterious and eternal. Love had found them, changed them, saved them. They were one now. No one could take that away.

Just let the universe try to take that back. Jenny tightened her embrace. *Just let it try.*

CHAPTER TWENTY-THREE

*J*enny leaned against the doorjamb of the bathroom and crossed her arms. Kathryn was submerged in the tub, her long dark hair languidly swirling about her face like Ophelia descending to the depths. Her leg was casually draped on the side of the porcelain tub, her foot tapping out a tune only she could hear.

Jenny smiled and looked at her watch, wondering how long Kathryn could hold her breath. Quite some time, apparently, and Jenny thought she should make her presence known before she startled her and she reflexively used the bar of soap as a lethal weapon, which she had no doubt she could do.

She lifted her foot and let her shoe fall to the floor before slipping out of the other.

Kathryn sat up with a whoosh and a splash as she guided her hair from her face.

"Hey, you."

Jenny grinned and greeted her drowned rat with a kiss. "Hi, baby."

She unbuttoned her suit jacket and looked at Kathryn's wet, dirt-stained clothes, piled in the corner. "You've been playing in the mud again."

"Yeah, we got caught in the storm this afternoon at the center. I was soaked to the bone."

Jenny slid the vanity bench over to the edge of the tub and pushed up her sleeves. "Warm bath feels good, I bet."

Kathryn slid further into the tub. "Mm ... divine."

Jenny loved coming home to find Kathryn's car in the drive. They'd been living together for over a month, and she marveled at the smooth transition. She'd been kidding about the shoebox and a few white shirts, but the totality of Kathryn's possessions amounted to little more than a few boxes and a garment bag filled with clothes. On moving day, as they covered the furniture that was left behind in her apartment, Jenny asked if she was sure there was nothing else she wanted to bring. Kathryn merely smiled and said, "I know where to visit it should I get nostalgic."

Kathryn seemed anything but nostalgic in the big house. Jenny was delighted at how easily she made herself at home. She even reorganized the art studio upstairs. She hadn't used it, but Jenny sensed a new calm and renewed interest that told her she might.

They cherished their weekend afternoons down at the dock and their late evenings together. Even lost in their own worlds, they were only a random thought away. When Kathryn played the piano in the study, Jenny would stretch out on the couch in the living room with a book. Soon, her imagination would turn to Kathryn's beautiful hands moving gracefully over the keys, which would lead to imagining her hands moving gracefully over *her*. The book would be abandoned, and the piano would become a silent bystander, as they'd wonder why they just didn't make love all day, every day.

It seemed they'd been together for years, as they fell into each other's routine with ease. Today was a Monday, and it was Jenny's favorite day because the club was dark and Kathryn would be home at a reasonable hour to greet her. Finding her naked in the tub was almost as good as last Monday, when she came home to find her on the couch wearing nothing but a fashion magazine.

She smiled at the memory and picked up the soap, holding out her hand for Kathryn's long leg, which was given without hesitation. Jenny lathered up the toned limb and picked up the razor and shaved slow, precise paths through the suds on Kathryn's calf.

"Mmm," Kathryn purred in delight. "I don't think I've ever had someone else shave my legs before."

Jenny grinned. "Better not have."

Kathryn laughed, but that laugh quickly became a rapturous exhale when Jenny ran her hand up her leg to check her handiwork. She met Kathryn's darkening gaze, and Jenny's wistful grin turned into a full-faced smile.

"This reminds me of the first day we met, when I straightened your seams in the ladies' room at The Grotto. Do you remember?"

Kathryn momentarily closed her eyes. "Mmph ... do I ever."

Jenny shook her head and chuckled. "Jeez, that made me hot."

"Me too," Kathryn admitted.

Jenny stopped what she was doing and shot her a disbelieving glance. "It did not."

"No ... it really did."

Jenny's jaw dropped, and she playfully splashed Kathryn with water. "You *did* moan!"

Kathryn laughed and wiped the dripping water from her blushing face. "I did. I shouldn't have, but, mmph, those hands."

Jenny grinned seductively and carefully set the razor on the floor.

"These hands?" She eased them onto Kathryn's ankle, guided them past her knee, and finally slid them up her firm thigh with definite intent.

Kathryn moaned and parted her legs in anticipation. With eyes ablaze, she leaned forward and reached out to capture Jenny's lips. "It still makes me hot," she said.

Jenny agreed wholeheartedly, and as their kiss intensified, she found herself heading for the bathwater. She pulled back just in time and issued a playful warning.

"Kathryn Hammond, if you ruin this suit, you're buying me a new one!"

"That's one way to get a new suit," Kathryn said with an evil grin.

Jenny wiggled from her wet grasp and shed her clothes into a heap by the door. She cursed under her breath as the zipper on her skirt jammed. Kathryn motioned her over with an impatient hand. Jenny eagerly sat on the edge of the tub, expecting help with her zipper, but wasn't surprised at all to find herself dragged into the water, skirt and all.

Happy Monday!

Kathryn cradled Jenny's head on her shoulder and mindlessly traced the tight muscles across her back as they lay in bed, limbs entangled. She sensed an urgency to their lovemaking that went beyond passion and pleasure.

Jenny seemed distracted. She was focused on their lovemaking, but the lust in her eyes was more searching than wanting. Kathryn couldn't place the emotions behind it. She thought maybe she'd imagined it. Jenny wasn't one to hide or redirect her feelings, but her blank stare and unusual silence afterward confirmed something was bothering her.

Things had never been better between them, Kathryn was sure of that, so, secure in their happiness, she could only assume it had something to do with work.

Well aware that details were suffered in silence, Kathryn thought Jenny might need a gentle reminder that, whatever her struggle, she would never be alone in it. She outlined Jenny's shoulder blade with a slow, deliberate finger.

"Where are you?"

Jenny blinked and settled deeper into her embrace. "Sorry. It was a day."

"What kind of day?"

"Just—" Jenny let her hand rise and fall back onto Kathryn's chest. "A day."

Kathryn kissed her head and let the silence do its work.

"I think one of our field agents was compromised," Jenny finally said. "He sent an incomplete code to his handler."

Kathryn knew it wasn't the first such occurrence and wondered what really had Jenny so out of sorts.

"Maybe he got interrupted."

"Well, at any rate, that's never good. It got me thinking. I hope he's all right. We rely on each other so much, yet we'll never even know each other's names."

Kathryn made comforting circles on the shoulder under her hand. "Don't get too attached to those agents. Things ... well, things happen."

"I know."

Kathryn intertwined her fingers with the hand on her chest and brought it to her lips, where she tenderly kissed it. There would be more to Jenny's confession, and she would patiently wait.

Soon, out of left field came, "What would have happened had Forrester gotten wise to you?"

Kathryn was pretty sure Jenny wasn't looking for the obvious answer, which was *I'd be dead.*

"I'm not sure what you're asking."

"Where would you go? Where would you be safe?"

Forrester would have killed her on the spot for such a personal betrayal, but on the off chance she survived his initial confrontation — "I would have been given a new life. New name, new place to live ... you know, new identity ... the works."

"You could do that? Just drop out like that?"

"It's really not a matter of choice, is it?"

"Mm."

Jenny was silent for too long after that, and Kathryn imagined her pondering the reality of it. In many ways, she probably felt she *was* living a new life. Her name was the same, and she lived in the same place, but so much had changed between finding out her father wasn't her father and her family's ties to the enemy that she may as well have picked up and started over. It probably would seem easier than the constant daily reminders that what used to be would never be again and what she knew to be the truth was anything but.

"That almost sounds appealing, if it weren't for missing Bernie and my aunt and uncle, I guess." She tightened her embrace. "You would have to come with me, of course."

Kathryn smiled and played along. "Of course."

"So, how did you wind up exposed? Aren't you supposed to use an assumed name or something when you go undercover?"

Kathryn shrugged. "Who says my name is Kathryn Hammond?"

Jenny snapped her head up, clearly hoping to see a humorous twinkle in Kathryn's eye. She found it and exhaled a sigh of relief, dropping her head back to its comfortable spot. "Don't do that to me."

Kathryn laughed and kissed the top of her head again in apology. "I didn't plan to be undercover. I was a desk jockey in D.C., working for the COI when, thanks to Luc, Dominic contacted me and offered me the job at the club. I transferred to the offices here and was minding my own business at The Grotto when Forrester took a fancy to me. I was asked by the OSS to take the assignment, and I agreed."

She was grateful, actually. Having been home for more than half a year, she felt stable enough to do more than push papers in the fledgling offices of the newly formed OSS. She wanted to get back into the thick of it—needed to get back into the thick of it. She was wasted in D.C. All her knowledge and experience, and they treated her like mended porcelain, held together with suspect glue. They dare not tax her strengths for fear the pieces would crumble. At one point, that may have been true, but she had worked hard to get well, and she was better, much better.

She was thrilled when given the opportunity to relocate. With Luc's recommendation, and a stellar audition, she easily landed the job at the club, and circumstances did the rest, pulling her back into active service, where at least she could begin to repay her debt to the men whose lives she lost.

"What did you do when you worked downtown?" Jenny ventured on.

Kathryn had no idea where Jenny was going. "I worked in Research and Analysis."

Jenny made a small noise of recognition. "That's right." She waited a beat and then asked, "Where do they put all that information when they're through with it?"

"Archives, I suppose." Kathryn furrowed her brow. "You know that."

"Well, what about things they're storing? Like objects they've acquired, outdated information. That sort of thing."

Kathryn craned her head to the side to get a good look at her inquisitive friend. It seemed her meandering questions were not a roundabout path to a confession but, rather, a fishing trip. "Say, what is this? If I didn't know better, I'd say you're trying to get something out of me."

Jenny remained silent. Inner turmoil had been plaguing her, and the last thing she wanted to do was involve Kathryn in something that could get her in trouble. She couldn't involve her without revealing the discovery of the storage unit and how she'd disobeyed orders to stay away from it. So, there she was, stuck in her own thoughts, wishing Kathryn could read her mind so that, technically, she wouldn't have to divulge anything but could still seek her advice.

Since moving in together, things had leveled to an even pace, and Jenny had begun to take stock of her recent past and the radical changes that had taken place in her life. She'd lost and found Kathryn—this time to stay—and in that regard, couldn't be happier, but she'd lost a part of herself when she learned about her family. Self-confidence that had always been a given had taken a blow, and finding the one thread back to something real about herself led her to thoughts of her mother and the mysterious box of her belongings.

For the past few weeks, she'd been nonchalantly asking around about record archives and storage buildings, only to realize, without some direction, her search was futile.

"What's going on, Jenny?"

Jenny had to plot her course carefully. She was hoping she could just casually lead Kathryn into an answer, but that unrealistic goal fell away quickly. To explain her situation without breaking protocol would be a neat trick, but she had to try. She'd reached a dead end and turned to the one person she knew she could trust. Kathryn couldn't read minds, but she was pretty good at connecting the dots.

"Something was taken from me."

Concern knit Kathryn's brow as she slid out from under her and propped herself up on one elbow. "Literally or figuratively?"

Jenny sat up. "Both, but I'm hoping the return of one will restore the other."

"And who is this thief?"

The tap dancing would begin. "The government."

Kathryn's first response was a logical one. She worried someone had broken into the house and stolen something. Jenny assured her it was nothing like that and that she had actually given them the items. Naturally, Kathryn was confused, until Jenny explained that the property in question belonged to her mother and that she was unaware they were among the other possessions. The next logical question was why didn't she ask for the items back? She was forced to explain she had done something she shouldn't have and that acknowledging their existence would expose her disobedience.

Kathryn shook her head. "I don't know what to say, Jenny."

"Say you know where to find this stuff," Jenny said breezily. She was hoping humor would cut the grim expression on Kathryn's face, but it seemed only to make matters worse.

"I haven't any earthly idea where those things might be kept. I'm still trying to process your blatant disregard for orders."

Disregarding orders wasn't really the point, and Jenny was a little disappointed at the lack of understanding and support.

"Would you tell me where they were if you knew?"

"That's not fair."

"I know. I'm sorry. I'm just so—I'm at my wits' end."

Kathryn pressed her lips together in sympathy, and Jenny was glad she didn't scold her for her lack of judgment or remind her that she wasn't thinking ahead. Instead, she sat up and put her hand on her shoulder.

"Jenny, suppose I knew where to find what you're looking for, and suppose I told you where to find it. Then what? Are you going to break into a secure government facility and steal it?"

Jenny was silent. It sounded like a good plan in her head.

"Jenny?"

"I just want to look at it."

Kathryn's eyes widened in disbelief. "Jenny, you cannot just break—"

"I'm never going to find it anyway," Jenny snapped in frustration, "so you can save your lecture." She threw the covers back and left the bed, stalking over to the window, where she leaned on the sill and hung her head.

Kathryn came up behind her and ran a comforting hand up her tense back.

"I'm sorry, honey. I just worry about you."

Jenny turned into her arms. "I know. I'm sorry I barked at you."

They sat on the window bench and Kathryn took her hand. "What's all this really about?"

"I just need to find my mother's belongings. I know that sounds simplistic, but I just need a touchstone to her. To find myself. To fill this awful void the truth about my family has left."

The empathy in Kathryn's eyes nearly made her cry, but ever the realist, she tried to temper her expectations.

"Honey, I don't mean to downplay the importance of what this means to you—"

"But ..."

Kathryn held tight to both hands. "Whatever you find out about your mother may satisfy your curiosity, but it won't change who you are. Everything your mother had to give you, she's already given you —it's inside you, in the same way finding out about your family doesn't change what they've already given you."

"I just want to know who I am. She's the only real connection I have."

"Jenny, the fact that Daniel Ryan was not your biological parent does nothing to refute the fact that he was your father, who loved you and raised you to be the outstanding person you are. You know you were loved, and nothing will change that."

Jenny knew it was true. It was something she felt still. No matter how much she tried to deny its value because of what her family did, every memory of them led to love. Why wasn't it enough?

"Besides," Kathryn went on, "you're the most self-assured person I know. If you don't know who you are, there's absolutely no hope for the rest of us."

Jenny smiled because she knew the statement was meant to comfort her, but she couldn't help the emptiness she felt. She looked into Kathryn's eyes and saw herself reflected in her love. She was strong and whole in that sea of blue, but she feared Kathryn admired a strength she didn't possess any longer.

That strength was out there. Her mother was out there, her legacy at least, waiting for her daughter to claim her and breathe life into her memory.

She would be strong for Kathryn and would continue to find herself in her eyes, hoping one day to justify the faith she found there.

Kathryn tenderly laid a hand on her cheek.

"Honey, so much has changed for you. Give yourself a chance to catch your breath. You'll find you're still the same strong, confident person you've always been, ready to take on any and all comers for what you believe in. That's who you are, who you'll always be. And if you forget, I'm here to remind you, because I see it so very clearly."

Jenny nodded and would rely on that until she could find her way. She snuggled into Kathryn's waiting arms. "I love you. Thanks."

"Anytime."

CHAPTER TWENTY-FOUR

The band on stage at The Grotto came to the end of another tedious song run-through, while Jenny pulled in the winnings from another friendly hand of poker with Smitty and a few of the staff at the club. Tensions were high in the front of the room, as frustrated musicians bemoaned the performance of a last minute replacement clarinet player struggling with some changes to the set.

In deference to the band, whose tempers were held in check by a thin thread of professionalism, the card players gingerly went about their game.

"I'm not playing with you anymore," Bobby whispered across the small table as he threw in his cards.

"You live to defeat me," Jenny said, smirking, as she gathered up the discarded hands.

"We all live to defeat you," Smitty added to a chorus of mumbled agreements.

The phone rang, and Bobby bolted for the bar to answer it before someone threw a drumstick at it.

"Kat, it's for you," he called to the stage.

"Tell them I'll call them back."

"It's important."

"For crying out loud," the bandleader grumbled, as he tossed his charts on the piano.

Kathryn threw a "sorry" over her shoulder as she hopped from the stage. She passed behind Jenny on the way to the bar and pretended to look at her cards as she rushed by.

"Throw 'em in now, boys, you'll never beat that."

"Hey!" Jenny pulled her cards protectively to her chest.

Kathryn laughed as she picked up the handset from the bar and the band resumed rehearsal without her.

Smitty looked up as he called for another card and saw Kathryn sink onto the barstool, putting her hand over her ear to block out the noise of the band. Between a beat in the music, everyone heard her say "Dead?"

The music trailed off, and all heads turned to listen.

"That's impossible. I just spoke with him. He was—"

Jenny cast a glance at Smitty and saw the same concern in his eyes. Could it be Luc? They scanned the club for Dominic, but saw no sign of him.

Kathryn put a hand to her forehead and closed her eyes as she nodded and listened in disbelief to the bearer of bad news go on with his explanation.

Jenny got up and went to her side, with Smitty close behind.

"Okay," Kathryn said solemnly. "Yes. I know. Okay. I'll be there."

She slowly returned the receiver to its cradle.

Jenny put a comforting hand on her arm. "Kat?"

"Tommy Wallace died of an overdose in his hotel room last night."

From the stage came a snort from the troublesome clarinet player. "Big surprise. What a dumb shit."

Kathryn turned to give him a piece of her mind, but Smitty took care of it. "Shut up, you, before I cram that licorice stick down your throat."

"Oh, like none of you saw that coming."

A few of the other musicians rose to Tommy's defense, and with everyone's patience frayed, the clarinet player was unceremoniously given the boot.

Jenny returned her attention to Kathryn. "I'm so sorry, honey."

"The funeral is Thursday. Will you come with me?"

"Of course."

Smitty looked up to see a stranger pass the departing clarinet player and head straight for Kathryn. It took a beat, but he soon recognized the man as no stranger. He quickly moved forward to intercept what he knew would be a confrontation.

"Now's not a good time, Clay."

"It's the only time I've got, John. I need to see my sister. Step aside."

Jenny watched as Kathryn took a deep breath and straightened her spine, shedding whatever emotions she'd allowed for Tommy and replacing them with cool indifference. She slid off her stool and patted her watchdog on the back.

"It's okay, Smitty." He moved out of the way, and she raised her chin, and her guard. "Clay."

"Kathryn."

"Aren't you on the wrong side of town?"

Kathryn's older brother stared her up and down, and Jenny could physically feel the animosity between them.

Clayton Hammond was the masculine mirror of his sister: the same dark hair, the same strong jaw, the same piercing blue eyes, though his peered out from behind wire-rimmed glasses. He had a broad build and stood just over his sister in height. It occurred to Jenny that Smitty was brave to step in front of him, especially when he seemed so determined. It would soon be apparent why.

"Dad's sick. He's in Memorial. I just came from there."

"Sorry to hear that."

"He's been sick for a while. He didn't want me to tell you."

Kathryn leaned on the bar and feigned interest in a cocktail napkin.

"Then why are you here?"

"He's dying, Kath."

She lifted her eyes.

"Cancer," he said.

She never thought it would matter, but she felt something at the news. She passed it off as sympathy for her brother, who would soon lose the father he loved. She softened her stance. "That's tough, Clayton. I'm truly sorry."

The softening of her brother's glare signaled that her words had awakened a long, dormant bond between them. She was a mere teenager when last they spoke, and she recalled words like obstinate and irrational hurled at her like daggers. His lanky baby sister had blossomed into a mature adult, and she assumed he expected her attitude had matured as well. He stepped closer.

"Sorry enough to see him?"

"We haven't seen each other in over ten years. There's no reason to start now."

She saw her brother bite down on his disappointment but not on his rising anger. Whatever infinitesimal progress they'd made was quickly stamped out.

"He's dying, Kathryn. He's your father. You at least owe him a goodbye."

She couldn't contain her dismissive smirk. "I don't owe him anything."

"Bullshit!" Clayton's voice echoed through the hushed space. He looked around, aware that his shout had drawn the attention of everyone in the club. He moved even closer and lowered his voice to continue his point.

"He gave you life. Made sure you were fed and clothed and had a roof over your head. When you took off after Mom died, you broke his heart. It was bad enough we lost her, but we lost you too. We were a family, Kathryn. You destroyed that."

Truths, lies, and blame were swimming in her head, but in the end, she said nothing. There was nothing to say. Her father would be dead soon, and she supposed she'd never see her brother again.

She'd lived more of her life without a family than she had with one, and she'd long ago accepted that would be the way of it. Her silence, however, did not please her irate sibling.

"You're the same selfish bitch you've always been. Why don't you think of someone other than yourself for a change? Look at you—" He looked around the room with disdain. "Hanging around with hoodlums and mobsters. You think wearing fancy clothes and working in a fancy club changes what you are? You're nothing more than a high-priced whore, Kathryn, and everyone knows it. I live in this town too, you know. You're a disgrace to the family name, and I thank God Mom's not around to see it."

Kathryn casually leaned on the bar again.

"I guess you've got me pegged."

Several musicians had risen to their feet with scowls on their faces, and Dominic stood with his hands on his hips at the entry to his office. Kathryn imagined Smitty digging his fingers into Jenny's shoulders to keep her from lunging at the man.

Her brother took note of the small army of defenders and knew it was time to leave—the club, and his sister's life. "You disgust me."

Kathryn watched her brother stalk away and decided that was not the way to end things. "Clay!"

He stopped at the end of the bar and turned with his jaw set in anger. Kathryn went to him and softened her demeanor, hoping to repair some of the damage done. She had nothing against her brother and sympathized with his frustration and pain.

"I'm sorry for your loss, Clayton. I mean it." She practically choked out, "And tell Dad I'm sorry too."

"Tell him yourself." He fished a small piece of paper from his pocket and slapped it onto the bar. "Here's the number if you get a backbone. Don't wait too long."

He stormed out of the club, leaving the front door swinging wildly and the entire room holding their collective breath.

Jenny was quickly at her side. "That son of a—"

"It's not his fault."

"The things he said to you, Kat."

"Skip it. It doesn't matter." She took the note from the bar and put it in her pocket.

Jenny followed her back into the main section of the club. "Are you going to see your father?"

"I wouldn't know what to say."

She cleared her throat and headed to the stage, where everyone looked at her sideways.

No one moved as she picked up her sheet music from the floor and took her place, front and center.

"All right, boys ... train wreck's over. Let's get back to it."

The bandleader put a sympathetic hand on her arm. "Listen, honey, let's take a break, hm?"

"I don't need a break."

"I do. We're short a clarinet. I've got to rework this."

She nodded and handed him the sheet music. She left the stage, and, with a tilt of her head, motioned for Jenny to follow her to her dressing room. Once there, she made a drink and plopped down into the large wingback chair, happy to get out from under everyone's curious stares.

Jenny sat on the bed beside the chair. "You okay?"

Kathryn took a drink while she sorted that out. She was torn emotionally. She understood her brother's attitude, but her mixed feelings about her father perplexed her. She had left him behind years ago, yet now, at the end of his life, she felt the need to reach out, not to forgive, but to somehow reconcile the past—hers and his—and in doing so, give them both peace.

She put down her drink. "I wouldn't know what to say to him."

Jenny took her hand and leaned in. "The question is, do you have something to say? Once they're gone, they're gone. You don't want unsaid things hanging over your head. Believe me."

"I know that."

Jenny sat back. "Given how I feel about my family right now, I guess that advice sounds a little hypocritical."

Kathryn smiled. Their situations were nothing alike. "Nonsense."

"Memorial is close by. I'll go with you, if you'd like."

Kathryn thought about the reality of it. "I don't want to see him. I can't."

"Okay."

Her hand closed around the number she hadn't even realized she'd taken from her pocket. When she hesitantly reached for the telephone, Jenny got up to leave.

"I'll be outside."

Kathryn looked up, slightly panicked. "Stay. Please."

Jenny sat while Kathryn apprehensively curled her fingers around the black handset.

"What should I say?"

"When you hear his voice, you'll know."

Kathryn was skeptical, but she put the handset to her ear and exhaled as she stretched the tension from her neck. Her hand trembled when she raised it to dial, and she made a fist and then shook it out.

"Jackson Hammond's room, please." Kathryn stared at the floor and nervously fingered the phone cord, words dancing in her head, but not a sentence to be found. She had an overwhelming urge to hang up, and almost did, when a woman finally answered.

"Hello?"

It took her by surprise. The thought that her father may have remarried or had a girlfriend never occurred to her. "Is this Jack Hammond's room?"

"Yes, ma'am. One moment, please. Mr. Hammond—"

Probably a nurse, she reasoned, and the distraction, though brief, was a welcome one.

"Yes?"

The voice caught her off guard. It was her father all right, but even with only one word spoken, he sounded frail and smaller than she remembered. It made her feel pity and didn't bring her any closer to something to say.

"Hi, Dad." Her voice was small and frail as well.

Silence greeted her from the other end of the line, and she imagined her father had about as much to say as she did, which was nothing. She heard an exhale of breath.

"Kathy," he said gently, almost like a prayer. "How's my girl?"

She could hear his smile and words filled with hope, like a ghost from the past trying to resurrect a life long dead. She was returned briefly to a time when they were a family, in a home filled with love and carefree days. It was a painful memory in the face of reality, and it made her want to back away from the telephone. She tightened her grip on the receiver and held her ground.

"I'm fine." She paused, still searching for something to say. "I guess I don't have to ask how you are."

"Poetic justice, don't you think?"

She found she bore him no ill will, least of all a slow, painful death. "I'm sorry, Dad."

"I made my bed."

An uncomfortable silence ensued, and Kathryn could feel her heart begin a panicked rhythm as her mind struggled against memories threatening to make her feel regret. She would not regret leaving her family behind—she could not. It was a pain she had no room for. She had to remind herself, this was the man who killed her mother.

"Say—" He cleared his throat. "You know, you did real well for yourself. Your mother would have been proud."

Kathryn frowned. How dare the murderer invoke her memory! "I don't need you to tell me that."

"*I'm* proud of you," he went on, ignoring her angry reply.

It made her take the receiver away from her ear, not wanting to hear anymore. Just the thought of him on the other end of the line, trying to make up for depriving her of a mother, made her feel sick.

Jenny put her hand on her knee. Kathryn worked her jaw and tightened her death grip on the handset, hovering dangerously close to the cradle. When Kathryn sought Jenny's eyes, Jenny whispered, "Last chance."

So many emotions went through Kathryn's head, but in the end, she knew Jenny was right. It was her last chance, because she certainly wasn't going to go through this again. She put the receiver to her ear and sat up straight. "Listen, I'm sure this is as uncomfortable for you as it is for me, but I wanted you to know—"

"Your brother just waltzed in," her father abruptly interrupted. "Good hearing from you." She heard him pass the phone. "Your sister."

That wasn't supposed to happen. She wasn't finished. "No. Dad ... Dad!"

"Kathryn?" her brother said, genuinely surprised.

"Put Dad back on, please, Clay."

She heard him offer the receiver. "Dad, here—"

"No, no, no."

"Dad, yes."

"No!" came the final stern declaration.

"Sorry, sis, it's a no go."

"Well, tell him ... tell him ..." She exhaled wearily. "Forget it." What did she want to say after all this time? Did it really matter anymore? To her? To him?

Her brother cupped his hand around the receiver. "Thanks for making the effort, Kath. I know it meant a lot to him." He paused. "And to me."

She couldn't control her need to lash out. Who were these people, thinking they could just fall back into her life and heart after so many years? "I didn't do it for him or for you. I did it for me. I'm selfish, remember?"

"Fine. I deserve that, but don't be sore at Dad. He's sick. He just doesn't want to talk right now."

"Don't tell me how to feel about that man, and for God's sake, don't make excuses for him!"

"There's some emotion," her brother remarked sarcastically. "I was wondering if anyone was alive in there."

She just barely cut off a *fuck you,* but she recognized a trace of his biting humor in the remark and decided there had been enough ugliness between them. Her brother was an innocent bystander, after all. She extinguished her short fuse and slowly counted to three to calm down.

"I've done all I'm going to do, Clay."

"Then you've done all you're going to do."

His comment fell somewhere in between absolution and condemnation, and Kathryn didn't know how to respond. It would probably be the last conversation she'd have with her brother, and such an ambiguous exit line would be fitting. She was about to hang up when he spoke, his voice softer.

"Listen, about before. The things I said. I didn't mean it. But you were just standing there like a statue, and just as cold ... it made me furious. I just wanted to get a rise out of you."

"Sorry to disappoint you."

He chuckled. "No need. I eventually got my rise."

Kathryn nodded. She sensed he knew they'd never have a relationship and that this was the end. He would never forgive her for breaking up their family, and she would never tell him the truth. They had only the formality of parting left between them.

"So long, Kathryn."

"Goodbye, Clay."

Jenny was dumbfounded by Kathryn's ability to channel her emotions. When she hung up the phone with her brother, she consigned her interrupted message to her father in a letter, which she sealed in an envelope and then called to have it delivered with a bouquet of flowers to his hospital room. Her only outward comment about the whole affair was, "Well, that's done."

She finished her drink in one swallow and went straight downstairs and continued the rehearsal like nothing had happened. Jenny expected some discussion of it later, maybe a few tears, but none were shed, save the few at Tommy Wallace's funeral two days later.

Two weeks after that, Jenny would see Jackson Hammond's obituary in the paper. She looked across the breakfast table at Kathryn, who was reading the sports section, and without looking up, simply said, "I saw it." And that was the end of it.

She did not attend the funeral, nor did she hear from, or contact, her brother.

Jenny secretly clipped the obit from the paper and tucked it away. Kathryn showed no interest, but it seemed wrong to let her father's life drift into the ages with no remembrance of it.

CHAPTER TWENTY-FIVE

In the ensuing days, Jenny became more sentimental about her mother and more determined to discover who she was. So much so that, in a last act of desperation, she finally risked approaching her uncle.

She picked a day—one that would allow her to broach the subject without suspicion, and chose a pleasant dinner at his home. She reasoned he would be relaxed and his guard would be down.

"Did you know my mother, Uncle Paul?" she casually asked.

He hardly paid attention to the question.

"No," he said between chews as he cut his chicken breast.

Jenny waited in vain for some sort of elaboration, until her aunt gracefully filled the expectant silence.

"Why do you ask, dear?"

Jenny shrugged. "Today is her birthday. Now that Dad's gone, I'm the only one left to celebrate it, and I don't even know who she was, what she was like."

Her aunt and uncle exchanged sympathetic looks. Paul put down his knife and fork and smiled sweetly.

"Why, she was just like you, kiddo ... beautiful and smart and—"

"I thought you said you didn't know her," Jenny broke in, not interested in platitudes.

He looked to his wife for help, who merely raised her brow and waited for his answer. "Well, I've seen pictures ... so have you ... and, why, you're the spitting image."

"Picture," Jenny corrected him.

"What?"

"One picture. That's all I've seen."

Her uncle wrinkled his brow in confusion and wiped his mouth with his napkin. "What do you mean, one picture?"

"There's only one picture in the whole house. The one in the study."

Paul looked at Betsy, who seemed just as surprised. "That doesn't seem right."

Jenny deposited her silverware on her plate with a clank, her appetite gone. "Nor is it fair to me."

Paul was at a loss. He turned to his wife and pleaded with his eyes for a little help.

"I'm sure there are pictures somewhere, dear. Have you looked—"

"I've looked in the attic, in the cellar, through all the family albums. There's nothing. Dad kept her all to himself, like he was ashamed of her or something."

Her uncle frowned at the accusation. "Now, see here, young lady—"

Betsy put her hand on his forearm to still him, then turned back to Jenny.

"Honey, you know that's not true."

"How would I know that, Aunt B?"

"Because you know your father loved your mother very much. You could see it every time he mentioned her, or looked at you, for that matter. You were his pride and joy, Jenny, everything he loved in her and more, all wrapped up in one beautiful little girl."

Paul smiled and sat back, amazed at his wife's diplomacy. Across the table, Jenny placed her napkin beside her plate and abruptly excused herself.

Paul looked to Betsy. "What is wrong with that girl?"

"Honestly, Paul," Betsy whispered. She skidded her chair back and then followed Jenny into the living room, where she found her crying, holding a family photograph in her hands that she'd taken from the mantle.

Jenny looked at the group portrait, specifically into her father's kind face, and knew he loved her mother. He loved her so much that the memory of her was too painful for him, and that's why she was so absent in their lives. Jenny knew he channeled that pain into the unconditional love and pride he bestowed upon her every day of his life, and she closed her eyes as the truth of it washed over her.

Betsy came up from behind and put her arm around her shoulder and led her to the couch, where they sat side by side.

"This is the last photo of us all together before Granddad died," Jenny said between sniffles, suddenly overwhelmed by happy memories being drowned in the fetid pool of the family's treasonous betrayal.

"I know. Gran's birthday."

Paul came into the room and stood awkwardly before the two women. "Everything all right in here?"

Betsy glared at him because the answer was obvious.

"Yes," Jenny said to the contrary, wiping her eyes as she tried to sort out her conflicting emotions. "Just missing everyone, I guess. Sorry I ruined dinner."

Paul shrugged and scratched the back of his head, obviously happy the tears had stopped. "That's okay." He hesitantly moved to the couch, where he sat beside his upset niece and searched for something useful to say. He reached over and caressed the dark wood frame in her hands.

"I miss them too."

In her own emotional turmoil, Jenny had almost forgotten these people were his family as well. He had been estranged, but she saw he loved them, nonetheless. It reminded her of Kathryn, pushing her father away for so long but unable to ever really let go, and, in the end, trying to find some sort of closure that made sense of their disconnected past.

Jenny found she couldn't let go of her family either, despite what she'd learned about their deeds. They had given her everything, and she had loved them. She couldn't regret that and was glad she didn't have to. It was too hard to live with irreparable mistakes. She sensed Kathryn was on the verge of regret, if she would allow it, and wondered if her uncle had found peace with his choices.

"Are you sorry you weren't closer to them, Uncle Paul?"

Paul ran his hand across the glass, tracing the smiling faces under his fingers.

"Not much I could do about your granddad. Oil and water, we two."

He offered a warm smile as his fingers hovered over his mother's face, and then Jenny watched it disappear when he landed on his brother.

"I miss your dad. I wish we—"

He stopped abruptly, and Jenny sensed he knew there was no point in wishes. No point in reimagining the past. She could hear regret and love in his voice and was glad he didn't know about the family's sordid past. She felt a bit like Kathryn, bravely sparing her brother the ugly truth about their father to keep their relationship intact.

"He was away so much," Paul went on.

Away plotting with the enemy, Jenny silently bristled. Her OSS training tapped her on the shoulder, and she was reminded that some of the best information comes from someone who doesn't know they have any information to give. It felt odd, mining her unsuspecting uncle for clues to her family's treachery, but she was presented with an opportunity to understand how her loved ones could have betrayed their country, and she was going to take it.

"He spent a lot of time overseas, didn't he?"

Paul shrugged. "When he was younger. It was the only place to get a decent medical education in the day." He wasn't telling her anything she didn't already know, so she pushed a little harder.

"Did he keep in touch with any of those people?"

Her uncle looked at her sideways, and she had to cover quickly. "I just thought one of his friends from back then may have known my mother."

"I think your granddad was more in touch with his overseas colleagues than your dad, but I wouldn't know. Sorry."

Jenny shrugged, masking the true impact of finding yet another dead end. "Worth a shot."

Paul saw her deflate in disappointment, and he came up with what he thought was a brilliant solution to her melancholia.

"You know, kiddo, I think that big house has gotten on your nerves. Why don't you close it up and take an apartment in the city? You used to love it there."

Jenny and her aunt turned to him in unison and had identical perplexed looks on their faces. Paul rephrased his idea. "What I mean to say is, the house is a reminder of ... well, everyone, and maybe living alone in all that empty space is finally becoming too much for you."

"Thank you for the concern, Uncle Paul, but it's not the house, and I'm not alone. In fact, I have a roommate now."

Her aunt subtly grinned, having a good idea who the new live-in was, and her uncle, as usual, was clueless.

"Since when? Who?"

"Last month. Kathryn Hammond. You remember her, don't you?"

Paul frowned and sat back, obviously disturbed by the news.

"Yes, I certainly do." He suddenly looked like dinner disagreed with him. "She's a grown woman. Doesn't she have a place of her own?"

"*I'm* a grown woman, Uncle Paul, and she's living with me."

"Well, I don't think that's a very good idea."

"I don't think that's for you to say."

"I don't want that woman parading her revolving door of strange men in and out of your house, Jenny."

"It is *my* house, Uncle Paul, and I assure you, there are no strange men parading in and out of it."

Paul looked to his wife, calling for her magical logic to save the day. "Talk to her."

Her aunt smiled and patted Jenny's hand.

"I think it makes perfect sense, dear. That house is so large, it's a wonder you don't get lost in it. You should have your friend to dinner sometime."

Paul glared at her, and she gave it right back.

"Shouldn't she, Paul?"

Jenny ducked her head to hide her smile. Her aunt was a formidable woman when it came to persuasion, and her uncle didn't have a chance of winning that one.

The arguing started before Jenny even reached the bottom of her uncle's front porch steps, but the raised voices were mercifully left behind with the closing of the front door. She was saddened by her uncle's attitude toward Kathryn but glad her aunt was on her side and accepting of her relationship.

"I'm so happy for you," she whispered in her ear as they hugged goodbye. "Don't worry about your uncle. I'll bring him around."

Of that, Jenny had no doubt.

She drove home, no closer to answers about her mother, and more confused than ever about her family. Her heart, her memories, every fiber of her being, told her they were good people, but all the evidence she'd seen proved otherwise. She wondered how her heart could be so wrong. Unable to reconcile the conflicting emotions, she felt helpless and confused. She couldn't wait to get home and fall into Kathryn's loving arms, where everything made sense and her heart was infallible.

"I told you never to contact me, Mr. Ryan," Holmes complained mildly into the telephone as he sat back in his chair and propped one outstretched leg onto the corner of his desk. "Especially for something so insignificant."

"I went through the proper channels, and the request is not insignificant to me. There were personal things in that storage unit that couldn't possibly be of any interest to you."

"I will decide what is and isn't of interest."

Paul gritted his teeth, knowing he didn't have a leg to stand on if Holmes wanted to be an ass about it. He'd made a simple request for the return of personal family mementos, the box of Bess Ryan's belongings among them. He felt bad for his niece and hadn't realized how important knowing something about her mother had become to her. It made sense though, that after losing her father, she simply wanted to reach out and discover her roots. He almost felt embarrassed that his wife had to explain to him such a simple human need. There was no reason Holmes should deny his request, other than he just enjoyed turning the screw.

"And how long will it take you to decide, Colonel?"

"I'll get back to you."

Paul was left with a dial tone in his ear, and he slammed down the receiver in frustration before roughly opening the phone booth door and disappearing into the crowded train station.

Holmes smirked as he hung up on his end and buzzed for his assistant, who burst into the office with all the eagerness of a fresh soldier on the battlefield, ready for duty.

"Yes, sir?"

"Brian, wait three hours and contact Mr. Ryan. Arrange to give him what he requested."

"Sir." He turned to leave.

"Oh, and Brian—"

"Sir?"

"Work up an exhaustive report on Bess Ryan. Get me everything you can find on her." He looked up from his paperwork. "I mean everything."

CHAPTER TWENTY-SIX

*J*enny squinted through the rain splattered side window of the taxi as it pulled up to her house, only to be disappointed when the headlights illuminated an empty driveway.

Monday was supposed to be her favorite day, but Kathryn had started nighttime training at the center, and she hadn't gotten in before one in the morning for the past week. Jenny had hoped with the lousy weather, tonight would be different, but the war didn't stop for bad weather, and neither would training.

She couldn't complain too much, but she sure could use a hug after the day she'd had. Her uncle invited her into his office after work and had proudly presented her with the box of her mother's belongings. She should have been thrilled, and for a moment she was, but the fact that her uncle now had possession of the items meant he had contact with Colonel Holmes, and that meant he most likely knew about the family's treachery, if not directly involved himself. More mysteries, more lies. It seemed every corner she turned led to a secret more painful than the last, tearing wounds open again before they had time to heal.

Her uncle stood before her, grinning expectantly. "What do you think?"

Jenny fondled the bright silk scarf she'd had in her hands once before, but the wonderment was gone, lost in the realization that all hope for some logical explanation about her family's activities was gone. She let the scarf fall from her fingers and closed the box to protect the only pure thing of her family left to her—her mother—from the ugliness surrounding her.

"Where did you find this?"

"Why, it was packed away with some old stuff I haven't seen in years. Hanged if I know how it wound up at my house."

She watched him lie, easy as you please, and she tried not to flinch when he moved to her side and put his arm around her shoulder. Disappointment, on top of disgust, was suffocating her, and she had to get out of there.

"I hope you find what you're looking for in there, kiddo," he said sincerely.

She closed her eyes and bowed her head, trying to gather enough strength to leave without confronting her uncle about what she knew.

Paul ducked his head to find her downturned face. "Hey, now, you're not going to cry again, are you?"

She took a deep breath and forced a smile.

"No, I'm not going to cry."

She swallowed her revulsion as she hugged him and thanked him and got out of there as fast as she could. He would assume she was overwhelmed, and that would do. Having a history of being emotionally unstable had its advantages.

Jenny opened the cab door, grabbed her precious box and purse, and dashed through the elongated darts of rain to her front door. She could hear the telephone ringing inside, and she hastily fumbled with her keys as she juggled her purse and the box on her knee. She finally unlocked the door but stumbled on the doorsill as she burst into her foyer. The box slipped from her hands and its contents skittered down the hallway.

"Fuck!"

She threw her keys and purse to the floor in frustration and then negotiated the debris field to the incessantly ringing phone.

"Yes!"

"Where the hell have you been?" A man's voice shouted.

"Who the hell wants to know?" she shouted back, out of patience.

"Get over to the training center. *Now!*"

It took her a few seconds to connect the panicked voice with the context.

"Smitty?"

"*Now!*"

The line disconnected, and Jenny was left paralyzed, with her heart in her throat and the humming receiver in her hand.

"Oh, God. Kat."

"She's fine," she kept repeating as she pushed her Cord's V8 past safe speeds for any condition, let alone a rainstorm. "She's fine."

She had to be. She would know it if she weren't. The call was about something totally unrelated. Her mind tried to convince her body, but the pounding in her chest and the sick feeling in her stomach told her it was losing, and fast.

She could see the lights of emergency vehicles as she came upon the center, and she sped on until she came to the guard gate. Her offered ID tag was met with a raised hand.

"Sorry, ma'am, no entry or exit to the center at this time."

She mustered all the calm she possessed. "I've got to get in there, Sergeant."

"Sorry, ma'am."

He motioned over his shoulder, and two soldiers in rain ponchos armed with rifles moved in front of her car.

"Tell your men to get the fuck out of my way or I am going to run them down."

"I'm going to have to ask you to back out of here, ma'am. That's an order."

She disregarded his useless order and revved her engine in neutral, with her hand on the shift, ready to throw it into first and mow them over if need be.

The soldiers raised their weapons at the threat moments before a jeep came skidding to a halt behind them. The driver hopped out and ran to Jenny's window, hiking up his jacket collar to keep the rain out.

"Are you Jenny Ryan?"

"Yes!"

"Park your car over there, ma'am, and come with me, please."

In no time, she was on a spirited ride to the infirmary building.

"What happened here, soldier?"

"Damnedest thing, ma'am. Hazardous storage next to the equipment shed went up. Looked like the Fourth of July out here. I think a coupla people got killed." He shook his head. "Damnedest thing."

That was not what Jenny needed to hear. *She's fine.*

"How long ago?"

"'Bout an hour." He looked her up and down. "Are you one of them special nurses?"

"No. What kind of special nurses?"

"Had a whole carload of high falootin' muckety-mucks race in here on accounta the hazardous materials." He stopped in front of the infirmary, mud flying. "Down the hall and to your left is the party, ma'am. Can't miss it."

Jenny's heart was racing and her whole body was shaking by the time she got to the entrance. It was by sheer will alone that her legs carried her down the long hallway.

Shouting, crying, retching, squeaky carts, and the metallic clatter of medical instruments echoed through the halls like the soundtrack to a horror show. She hustled into a quick jog with equal parts concern and dread. She turned at the first left and could see Smitty's tall form up ahead, shifting and walking in small circles, his hands clasped behind his head, as if he were trying to block out the commotion. An instrument tray hit the floor, and he darted into the room in front of him, only to be shoved back into the hallway a few seconds later by latex-gloved hands at the end of white sleeves.

"For the last time, get out of here!" an orderly shouted through his surgical mask, "or I'm calling the MPs!"

"Then fucking do something!" Smitty screamed.

Jenny ran toward him.

"Smitty!"

He looked shocked to see her and glanced back into the room before taking off to intercept her before she got to the door.

"Jenny, wait!" He held her back.

She could hear the voices sounding more desperate in the background.

"What the hell is this stuff?" someone asked.

"I've never seen it activate this quickly before," said another.

"Shut up and get me that syringe ... and for God's sake, wipe up that blood."

Blood was all Jenny needed to hear. She looked briefly into Smitty's fear-filled eyes and broke from his grasp, coming to an abrupt halt in front of the open door.

"Oh my God!" Her hands went instinctively to her mouth and then to the doorjamb, as she steadied herself from the gruesome sight before her. Bloody towels were strewn about the floor, and masked attendants and nurses were standing around helpless, unsure of what to do.

Kathryn was lying on her side on a gurney, facing her, writhing in obvious pain and holding her chest while coughing. A nurse was holding a clean towel to her mouth, which was quickly stained with blood with every cough. Kathryn's hair was wet and clung to her red contorted face in stringy patterns. Her eyes were tearing and almost swollen shut. Her exposed skin was bright red, and a nurse was trying to apply some sort of lotion, which was nearly impossible because of Kathryn's constant thrashing.

Smitty pulled Jenny away to prevent her from entering the room, but it was unnecessary. She was paralyzed with disbelief and horror. There had been another patient in the room, but they were dead now. Jenny followed the trail of blood to a gurney sticking halfway out from behind a screen in the corner, where a blood-soaked sheet was draped haphazardly over the bulk of the body. A pile of bloody towels lay at the feet of that body, and Jenny panicked, fearing the same outcome for Kathryn. She had to go to her.

"Let me go, Smitty!"

"Stop, Jenny! We can't help her."

Jenny struggled briefly, but she knew she'd only be in the way. She put her hands over Smitty's to thank him and comfort him as they both stared helplessly through the large glass windows, into the open room.

"I ... can't ... breathe," Kathryn managed to get out between gasps and coughs. Her voice was unrecognizable, low and gravely, like walking on stones, and Jenny would have fallen to her knees had Smitty not held her up.

"Jesus Christ," she whispered.

"Here we go," said the doctor. He seemed to be the only one not traumatized by the situation. He looked at the empty oxygen tank next to the body in the corner. "Where's that damn tank?"

"Where's that damn tank!" Smitty bellowed down the hallway. An orderly nearly ran him down as he barreled around the corner with a large oxygen tank strapped on a dolly.

"Coming through!"

They hooked up the equipment, and Kathryn clung to the mask placed on her face, the only lifeline to save her from her closing respiratory passages. She moaned into the soft plastic, first in relief, then in pain, as more coughing ensued, and then in fear when the oxygen didn't ease her breathing. The nurse briefly removed the mask to clean it of blood, and Kathryn's fear turned to panic, as she realized the oxygen wasn't going to save her and it was becoming harder to breathe by the second. This was it. She would suffocate in her own blood, like Sergeant Johnson had beside her.

"Just relax," the doctor commanded sternly. "You are not helping yourself by panicking."

Then help me! she would have screamed if she could. She imagined he saw the terror in her eyes, because he softened his demeanor.

"We're going to help you," he said, as he rubbed her back. "Hand me that," he said over his shoulder as he held out his hand. A nurse quickly handed him a syringe, while another cut off Kathryn's wet sleeve.

"This is going to help you relax, and then we're going to help you breathe, okay?"

Kathryn nodded, clinging once again to the mask as she ignored the searing pain it caused against her chemically burned skin.

The doctor calmly injected the contents of the syringe into her arm and addressed his assistant. "Bring it here," he whispered sternly.

"But, sir—" The assistant eyed the dead body in the corner.

The doctor snapped his eyes to him in a warning and didn't have to tell him again. The assistant glanced at the audience in the hallway before producing a small vial and a fresh syringe from a flat brown leather case on the counter.

The doctor emptied the contents into her arm and straightened. "Keep her on her side until you're sure her airway stays clear," he instructed the nurse.

The nurse pressed her lips into a grim line. "If the blood continues?"

The doctor glanced to the hallway and then back to the nurse. "Make her as comfortable as possible until it's over." He handed her some vials of morphine from his pocket.

Jenny and Smitty watched the doctor go into the outer room and shed his mask, gloves, and gown, and wash his hands. He turned his back to them as he dried his hands and surveyed the scene before him and then tossed the towel onto the floor beside his gown and slowly emerged.

Smitty still had his arms wrapped around Jenny's shoulders, and only when the doctor held out his hand in greeting did he let her go and step forward. "What's happening, doctor?"

"I'm Dr.—"

"I don't care who you are," Smitty said anxiously. *"What is happening?"*

"This woman—"

"Kathryn," Jenny interjected.

The doctor paused, acknowledging her name. "Kathryn was exposed to something called Lewisite."

Jenny frowned. "What the hell are we doing with Lewisite here?"

"That's not my concern, miss."

Smitty looked at Jenny and then the doctor like they were from Mars. "What the hell is Lewisite?"

"It's a vesicating gas."

"Look, Doc, speak English, for crying out loud," Smitty complained.

Jenny took it for the sake of expediency. "It's a blistering gas developed by the Germans at the end of World War I."

"Like mustard gas?"

"Quicker." She turned to the doctor. "Please, how is she?"

"We've made her as comfortable as we can for the time being."

"What does that mean?" Smitty asked.

The doctor turned to him. "We've made her as comfortable as we can."

"Did you have BAL on hand?" Jenny asked. "How soon was it administered?"

"Bee ... what?" Smitty asked.

"British Anti-Lewisite." She turned back to the doctor. "Did you have it?"

The doctor blinked at her in surprise. "Yes, we did. Within the first twenty minutes."

Jenny rubbed her forehead. "God. Better within the first five."

Smitty and the doctor exchanged looks, both wondering how she knew so much about it.

Jenny peered into Kathryn's room, satisfied they'd done all they could. "What's her prognosis?"

"She was lucky. It was a relatively small exposure to the gas, and the rain helped dilute its effect on her skin until we could get her into a decontamination shower. She'll have some blurred vision and some upper respiratory issues for a couple of weeks, but that should clear up completely."

"Her skin?" Smitty asked.

"I feel we acted soon enough and that there will be no blistering. Consider it a very bad sunburn."

Jenny wandered back to the window and watched as one nurse was coating Kathryn's eyelids with some sort of salve and another was coating her burned skin, which was an easier task now that the patient was quiet.

"What else was she exposed to?"

The doctor came up behind her. "What?"

She looked at the body in the corner. "That man didn't die of Lewisite exposure, and such a small amount of the gas wouldn't cause expectorating blood. What else was she exposed to, Doctor?"

"I assure you, miss, Lewisite can, and did, cause those injuries. Excuse me." He left abruptly, disappearing down the hall.

Smitty moved to Jenny's side. "He's lying."

"Yes."

"She will be all right, though, right?"

"From the Lewisite? Probably."

They both eyed the assistant discarding his gown in the room in front of them.

"I'm on it," Smitty whispered. He watched the man leave and then turned to follow him.

They wound up in the men's room, where Smitty slammed the small bespectacled man up against the wall. "What was she exposed to?"

"Lewisite!"

He leaned in harder. "What else?"

"N-nothing!"

Smitty pulled his gun. "What else?"

The frightened man looked to the hall and whimpered, "They'll kill me."

Smitty forced his gun into the soft underside of the man's chin. "*I'll* kill you! What else?"

"It ... it's some sort of experiment ... a virus! I don't know! I've never seen anything like it!"

"But you gave her something for it."

"It doesn't work! The serum doesn't work! You saw that man die!"

He did see it. Bleeding out of every pore, it seemed. The man died in agony, and he was thankful Jenny wasn't there to see it.

He pressed even harder. "Will she die like that?"

"I don't know!"

Smitty had thought Kathryn was out of danger, but now he started to panic, imagining her writhing in the throes of a horrible death while he leaned on this worm for information.

"What do you mean, you don't know?"

"She should have died already. It's not affecting her like it did him. I don't know! Please!"

Smitty loosened his hold and the man slid down the wall.

"Please, they'll kill me if they find out I've told you anything."

"Then I suggest you get out of here and forget the whole thing."

The little man nodded and scampered to the door.

Jenny was leaning against the wall outside the men's room when Smitty stepped into the hallway, straightening his tie. "It's a virus."

"I heard."

"How is she?"

"Seems to have stabilized. They wouldn't let me see her. They're getting her ready for transport in twenty minutes."

"Let's get back."

They took purposeful strides, side by side, down the hall.

"Thanks for calling me, Smitty."

He looked at her strangely. "I didn't call you."

She stopped walking. "Well, then who—?" They both looked at each other and had the same paranoid thought. They took off at a run and came upon an empty room where Kathryn and the body used to be. They immediately headed for the exit, only to be intercepted by armed MPs.

"Come with us, please."

"Where have you taken her?" Jenny shouted.

"Come with us, ma'am."

"Bullshit!" Smitty shouted. He tried to push past but found himself the target of their weapons.

"On the floor, sir, now! Do it!"

"Okay, okay."

They settled on hands in the air and a calmer attitude.

"Just tell us where they've taken her."

"Come with us, sir, and everything will be explained to you."

They knew it was a lie, but they had no choice. They waited in an empty room for over an hour before some private informed them they could go. Due to the nature of her exposure, Kathryn would be kept in isolation for evaluation, they were told. No time frame, no information about her condition, no visitations—just a phone number to call for inquiries.

Dawn was breaking as Jenny pulled into her driveway. She couldn't remember the drive home. She was haunted by Kathryn's screams and her panicked eyes, pleading for something, anything, to be done. Jenny didn't know if she even knew she was there. She never got to say *I'm here, I love you, you'll be okay*—all the things that give hope and comfort in times of distress.

Once inside her front door, she was confronted by her mother's belongings, strewn where they fell down the foyer hallway. It was too much for her. It was all too much. The door closed behind her and she collapsed to her knees in tears. She picked up her mother's scarf and held it to her heart, wishing she were with her now for strength. She sank the rest of the way to the floor and curled up on her side, sobbing uncontrollably into a musty silk scarf as she tried to find comfort in the scattered remains of a stranger.

CHAPTER TWENTY-SEVEN

*J*enny was scrubbing the kitchen floor on her hands and knees when the doorbell rang. She'd cleaned her house from top to bottom in the last two weeks, trying to keep from going insane with worry about Kathryn. She'd tried everything to locate her, even threatening brass with writing to the president, if she had to. It was a matter of safety and national security, she was told. To hell with that. She just wanted to be with Kathryn, to see her with her own eyes and know that she was all right. Even Smitty, with all his contacts, had come up against a brick wall in his search, and she knew if he couldn't find her, no one could. When she asked, "Now what?," he simply said, "We wait."

So, she waited, but she couldn't get the horrific images and sounds out of her head. She couldn't sleep or eat. She went through her days on automatic, doing what she had to do before coming home to a dreadfully empty home, where every excruciating minute reminded her of what had happened and the pain and suffering Kathryn was going through.

Jenny called the number they gave her three times a day, every day, begging to speak to Kathryn, but each time, she was refused, with the person on the line claiming the nature of Kathryn's injuries had rendered her unable to speak for the time being.

"Then just let me hear her breathe," she pleaded, desperate for any contact. "Or at least let her listen to me. I need to speak to her. Please!"

Her pleading fell on sympathetic but deaf ears. She had received a letter after the first week. It was supposedly from Kathryn, but it was not in her hand, and Jenny couldn't help but doubt its provenance. The letter claimed she was all right, but they wanted to keep her for tests and observation to be sure. She claimed she couldn't see well yet, so she had a nurse write the note for her. She asked her to please not worry and said she missed her like crazy, and she signed it K, which seemed like Kathryn, but without actually seeing her handwriting, Jenny was wary. She had seen enough of the spy world to doubt everything and anything unless she had concrete proof, and concrete proof would be nothing less than Kathryn safely in her arms again.

Her incessant calling paid off in the middle of the second week, when she actually got to speak to Kathryn on the phone. She sounded terrible, her voice barely audible and painfully raw, but she assured her she was doing well and should be fine soon. She had no idea where she was or when she would be coming home, but the thought of it, and thoughts of her, kept her going. Their call was cut short when Kathryn suffered an awful coughing fit, and the nurse took over the phone, complaining she shouldn't be talking at all.

Kathryn managed to wrangle the phone back long enough to say she missed her and loved her and would call her back soon. It was some measure of relief to finally speak to her, but she needed to see her, to have her home, to take care of her until she was completely well.

Jenny let the doorbell go. Whoever it was could come back another time. She was filthy from cleaning, had suds up to her elbows, and was in no mood for some Joe selling vacuum cleaners.

The bell tolled on until Jenny finally threw down the scrub brush and struggled to her feet.

"For crying out loud," she complained, as she slogged down the hall, drying her hands on a kitchen towel. She yanked open the door.

"This better be—" She stopped dead in her tracks. "Oh my God."

"Not quite," Kathryn whispered, as she removed her dark sunglasses. "Sorry, I don't have my key."

Jenny fell into her open arms and held on for dear life.

"Kat. Oh my God. Oh my God," she kept repeating as she rocked her back and forth.

She abruptly let up and held her at arm's length. "Am I hurting you?"

Kathryn smiled. "Best thing I've felt in weeks."

Once inside, Kathryn put her glasses on the console table in the foyer and slowly took off her light jacket and hung it on the hall tree. Jenny watched her carefully. She looked tired but, otherwise, seemed all right, except for her strained voice. Her skin looked normal again, albeit slightly darker from the burns, she imagined, but she saw no signs of blistering or scarring. Outward appearances aside, Jenny couldn't hide her concern for what was going on inside after such a traumatic experience. She knew she was a mess. She couldn't imagine what Kathryn had gone through emotionally.

Kathryn put her arms around her again and whispered, "I'm fine."

As they stood in the hallway, Kathryn found her embrace becoming tighter and tighter. Jenny became the only thing in her world she could believe in. She tried to hold herself together, but anger at what had happened to her, fear, and the relief of finally being home, all washed over her at once, and suddenly, Jenny was the only thing holding her up. Her strength drained, and her brave front evaporating with it, she broke down and sobbed.

Jenny held her tight. "Oh, baby, I know. Let it go. I'm here. Let it go."

She did let it go. They both did. There would be time enough to sort out the bigger picture, but for the moment, they had each other.

Their tears washed away the horrors of the past two weeks, and they would sleep the night fitfully, but thankfully, in each other's arms, gathering strength for whatever was to come.

Jenny let the drawn curtain in the living room fall back into place. "Smitty's here."

"I'll get the door," Kathryn whispered, as she got up from the couch. She had spoken to Smitty on the phone, but Jenny hadn't left her side since she'd gotten home the previous afternoon, and she desperately needed some private words with him.

She opened the door and found him with his hat in one hand, a beautiful spray of red tulips in the other, and the widest smile she'd ever seen.

He kissed her cheek and embraced her gently, holding the flowers to the side. "It's so good to see you, honey. I looked everywhere for you."

"I need to talk to you," she whispered in his ear.

He backed off, a little surprised at the urgency.

She flicked her eyes in Jenny's direction, indicating it was business related, and he nodded.

Jenny approached from the living room and took the flowers. "Oh, how pretty."

Kathryn caught a whiff of the bouquet and nearly retched.

Smitty took her arm. "What's wrong?"

"The flowers—"

"Shit." Jenny took them away immediately.

"What?" Smitty asked.

Jenny was already halfway down the hall with them when she called out, "Lewisite smells like flowers."

He turned to Kathryn. "I'm sorry, honey, I didn't know. We'll throw them out."

"No, they're beautiful, just—" She swallowed her nausea and stepped outside for some fresh air.

"You sure you're okay?"

She nodded and shielded her sensitive eyes against the bright afternoon sun.

"Say, you're a wreck," Smitty joked.

"You have no idea."

Before they could talk, Jenny stuck her head out the door. "Everything okay?"

Kathryn nodded, and they all moved into the darkened living room, where Jenny played the perfect hostess.

"Can I get you something? Water? Tea?"

Kathryn saw an opportunity. "I'd like some tea, honey. Thanks."

"You got it."

As soon as Jenny was out of earshot, Kathryn turned to Smitty.

"Bouchaule is back," she whispered. "He took my blood while I was in that facility."

"What?"

She'd been in isolation for a week when she was awakened from sleep by someone taking blood, which wasn't unusual. She rarely got more than a half hour's rest at any given time, due to all the poking and prodding of the medical staff, but this person lingered long after the vial was filled. She opened her eyes, which was an exercise in futility since her vision was still blurred, but she smelled a familiar cologne, and on the off chance, uttered Bouchaule's name. The man didn't move for a second, but then he gently placed his hand on her wrist, just above the burns on her exposed hands, before disappearing. He did not visit again.

"It was him." She paused and winced at her sore, dry throat before pressing on. "I know it."

Smitty put a sympathetic hand on her arm as they sat down on the couch. "He was one of the doctors there?"

"No. The usual attendant came in after, right on schedule."

"Have you told brass?"

"No. I haven't told anyone."

"What are you waiting for?"

"I want to know what he wants, and then I want to know what he knows."

"You should tell brass, Kat."

"You don't understand, Smitty. They did this to me."

He was stunned for a beat. "What are you saying?"

"To lure Bouchaule back here."

"That's screwy. You could have died. A man *did* die. They wouldn't do that."

"Holmes would. He was desperate for Bouchaule to return. Now he has."

Smitty sat up straight, his anger growing at the possibility of such a despicable scheme. "If that's true, I'll kill that son of a bitch."

They both clammed up about it when they heard Jenny coming down the hall with the tray of tea.

They carried on, making small talk, until Smitty made his excuses and got up to leave.

Jenny volunteered to walk him out.

When Jenny got to the door, she stepped outside with Smitty and closed the door behind her.

"Smitty, does she seem all right to you?"

"What do you mean?"

"She seems ... I don't know ... distant."

"Well, she's been through a lot, and she really shouldn't be talking much, so maybe that's it."

Jenny nodded, but there was more, and Smitty needed to know it.

"I think this is all my fault."

"How so?"

"Remember when you asked me how I knew so much about Lewisite?"

He nodded.

"It was in my father's papers. The classified reports I saw. I looked it up after that."

Smitty looked around like someone might be watching. "Jenny, I don't think you should be—"

"Fuck them, Smitty," she said under her breath. "They did this to her to see if I would do anything to save her."

He eyed her warily. "Who did what?"

She hadn't worked that out yet.

"Forrester's remaining associates? German subversives? I don't know, but that was my father's virus she was exposed to. I know it. It's all too much of a coincidence."

"Your *father's* virus?"

"It was in the reports. They're trying to use it as a weapon. The Lewisite is used to prime the lungs. The virus acts much faster on the damaged tissue, and the patient drowns in their own blood, while their immune system tears the lungs apart, trying to destroy the virus."

She watched Smitty seethe as he pictured a sinister plot with Kathryn the expendable pawn. When his thought process got to the who and the why, anger turned to confusion.

"But ... she was exposed."

"She couldn't have been, or she would have died like that soldier who was with her. There's no cure, Smitty."

"Have you spoken to Kat about this?"

"No. I wanted to speak to you first. I don't want to upset her. Better she thinks it was an accident."

"Yeah," he drew out, as he put his hand on her shoulder. "I think that's the right thing to do. Listen, I'll sniff around and see what I can see. You just take care of her, will ya?"

Jenny nodded and gave him a hug before going back inside.

Smitty turned around with his hand on the back of his neck, overwhelmed by the treacherous machinations beyond his control. He put on his hat as he descended the steps, unsure of where to turn for answers.

Colonel Holmes rolled down his car window as the bespectacled doctor's assistant walked past his headlights and came to his side.

"Here's your report, sir." He handed over a manila folder through the open window.

"I'm a busy man, Saunders. What does it say?"

"It's not there."

"But she was exposed."

"Yes, sir, she started to react, but then just ... stopped."

"Then the serum worked on her."

"No, sir. The reaction stopped before she was given the serum."

"And what did Ryan do?"

"Nothing."

"Did she know what was happening?"

"Oh, yes sir. She knew all about the Lewisite, and I'm sure she put two and two together about the virus."

"And she did nothing?"

"Nothing. It wouldn't have mattered. The crisis was over by the time she arrived."

Holmes glared at the man.

"She wasn't home. There was nothing I could do."

"That was careless planning."

"I tell you, it wouldn't have mattered, sir. Ryan didn't do anything to save her, and the woman shed that virus like a dead skin cell."

"Just like Daniel Ryan."

"Yes."

"Her blood?"

"Useless, like his."

Holmes faced forward and stared into the blackness of the empty field.

"Thank you, Saunders."

The assistant nodded and walked to his car.

Holmes put the folder on the seat beside him and pulled a gun from his glove box. He stuck his head out the window.

"I say, Saunders—"

The man turned. "Sir?"

"How are your wife and children?"

"Alive and well, and I intend them to stay that way."

Holmes smiled. "We understand each other."

"Perfectly."

CHAPTER TWENTY-EIGHT

Kathryn sat at the dining room table and absentmindedly stared at the pile of get-well cards scattered over the seven-week-old newspaper bearing the false report that she'd been in a car accident involving a chemical truck. The planted story came complete with photos and eyewitness accounts of the late-night incident, and Kathryn marveled at the efficiency of the OSS propaganda department's explanation of her injuries for public consumption.

She put down her fountain pen beside the stack of blank thank-you cards and rubbed her tired eyes. She'd stopped by The Grotto on her way home from a meeting at headquarters and was met with a dressing room full of get-well wishes from all over town. There were sweet notes from strangers who had enjoyed her performances in the past and touching messages from professional acquaintances and musicians she knew only by reputation.

It was a bittersweet feeling of support, gathering up the goodwill from so many admirers on the same day she tendered her resignation to her boss at the nightclub.

Giving up her singing gig was just turning the knife that had been firmly plunged into her heart by the rest of her day.

It began with her meeting with brass, which confirmed her suspicions about being a pawn in Holmes's deadly game to bag the elusive doctor. He claimed the incident resulted from petty revenge by a disgruntled rival that was aided by a freak accident. The explanation put him above the fray and above suspicion, but she was not fooled.

"Operation Pastorius," Holmes announced ominously as he threw the open file on the table in their morning meeting. Photos of eight men stared back.

"As you may recall, last year, these men came ashore on Long Island and Florida, bent on destroying and crippling industry and transportation on your East Coast."

Nods went around the table, as the story was remembered well.

The men had emerged from German U-boats anchored off the East Coast. Upon reaching shore, they buried crates of explosives, timing devices, and detonators, and waited for instructions to proceed. One of the members was caught and exposed the plot, and all eight were captured and their cargos recovered before their plan was put in motion.

"So?" Smitty asked, wondering what it had to do with them.

"Not only were these gentlemen bent on disruption and destruction, they had planned mass panic and murder as well." Holmes slid another paper stamped *Classified* in red across the table, and it came to rest in front of Kathryn.

"Also found buried on the beaches were crates of gas canisters."

Kathryn looked up, suddenly interested.

"Yes, your canisters, Miss Hammond."

Kathryn took exception to the notion of ownership and showed her disapproval with a glare from under her furrowed brow.

"That is to say," the colonel clarified, "the canisters are the ones with which you had your unfortunate encounter. The papers you are holding illustrate the plan in which they would be used against the people of these United States."

It was in German. Kathryn knew enough of the language to make out a skeleton plan, but Smitty was the German expert. She offered the papers to him, and he shook his head as he skimmed through them.

"Good God. This would have been catastrophic."

"Quite."

Holmes took the papers back and tucked them neatly into the folder.

Smitty leaned back in his chair. "You think they were trying to finish what they started?"

"At some point, yes, but I think what happened here was just an unfortunate accident for you, Miss Hammond."

"And Johnson," she reminded him.

"Yes," he acquiesced. "Sergeant Johnson as well, of course, but it did expose the existence of these canisters and perhaps avert a larger disaster in the future."

"And?" Smitty leaned back in, waiting for something better than *it was all just a tragic accident.*

"And those remaining canisters have been directed to the proper secure depots. If that had been done correctly the first time, this could have been avoided."

The two men stared at each other. Smitty was glad his departure overseas had been delayed. He wasn't sure what was going on, but Colonel Holmes was curiously avoiding the virus issue altogether, and he wanted to be there to keep an eye on him, especially if he had Kathryn in his sights, as she suspected.

Holmes gathered his papers. "There are some interdepartmental issues that I will let Colonel Forsythe discuss with you." He snapped his briefcase shut. "That's it then. Gentlemen?" His two sheep rose in unison. "Good seeing you on your feet, Miss Hammond. Do take care."

Kathryn watched the British group file out of the room in silence. Brian, the dark-haired attentive one, offered a sympathetic half-smile as he passed.

. . .

The final report claimed no one knew how one of the crates of German canisters wound up at the training facility. They certainly weren't manifested there. They determined it was a clerical error. Kathryn could barely contain her skeptical snort. The plot was so clear to her. Watching Holmes lead the others through hoops to legitimize his scheme was merely a sideshow, doing little more than trying her patience.

After the British contingent left, Kathryn stood and turned to Colonel Forsythe. "Interdepartmental issues? That's an understatement. Please tell me you have something, because I'm not buying this resurrected plot to poison our largest cities."

Forsythe cocked his head, considering it a possibility. "Those canisters did come from last summer's failed plot."

Kathryn crossed her arms. "And the classified German document?"

"Never saw it before," the colonel admitted. "But that doesn't mean anything."

"Bogus," Smitty grumbled, as he rose to join her. "What the hell is going on?"

Forsythe chewed on the question a moment. "Something."

It was the first good news Kathryn had heard all day. Maybe now they'd get some answers.

The officer removed a box from under his desk and pulled out a large, scorched gas canister.

Kathryn backed up instinctually, her chest tightening at the sight of it. Smitty put a hand on her back as she bumped into him. Forsythe apologized and assured her it was safe.

She took hold of Smitty's arm for support, as the memory of the sickening hiss of the escaping gas seemed real for a moment and that fateful evening came rushing back.

She and Johnson had been laughing as they commiserated about the late hour at the equipment depot before all hell broke loose. She'd been surprised to see him there, but he explained he was working overtime, doing inventory, so he could take the next night off to be with his gal. It was her birthday.

They'd heard an explosion behind them in the hazardous materials room. A metallic shelf had collapsed and there was a fire in the corner. A teargas canister used for training, or so they thought, had gone off when it hit the floor. Kathryn had grabbed the gas mask from her equipment sack and put it on. Johnson opted to hold his breath for the moment as they both grabbed fire extinguishers and headed for the fire. Kathryn found her mask worthless, as she was quickly overcome by the toxic fumes, and Johnson never made it to the equipment shelf to grab one of his own. They'd screamed in pain as their eyes, lungs, and skin burned, and they'd dragged each other from the building as fire consumed it.

She blinked to find the colonel staring at her, and she swallowed the memory and released her partner's arm. "Sorry."

Smitty rubbed her back and addressed the officer. "What gives?" He pointed at the canister.

Forsythe went on to explain the mechanics of the device—the same device Smitty had seen in Forrester's papers—which was all very interesting but of no use to them now.

"The point is," the colonel explained, "normally, this is a binary toxin device. When activated, the caustic gas eats through the membrane into the lower chamber, where they mix and become the intended poison. In this case, though, the lower chamber was never filled, and the upper chamber carried very little gas."

"Enough to do damage," Smitty reminded him.

"Yes, to do damage, but it wouldn't have killed anyone. Not even Kathryn or Johnson in the same room. It was spent almost as soon as it was released."

Kathryn leaned in. "So, the doctor's assistant Smitty questioned the night of the incident wasn't lying about the virus. That's what killed Johnson."

The colonel raised his brow and pursed his lips, clearly uncomfortable with the mention of the virus. "So it seems."

Kathryn saw something in Forsythe's eyes. "Something's screwy, isn't it?"

The colonel looked away, his business face back on, and for the moment, his evasion. "Whatever's going on was done deliberately." He pulled a gas mask unit out of the box. "This is your mask, Kathryn, the one you donned that night."

Smitty pointed at it. "That gas ate right through it in a matter of seconds."

Forsythe picked up the face mask. "No. It wasn't that type of gas." He ran his hand down the ribbed rubber hose to the canvas-encased respirator pack. He squeezed the hose, revealing a slit. "This has been cut."

Smitty looked up, shocked. "Sonofabitch."

Kathryn closed her eyes. It was one thing to have her theory—to believe it, even—but to see the proof before her, to know for a fact that her health, her very life, was worth little more than someone else's desire for results, infuriated her. She looked at Forsythe and wondered whether he was part of it all.

"Why?"

He looked at his agent, wishing he had an explanation. "We don't know."

Smitty stepped forward, outraged. "You don't know? She could have been killed!" He pointed at the sabotaged mask. "Someone did this deliberately. This happened in our own backyard, and you don't know?"

"Easy, John. No one wants to get to the bottom of this more than we do."

Smitty restrained a curse and turned away before he really lost his temper.

Kathryn exhaled in defeat and sat down. There would be no answers for her today, but Smitty wasn't done.

"What of this virus? Where did it come from? Why didn't Kathryn get sick?"

The colonel looked at his agents and their stark contrasts in disposition and decided to address the less agitated of the two.

"The doctor's report says there's no evidence you were infected, Kathryn. Assuming it was an airborne contaminant, you were closer to the fire, so they think your mask gave you just enough protection and that the heat of the blaze consumed the virus before it could do any damage."

Kathryn knew that wasn't the case, and she shifted in her seat, tired of the convenient excuses. She was no closer to the fire than Johnson, and her mask afforded her nothing. She swallowed a lungful of the gas all right—that much was certain. As for the virus, well, she had her theory about that too.

Colonel Forsythe questioned her reaction. "You disagree?"

Smitty casually put his hand on her shoulder, warning her against unleashing her theory.

She ignored him. "There's no evidence I was infected, because I wasn't. There was no virus released from that canister. Johnson was infected afterward, in the infirmary—by our doctors."

Forsythe was dumbfounded. He looked at Smitty, who had turned away, distancing himself from Kathryn's conjecture. "You're talking murder. And to what end?"

"I think the whole thing was planned to lure Bouchaule back here. It would look like we were both infected, but I survived. Nothing would bring Bouchaule running faster than the rumor of a vaccine."

"Then where is he?" Forsythe shouted, obviously insulted by her accusations.

Smitty glanced at her, and she could tell he wondered if she would reveal Bouchaule's return.

She said nothing and looked away.

"I'm appalled you would even think us capable of such a thing, Kathryn. Truly."

Kathryn cut her eyes to the officer. "Imagine how I feel."

Forsythe gathered his shock and temper and retreated to the safety of his paperwork. He shifted a few papers around with his fingertips before sitting and folding his hands across them. He looked at his prized agent with pity and disappointment.

"I question your state of mind, Kathryn."

She frowned. "And what does that mean?"

He uncapped his pen and made a note in her folder.

"You're on leave until further notice."

"Because what I said makes sense and is probably the truth?"

"Because you obviously need more time to recover your faculties."

"My—"

Smitty moved in before she really said something she'd regret. He needn't have. Kathryn had nothing else to say. She'd been verbally slapped and dismissed by someone she respected above all others, someone she thought respected her, and her opinion, at the very least.

"It was an accident, Kathryn," Forsythe insisted sternly. "It would be unconscionable for any member of this, or any, agency to do what you've suggested." He paused and rolled his pen between his fingers, softening his demeanor. "I know you've been through an ordeal, but you're letting your feelings about Holmes cloud your judgment. He has been fully vetted and is above reproach."

That was no comfort to Kathryn. It merely raised doubts about the agency's vetting protocols.

Smitty picked up the damaged gas mask again, noting that Kathryn's concerns were not altogether without merit.

"Someone did this, Colonel. Someone with access at the center."

Forsythe looked at his irritated agents. "Any ideas?"

Smitty looked at Kathryn, and when their eyes met, he knew their prime suspect was the same.

"Yes," Smitty said gruffly. He threw the mask down and headed for the door.

"Smith!" Colonel Forsythe called to his back, to no avail.

Kathryn stood and picked up her purse and broad-brimmed hat from the table. "I suggest you call over to the center and get an armed guard for Lieutenant Branson. He's going to need one."

Kathryn stared at Smitty's raw knuckles as he drove her home from her afternoon meeting at The Grotto.

"Did you break anything?" she asked.

He flexed his hand. "Nah. I'm all right."

She smiled. "I meant Branson's face."

Smitty just grinned.

"You can't make me talk, Smith," Branson warned, even as he backed up in fear.

"I'm not here to make you talk, Branson." Smitty slipped off his jacket. "But you're going to wish you had, if for no other reason than you'd be out of my reach right now." He rolled up his sleeves and slammed the door to Branson's empty classroom.

He got in a few good licks before security pulled him off, but Branson sang like a canary after that. A very well-trained canary.

He claimed he cut Kathryn's mask to embarrass her in front of her students when they trained for the gas simulation that evening.

During a simulation, the group is shut in a small building with a live canister of teargas and then instructed to remove their masks, to get a feel for the situation, to learn not to panic. It's uncomfortable, to be sure, but not dangerous, and he planned to delight in the sight of her coughing and retching with her recruits as they stumbled out of the building, clambering for fresh air.

She didn't run the simulation that night, though, taking advantage of the foul weather to get them accustomed to functioning in adverse conditions instead.

Kathryn didn't know what would become of Branson, nor did she care. She was confident she had her answer. She'd been used, and in the worst possible way. Colonel Forsythe was right that it was unconscionable. She felt violated by the very people to whom she'd sworn her allegiance. She didn't know whether Holmes was acting alone or whether it was a larger SOE plot, but as Smitty said, it happened in her own backyard, under the nose of the OSS. She felt abandoned, expendable, and deeply wounded by Forsythe's rebuke.

As an agent, she always considered herself expendable to the larger picture, but the notion of dying proactively for the greater good was easier to swallow than the reality of dying as a helpless victim, a forsaken cog in a large, unyielding wheel.

Colonel Forsythe offered nothing but a cold shoulder and his blind devotion to his government's cause. Branson's confession about the mask only reinforced the OSS's position that the whole incident was merely the result of a string of unfortunate events, producing a tragic outcome, and she was left looking like an unstable woman with delusions of prosecution.

Smitty took out his frustrations on Branson and didn't say either way what he believed was the truth of the situation, but he did point out that he didn't think she was serving her cause by her outburst.

"You should have kept a lid on it, Kat."

"Maybe so," she admitted. "I just want answers."

"It might help if you report Bouchaule to brass."

"They're not listening to me, Smitty. They're not even considering what I'm saying could be the truth. That tells me all I need to know. I've been fucked by them without so much as a kiss, and when Bouchaule comes back again, I want first crack at him."

"What if he doesn't come back?"

"Then it won't matter, will it?"

Smitty looked at her sideways, worried that Forsythe was right, and that she'd been pushed too far this time.

"Do you really think they killed Johnson?"

"We were two feet away from each other in that room, Smitty. If he was infected there, I was too. But, obviously, that didn't happen. Besides, if I really did survive exposure to the virus, do you think the government scientists would let me out of their sight? No. I'd still be in that facility, and I'd still be the resident lab rat. They don't need me, because I'm of no use to them. Brass wants to keep me on leave because they think I'm crazy? Fine. Nuts to them."

It occurred to her that if the government had no use for her, Bouchaule wouldn't either. If her blood was clean, he would know it because he took a sample, which meant he wouldn't be back for her. She quickly dismissed the notion it was all over, hoping against hope that he at least had feelings for her, and that would be enough. It had to be enough.

Perhaps she was losing her faculties. It wouldn't make for sanity, plotting her moves on wishful thinking, but Bouchaule had to come back for her, or the suffering, the pain, the loss of her singing voice and career—it had all been for nothing. She couldn't accept that. She wouldn't accept it.

Smitty was silent for a moment while he married his partner's assumptions with Jenny's suspicions. He supposed Kathryn had every right to blow her cork, and he wasn't far behind when Colonel Forsythe conveniently ignored his question about the virus's origin. He couldn't deny he doubted the official report that claimed everything had been a tragic accident, and if anyone deserved to know the going theory, Kathryn did.

"The kid thinks this all happened because of her. She thinks the virus was her father's mysterious project. Actually, she's sure of it."

"Where did she get that idea?"

"References to a virus were in those classified papers. She thinks German subversives were trying to coax her father's miracle cure from her—assuming there is one—by getting you sick."

"Did she tell you that?"

"When you came home. She didn't want me to tell you. Thought it would be easier on you if you believed it was just an accident."

Kathryn exhaled and rested her head on the back of the seat. "That's going around, apparently."

"Don't be angry with her for not telling you."

"I'm not."

Her wistful smile told him she wasn't.

"I won't tell her you told me."

"I appreciate that."

·　·　·

Kathryn took his hand, thankful for the truce he'd formed with Jenny. The two were her strength now in the midst of madness, and she was glad they were supporting not only her but each other.

It made sense the virus would be the secret weapon Daniel Ryan was supposedly selling to the Germans. She'd seen enough doctors and scientists jockeying for position in Forrester's negotiations that she should have guessed it herself.

She could only assume Holmes thought Bouchaule had the key to the coded documents and that's why he was so desperate for his return.

The doctor did have something, but, apparently, not everything, or he wouldn't have come back and taken her blood. Bouchaule had all the answers now, and, ironically, the only other person who seemed to realize that was Holmes. Not exactly comforting.

She hated the man and what he'd done to her, but Bouchaule had come back, as planned, and he would contact her again—he had to— and when he did, she would be ready, armed with enough hatred and resentment to bring them all down.

CHAPTER TWENTY-NINE

Jenny shouldered open her front door and was surprised to find no lights on, which was odd because Kathryn's car was in the drive, and she could hear music drifting through the house. She would have called out but thought Kathryn might be sleeping, so she slipped out of her shoes and tiptoed to the master bedroom, only to find the bed empty. She turned on the hall lights and moved to the dining room, where she found the table and floor littered with Kathryn's get-well cards and blank thank-you cards, as if she had pushed it all aside and left abruptly.

"Kat?" she called out, a little concerned as she headed toward the music.

Jenny initially thought it was the radio and wondered why Kathryn was listening to such a somber piano recital, but as she entered the living room, she realized it was coming from the study and that it was Kathryn who was playing.

The study was dark except for a small floor lamp beside the piano, and Kathryn's perfect posture was silhouetted against its warm glow. Jenny leaned on the partially closed sliding door and just watched her play.

. . .

Kathryn couldn't see through the tears in her eyes, so she closed them and let the music carry her far away from her day and, for the moment, her life.

She was glad Jenny was working late, because she wasn't fit for human company. She thought her day couldn't get any worse, but it had, and she didn't want to see anyone or talk to anyone. She thought about spending the night at her place but loathed the effort it would take to explain to Jenny why.

She decided instead to get lost, and hopefully found, in her music. Satie's Gnossienne No. 3 was one of her favorite escapist pieces. It was melancholy to some, but she always found it soothing —haunting and ethereal. When she closed her eyes, she always pictured water ... water so deep, it appeared black and still, with silvery highlights from a mysterious light source that was everywhere and nowhere.

The notes echoed in this dark void, like water dripping in a cave. They took their time as they fell, purposeful and constant, one after another, each glad to follow the one before as they floated down to the black watery surface like fallen leaves in autumn and drifted away on the lazy, swirling current, taking her troubles with them.

Kathryn felt lost, unsure of her professional future, of her place in the OSS, and of her relationship with Jenny once Bouchaule came back. What then? What would she tell her? What *could* she tell her? Jenny said she should always do what she had to do, that it would be all right, but how could it be? She tried to imagine if their places were reversed. The thought of Jenny giving the most intimate parts of herself to someone else was anything but all right.

Kathryn feared the return of Bouchaule would spell the end for them, no matter how determined they were to prevent it. The thought that he wouldn't return was equally as debilitating, and she couldn't keep it from invading her thoughts. The music ceased to be a comfort, and she found herself desperately clinging to her water-logged dreams of a happy future as she slowly slipped below the water's shining surface and drowned in its cold, endless depths.

. . .

Jenny watched Kathryn abruptly stop playing. Her shoulders slumped and she put a hand over her eyes as she cried.

Jenny immediately went to her side and sat facing her on the piano bench.

Kathryn was startled and sat up straight, as she wiped away her tears and cleared her throat. "You're early."

Jenny took her hand. "No, baby, I'm late. Sorry."

Kathryn looked at the grandfather clock in the corner. It was half past eight. "I lost track of time."

Jenny shook her head as Kathryn did her best to pretend nothing was wrong.

"Bad day?"

Kathryn attempted a smile. "The worst."

"I see you visited the club."

She looked in the direction of the dining room. "The cards. Sorry about the mess."

"Don't worry about it. How'd it go?"

"I gave Nicky my resignation."

Kathryn had talked about it, but Jenny was hoping she'd hold off.

"And?"

"He refused it."

"Naturally."

"Then I invited him to the USO rehearsal." She absently wiped a speck of dust from the black surface of the piano. "Now he knows I don't belong at The Grotto."

"Did he say that?"

"He didn't have to. It was in his eyes. He knows."

Jenny could imagine Dominic's kind but reluctant smile when he gave Kathryn some platitude about her progress. She had gotten her voice back, for the most part, but it certainly wasn't like it was before. She'd started doing backup vocals at small pubs and then had taken to doing a few lead numbers every other night at the canteen, run by the USO, to get back into form, but she wasn't happy with her performances. Jenny always did her best to be optimistic.

"You're getting stronger every day, Kat. You'll be back there soon."

Kathryn shrugged. "The USO is fine. If I stick to jive numbers, I can fake it." She smiled grimly. "You only have to hit the note ... you don't have to hold it. Any ol' singer can do that."

"You're hardly just any ol' singer."

Kathryn turned her head. "No. I'm worse. I'm a known singer who will never be what she was."

Not one to give in to such a defeatist statement, Jenny perked up. "Well, then it's a good thing you were ten thousand times better than everyone else, because even with a bad break, you're still better than most."

Kathryn smiled for a moment, but it didn't last long. Jenny tugged on her hand, trying to coax it back.

"Don't give up, honey. You see the throat specialist in—"

"I saw him this afternoon."

Jenny stared at her. "Why didn't you tell me? I wanted to go with you."

Kathryn dropped her gaze to the piano keys. "I was afraid of what he might say."

"Which is why I wanted to be there, Kat."

Jenny exhaled in frustration, knowing it was the wrong time to be upset with her. "Well, what did he say?"

Kathryn caressed the smooth ivory surface of middle C. "There's scarring on the vocal cords." She looked into Jenny's concerned eyes. "It's not going to get any better."

"Oh, Kat."

"So," Kathryn chirped dismissively as she closed the fallboard on the piano *and* her vocal career, "disappointment all around." She stood, obviously trying to shed her lousy day before she let it drag them both down. "Come on, I'll make us dinner."

Jenny took her hand and stepped around the bench. "Baby, you can't cook."

Kathryn smiled and kissed her hand. "Okay, *you* make us dinner."

Jenny was busy preparing dinner in the kitchen while Kathryn picked up the mess she'd made in the dining room.

Overwhelmed by the outpouring of caring from friends and perfect strangers alike, and irritated by her bad day, she couldn't face writing cheery thank-you card after cheery thank-you card and had simply pushed it all away in frustration.

She smiled now as she picked up the cards. Ever thoughtful, Jenny had written descriptions of the bouquets that arrived in her absence and paper clipped them to the appropriate cards so that she'd know who sent what and could respond accordingly.

The evening was turning out better than she could have hoped, considering. News of the final report had spread through headquarters, and Jenny had expressed relief that it was deemed an accident and had nothing to do with conspiracies about her father's work. Kathryn let her go on believing that. There was no need for Jenny to think otherwise.

Kathryn was gathering the last few wayward cards when the phone rang.

"I'll get—"

She saw Jenny pick it up in the kitchen.

"Hello?"

Jenny glanced her way but quickly turned her back and spoke softly. Kathryn moved into the hallway to get a better look, but Jenny, with another odd glance, had already hung up the phone.

"Who was it?"

"Hm?" Jenny answered, as she put a head of lettuce back in the refrigerator.

"On the phone. Who was it?"

Jenny untied the apron from her waist, took her time folding it and laying it over the chair at the kitchen table, and walked down the hall until she stood at Kathryn's side.

"Jenny?"

Jenny put her hands on her hips.

"That was your brother."

"My—"

"He called from the station. He'll be here in a minute."

Kathryn was flabbergasted.

"Why? Why did you tell him he could come over? I've got no reason to see him."

"I think you should."

"You think? Did you plan this?"

Jenny opened her mouth to speak, but Kathryn was quickly feeling manipulated, and after the day she'd had, she had no patience left.

"I don't need you to be a family counselor, Jenny. If I wanted to see my brother, which I don't, I could arrange that on my own. I don't need—"

"I didn't plan anything, Kathryn, but I do think you should see—"

"And I think you should mind your own—"

The doorbell cut her off, pausing the argument. Jenny held up her hands in surrender before heading to the door. Kathryn shook her head while exhaling her exasperation.

Jenny took Clayton's hat and jacket, and, after putting them on the hall tree, picked up her purse and keys.

"Where are you going?" Kathryn asked, slightly panicked to be left alone with her sibling.

Jenny turned to him. "Clayton, your sister is notorious for burning dinner. If that meatloaf is not out of the oven in twenty minutes, you are taking us all out to eat for the next three days. I will be back in thirty minutes. Have the salad made, okay?"

The two Hammonds blinked at the closing front door and then at each other, until the eldest spoke first.

"She's ... interesting."

Kathryn said nothing.

Clayton scratched the back of his head and looked around.

"Nice place."

"Being the town whore does have its advantages."

"Aw, Kath, don't be like that. That's not why I'm here."

Kathryn crossed her arms. "Why are you here, Clay?"

He shifted uncomfortably. "I read about your accident and I wanted to make sure you were all right."

"Mm, I see. That happened almost two months ago. Glad you rushed right over."

"Cut it out, will ya? Can't you see I'm trying?"

"Trying what? Why?"

"Because you're my sister, and I want you back in my life."

Kathryn shook her head. She didn't know what he and Jenny were up to, but ... "This isn't going to happen."

"Why? Because you truly despise me or because you think I don't know Dad was the drunk driver who killed Mom?"

Kathryn snapped her eyes to him in surprise and then to the front door in anger. "Jenny had no right to say anything."

"Jenny? I don't know what you think Jenny has to do with this, but Dad told me. He left me a letter in his safe deposit box. He told me everything ... what he did, why you left."

Kathryn needed to sit down. Her world was shifting on its axis. She had given up everything to keep that secret, and, in one fell swoop, her father reached out from beyond the grave and made it all worth nothing. She sat at the dining room table in stunned silence. How much more could her father take from her? She put her elbows on the table and put her head in her hands.

Her brother sat beside her and put his hand tenderly on her arm.

"Why didn't you tell me, Kathy?"

Addressing the part of her lost so long ago made her mourn the loss of it even more now that her brother knew the truth, and she turned away from what he was too blind to see.

"Don't call me that. She doesn't exist anymore."

He regarded her sadly. She knew there was very little of the sister he loved left in her tired eyes.

"What happened to you, Kathryn?"

She sat back in her chair, breaking the physical contact. "Nothing you can change."

Clayton sat back as well, and Kathryn could see he was defeated and hurt. He longed for something she couldn't give him, and he would have to settle for something she could.

"I feel no malice toward you, Clay. I never did."

He leaned forward, eagerly. "Then why, Kathryn? Why didn't you tell me?"

"It wouldn't have brought Mom back, and I thought there'd already been enough loss."

Anger flashed in his eyes. "Don't you think I deserved to know the truth?"

"I would have given anything if someone could have taken that truth out of my head! Do you think I wanted to lose my father? Do you think I wanted to lose you? Do you think I wanted to—" She cut herself off and exhaled. The whole conversation was water under the bridge and pointless. "I couldn't bear to stay, and he couldn't bear the sight of me, and now it doesn't matter. What's done is done."

"What matters now is that you know I would have done anything to keep us together. If only you had come to me with the truth."

Kathryn smiled. Her brother seemed to have forgotten he was in his last year of college, with a good job lined up, and a fiancée waiting in the wings.

"What would you have done? Smuggled your fourteen-year-old little sister into your dorm room for the duration?"

"You let me go on loving that murderer. He should have paid dearly for what he did to Mom. To us! Instead, he got off scot-free!"

His accusation struck a chord. There was a time she thought the same, but not anymore. "He didn't get away with anything."

"And now you're defending him?"

"I'm not defending him." She looked him in the eyes and then vaguely away, feeling the hollow ache of her own battle with guilt. "Her death was his fault. He had to live with that every day of his life. Every day he took a breath and she didn't, he paid. Believe me."

Her brother stared at her, and she knew he saw unsettling traces of a woman haunted.

"What happened to you?"

She raised her chin, putting up a wall between them once more.

He would find no comfort in her past, no panacea in their reunion. They were strangers going on about their lives with the numb denial of survivors wandering through the crumbled wreckage of some catastrophic disaster.

Clayton was struck by what his sister had sacrificed for him. In the fleeting glimpses he'd had of her adult life, she seemed to have risen, unscathed, above the havoc she'd caused. It always made him furious, but seeing her now, seeing her pain, it humbled him. He didn't know the details, but he knew her decision had cost her dearly. She did it for him, all to spare him the horrible truth about their father. It broke his heart, and he had to turn away.

"Hey," Kathryn reached out.

"I ... uh ..." He stood and cleared his throat. "I left something in the car. Be right back."

Kathryn lifted her hand, as if she had something to say, but he ignored it and rushed out the front door.

Clayton opened the trunk of his car and leaned on the cold steel for support. He had let his sister down when she needed him most. He berated himself for not realizing her behavior was more than just a rebellious teenager mishandling her grief. The fact that she couldn't come to him with the truth and that he didn't fight to keep her in his life ate him up inside, and he covered his eyes to deny his tears.

He gathered himself and went back inside, his demeanor all business when he opened his briefcase on the table before them.

"There's some legal business about Dad's estate we have to go over."

"What's that got to do with me?"

He pulled out a multi-page document. "He left you the beach house. We've been renting it out during the summer seasons, but you don't have to do that. Nice supplemental income though. Here's the deed." He took out his pen. "Sign this, this, this, and this, and it's yours."

"I don't want it." She pushed the papers back to him.

"Then sell it." He shoved them forward.

"You sell it. I told you, I don't want it."

"Don't be stupid just to spite him, Kathryn. He's dead. He doesn't care. You loved that house. Mom did too. It's yours. Like it or not."

"Not."

"Fine." He capped his pen. "You think about it. Here are the papers. Lawyer's name and address are at the top. Do what you like."

Kathryn tossed the deed on the pile of unwritten thank-you cards and leaned back. She glanced into her brother's neatly organized briefcase, only to have a familiar sight catch her eye.

"That's my letter to Dad." She pulled it out and turned it over in her hand. "The one I sent to the hospital." It was unopened. "He never read it."

Her brother said nothing. Clearly, he had run out of excuses for the old man.

Kathryn sat back in disbelief. "He doesn't know."

Clayton raised his brow in surprise, and she suspected he wondered why she cared.

"You called him, Kathryn. I can't tell you how much that meant to him."

She stared at the letter and shook her head before tossing it too on the pile to her right. Closure was one more thing denied her.

Clayton took out a leather bound album and set it on the table before her.

"This is yours too."

Kathryn slowly opened the album and was met with page after page of newspaper clippings, all about her: singing engagements, occasional run-ins with the law, appearances at social events with Forrester, reviews of performances, everything that ever appeared in print, it seemed. She turned each page slowly, imagining her father doing the same as he clung to his lost daughter through yellowing scraps of newsprint. To her surprise, she came upon a cocktail napkin from The Grotto tucked away between the last two pages. She lifted her eyes to her brother, who closed his briefcase.

"He went to hear you sing ... beamed about it for a week."

She closed the album, unable to deal with her father's unconditional love, and added it to her pile of neglected responsibilities.

"Did you ever hear me sing at the club?"

With obvious regret he shook his head. "No."

Kathryn figured as much. "Too bad. I was pretty good."

She could see he was confused by the past tense, but then his eyes drifted to the end of the table and he saw the newspaper account of her accident.

"I thought you were all right?"

"For the most part, I am. My vocal cords were damaged though. I've lost half an octave from my range, and I can't hold a decent note to save my soul. I had to give up my job at the club."

"Gosh, Kathryn, I'm awfully sorry. What are you going to do? Are you okay? I mean financially? Do you need some money?"

Kathryn almost laughed at him—a banker through and through. "Does it look like I need money?"

She was sure Clayton preferred not to know how she afforded the house she was living in, so she wasn't surprised when he dropped it and looked away.

Kathryn didn't miss the disgusted look on his face.

"What do you want from me, Clay?"

"You're my sister, Kathryn."

This time she did laugh, albeit gently. "I haven't been your sister for a long time, and the girl you knew—"

He took her hand, stopping her. "The girl I knew turned into a woman. And I would very much like to know her."

Kathryn stared at him, unsure of her feelings. Her brother was reaching out, giving them a chance to rebuild what was destroyed. For some reason, squeezing blood from a stone became a prominent analogy in her mind, as she felt she had nothing to offer him.

Her brother, to his credit, was not willing to give up that easily.

"I loved you once."

Kathryn raised a challenging brow. "You hated me once too."

He smiled. "Well, between the two, I think we can make something of it."

Kathryn finally smiled too, and thought, perhaps, it was as easy as just taking the first step.

"Come to dinner." Her brother insisted. "Bring your friend."

"I thought you didn't like Smitty?"

Clayton chuckled. "He had designs on you."

"He still does."

"Of course he does. I meant bring Jenny."

Kathryn merely stared at him, a little dumbfounded.

"You're together, right?"

"How—"

Her brother laughed out loud. "Oh, it's obvious. I thought she was going to clock me that day in the club."

"Lucky for you she didn't. She's got a mean right hook."

They both laughed easily, and it felt good—right.

"Come to dinner."

"And how will Nan feel about that?" She paused. "You did marry Nan, didn't you?"

Clayton smiled. "Yes."

Kathryn was glad. "You were crazy about her."

"Still am. We have a daughter."

"No kidding?"

"No kidding. She's eight."

"Good heavens."

How much she'd missed. She watched her brother's eyes light up at the mention of his daughter, and it made her smile. "I'm sure she's a great kid."

"They change your world. She's got me right here." He held up his pinky finger with a grin.

Kathryn could see a precocious little girl with mousy brown hair, the perfect blend of her father's dark locks and her mother's strawberry blonde, charming her darling daddy out of all manner of things, with one disarming look after another. She smiled wistfully.

She was that girl once.

"You're my sister, Kath. I want you to meet my family." He took her hand. "*Your* family."

She let him keep her abbreviated nickname. She liked the notion that he thought there might be something of that lost girl in her after all.

"I'd like that."

<hr>

Jenny gingerly pressed her car door shut with her hip, careful not to make a sound. The law hadn't designated her home a crime scene yet, so she reasoned no one had killed anyone inside.

Kathryn's brother had called her the week before at her desk at the *Daily Chronicle*. He had apparently gotten her number from someone at the club who thought she should be the judge of whether Kathryn's brother should be given access to her.

He had a lot of nerve, she recalled thinking, after his scene at The Grotto, but anyone who would crawl back after that at least deserved a listen. He wanted to see his sister. Jenny warned him that if he was going to berate her again, or upset her in any way, he could just go to hell. He found her protective stance amusing for some reason and assured her he had only the best intentions in mind.

He said he'd try to get over to the house soon, and Jenny gave him the number. It seemed like a bad day to dump a surprise visit on Kathryn, but maybe, like pulling a Band-Aid quickly from a wound, it would only hurt for a few seconds.

Her thirty minutes were up, so she tiptoed onto the front stoop and put her ear to the door. To her great surprise and relief, she heard laughter and proceeded inside. Brother and sister were still sitting at the dining room table.

"Hey!" Kathryn beamed as she looked up. "I'm an aunt. Look!" She held up her brother's wallet, filled with family photos.

Jenny smiled as she put her hands on her hips. "Congratulations. How's that salad coming along?"

The siblings looked at each other with sudden dread. "The meatloaf!"

Jenny rolled her eyes and threw her hands up. "Good grief, it's genetic." She shook her head and headed for the kitchen.

She saw Kathryn and Clayton cringe at each other.

"Sorry," they cried in unison.

"Don't worry," Jenny called out, pleased with the evening. "I left it on low. Dinner in ten minutes. Now get your absentminded behinds in here and make the salad."

CHAPTER THIRTY

*J*enny drove slowly down the tree-lined street in Pelham Gardens looking for Clayton's address. Kathryn checked her look in her compact mirror for the third time.

Jenny smiled. "Nervous?"

"No."

Kathryn snapped the compact shut and dropped it in her purse. "What's there to be nervous about? I have a niece I've never met, a sister-in-law who only knows me as the bratty little sister who destroyed her husband's family, and a brother who's decided his new mission in life is to right a thirteen-year-old wrong. Me? Nervous? Nah."

Jenny took her hand. "It'll be great. You'll see." She spotted the address. "Oh, here we are."

Kathryn blew out an anxious breath as they pulled into the driveway of the immaculately kept two-story colonial-style brick house.

Clayton peered through the airy marquisette curtain draped from the large bay window in the living room and smiled as his sister opened the suicide passenger door of the Cord and unfolded herself from the maroon convertible.

His wife peeked over his shoulder. "Good heavens, Clay. That's lanky little Kathy?"

"That's her."

He looked over his shoulder. "Don't call her that, remember?"

"Oh, right ... Kat."

"I wanna see! I wanna see!" Stephanie came bounding onto the window bench seat and settled under her father's outstretched arm.

"Wow! What a dish!"

"Stephanie," her mother scolded. "I've told you, watch your slang, and shoes off the cushions."

"Yes, Mother," the young girl said, already on her way to the front door.

Stephanie waited patiently while the adults greeted each other and then she grinned as they settled into an awkward silence. She'd been taught not to interrupt when grownups are speaking, so she took full advantage of the pause in the conversation.

She put her hands behind her back, mirroring her father's stance, and peered up at her tall aunt. "I had a piano lesson today."

Kathryn leaned down and looked thankful for the distraction. "You did? And how long have you been taking piano lessons?"

"Since I was five." She held up her hand, fingers spread.

"Wonderful! And what did you learn today?"

She took her aunt's hand. "Come on."

Kathryn let her niece drag her to the piano in the living room, where she pulled out the piano bench and sat on the edge so that her feet could reach the pedals. Kathryn sat beside her and smiled, as the young girl sat up straight and opened her music.

"This is Daddy's favorite."

The sheet music was a simplified version of "Clair de Lune," and

Kathryn looked across the room to her brother, who smiled as they shared their affection for the song and spared a moment for their mother's memory.

She knew Clayton was comparing the scene with many similar recitals growing up, watching his mother turn the music for her.

Jenny and Nan sat around the long coffee table in front of the sofa as they listened to the recital.

Nan sat on the edge of her seat, legs crossed at the ankles, hands clasped in her lap, nodding her head to each note as she willed them to be perfectly executed, which they were.

She clapped enthusiastically, as did the others, when the piece was through, and Stephanie acknowledged it with a polite bow before turning to her.

"Daddy said you used to play. Would you like to try it?"

Kathryn feigned chagrin so as not to steal her niece's moment. "Oh, well ... gosh, it's been a while."

"You must try," Stephanie insisted. "Here—" she chased her up and scooted the bench back.

Kathryn stepped to the center of the seat and smoothed her tailored slacks under her as she sat down again and pretended to study the sheet music.

"Let's see here ..." She put her hands in position. "This is middle C, right?"

"Tst," her niece said with a giggle. "Everyone knows that. Come on, Aunt Kathryn."

Kathryn picked through the piece like someone with rusty musical skills and asked Stephanie to help her along when she pretended to have forgotten what note was what.

"You need to practice," Stephanie scolded when she was through.

"Well, I promise I will do that."

The rest of the adults sat in silence again. Nan stared at her new manicure, and Clayton was perfectly happy to watch the two of them engage in the universal piano duet, "Chopsticks."

"Nice wallpaper," Jenny finally said, obviously trying to save Clayton's wife.

"Why, it's just new this last month," Nan volunteered cheerfully. "Would you like to see the house? We just had it redone."

Stephanie stopped playing abruptly and didn't hesitate to direct traffic. "You and Daddy show Jenny the rest of the house. I'm going to show Aunt Kathryn my room first."

She led Kathryn to her room upstairs and shut the door behind them.

The space was bathed in yellow and white, with flowered curtains that matched the bedspread, and Kathryn smiled at the cheery decor. "What a lovely room."

"Sit."

Kathryn blinked at the girl's demeanor, which seemed suddenly older. "What?"

"Sit on the bed."

Kathryn complied, and her niece stood before her with her hands on her hips.

"You know, Daddy said I had to be extra nice to you, so I got worried and thought you would be boring and smell funny, like Mommy's Aunt Clara, but I think you're pretty swell, and I would have been nice to you even if Daddy hadn't told me to."

"Well, thank you."

"Certainly."

Stephanie sat beside her.

"I heard Pop Pop talking about you once. Daddy got mad and said he didn't ever want to hear your name in his house again."

Kathryn sat back slightly. "I see."

"Adults don't think kids hear things, but they do."

Kathryn thought back to her childhood and the whispers that changed her life forever.

"Yes, they do."

"I'm glad you made up with Daddy."

"Me too."

"Oh," the little girl chirped, "and thank you for going along with me at the piano." She nudged her with an elbow and giggled. "You're really good at fooling."

Kathryn looked at her quizzically.

Stephanie patted her knee. "I know you can play the piano."

"Oh? And how do you know that?"

"Pop Pop told me."

Kathryn tilted her head. "And what else did your Pop Pop tell you?"

"He told me you were as pretty as Nana and could sing like an angel. He also told me I'd meet you one day and we would be great friends."

Kathryn stared at her niece as pieces of her broken life started falling together. Her father had planned for this day. Set it up, in fact, with his letter of confession. She thought he'd taken something from her when he revealed the truth to her brother, but she realized he'd given her a chance to have her family back. She looked at the ceiling and struggled to place her swirling emotions. She suddenly found her hand taken into two smaller ones.

"It's okay, Aunt Kath. It'll be our secret." Stephanie held up her hand, little finger extended. "Pinky swear?"

Kathryn looked into Stephanie's innocent, wide eyes and, in them, she found everything she'd lost—herself, her brother, her mother, her father, and a future filled with love and promise.

Her niece would have all those things and more, and she was honored to be part of it.

"Pinky swear." She hooked their fingers with a full-faced grin and pulled her into a hug.

"Dinner!" they heard called from the stairway.

Stephanie hopped off the bed and held out her hand. "Come on. Time to act five again."

Kathryn took her hand. "Five?"

"Mother and Father treat me that way, so I play along," her niece explained. "You hear more that way, anyhow, because they think you're just a silly little child, paying no mind to their adult talk."

Kathryn raised her brow.

"Now, I'm a good daughter ..." Stephanie went on. "*Yes, Mother dear*, and *certainly, Daddy darling*," she mocked. "But I'm not a baby." She stopped and turned to face her before opening the door. "They are just going to have to realize that I'm almost nine, and I will be ten before they know it, and then, eventually, a teenager." She threw her hand up and opened the door. "What are they going to do then?"

Heaven help them. Kathryn shook her head, enchanted. "You're pretty smart, aren't you?"

Stephanie shrugged confidently. "I'd say."

She led her to the dining room, and Kathryn beamed inside. Children change your life, her brother had said. She'd only had a glimpse of what he was talking about, but, already, her niece had wrapped herself around her heart.

Dinner was a pleasant enough affair; even Nan loosened up as she and Kathryn discussed fashion and the latest trends in makeup. There wasn't much about Kathryn's life that could be discussed, especially in the presence of an eight-year-old, so catching up really wasn't on the agenda. That was fine with her, as she sat back and watched the family dynamic in action.

Clayton and Nan obviously adored each other. Their loving interaction was rivaled only by the adoration they bestowed upon their daughter. It was a sweet family unit, and everyone was at ease and comfortably stuffed by the time dessert and coffee was served.

Nan set her cup in its saucer and turned to Jenny. She had made sure she included Jenny in the conversation all afternoon, but Kathryn could tell she still wasn't sure why she was invited in the first place.

"So where do you work, Jenny?"

"I work at the *Chronicle*."

Nan sat back. "Oh. Don't care much for its politics, but a job is a job these days, I suppose."

Jenny smiled and didn't take the bait. "Well, I'm the *About Town* columnist in the *Arts and Entertainment* section, so I don't have much say in the paper's politics."

"Oh, say, I've read that ... why, Jenny Ryan. My goodness. I didn't put the two together. We have a celebrity among us."

Jenny merely grinned, and Kathryn noticed it seemed to take the sting out of the paper's politics for the woman.

"So you did a piece on Kathryn? Is that how you met?"

Jenny smiled across the table at her. "Sort of. I was working on a story that brought me to The Grotto."

Kathryn shook her head slightly and chuckled, remembering the scene Jenny made as she departed the club the first time they met.

"Then she graciously agreed to sing at an event I was organizing, and we became fast friends after that."

Kathryn suppressed a laugh at the lie. She had been anything but gracious when Jenny asked her to perform at the armory, and their friendship had been anything but expeditious. It all seemed a lifetime ago, and none of it mattered now. Jenny's face was glowing with love, and Kathryn couldn't help the broad smile that split her lips in return.

Nan looked at Jenny, then at her, and then nearly dropped her cup, as the reason Jenny was invited to the family get together dawned on her. The truth slid down her well-bred polite expression like a landslide devouring a pristine hillside. Her eyes snapped to Clayton, who could already see the storm brewing, and she politely set her napkin on the table and excused herself.

"Nuts," Clayton exhaled, as he quickly got up and followed her into the kitchen.

Jenny looked at Kathryn and mouthed, *He didn't tell her?*

Kathryn rolled her eyes and glanced at her niece before gesturing outside with a tilt of her head.

Jenny turned to Stephanie, who was sitting next to her. "Say, Steph, how would you like to go play on the swing set?"

"Sure!" The girl bounced out of her chair.

She ran up behind Kathryn and cupped her hands around her ear. "If they're mean to you, remember, I still love you."

Kathryn grinned and said, "I will," with a wink.

Stephanie and Jenny went outside, and Kathryn exhaled slowly as she took a last sip of coffee and pushed away from the table. She couldn't believe her brother didn't tell Nan about Jenny and her. Although, meeting her again after so many years, perhaps he knew best. The last thing she wanted to do was cause trouble between them, so she decided to put an end to the argument.

She approached the kitchen and heard Nan in mid-restrained shout saying, "Nothing but trouble, Clayton! She always has been."

"You know what she's been through, Nan. I can't believe you're behaving—"

Kathryn came up behind her brother and cleared her throat. "Sorry to interrupt, but we're leaving now."

Clayton turned, and his wife straightened, embarrassed to be caught arguing.

"I'm sorry, Kathryn," Nan said in clipped tones. "I don't mean to make you feel unwelcome."

The Hammond siblings stared at her expectantly, wondering what exactly she did intend.

"For myself," Nan went on, "what you do in your personal life is your business, but I have a very impressionable young daughter here, and I don't want her exposed to your—" She looked her up and down but was at a loss for words.

Kathryn raised her brow. "My polite conversation? What, Nan? What do you think I'm exposing her to?"

Nan raised her chin. "If you were a mother, you'd understand. I'll not have it in my home."

"That's not for you to decide," Clayton broke in angrily. "She is my sister. You'll not treat her—"

"Okay—" Kathryn stepped between them.

"No!" her brother barked. "It's not okay!"

"Yes. Come on." Kathryn put her arm across his chest, pulling him from the kitchen. "Thank you for dinner, Nan," she called over her shoulder while pushing Clayton into the other room. "I'm sorry my visit was so upsetting."

Clayton was incensed as they came to a halt in the middle of the living room. "You don't have to apologize. This is my house, Kathryn, and what I say—"

"Don't be a caveman, Clayton. This is her house too. She's uncomfortable."

"Because of two people in love?"

"Two *women* in love. You should have warned her."

He wriggled from her grasp.

"It shouldn't make any difference."

"Yes. Well, in my perfect world ..." She smiled and hoped it would help calm him.

Clayton shook his head. "I'm sorry, Kath, I never thought ... this is so unlike her."

"Just let the dust settle."

"I thought if she met Jenny first, got to know her ..." He looked out the window at Jenny pushing his daughter on the swing, both laughing.

Kathryn stood by his side and smiled as Stephanie waved at them. "She's a beautiful little girl. How do they get so smart, so fast?"

He grinned proudly, and the tension instantly washed away. "She *is my* kid."

Kathryn pinched his side and they both laughed.

Stephanie launched herself from the swing at the top of the upstroke and flew in midair as the three paralyzed adults gasped. She made a perfect landing and giggled as the grownups exhaled a sigh of relief. She ran to the backdoor and threw it open with a mighty heave from both hands. Jenny was right behind and apologized to the slightly traumatized father.

"Sorry, Clay. I didn't know she was going to do that."

He turned to his impish daughter and wagged his finger at her. "Yes, well, she knows she's not supposed to do that."

Stephanie tugged on the warning digit "Oh, Pops. You worry too much." She scampered to the couch and plopped herself down with an energetic pounce.

"Pops?" Kathryn whispered with a grin.

Clayton rolled his eyes. "She just started that last week."

Nan appeared from the kitchen, and, without a word, began clearing the table.

"Here, let me help you," Jenny said as she made her way over.

"No, thank you."

"We're going to go," Kathryn said.

"No," Stephanie whined. "You just got here."

Nan set down the dishes, obviously happy to expedite their exit. "Stephie, your aunt is very busy. Don't be a pest."

"You're not being a pest, are you, pumpkin," Clayton said with a warning glance to his wife. "Come on." He held out his hand. "Kiss your Aunt Kathryn and Jenny goodbye."

Kathryn knelt before her niece and tickled her pouting cheek. "What's this, a frown?"

Stephanie lowered her eyes. "Will I see you again?"

"Of course you'll see her again," Clayton assured her.

The little girl looked to her mother.

Nan wiped her hands on her apron and came to her daughter's side.

"She's your aunt, honey. Of course you'll see her again."

Clayton straightened and put a thankful hand on his wife's lower back.

"See?" Kathryn smiled at the girl. "You'll see me again before you know it."

Stephanie looked past her shoulder and beamed. "Jenny too? I like her. She's funny."

All eyes shifted to Nan, who had the grace to acquiesce for her daughter's sake.

"Sure, sweetie, Jenny too."

Jenny smiled. "I'd like that."

Pleasant goodbyes were forced, and Clayton apologized as he walked Kathryn to the car.

"Sorry, Kath," he said, as he opened the door for her.

She put her hand on his chest and glanced at the front steps, where Nan stood holding Stephanie's hand. "Don't push things with Nan. It'll work itself out."

He pursed his lips, expressing disappointment in his wife.

"Promise?" She cupped his face in her hands. "I remember her as a good, rational person. It'll be all right. Just give her time."

"Okay," Clayton relented.

"Promise?"

"Promise."

The siblings embraced and Kathryn gave her brother an extra squeeze before she let him go.

"Thank you, Clay. You don't know what this means to me."

"I love you, Kath."

She kissed his cheek. "I love you too."

Kathryn blew a kiss to her niece as they backed out of the drive, and the little girl jumped up and caught it, waving it proudly as her father joined her on the top step.

Jenny shifted into first and they started down the street.

"Are you upset?" she asked.

"About Nan? No. She'll come around or she won't. You know how it is."

She smiled, putting thoughts of her sister-in-law far behind. "Isn't Stephanie something?"

"I'll say. That little girl is sharp as a whip. They're not putting anything over on her."

Kathryn laughed. "I know!"

She grinned and shook her head when, almost absentmindedly, her eyes were drawn to a dark car parked on an otherwise sparsely populated street. She followed it with her eyes, and as they passed, the driver slowly ducked his head and pulled his hat over his eyes.

Her senses went on high alert and warnings went off in her head. She couldn't see the license plate in the side-view mirror, and she couldn't tell Jenny what she thought was going on, so she stared helplessly out the windshield, fearing the reunion with her family had opened up a new avenue of danger.

As soon as they were out of the area, Kathryn had Jenny stop at a restaurant on the pretense of using the restroom. Jenny waited in the car, and Kathryn went right to the phone cabinet at the back of the dining room and called Colonel Forsythe.

"Are you sure he was ours?" she asked again.

"Yes, Kathryn. Who else would it be?"

She was silent.

"It's procedure, you know that. Once you renewed relations with your family, they had to be investigated."

"I don't want his life disrupted."

"He will be unaware, I assure you."

She almost laughed out loud. "It took me two seconds to spot your man."

"But you missed him on the way in, didn't you?"

She was so busy being anxious about her visit that she had to admit she didn't notice. She shook her head at her carelessness.

"Don't worry about it, Kathryn. It rather defeats our purpose to be noticed."

Kathryn had to agree. She hung up the phone and stared blindly at the small fan in the upper corner of the booth. The investigation may be standard procedure, but it reminded her of how easy it would be for someone to harm those she loved, if one was so inclined. She weighed the wisdom of reconnecting with her family at this point in her life and made a decision as she made her way back to the car. Once there, she pretended everything was fine.

Jenny pulled out onto the busy street and then glanced at Kathryn. "Everything all right?" she asked, not letting on that she had changed her mind about using the restroom and saw her on the phone.

"Mm," Kathryn said with a smile, but Jenny could tell she was masking a distinct feeling of dread. "I think I'm really going to love being an aunt."

Jenny smiled. "You're going to make a great one."

She wouldn't ask Kathryn who she called or why she lied about stopping. Kathryn had a life, a whole world, outside theirs, and their relationship was built on trust. If Kathryn was keeping a secret, Jenny knew it was for a good reason and had nothing to do with their life together. That's what she would keep telling herself. She would tell herself that until the need to know stopped niggling at her brain and the sting of exclusion melted away with the next loving look, word, or touch.

CHAPTER THIRTY-ONE

Kathryn closed her eyes and leaned on the phonograph cabinet as she listened to the recording she'd made for Jenny. Her voice was clear and true in a way that it never would be again. She savored it, marveled at its clarity and tone, and then, with a dismayed exhale, she gently lifted the needle from the record mid-song and turned off the player.

Silence filled the empty house, and she resisted trying to emulate what she heard in the recording. Her voice had gotten notably better in the weeks since she'd resigned from the club—inexplicably so, according to her doctor—but nowhere near what it once was. At times, she would almost convince herself she'd worked her way back, but then she'd listen to the record, and the truth couldn't be denied.

It was painful to hear at first, a physical reminder of what she'd lost, but then she found comfort in the permanent record of her talent. A permanent record of her love for Jenny.

She had recovered her lung capacity and enough of her voice to resume her career, but she was still getting used to her limitations. Considering what she'd been through, she knew she was lucky, but she couldn't help wondering if this particular brand of luck was more design than chance.

"This is remarkable." The throat specialist had said as he closed his file at their afternoon appointment. "The scarring seems to have ..." He paused, as if trying to wrap his brain around what he was about to say. There was only one way to describe it, and though it made no medical sense, he said it anyway, and with confidence. "Well, it seems to have healed significantly."

Kathryn stared at him. "Is that possible?"

The doctor smiled. "Evidently."

"But is that possible?" Kathryn reiterated doubtfully.

The doctor smiled again, this time in a condescending way, and avoided the question. "The human body is an amazing machine. It does incredible things, often with no—"

Kathryn's skeptically irritated stare told the man she wasn't buying it and that the truth would better serve him.

"Not usually. No."

"Any explanation?"

"Good genes? Don't worry about it, Miss Hammond. Just rejoice in your good fortune. Your hard work and excellent technique helped quite a bit in retraining your voice, I would imagine." He paused. "I mean, obviously."

"And the damaged cords?"

The doctor looked at his report again, and Kathryn could tell from his slightly raised brow that he was without a good explanation.

"Not as bad as we originally thought, apparently."

She shook her head as she closed the phonograph cabinet lid. His explanation didn't make sense. The original diagnosis was fairly conclusive—not much room for misinterpretation—and he was not the only one she'd consulted.

She didn't know what to make of her progress any more than her doctors did. As for her voice, what she'd lost in range and purity, she gladly allowed her resurrected vibrato to subtly conceal.

Resting on the turntable was the only remnant of her pristine voice, and she placed her hand reverently on the phonograph lid. It was true it would never be like that again, but it was good enough. Good enough for Dominic to ask her to return to the club after seeing her latest performance at the USO. She agreed, putting aside the perfectionist in her, and accepted her vocal abilities for what they had become.

It was a good day—she should be ecstatic—but the unknown and the nonsensical swirled around her like a dense fog hiding the plot of some sinister Dashiell Hammett mystery in its dark, heavy dampness.

She wondered whether something had been done to her after all and whether it had anything to do with her unusual recovery. Again, her thoughts turned to Bouchaule. He would know. He held the answers. Every day, she expected him to show up, and every day he didn't, she worried she was wrong.

It had been nearly three months since the incident at the center. Surely Bouchaule would have contacted her by now. Maybe it wasn't him at the hospital. Maybe the whole thing had been a tragic accident, like the report said. She didn't know what to believe.

She rubbed her forehead. Sometimes she felt like she was going mad. What was the truth? What was a lie? When was a shadow just a shadow, and when did it hide something menacing that would bring her world crashing down around her? She used to relish the unknown. She found it intriguing, exciting. It energized her, gave her purpose. But that was before she had anything to lose. She was trying so hard to hold on to everything now—Jenny, her new family, her future. She felt consumed by her paranoia. For months, it had poisoned her every thought, her every move. She felt constantly watched, whether it was a trip to the grocery store or a day at the zoo with her niece. Her guard was never down.

The waiting for everything to come undone hung over her like a foregone conclusion. She thought she saw Bouchaule everywhere. She'd made a fool of herself more than once, rushing through crowds to get a glimpse of a stranger's face because he wore his hat just so, and she had taken to habitually doubling back on the street because she was sure she was being followed. The stranger was never Bouchaule, and she could never prove she was followed, but the unnerving shadows in her mind's eye remained.

She shook her head, aware she had to get hold of herself. She was going stir crazy with so much free time. She'd taken up painting again—still lifes, or the beautiful autumn landscape outside the huge upstairs studio window—anything pleasant and safe, unwilling to reveal the ominous thoughts in her head to Jenny or anyone else. She hoped the simple distraction would help. Paint something beautiful and the mind will follow, except it never did. The dull exercise merely allowed her to cultivate her paranoid schemes. She was becoming obsessed, she could feel it, and she feared she could no longer hide behind her pleasant smile and composed façade.

Straddling the line of trust and mistrust was destroying her. She had to face her fears as unfounded, or act on them to protect those she loved. It may cost her dearly, but she chose the latter as a matter of necessity. She couldn't afford to be wrong.

She decided to embrace her instinct and mistrust those she worked for. It was time to get back there, to play out their twisted little game. They would never know she had a game of her own in mind. For the first time in a long time, she felt a spark of excitement at the prospect and anxiously awaited the return of Bouchaule—the one thing she had and they didn't.

She glanced at the clock. Six. Jenny would be home soon. Thoughts of plots and their consequences were set aside in favor of a pleasant evening at home with her girl. It was the only thing keeping her sane. Jenny had been so patient and understanding throughout the whole ordeal. She never pressed or complained, and Kathryn was well aware of how lucky she was.

Jenny practically leaped into Kathryn's arms when she told her Dominic had asked her back to the club. She scolded her for waiting all through dinner and coffee before saying anything.

"I knew he would ask you!" she went on as they cleared the table. "You know he came to see you every Wednesday."

"You didn't tell me that."

"I didn't want to make you nervous."

Kathryn laughed.

Jenny had watched him show up for weeks. He would stand inconspicuously off to the side and watch his favorite singer perform. The first time Jenny saw him, she saw the disappointment, dismay, and sadness that Kathryn must have seen in his eyes. He didn't stay long, but every week, like clockwork, he would be back, hopeful. Jenny caught his eye once, and he smiled and came over to greet her.

"I think she's getting better," he said.

Jenny agreed but could see Dominic's regret that *better* still wasn't good enough.

Slowly, Kathryn added ballads to her set, testing her abilities. Dominic would stay longer and leave with an encouraged smile instead of a frustrated scowl.

Last night, during Kathryn's brilliant rendition of "I'll Be Seeing You," Jenny watched Dominic lose himself in Kathryn's performance and her returned confidence. He closed his eyes to focus on her voice, his body language anticipating every note. He smiled with pride and satisfaction when each one was hit and held perfectly. Jenny knew it wasn't the voice he knew so well but, rather, a new version of it, still technically flawless and just as emotive.

When the set was over, he clasped his hands together in victory and left with a full-faced grin.

Jenny looked to the stage, where Kathryn smiled and waved good night to the applauding crowd. She was happy for her. It wouldn't be long now. Dominic would have her back, and everything would get back to normal.

It had been a trying three months. She was worried about Kathryn. She had been through a lot, and though she tried hard to hide it, the cracks were beginning to show. Jenny could feel her discontent, her restlessness, the muted anger behind her eyes.

Their physical relationship was better than ever, but they hardly spoke about anything of import. Jenny had given Kathryn the space she felt she needed, but it didn't help. She just drifted further into herself.

Tonight was a welcome exception. The house glowed with

candles and classical music. A wonderful dinner proved that Kathryn could actually cook when she put her mind to it.

They stood side by side at the sink—Kathryn washing, Jenny drying—and they were perfectly content, a stark contrast to months of uneasy silence or mindless babble brought on by things not said and secrets not shared.

Jenny absentmindedly toweled the dish in her hand as she watched Kathryn's hands move gracefully through the mundane task of washing and rinsing.

Those hands knew her body so well, and she couldn't escape the rush of arousal that swept through her. She involuntarily closed her eyes, and when she opened them, she found Kathryn staring at her, drying her hands—those beautiful hands. Jenny blushed, and Kathryn took the dish with a knowing smile.

"I think it's dry."

"Yeah."

Jenny swallowed and reached for the next dish as Kathryn stretched behind her to put the other away in the cabinet above their heads. Soft breasts pressed against her back, and Jenny clutched the plate in her hand, fearing she would drop it. A warm breath on the back of her neck weakened her knees as Kathryn nudged her robe aside and planted slow, sensual kisses across the top of her now bare shoulder. Jenny lost all sense of her task, and soon her robe's belt fell away, and Kathryn relieved her of the dish.

"I think you'd better put this down," she whispered in her ear.

"Good idea," Jenny answered breathlessly.

She tried to turn, but Kathryn surrounded her from behind, doing things that she had no intention of interrupting. The robe now hung limply from her elbows as Kathryn's hand cupped her breast and caressed her hardening nipple with her thumb. Jenny reached back to touch her, but Kathryn held her tighter and slid her hand down her abdomen and below her belly, until it disappeared between her legs.

"God—" Jenny melted forward and then slowly arched back again as Kathryn's fingers brushed teasingly across her awakened center.

Her mind went blank and there was nothing but Kathryn's touch, sending wave after wave of desire. A throaty moan rumbled from deep within as long fingers dipped into her and were welcomed with wet anticipation.

Kathryn exhaled an aroused breath into her ear. "Mm. What have you been thinking about?"

Jenny moaned again as Kathryn pulled her fingers through her folds, temporarily disabling her baser functions like standing and breathing. Kathryn mercifully stopped and allowed her to catch her breath and her balance. Jenny craned her head back against Kathryn's shoulder, and with love and lust in her eyes said, "You. Your hands on me. Your hands in me."

Kathryn captured her mouth, and Jenny twisted her body around so that they were facing in an embrace. She attempted to get inside Kathryn's robe, but she captured her hands and gently pushed her toward the kitchen table.

The tablecloth slid beneath her as Jenny lay back and surrendered. She closed her eyes and immersed herself in the sensations as Kathryn taunted and teased her most sensitive spots with loving hands and an eager mouth.

The intense foreplay suddenly diminished into soft caresses on her breasts, and Jenny opened her eyes to find Kathryn hovering over her face.

"I love you, Jenny," she said.

A vulnerable hollowness lurking behind Kathryn's eyes tore at Jenny's heart. Everything Kathryn was and wanted hid there, crying to escape, crying to be felt. It was honest and raw. It was the woman Jenny knew and loved and a resurrection of the connection that bound them. The moment was too brief, too fleeting. Jenny wanted to reach into the dark recesses of Kathryn's mind and pull her out, this woman she knew. She would save her from the demons at her heels, the thing tearing them apart. Together they would fight. Together they could withstand anything.

She reached up, letting her love, her compassion, and her hope pass through her fingertips as she traced Kathryn's cheek.

Please stay with me, she wanted to say, but instead she whispered, "I love you too."

She wanted to take Kathryn in her arms and force her to stay present, force her to tell her everything, but Kathryn's vulnerability was quickly replaced with purpose.

Jenny could see Kathryn needed to make love to her, as if she had to prove their love was real, maybe to her, maybe to herself. Jenny let her take her. She let her worship her body with hungry kisses, let her kneel before her parted thighs, and let her drink from her sex until she'd coaxed all coherent thought from her head and made her come and then come again.

She knew Kathryn needed it, to feel close, to feel as one, to know they still belonged together and would make it no matter what. Jenny stared at the ceiling, breathless and ravaged, and admitted she needed it too.

***

Jenny lay on her side in bed and stared at her sleeping lover. She traced her prone profile with bittersweet eyes. It was always this way. They'd make passionate love, and for that time, and in the calm moments after, they felt renewed, hopeful that it would carry over into the rest of their lives, but it never did. Kathryn would wake, and the cycle of polite but distant cohabitation would resume.

Jenny saw Kathryn's eyelids flutter and quickly pretended to be asleep. She heard Kathryn turn her head, felt her eyes upon her, and wondered if she was lamenting the same thing. She waited until she turned away again and listened to the long, controlled exhale that always followed.

Slowly opening her eyes, she saw Kathryn staring dejectedly at the ceiling. Jenny couldn't take it anymore. The moments of truth were so powerful that the half-life they lived outside of those moments diminished them all. She couldn't live that way, and she couldn't let Kathryn live that way. It was destroying her, destroying them.

"Are you all right?"

Kathryn smiled her perfected polite smile. "Mm. You?"

"Swell."

Jenny propped herself up on an elbow and ran her fingers through a lock of Kathryn's long dark hair while her frustration slowly burned. They were going to talk it out tonight. If it killed them, they were going to talk.

For weeks she had tried the gentle, understanding approach. Each time, Kathryn would deflect her inquiries with humor or distract her with sex. Kathryn definitely wasn't all right, and Jenny had to do something before it was too late.

"You know, baby, there's more to a relationship than incredible sex."

Kathryn smiled. "Is there?"

Jenny sat up, annoyed. "I'm serious, Kathryn."

Kathryn became defensive at the shift in mood. "I can see that."

"I hope you do."

Soft, sated blue eyes suddenly turned cold. "Is that all you think we are?"

Jenny held back for a moment, startled by the intensity of Kathryn's accusatory stare.

"Something is terribly wrong, Kat. I can feel it. And, lately, yes, sex is about the only thing we share."

Kathryn looked away. "We've had this discussion, Jenny. There are things—"

"We can't talk about. Yes, I know. But you've been on leave for months, and I find it hard to believe that any of this has to do with classified information or assignments. It's not fair to use that as an excuse to hide behind whatever it is that's tearing you up inside."

Kathryn was silent.

"Hey ..." Jenny hovered over her until she looked in her eyes. What she saw there frightened her. Kathryn's hooded eyes telegraphed not only anger but indifference. Jenny had experienced the anger and had seen the indifference directed at others, but she had never been the recipient.

Kathryn was shutting down—the very thing she was trying to prevent. She sought Kathryn's hand, which was as indifferent to her touch as the empty stare that dared her to continue.

Jenny pressed on, running her hand up the tense arm, across the shoulder to the stone cheek, where the cold apathy became too much, and she pulled her hand away.

"I don't want to upset you, Kathryn, and I don't want to hurt you, but you're getting further away from me, and it scares me." She lifted her hand. "Like now. Who are you?"

Kathryn's eyes softened and her tense form followed suit. Sometimes she didn't know. She closed her eyes briefly and swallowed. When she looked into Jenny's eyes again, she was more honest with herself than she had been in weeks.

"It scares me too."

Jenny moved in earnestly, no doubt thankful the stranger was gone. "Honey, what can I do?"

Kathryn didn't know. She only knew she needed her. "Just love me."

Jenny deflated back onto her outstretched arm, uttering a clipped, "I do."

She was upset, and Kathryn knew the fall had begun. Jenny slipped from the sheets and gathered her robe from the end of the bed.

"I hope that's enough, Kathryn."

Kathryn propped herself up on her elbows. "Hey—"

Jenny disappeared into the bathroom and started a shower.

Kathryn stared into the empty space at the end of the bed and then collapsed onto the pillow. Clearly, Jenny didn't think it was enough, nor should she. Kathryn weighed the fear of losing the one person holding her together with the knowledge that overcoming that fear could be the thing that would push her away. She couldn't blame Jenny, only herself for wanting it all and thinking she was strong enough alone to get it.

. . .

The hot water on Jenny's face made her tears feel cold in comparison. She wondered if she had done the right thing. The last thing Kathryn needed was one more thing to worry about, but she was slipping away, and she didn't know what else to do.

Kathryn had refused to see the agency psychologist. Jenny had overheard her vehemently complaining to Smitty that she didn't need a head-shrinker, she needed the truth. That's all Jenny needed too, but she would settle for something, anything, to bring Kathryn back to her.

It wasn't just *their* relationship. From Kathryn's conversation with Smitty, she could tell relations were strained not only with him but also with the OSS.

Even the reunion with her family had lost its luster, as Kathryn physically distanced herself from them. At first, Jenny thought it was out of respect for Nan's feelings, but they'd been to the house several times since then, and they seemed to have made peace with their differences for Stephanie's sake, if nothing else.

Kathryn kept in touch with her niece by phone—the only true moments of joy she seemed to have—but the joy was fleeting, as introspection quickly resumed its grasp. Kathryn hid it well for the most part, and most would be fooled, but Jenny watched her in the quiet moments, when she wasn't "on" or otherwise engaged, and she could see the emptiness clearly. She was playing a part, and whatever the reason, it started after the accident at the center.

Jenny blamed it on the trauma of the event, which was completely understandable, but she'd be damned if she would let Kathryn succumb to the tortures of her mind and sacrifice their relationship as a matter of course.

She felt the cold rush of outside air as the shower curtain was gingerly pulled back and Kathryn stepped into the shower and stood at her back. Jenny rinsed the suds from her arms and put up a wall to give her strength. She handed Kathryn the soap and stepped out of the shower without a word.

Kathryn tied the belt on her flowing robe as she entered the living room and found Jenny in the center of the couch, legs tucked under, reading a book.

She sat on the coffee table opposite her, and Jenny snapped the book closed with a defiantly expectant glare. Kathryn smiled to herself. Jenny had been "reading" the book upside down.

"I'm sorry, Jenny."

"Do you even know what you're sorry for?"

Kathryn shrugged and smiled. "If you have a list, I'll own up to all of it."

"Damn it, Kathryn." Jenny slammed her book onto the couch and got up.

Kathryn put her hand on Jenny's arm. "Okay, okay."

Jenny settled back into her seat and crossed her arms, waiting.

"I know things have been a little nuts lately."

Jenny tilted her head, requiring more honesty than that.

"Okay, *I've* been a little nuts lately."

Jenny raised her chin without comment.

Kathryn expected a little help, but it was soon apparent she would get none, which didn't sit well.

"It's to be expected, isn't it? I've been through hell. You don't even know."

"And why is that? Could it be because you're shutting me out?"

Kathryn exhaled a disgusted breath and sat back, struggling to stay in the room. After all she'd done to try and keep some sense of normalcy for them, to preserve what they had, it was all for naught. Hateful retorts, brought on by frustration, piled up in her throat like patrons jamming the exit of a theater after someone yelled *fire!* Kathryn swallowed them down. It would be so easy to turn it around, to avoid the truth. If it were anyone else, she would beat them down with guilt until they were the one begging for forgiveness. But it wasn't just anyone. It was the woman she loved, and righteous indig-nation was not going to save their relationship, if there was one to save after their ensuing conversation. Kathryn would make one last-ditch effort to avoid testing their resolve about their future.

She lifted her hand in surrender. "Look, it's been hard on both of us. If you can forgive me for these last few months, I promise things will be better. I'll be better."

Jenny stared at her for a few moments and then threw her hand up in disbelief. "You don't get it, Kathryn," she snapped. "It's not about you *pretending* to be someone else to appease me!"

Unmasked and exposed, Kathryn lashed out. "It's always about being someone else!"

"Not for us!"

Kathryn was struck by the panic in Jenny's eyes. For a split second, Jenny believed that their relationship was just another performance on her part. She watched a tear fall down Jenny's pained face and recognized the fear and desperation of trying to hold on to something out of your control.

She waited a breath for the tension to dissipate and then held out her hand, thankful when Jenny took it. "No, honey, not for us."

Jenny closed her eyes and nodded weakly in relief.

Kathryn added her other hand to the union. "You believe that, don't you?"

"Yes. I know we're real. I know you love me. I do." Jenny wiped the tear from her cheek and shook her head, unable to keep up her brave front. "I don't want to lose you."

Kathryn tightened her grasp. "You're not going to lose me."

"But I am, Kathryn. Everyone is. Smitty ... your family." She paused. "Your *family*. Stephanie adores you, and I know you adore her. What are you doing?"

Kathryn sat back and pulled her hands away. There would be no reprieve this time. Jenny had a choice to make, just like she had made hers. A few months ago, Kathryn had no doubt what Jenny's choice would have been. But now, considering her frustration and all she'd been put through, she wasn't so sure. Kathryn could only do what she had to do and hope that Jenny would do the same.

"I'm protecting those I love."

"From what?"

Kathryn looked at the floor. "I just don't think it's safe for them to be in my life right now. I may have to let them go for a while, so I don't want them to get used to having me around." She looked up. "I want to prepare them, to make it easier when it happens."

Jenny frowned. "Are you preparing me? Is that what this is about?"

Kathryn blinked. Was she? Or was she preparing herself.

"Kat?"

"No. I told you ... you're not going to lose me."

Jenny stared at her, concern knitting her brow. "You don't seem so sure."

Kathryn straightened and rubbed her hands on her thighs.

"No more running," Jenny demanded. "Please."

Kathryn exhaled. She stopped running and stood her ground. "I'm going to call Forsythe and see if I can get reinstated. I'll do the psych eval, apologize ... whatever he wants."

Jenny raised her brow in surprise, clearly expecting something bad. "Good. That's very good."

Kathryn didn't think so.

"Is that a problem?"

Here we go, Kathryn thought. How Jenny responded to what she was going to say would determine everything. They had talked about it, but the blade of reality was always sharper than its vague concept. She put her trust in their love and continued.

"Do you remember the day we parted at the shore ... on the pier?"

"Yes."

"I told you I had done some things while we were apart but that they didn't matter anymore."

"Yes."

Kathryn looked at her and waited until Jenny caught the drift, which didn't take long.

"If you get reinstated, they're going to matter."

Reinstated or not, it would matter, but the OSS was a nice distraction from the lack of details. "Yes. I'm fairly certain."

"I see."

Kathryn watched Jenny carefully and wondered if she really did. "I know this isn't fair to you, and I know I made you a promise that I wouldn't use my body to—"

"How many times do I have to tell you to do what you have to do? We're at war. We don't have the luxury of choice."

Kathryn paused for a moment, holding on to her relationship for as long as she could. "You do."

"What?"

"I don't have a choice, Jenny. If this plays out like I think it will, I will do what I have to do, but that doesn't mean you have to stay. That we—"

"Are you kidding me?" Jenny said incredulously. "After everything we've been through, you're asking me to leave?"

"I'm not."

"Good! Because that's ridiculous."

"I want you to have a choice. I don't want you to feel obligated."

"Obligated? We're not talking about a business contract! We're talking about our lives, our love!" Jenny got up and started stalking the room. "*Obligated?* Jesus."

Kathryn rubbed her forehead and then got up and followed after her. "Think about it, Jenny."

"What the hell am I thinking about? Here I am, worried about losing you, and you've already tossed me out with the garbage!"

Kathryn grabbed her shoulders. "Stop for a minute and listen to me."

Jenny tried to escape. Kathryn recognized the panic of being caged with no way out, so she let her go, knowing she wouldn't wander far.

Jenny couldn't hold back the tears as she spoke. "We talked about this. Whether it was Forrester, or whoever this other assignment is, you would do your job, and I will be fine with it."

Kathryn moved closer but made no attempt at contact. "I've told myself that every day. Just do what you have to do, because Jenny loves you and she'll understand."

Jenny turned, hopeful. "Yes. That's right."

"I don't think you've really thought it through."

"Don't tell me what I think!"

Kathryn put her hands up, not looking for a fight. "Listen, I've put myself in your place. Imagined how I would feel if someone else … if you …" She had to stop. "It makes me physically ill to think about it. I can't imagine how you …"

Jenny raised her chin, her emotions under control, determined. "There's nothing to think about. I'm not letting you go. Will it be hard? Yes. Will it be painful to bear? Probably. Will I cry? Most definitely. But walking away is not going to make it hurt less. It's only going to let them win, and we're not going to let that happen. Are we?"

Kathryn stood in awe. Jenny was going to stick it out. In her heart she felt she would, hoped she would, but her mind told her no one would bother. Not for her. She wasn't sure Jenny was fully acknowledging the reality of what she had to do, but she was right about walking away, so they would work through it together. There was only one more thing.

"Do you want to know?"

"Do I want to know what?"

"When the assignment starts."

Jenny paused for a moment, and Kathryn sensed that, for the first time, she was truly thinking about what was going to happen. She raised her chin, resolved to not let this come between them.

"Yes. I want to know."

Kathryn nodded and took her into her arms.

"I'm so sorry, honey. For this mess. For everything."

Jenny melted into her embrace. "Please don't ever doubt that I'm always going to be here for you."

"I won't."

Jenny bravely smiled into her chest. "Besides, you've got the hard part. I only have to love you."

Kathryn found this hilarious and threw her head back in laughter. "Glutton for punishment, that's what you are."

Jenny agreed with a lighthearted chuckle, and Kathryn pulled back, encouraged to see the love and determination in Jenny's beautiful green eyes.

"I'll love you till the day I die, Jenny. Please tell me that's enough."

Jenny answered with an earnest kiss that quickly deepened, as both women poured their dedication and desire into each other's souls.

Kathryn suddenly stopped and gently pushed Jenny away with a hand on each shoulder.

"You know, honey, incredible sex does not a relationship make."

Jenny smirked. "Shut up and kiss me."

CHAPTER THIRTY-TWO

"So, what do you think, Mr. Smith?" Holmes asked.

Smitty took a final drag on his cigarette and smashed it into the ashtray on the desk before him.

"You've got the psych evaluation. What does the doc say?"

Holmes leaned forward. "We don't appreciate your evasive attitude, Mr.—"

Forsythe stalled his British counterpart with a raised hand and then turned to his agent.

"John, with the exception of the security of this country, nothing is more important to us than Kathryn's safety, and that is bound to her mental health. There's no room in this business for indecision or divided loyalty. We need to know she's ready to come back to us and get this job done."

"Divided loyalty? What are you inferring?"

Holmes leaned back and crossed his arms. "She made some rather scurrilous accusations against this agency."

Smitty glared at him and then offered a disparaging glance at Forsythe for sharing the information. It didn't really surprise him though. The SOE and the OSS were like incestuous twins.

"She was upset."

Forsythe nodded. "As were we all."

The two colonels stared at him, waiting for his answer.

"So, what ... are you asking me if I think she's going to turn into a Nazi or something?"

Holmes raised his brow. "The mind can be a fragile thing, Mr. Smith. Our Miss Hammond has been *through the ringer,* as you Americans say. I've seen good people broken by less."

Smitty didn't like the man's tone or his implication, and he liked even less his assumption of possession. He may have had questions about what Kathryn still thought about the accident, but her loyalty was not one of them.

"No one hates those Nazi bastards more than she does, and she'll do anything to bring them down."

Holmes smirked. "You're saying she finds us the lesser of two evils?"

He looked at the man and wanted to say, "Aren't we?," but merely said, "Yes."

Forsythe nodded and closed the file on his desk. "Thank you for your honesty, John. You may go."

The two colonels waited until the agent was gone and then sat in contemplative silence for a moment.

Forsythe exhaled. "Not a very glowing endorsement."

Holmes smiled. "Miss Hammond needn't like us, Walter, or necessarily trust us. She need only hate them." He walked to the window and gazed at the busy streets below. "Shame about the hostility towards us, but I dare say I've grown fond of your lovely agent. She seems to have *the stuff,* don't you think?" He turned. "Recognizes the larger picture and accepts her place in it. She'll serve us well."

Forsythe glared at him as he came to his side and gloated like a puppet master pleased with the performance of his marionettes.

"You're a cold, ruthless bastard, Holmes, if you don't mind my saying."

Holmes grinned. "Not at all. I take it as a personal compliment.

And may I say, you are not, nor are most in your employ, and that is why the SOE will always be the superior agency."

He laughed at Forsythe's seething disdain and put a hand on his shoulder.

"Don't trouble yourself about it, old chap. We've been at this a bit longer than you Yanks, and we better understand the world view, as it were."

He pulled a pipe from his pocket and leaned on the intercom lever.

"Send in Miss Hammond, please, and if it wouldn't be too much trouble, could you be a dear and find me a cup of tea?"

<hr>

Kathryn smiled from the stage of The Grotto as the audience applauded the final song of her set. She'd been back for a week and had played to an unusually packed house each time. Dominic claimed it was evidence of how much she was missed, but Kathryn dismissed it as the result of the club owner's extensive ad campaign announcing her return and curious onlookers eager for a glimpse of the hard-luck musician triumphing over near tragedy.

Kathryn didn't care. She was happy for Dominic and glad to give the local papers a warm and fuzzy human interest story to break up the drudgery of the war headlines. Jenny had written a particularly moving article in her *About Town* column, and Kathryn treasured it even more when she learned Jenny had written it weeks before Dominic had invited her to return.

She was in the audience tonight, along with Clayton and his family, in honor of Stephanie's ninth birthday.

Kathryn grinned as she came up behind her niece and kissed her on the cheek. "Say, who let you in here?"

"Hi!" Stephanie beamed with stars in her eyes as she looked up at her glamorous aunt. "Gosh, you were swell!" She ran her small hand across the sequined gold dress, mesmerized. "So pretty."

"Thank you, sweetie." Kathryn held out her arms. "Come on, give me a hug."

Stephanie hopped from her chair and wrapped her arms around her stooping aunt.

Kathryn held her tight. It had been too long since she'd seen her, and she didn't know when she'd see her again.

"Mmm," she hummed in her ear as she squeezed. "Happy Birthday, pretty girl. I love you."

"I love you too, Aunt Kath."

Kathryn couldn't bring herself to let go.

Stephanie giggled as she squirmed to escape. "You're squishing me."

"Sorry." Kathryn held her at arm's length, hoping in the dimly lit club that no one could see the tears in her eyes. "You look beautiful! Nine agrees with you."

"Mommy made my dress."

Kathryn looked up at the politely smiling woman. "It's beautiful, Nan." She stood and greeted her sister-in-law with a peck on the cheek, as she did with Jenny, and then she gave a warm hug to her brother.

"Thank you for coming, and thank you for bringing Stephanie."

Nan grinned. "We couldn't keep her away. It's all she wanted for her birthday."

"It's all she's talked about all week," Clayton added. "Thanks for getting her in."

"Well, when Dominic gets shut down for serving alcohol to a minor, I'll send him to your office to complain." She slid Clayton's champagne glass away from his daughter's slowly reaching hand.

Nan scolded her daughter and Clayton laughed.

"You were fantastic, Kath."

"Thanks," she said, as everyone sat down.

Kathryn surreptitiously glanced around the room while everyone else got settled. Jenny noticed and questioned her with a subtle tilt of her head. Kathryn nodded discreetly, acknowledging the start of her next assignment. Jenny closed her eyes briefly and gamely put on a smiling mask for the rest of the evening.

It was far past Stephanie's bedtime by the time the little girl lay sleeping on her father's shoulder while they waited for the valet to bring the car around.

Kathryn watched him set his sleeping daughter in Nan's lap in the passenger seat and gently close the car door.

"Nothing wakes her up," he said, as they rounded the back of the car. "Say, are you coming over next weekend? We're having some friends over and I'd like to—"

Kathryn put her hand on his arm. "Listen, Clay, I need to talk to you a minute."

"Out here?" He rubbed his hands together against the chilly winter night.

"It's important."

"Okay, well, here—" He took off his overcoat and offered it to her.

"No, I'm all right."

"Don't be silly," he insisted, as he wrapped it around her exposed shoulders.

Nan waited a few minutes and then craned her head around to look out the back window of the car, wondering what was taking so long. Her husband was gesturing in an agitated manner, and her sister-in-law was ineffectually trying to calm him. This mysterious ballet went on for a few more moments, until Clayton got in the car, angrily tossed his overcoat in the backseat, and slammed the door.

"*Clay*," Nan said in a whisper, putting her hand over her daughter's ear. "You'll wake her up. What's wrong?"

Clayton shoved the car in gear. "Give me a minute to calm down," he growled, and then he drove off.

Jenny lay in bed, staring into the darkness above. The cold, empty space beside her was a bitter reminder that Kathryn was sleeping in someone else's arms tonight instead of hers. That's what she assumed anyway. It was past three a.m., and she'd heard nothing from Kathryn since they parted with regretful smiles across the table at the club. It was awkward and frightening for Jenny—leaving her love to the unknown—but her promise to handle it carried her gracefully from the club to home, where she promptly allowed herself to fall apart in her foyer.

She supposed she'd better get it out of her system. This would only be the first of many evenings spent wrestling with her revulsion for the situation, and the sooner she got used to it, the better it would be for both of them. She closed her eyes. Who was she kidding? She would never get used to it. The thought of someone else's hands on her lover, their mouth drinking from her lips, tasting her body, exploring her most intimate places, places meant only for her—God. She imagined Kathryn moaning for them, coming for them, and even though make-believe, it made her sick. Just like Kathryn said it would.

Jenny felt like a daft person, unable to control her torturous imagination. Would Kathryn sound the same with this stranger? Would her cries of ecstasy bring her partner to climax as it did her? Would her playacting arouse her? Would she come in spite of herself, in spite of their love? Was she acting, or did she enjoy it? Jenny swallowed her nausea and sat up, gasping for air.

She despised herself for such thoughts. She reminded herself she had the easy part, and then she remembered Kathryn's past as a prostitute and wondered if it was true. Maybe Kathryn had the easy part. Sleeping with strangers was as simple as switching pairs of shoes. Revulsion turned to anger, and Jenny welcomed it. She couldn't say with any certainty the target for her anger—Kathryn, the war, the past, the future—but it caused a relentless ache in her gut that was bursting to free itself from the confines of her body.

She leaped from the bed with her hand pressed to her mouth and scrambled to the bathroom door, where she leaned on the doorjamb and waited for her churning stomach to make up its mind. She heard a car swing into the drive and saw its headlights illuminate the bedroom wall like a prison searchlight looking for her AWOL promise to handle it. Jenny had a moment of panicked indecision, knowing she couldn't let Kathryn see her in such a state. She hurriedly climbed back into bed and pretended to be asleep.

Kathryn carefully eased the front door closed until she heard the dull click of the lock. She gently laid her keys in the porcelain bowl on the side table in the foyer and slipped out of her shoes. Thank goodness the house was dark and quiet. She wasn't ready to face Jenny. She felt awkward, like an intruder in someone else's happy home. She'd become someone else to convince Bouchaule she still belonged to him, and to her surprise, falling back into that role was easier than falling back out.

She stood at the bedroom door and gazed at Jenny's sleeping form. This was her home. Jenny was her home. She closed her eyes and reached inside herself to find the woman who belonged here, the woman who was loved here. She silently exhaled in relief when her alter ego fell away and she felt herself again. She smiled at her triumphant transformation and tiptoed upstairs to use the shower.

Jenny rolled onto her side and listened to the water run down the pipes in the wall. She imagined Kathryn washing the stranger from her body. Then, she would come to bed and expect what? Absolution? Ignorance? Denial? Jenny rolled onto her back and covered her face. She had to give Kathryn all those things. She had to pull it off. She promised she would handle it.

The water stopped and she soon heard the telltale creak of the wooden floorboards, as Kathryn padded across the bedroom and quietly slipped into bed.

Kathryn gently kissed her on the cheek and settled onto her side.

Jenny knew she should respond, but she was paralyzed, caught between proving ownership with a blinding kiss and bursting into tears because she felt personally violated on Kathryn's behalf. She took the coward's way out and pretended to be asleep, but at least she was handling it.

"Nothing happened," Kathryn whispered.

Jenny slowly opened her eyes.

Kathryn took her hand and brought it to her lips, where she kissed it. "Nothing happened."

"You don't have to tell me anything," Jenny whispered, so the lump in her throat wouldn't betray her inner turmoil.

She heard Kathryn smile and felt her soft breath on her knuckles when she said, "I'd want to know."

Jenny was silent for a moment, corralling her emotions. The darkness hid a myriad of sins, and she was thankful, as she reached out and caressed Kathryn's face. Together they would do this. Only through trust would they survive. Kathryn had played her part tonight, and now Jenny had to play hers. She leaned in and tenderly kissed Kathryn on the lips as a thank you.

Apparently, they would both sleep on the things not said and, more than likely, ignore them in the light of the new day. And so it would go.

Jenny let her hand fall away.

"I love you. Nite."

"Love you too."

Jenny stared into the awkward silence and shut her eyes against her rapidly forming tears. Kathryn eventually rolled onto her back, and Jenny couldn't help but feel abandoned. She didn't know what she expected the woman to do, but they were failing their first test. If they didn't get it right now, they would never get it right. They would set a precedent that would do nothing but drive a wedge between them. She was doing the very thing she accused Kathryn of doing— shutting her out. They had nothing if not emotional honesty, and Jenny needed to show her love, feel their love.

She leaned over and pulled Kathryn into a kiss. It was tentative at first, but then passionate, as she claimed what was hers. Kathryn gave her what she asked for and offered even more, which was greedily taken.

Their fervent kiss became a vessel of truth, as Jenny lost the tenuous grasp on her emotions and pulled back. She pressed her forehead to Kathryn's in an attempt to regain control, but she began to cry and then sob. She tried to push away, managing a blubbering, "I'm sorry," but Kathryn wouldn't let her go.

"Shh. It's okay." She cradled Jenny's head protectively onto her shoulder and urged her to let it out. "It's okay."

Jenny didn't know what to say. She didn't know if she was relieved that nothing happened, appalled at what she had to look forward to, or ashamed for not thinking until too late that Kathryn might be the one in need of support.

"I'm sorry," she said again.

"I know, honey. It's okay." Kathryn stroked her hair. "It's okay." She kissed her head. "I love you. We're in this together. They don't win, right?"

Jenny nodded.

Kathryn stared at the ceiling and nodded too, but she doubted the state of their personal war with the enemy. She'd already lost her family. There would be time enough to mourn that, but this was not it. Nor was it the time to take stock in what else she might lose. There was no room for weakness. She had work to do. She comforted Jenny and processed her reintroduction to Bouchaule.

CHAPTER THIRTY-THREE

"What now?" Kathryn had asked the cab driver as they sat at a desolated crossroad outside the city.

"Now I drop you off."

"Here?" she said incredulously. "There's nothing here. Not even a streetlight."

"Look, lady, I got my instructions, see? And when people pay that kinda do-re-mi for a cab ride to nowhere, you forget your own name if they tell you to, get me?"

Kathryn exhaled and exited the cab, which quickly drove off. She stood in the pitch dark, still in her club attire, and watched the cab's taillights disappear into the distance.

She'd found a note slipped under her door when she arrived at her dressing room that evening. It was handwritten from Thierry Bouchaule, which said he needed to see her and that he'd meet her after the show. She assumed he was somewhere inside the club, so she hung around until most everyone had gone for the night, giving the man ample opportunity to show himself. When he didn't, she went to her car, parked in the back alley of The Grotto, and found it wouldn't start. A cab drove up on cue to her frustrated curse, and here she was, standing in the dirt, with her overcoat draped elegantly over her shoulders, waiting for Bouchaule's long-anticipated appearance.

She waited a disproportionately long time compared with the perfect timing of the cab at the club, but, soon, headlights appeared from the road ahead, and a long dark sedan pulled alongside. The driver got out and politely opened the back door. She smiled. Thierry Bouchaule had gone to a lot of trouble to see her again.

To her surprise, Bouchaule was not waiting inside. Instead, she found two men identifying themselves as FBI agents. One got out and extended his hand for her to enter.

She played dumb.

"Say, what is this?"

"You're the one standing in the middle of nowhere. Why don't you tell us?"

"I'm getting some fresh air. Is that illegal?"

The man inside turned on the floor courtesy light, tilted his hat back off his forehead, and stretched out his leg.

"Have a seat."

She straightened. "Or what?"

The burly man beside her grasped her arm. "Or we all forget we're civilized."

Good cop, bad cop, she surmised. She got in the car with a practiced sneer, and the man on her arm slid in beside her while the driver shut the door and stood guard outside.

The two agents waited for her to comment, but she knew better than that. Good cop to her right chuckled.

"You have a penchant for trouble, Miss Hammond." He looked her up and down with equal parts lust and disdain. "Questionable men. Questionable circumstances."

She settled into her seat, amazed the arrogant G-Men had no idea who they were dealing with. She crossed her legs and smiled as she smoothed her shimmering dress across her knee.

"What can I say ... I lead an interesting life."

The fellow took a moment to appreciate her poise and her shapely leg and then calmly asked, "Where is he?"

She turned to him conversationally. "You know, I look in the mirror and ask myself that every day. I'm an attractive woman, don't you think? The man of my dreams is out there, yet I haven't had a date in months. Where is he? Am I *too* attractive? Is there such a thing?" She leaned into his personal space. "Do you find my beauty intimidating?"

She watched his nostrils flare as he inhaled the possibility of her smiling lips.

The burly bad cop on her left leaned forward. "Look, dolly, don't play cute with us. You're dealing with the U.S. government here."

Kathryn could barely contain her laughter as she leaned into the titillated man on her right. "Hold me, brother, I'm shaking."

"Knock it off, you!" Bad cop grabbed her arm again. "Save the immoral sexual game for your next meal ticket. It has no power here."

She looked him up and down. "Oh, I see." She smiled sympathetically and patted his knee. "I've heard about men like you."

The object of her insult balled his hand into a fist.

"Easy, boy." The man on the right reached across. "She's teasing you."

Kathryn looked over her shoulder at him. "Actually, I was teasing *you.* I'm quite serious about him."

Good cop smiled and looked to his partner. "What did I tell you? Clever girl."

His partner grunted at being played and listened while the other took over.

"Miss Hammond, Mr. Bouchaule is a very dangerous man. A threat to this country."

She crossed her arms, feigning disinterest. "Well, whoever this man is, perhaps you should be out apprehending him instead of pestering me."

Bad cop showed her a photograph of them dancing together at one of Forrester's fundraisers.

She shrugged. "I dance with a lot of men."

Photograph after photograph appeared in quick succession, chronicling every public occasion of their meetings.

"Shall we stop playing games now?"

"So I know him. So what? I haven't seen him in ages."

"We know he contacted you tonight. We know you were to meet him here."

"I don't know what you're talking about. A cab driver and I had a disagreement over a fare; that's how I wound up here. So, if you are any kind of gentlemen, you'll give me a ride home and we can put this little incident of mistaken brilliance behind us. No hard feelings."

"I suggest you cooperate, Miss Hammond," said the good cop. "We can make your life very difficult."

She laughed. "Get in line."

He smiled. "Yes, well, I understand the road has been a bit bumpy since your unfortunate mishap, but you seem to be holding up well."

She had no comment.

"We'd like to see you continue to do well. We'd like you to keep your job, for example ..."

Kathryn smirked. As if they could influence Dominic.

"A job which you do very well," the man went on. "Loved the show tonight. Nice family. Cute little girl."

Kathryn did her best to control her sudden rage, but she knew the men saw it, evident by their ever-widening grins.

"I don't know what you want from me," she said as evenly as she could. "I told you I haven't seen Bouchaule, nor do I expect to."

Bad cop reached under the seat and presented something wrapped in a handkerchief.

Kathryn looked at it. "What's that?"

The agent smiled. "The distributor cap for your car."

Kathryn slowly cut her eyes to him. The trip out there had been a ruse. They knew nothing of Bouchaule's note, the timing mere coincidence, but the fact that she'd readily accepted the cab ride and waited in a deserted field told them she expected to hear from Bouchaule eventually.

She chuckled. *Touché.* "Who's clever now?"

Bad cop grinned and tapped on the window beside him with his knuckle.

"We'll be watching you, and we'll be in touch. Count on it."

The driver opened the door, and the agent got out and extended his hand to help her out.

Kathryn looked at good cop. "You're leaving me here? Are you kidding me?"

"Does he look like he's a kidder?"

She snorted derisively and stepped out of the car without taking the offered hand.

"You'll need this," bad cop said, as he handed over the distributor cap.

"And what am I supposed to do with this?"

"You'll need it when the cab takes you to your car."

She stared at him as if she hadn't the faintest idea what to do with the thing.

"Just bat your eyes, honey. I'm sure the cabbie will put it in for you." He grinned. "The distributor cap too."

The car drove off, and she stood in the still, black night, holding the bundle by the corners like a dirty diaper.

Kathryn straightened from the engine compartment of her car and pulled on the handle of the split hood, letting it slam into place. She had no words for the cab driver on the ride back, and she could plug in her own distributor cap, thank you very much.

She had nothing but curses for the FBI as she wiped her hands on the agent's handkerchief before unlocking the back door of the club and going inside.

She was furious. If Bouchaule was waiting for her tonight, he surely would be gone by now, and if he saw the FBI watching her, they had just made it that much harder for her to convince Bouchaule she was on his side. She found some comfort in the Bureau's surveillance, though, if only to confirm her sanity. She had been watched. She wasn't just paranoid. How two agencies in the same government could be so out of touch with each other was beyond her. The OSS would hear about how the FBI's meddling had cost her a reunion with Bouchaule—and maybe his trust.

She shook her head as she scrubbed the dirt from her hands at the small sink behind the bar. She seethed at the veiled threat to her niece, and playing the scene over in her head, wished she'd done the man bodily harm. She dried her hands and paused mid-violent thought, as she sensed a presence at her back. She squinted into the mirrored wall across the room, confirming her intuition.

"Thierry!" She turned in mock shock as she fell back against the sink for support.

He held up his hands with a queer sort of smile, glad and unsure all at once. "Do not be frightened, darling."

She remained speechless, allowing him to pace the reintroduction, and allowing herself to get into character.

"I tried earlier, but someone was watching."

"Yes," she said angrily, not altogether acting, "and do you know who that someone was? The FBI!" She paused for effect. *"Don't be frightened, darling,"* she mocked. "I'm not frightened. I'm furious! Do you know how long they've been watching me?"

"Yes," he said meekly. "That is why—"

"Yes? Did you know they threatened my family? My family, Thierry!"

"I am sorry. I did not know."

"You're sorry," she spat. "I have half a mind to pick up that phone and call the FBI right now."

"I will call them myself if you agree to stand by my side."

She stared at him, wondering what kind of game he was playing.

"Don't be foolish. That would be madness."

He stepped closer. "You care?"

She lifted her chin, putting up a wall against his advances. "I care about the safety of my family. I care about getting my life back, and I assure you, that life will not include you. I want you to walk out of here, and I never want to see you again."

He moved even closer. "I cannot do that."

"Well, you had better try, because—"

Suddenly his hands were on each side of her face and she found her lips captured in a hungry kiss.

She ducked from under his hands and mouth and struck him sharply across the face with her open hand.

"How dare you!"

Bouchaule barely flinched. "I love you."

She tried to slap him again, but this time he was ready with a lightening quick hand around her wrist. "I love you," he repeated emphatically.

"You're lying. You're here because of what was done to me. You want me to be your lab rat, so you can poke and prod me like they did."

He pulled her wrist down to her side. "I am here because I miss you and I was worried about you."

"Like you were worried about me in the hospital when you stole my blood?"

He slowly raised his chin, but said nothing.

"Do you know what they found? They found nothing. *Nothing!* So you can go home and stop pretending that you give a damn about me."

He paused, as if deliberating.

"They do not know what they are looking for."

She yanked her arm away and put some distance between them. It was the first confirmation that something had actually been done to her beyond the gas exposure. She found herself shaking, as the line between real anger and controlled manipulation blurred. She had to stay in the moment, had to draw out his intent.

"Is that why you're here? To take another sample?"

He didn't answer.

So much for love, she thought bitterly. One more person to use her. One more person to control her. "What do you want from me, hm?" She grabbed a knife from a cutting board at the bar. "You want my blood? Here!" She meant only to hold the knife against the vulnerable underside of her wrist, but she found herself pulling it across her skin, drawing blood. "Take it all, and go to hell!"

"*No*, Kathryn!" Bouchaule lunged for her wrist and the knife, procuring one and disposing of the other. He quickly produced a handkerchief and wrapped it around the wound.

Kathryn was momentarily stunned. To her surprise, she found her actions frighteningly liberating, like a disillusioned nun finally discarding her habit. She blinked and found Bouchaule on his knees, kissing her palm while he pressed the handkerchief against the superficial wound.

"No, darling, no," he kept whispering between kisses.

Kathryn closed her eyes. She felt drained and lightheaded, and it had nothing to do with the sight of blood. She was caught up in the drama of the scene and realized it wasn't just a scene, it was her life, and like a cruel Rosetta stone, this man was the only one who could help her make sense of it.

"At first, I thought it was just an accident," she said, as if in a trance.

Bouchaule looked up as she went on.

"But now I realize it was because of you. They did this to me because of you."

The doctor wrapped his free arm around her waist and pressed the side of his face to her abdomen. "I am so sorry."

"You left me here."

He looked up again and slid his hand to her hip. "What?"

She looked down at him and pulled her wrist away, replacing the pressure of his hand with her own. She found herself lost in the moment, really wanting to know. "Why did you leave me here?"

He appeared remorseful, but silent, and she walked away, finally rounding the bar and taking a seat at the end.

Bouchaule got to his feet and followed, sitting beside her.

"I had no choice, darling. I could not ask you to come with me."

Kathryn looked him in the eyes. "*Come away with me, Kathryn. How hard is that?*"

Bouchaule was speechless for a few bewildering moments. "I had no idea you felt so strongly."

She looked away, disappointed. "You wouldn't."

"That is not fair. You were the one keeping me at arm's length."

"Because of Forrester. For your safety. Couldn't you see that?"

They were both silent. Bouchaule was processing the past while Kathryn was considering the present.

Bouchaule reached out his hand. "I did not know."

She looked into his expressive hazel eyes. "Would you have taken me, had you known?"

He leaned in, with no fear of another slap, and kissed her until she returned his passion in kind. They stopped kissing and embraced. Then Kathryn whispered in his ear. "What are we going to do?"

He gently pushed her away, held his index finger to his lips for silence, and pointed around the bar area. Kathryn frowned in mock confusion and then nodded, letting him know she understood his concern that the club was wired. It was, of course.

He dragged a cocktail napkin over and took a pen from his jacket pocket, carefully removing the cap before leaning in for another kiss. Kathryn moaned for effect, and he smiled as he pulled away. He scribbled a time and place on the napkin, kissed her again, and made a vocal production as he ended it.

"I must go now, my darling."

"But—"

"It is not safe here."

"When will I see you again?"

"Soon."

<hr>

Kathryn, Holmes, and Forsythe sat at a table at HQ, huddled over the wire recording of Kathryn's meeting with Bouchaule. When it got to the part where the FBI threatened her family, Forsythe stopped the playback. "Did the FBI do that?"

Kathryn nodded.

The American colonel frowned. "That was wholly inappropriate."

Holmes quietly smirked and shook his head.

Kathryn knew that in his world, nothing was inappropriate. She ignored him. "Is the Bureau cooperating?"

"Completely. They have been informed of your status, acknowledged their presence is a threat to your assignment, and have agreed to turn jurisdiction over to us."

"I imagine they weren't very pleased by that."

"To say the least."

The intercom buzzed and Holmes mashed the switch. "Yes?"

"The gentlemen are here, sir."

"Send them in."

The two FBI agents were led into the room and introductions were made.

Agent Eric Burnes, the good cop, was still outgoing and greeted Kathryn with an easy smile. Agent Gus Casey, the bad cop, was still grumpy, but considering he and his partner had just been relieved of their case, Kathryn couldn't blame him.

"You are here as a courtesy, gentlemen," Forsythe said. The animosity between the two agencies was legendary. "As you know, your superiors have already turned over your case files. We want you to know we appreciate all the hard work you've put into this, and we assure you, the case is in good hands."

Casey's eyes drifted behind Forsythe to the boxes of their records stacked along the wall.

"Our hands were just fine," he grumbled.

"Fine but not very productive," Forsythe countered sternly, aware of the agent's hostile nature. "Did you have The Grotto wired last night?"

Casey shrugged. "She hadn't worked there in months."

"Three to be exact," Forsythe continued. "But she worked there last night, and last night is when Bouchaule showed up."

The two FBI agents looked at each other and then at the indifferent singer. Forsythe turned on the playback, to the part where

Kathryn threatened to call the FBI and told Bouchaule she was done with him.

The burly agent frowned at Kathryn's seemingly counterproductive tirade, but not for long, as the kiss and the ensuing slap played out.

Burnes smiled, as he realized Kathryn had been kissed, and he was not shocked when he heard the ensuing slap. He absentmindedly rubbed his jaw, obviously wondering if that would have been him had he given in to his baser instincts.

The two G-Men raised their brows when Bouchaule professed his love, and then Forsythe fast-forwarded past details that were no longer the FBI's concern. He let them hear the end to convince them Bouchaule was well in hand.

Burnes stared at Kathryn. His respect for her grew as the recording went on. Casey glowered, as if lunch disagreed with him.

The two men leaned in as the conversation ceased, and they tried to interpret the creaks and miscellaneous noises. A grin of recognition split Burnes's lips, and he clasped his hands on the table, as Casey, clueless and exasperated, frowned and pointed at the machine.

"What's going on here?"

"He's kissing me."

The agent narrowed his eyes, registering a look caught between disapproval and disbelief, as the noises continued a little too long for his comfort.

Kathryn merely shrugged and smiled. "He's very good."

Burnes sat back and chuckled as the recording played out, and Forsythe turned off the machine.

"So, you see, gentlemen, our agent has the matter well in hand."

Burnes raised his brow and nodded. "Safe to say."

Casey looked to Colonel Forsythe. "Well, I'm not so sure I like her methods."

Forsythe was about to defend his agent, but Kathryn defended herself.

"Mr. Casey—"

"*Agent* Casey," he countered.

She nodded curtly. "My apologies. Agent Casey, perhaps if you had spent more time keeping track of your subject and less time intimidating possible allies, *you* would have someone on the inside, and we would be sitting in *your* offices instead of ours, but as it happens—"

"You'll have to excuse my partner," Burnes said, as he leaned forward and addressed the group. "We worked very hard to secure Mr. Bouchaule, and, understandably, we are disappointed that the opportunity to finish what we started has passed us by." He eyed his partner, who reluctantly agreed as he shifted and cleared his throat.

"Yeah, disappointed."

"Disappointment aside," Burnes continued, "after witnessing Miss Hammond in action, I am confident the case is in very capable hands, and we are eager to assist you in any way we can."

Casey clasped his hands, out of ammo, and dropped the attitude. "What do you want to know?"

Once the bruised egos were soothed, the group settled down to business. The FBI admitted they had been unable to track Bouchaule upon his return, so they started trailing Kathryn, hoping he would contact her again. They had the right idea but the wrong approach, and even Casey conceded their less than productive results. Clearly, Kathryn had the inside track on Thierry Bouchaule, and, clearly, turning over the case was the proper thing for the Bureau to do.

When the men got up to leave, Burnes approached Kathryn and shook her hand.

"I really am very impressed, Miss Hammond. Be careful, and good luck."

"Thank you, Burnes."

Casey was next, holding out his hand.

Kathryn looked at it like it was a fifty-cent piece when she was expecting a dollar.

He shrugged with a grin.

"I hate to lose, doll. No hard feelings, eh?"

She understood his type and shook his hand. "No hard feelings." She briefly held on. "I'm not going to let us lose, Casey."

He nodded, satisfied.

The trio watched the FBI agents leave, and Holmes got right down to business.

"Tell us about the second meeting."

Kathryn immediately leaned forward, anxious to get on with it as well.

"We've got a problem."

The second meeting with Bouchaule started innocently enough when a car picked her up at the appointed time and place, and this time, to her surprise, Bouchaule was in the backseat to greet her. She thought it bold, his appearance in broad daylight, but he seemed unconcerned, almost giddy, as he held her hand and they rode aimlessly around the city.

It would be a thin line between truth and lies when it came to dealing with the doctor, and the first major hurdle would be how Bouchaule would deal with the intrusion of the FBI.

"How can you be so calm?" Kathryn had asked as she looked around. "I'm a nervous wreck."

Bouchaule had merely smiled.

She admired his confidence. He always seemed one step ahead and undaunted by the future. He dismissed the FBI as one would shoo away a gnat and kissed her hand, obviously pleased to be in her company.

"I am going to take good care of you, darling. Do you trust me?"

Kathryn had seen her share of liars, cheats, and generally despicable men, and no matter how smooth an operator, the truth was always evident in their eyes. She saw nothing ignoble in the Frenchman's gentle eyes when he looked at her. Either he was sincere or he had cultivated the most incredible façade she'd ever seen.

"Yes, Thierry, I trust you."

He smiled and kissed her hand again. "I have taken care of your government. You need not be concerned."

She suppressed a flash of panic. "What do you mean, you've taken care of my government?"

He patted her hand, a conciliatory gesture on the way to more important things. "Friends in high places afford one many things. Now, are you free for a late dinner tomorrow evening?"

Forsythe offered a momentary glance at Holmes, and both men frowned, chanting in unison, "Friends in high places?"

Kathryn sat back. "Exactly. Now, either he's lying, which wouldn't make any sense, or one of our agencies is running a higher table."

Holmes put his hands on his hips, as if doing his best to control his exasperation with these amateurs in the spy trade. "Perhaps there *is* a mole in your government assisting him."

Forsythe refused to believe that. "I'll get to the bottom of this."

"That will be near impossible if you've got a mole," Holmes rightly pointed out.

Kathryn rubbed her forehead, her demise practically guaranteed if the latter was the case.

Holmes couldn't resist stating the obvious to his American counterpart. "I'm sure I don't have to tell you what a precarious position your agent is in. She could already be exposed to Bouchaule, and once he gets whatever it is he came back for—"

"Well aware, Holmes," Forsythe snapped as he reached for the phone. "Patch me through to the director."

Pause.

"Yes, the director."

"I'd hate to see you become a sacrificial lamb," Holmes commented dryly as he and Kathryn walked side by side down the hallway toward the elevator bay.

You mean again? Kathryn wanted to say.

"I appreciate your concern, Colonel. It's quite touching."

He laughed. "You don't care for me, do you, Miss Hammond?"

"The feeling's mutual, I'm sure."

"On the contrary. I find you an extraordinary woman. Pity the SOE couldn't keep hold of you."

She looked at him sideways, his crooked smile sincere and just as bizarre as the rest of her day. Her one and only mission for the SOE was an unmitigated disaster, and she doubted the SOE wanted anything to do with her after that.

"I think the SOE was very happy to have me out of their jurisdiction, Colonel Holmes."

"You were a loose cannon after your ... incident, Miss Hammond, and you know it."

She couldn't deny reckless behavior that could only be described as a death wish.

"And now?"

The colonel smiled. "Now you are a fine-tuned cannon, and we are pleased to have you on our side."

"I suppose I should say thank you, but I won't."

"Quite all right. Your continued participation is thanks enough."

She could only shake her head.

Holmes cozying up to her, moles in the government jeopardizing her cover—she didn't need any more distractions or bullets to dodge.

If Bouchaule was on to her, he certainly didn't show it during their afternoon meeting, but then again, he was just charming in that way.

He kissed her passionately before they parted, and Kathryn did her best to flush out where he was staying.

She pulled back from their kiss, breathless, eyes half-lidded, feigning desire. "Is there somewhere we can go?"

She could tell he thought about taking her right there in the car, his driver and passersby be damned, but instead, he said, "I cannot today ... business, you understand, but soon, my darling."

She kissed him again and made sure that *soon* couldn't be soon enough.

He pulled away this time and licked his lips, as he shifted in his seat to allow for his growing erection. He looked at his watch and cursed under his breath in French.

"Soon," he repeated purposefully.

Kathryn smiled, enjoying the small victory. At the time, she couldn't allow herself to comprehend what it would mean if her cover had been compromised. She couldn't afford even the slightest slip of character. She would save her concerns for her ride to headquarters, where even her victory turned into a bitter pill when she realized it wouldn't be long before her intimate relationship with Bouchaule would resume.

It was a day of steely resolve. Stay the course with Bouchaule, hope there was no mole, and trust that her relationship with Jenny was strong enough to withstand the next step.

The price of being an agent never seemed higher, but she was reminded it was never high enough when she and Holmes turned the corner and ran into an argument between Jenny and her supervisor outside the code room.

"Someone should at least try!" Jenny shouted.

"You know better, Ryan."

"Problem?" Holmes calmly queried.

The supervisor handed him a communiqué. "We lost a team. The Germans cracked a cell, knew where they were dropping and when. They probably never made it to the ground."

"But you can't be sure," Jenny insisted.

"That's a shame." Holmes passed the communiqué to Kathryn.

"That's a shame?" Jenny spat. "That's all you have to say?"

Holmes stared at her. "Welcome to war, Miss Ryan."

"You cold son of—"

Kathryn stepped in and took her by the elbow. "May I speak with you a moment?"

Holmes and the supervisor went about their business with synchronized shakes of their heads while Kathryn led Jenny down the hall and around the corner.

"What are you doing?"

Jenny pointed at the paper in Kathryn's hand. "Did you read that? They were from our group ... Johnson and Hendricks."

"I know that."

"They were our friends, Kathryn!"

"They were agents."

Jenny stared at her in disbelief. Kathryn was sure her cold response drove the point home like a stake to her heart, and she put her hand on her shoulder as Jenny turned from her.

Jenny all but brushed the touch aside and snatched the communiqué from her hand, announcing coolly, "They were my friends," as she turned and walked away.

"Jenny—" Kathryn called to her back.

Jenny lifted her hand dismissively and kept on walking.

Kathryn set down her keys and walked through the quiet house, finding no sign of Jenny. Her keys were in the bowl in the foyer, so she knew she was home. She didn't think Jenny was mad at her, per se, just upset about the loss of her friends and lashing out with the helpless frustration of their meaningless deaths.

Kathryn completely understood and knew she could have been more sympathetic in her response. Just because she had hardened her heart to such eventualities was no reason to expect the same from others.

She looked out the kitchen window and saw Jenny leaving the dock in the dwindling daylight. Instead of heading for the house, she started along the lake, toward the woods. Normally, Kathryn would have given her the space she obviously needed, but she had dinner with Bouchaule to get ready for, and she didn't want to leave things with Jenny as they were.

She put on her coat, grabbed the flashlight from beside the back door, and followed after. She stayed a good distance behind and just watched as Jenny meandered along a seemingly abandoned path with no intent or direction. She had a long twig in her hand and swept it lazily along the trail like a blind woman only half-interested in finding her way.

The overgrown path eventually led to an equally overgrown

former clearing, where a moderately sized greenhouse, long abandoned, stood in an advanced state of decay. Most of its glass was broken or missing, and its door hung loosely on its hinges. Jenny went inside, and Kathryn approached and stood just outside the entrance. She watched as Jenny swiped at spider webs with her stick and then stood looking at the wreckage of what once must have been a glorious oasis.

Jenny poked at the decaying leaves and branches on the table by her side and pushed the remains of a broken terracotta pot off the edge. It shattered into more pieces when it hit the wooden floor, and she imagined it like Johnson and Hendricks, as they fell from the sky, with no one to care about their broken remains on the ground.

She looked up, startled to find herself being watched through the broken pane of glass in the door.

"Jesus!" She put her hand to her chest. "You scared me."

Kathryn opened the door and stepped inside. "Sorry."

"I didn't expect you home. Don't you have a show?"

"It's Monday."

"Oh, right." The day no longer held its charm or its promise of good things to come.

Jenny looked to the ground and planted the point of her stick into the frayed weave of an old ratty rug beneath her feet, unsure of what to say.

"I didn't know this was out here," Kathryn began conversationally. "Kinda neat."

Jenny smiled without much emotion behind it and gave a half-hearted glance around. "Once upon a time it was. I remember when I was a kid, Gran had it filled with exotic plants and beautiful flowers." She kicked the pieces of broken pottery at her feet. "Hard to believe anything beautiful ever existed here."

Kathryn was silent for a moment and then tentatively moved closer.

"Listen, Jenny, about this afternoon ..."

Jenny cut her off with a raised hand. "I apologized to Colonel Holmes. Guess I owe you one too."

"No. They were your friends. You were upset, and rightly so. I'm sorry I wasn't more sensitive to that."

The apology wasn't needed, and in all honesty, in her current state, she should probably tell Kathryn she just wanted to be alone for a while. "We should get back. It'll be dark soon." She tried to brush past.

Kathryn stopped her. "Hey, I said I was sorry."

Tears welled in Jenny's eyes as the reality of her new life, and Kathryn's accumulated experiences, hit her full on. "I don't want to be like you, Kathryn. So ..." She wanted to say cold, but settled on, "detached."

Kathryn let her hand fall away.

"I don't want you to be like me either."

"But I will, won't I? Eventually."

Kathryn dropped her gaze to the broken pot on the floor, and Jenny imagined she found a kinship there. She straightened her spine and defended what didn't need defending.

"Maybe you're stronger than I am, Jenny. But I can't afford the emotional investment. I just can't."

Jenny took her hand. "I know, honey, I'm not ..." She didn't know how to describe her feelings. Angry? Disappointed? Frustrated? All of them, she supposed, but not toward Kathryn. "It's so pointless. They never even reached the ground."

"I know."

Kathryn offered her arms, and Jenny fell into her embrace without hesitation. Why she ever thought being alone would be better than this, she didn't know. Safe in Kathryn's arms, fear, relief, and guilt took over.

"That could have been me."

Kathryn tightened her hold.

"I know."

· · ·

The broken glass crunched beneath their feet as they left the dilapidated building, and as the front door swung closed, its top hinge gave way and the door fell with a thud and came to rest diagonally across the entrance like a barricade.

Jenny yelped as she hopped out of the way and then laughed. "Oops."

Kathryn put her arm around her, glad to see the smile.

"When was the last time you were out here?"

"Gosh, years. Not since I was a teenager. I almost forgot it was here." She pointed to an overgrown patch through the trees. "We had some cows, a pig, and a few chickens in that field over there when I was a kid."

Kathryn chuckled. "Old MacDonald's farm."

"*Ee-aye-ee-aye-o*," Jenny sang.

Kathryn laughed, but as they walked home, she couldn't resist glancing over her shoulder at the decaying greenhouse and wondering who recently moved the rug on the floor and why.

CHAPTER THIRTY-FOUR

*K*athryn watched with fascination as tears streamed down Thierry Bouchaule's cheek. An extravagant private dinner in his room at one of the most expensive hotels in the city turned into opening night at the opera, something for which Kathryn was ill prepared. Bouchaule, naturally, had everything well planned, providing a long black evening gown with jewels and a fur coat for the occasion. It reminded Kathryn of Forrester—branding her with his likes and dislikes—and Bouchaule did not miss the contempt in her eyes.

The doctor was quick to apologize and was more than happy to skip the performance entirely. Kathryn knew skipping the performance would leave them plenty of time for other activities, so, delaying the inevitable for as long as possible, she chose the opera.

The performers were stellar, but the Russian tragedy was not one of her favorites, especially when sung in Italian. The management chose that particular opera for the opener as a tribute to the country's new ally, the Soviet Union, and she supposed it only fitting for another season in the midst of war.

As they sat in the dark upper balcony, Kathryn's mind drifted through most of the first and second acts. She was consumed with thoughts of Jenny, their life together, and what she was doing now with Bouchaule, trying to justify it all to herself. She glanced at her assignment, who was utterly lost in the bleak landscape of the Russian opera, and she was struck by his unabashed display of emotion. It brought her back to the present, back to her character, and she marveled at the depth of the curious man beside her.

At the end of the last act, she offered him her flowered handkerchief, which he took without embarrassment and dried his tears.

"Good men brought to ruin by greed and a lust for power," he announced matter-of-factly, "and always it is the people who suffer." He stood and held out his hand as the curtain fell.

As open as he had been in broad daylight that afternoon, he was equally as secretive in the evening. They arrived late, entering the auditorium just under the preperformance warning chime, and they left just as the lights went up. His desire to come and go unnoticed was obvious.

"I thought you said you have friends in high places," Kathryn said as soon as they were settled in the backseat of his chauffeured car.

He smiled. "I have many enemies in high places as well."

"Then why risk nights like tonight ... this afternoon?"

"I do not want you to feel like a criminal, darling." His eyes swept up her body, admiring her beauty. "You deserve fine things. You deserve the lifestyle in which you have become accustomed."

Kathryn stared at him. Thierry Bouchaule was a challenging case. He seemed devoid of insecurities, so it was impossible to exploit them, and he was difficult to manipulate because his motives were unclear.

They were both masters of the game, that much was certain, and Kathryn knew the approach she had taken with Forrester and so many of her conquests would not work on Bouchaule. He had seen it all, he had done it all, and he would see right through her.

Doctor Bouchaule would require a delicate balance of truth and deception. She would give him what he wanted, and what remained, if anything, would reveal the truth of his intentions.

"This is not my lifestyle. I lived in a small apartment, just barely making rent when I met Marc. Things of late have been difficult, as you can imagine, and now I share a place with a friend because that is what I can afford. I don't belong to this world." She tugged impatiently at her silk-lined fur coat. "This was Marc's world, your world—a fantasy. I have no use for fantasies or the men who dream them. I just want my life back."

Bouchaule smiled. "Was tonight not beautiful?"

"Of course."

"Then let me do this for you, not because I am a man who needs a woman to be like this or that but because I want to give you beautiful evenings and stars on a string." He eyed the diamonds around her neck and stroked her cheek.

She offered him a reluctant smile. "You make it hard for a girl to resist."

He leaned in and kissed her gently on the lips. "Precisely."

"Seriously, Thierry ..."

"Were we not being serious?"

Kathryn could see how his charm could get him almost anything, but she was no slouch at getting what she wanted either.

She looked around and then at the back of the driver's head, like she was uncomfortable with the company. Bouchaule asked him to pull the car around the corner and wait outside.

"These enemies," Kathryn began. "The men from Chicago?"

The doctor nodded.

"I've seen these men in action. They play for keeps. Forrester is proof of that. You can't expose yourself like this."

He leaned back with a frustrated exhale. "I have been living here like a caged dog for months. I do not wish the same for you. I want to dance and laugh ... I want to be alive again."

Bouchaule wanted something all right, Kathryn could tell, and it was more than her, more than her blood.

"When you left here you seemed ... satisfied. Why have you come back?"

He looked her up and down like she was mad for asking. "I would have thought that obvious."

"I'm not naïve. You didn't have to come back here. You could have sent for me. I think you know I would have come."

"I did not dare presume."

She turned away from him and stared straight ahead, upping the ante of their game. "I think after what I've been through, I deserve the truth."

They sat in silence like the strangers they were, until, finally, Bouchaule spoke.

"I do need you for my work."

Kathryn nodded silently as she mindlessly rubbed a seam on her gloved hand and absorbed the blow to her character's ego and, surprisingly, a bit to her own.

He stilled her hand. "Would you believe me if I said it was more than that?"

She pulled her hand away, still refusing to look at him. "Everyone has lied to me. I've been used, threatened—" She shook her head. "It doesn't seem to matter what I believe."

His next move should have been to convince her of his devotion, but he merely nodded and folded his hands across his lap. She held her breath, wondering if she had gone too far.

"I have no right to ask," he began softly, "but will you help me?"

His voice was sincere, absent any hint of manipulation or threat of force, should she refuse. Of course, she had no intention of refusing, sincere or not, not if she wanted answers.

"Are you working against the people who did this to me?"

"Yes."

"Then I'll help you in any way I can."

"Even if those people are in your own government?"

She looked him in the eyes, the validation of her suspicions stirring up a suppressed rage she barely managed to contain.

"Especially if they are in my own government."

He nodded and tapped on the window to retrieve the driver. To her surprise, that was the end of their evening. Gone was the suave lover, replaced by a man more serious and businesslike. Kathryn was dropped off at the club, and Bouchaule bid her good night with a polite kiss on the hand.

They arranged to meet again the next evening after her show to get on with their new partnership, but until then, Kathryn was left to contemplate whether her moves had been the right ones or whether she had overestimated her allure and slammed the door on her inside track.

Jenny dreaded arriving at the house and finding the driveway vacant. She'd stayed out late after the double feature because she couldn't bear to come home to an empty bed and a vivid imagination. Tonight, she was greeted by Kathryn's car in the drive.

The bedroom light was on, and Jenny was delighted to find Kathryn in bed with a book.

She sat up and wrapped her arms around her knees as she pulled them to her chest.

"Hi, cutie, I was worried about you. It's so late."

Jenny grinned as she slipped out of her shoes and crawled across the sheets to a waiting kiss. "Sorry."

"Mm," Kathryn hummed as their lips parted. "I'll take another one of those. I missed you tonight."

Jenny surrendered another kiss and curled up beside her. "I missed you too. I'm so glad you're here."

Kathryn put her arm around her. "Me too. What did you do tonight?"

"Double feature at the Colony ... chatted up some folks at Joe's."

Kathryn's downturned smile betrayed her regret that Jenny chose a twenty-four-hour diner over her own home just to stay occupied, and she offered a sympathetic squeeze in lieu of the *sorry, honey*, that Jenny knew was dying to escape.

They had both agreed they were no longer going to apologize for things out of their control, and as promised, each was doing what they had to do to deal with the situation.

"How was the double feature?"

Jenny put her head against Kathryn's shoulder and cheerfully recounted her evening, leaving out the angst that had distracted her for most of the night, as she struggled with her thoughts and ineffectually tried to reign in her jealousy. All that dissipated the moment she saw Kathryn's car in the drive. Whatever did or didn't happen with her assignment, she was home now. She was hers.

Nothing in Kathryn's adoring eyes gave away the intimate details of her evening, and if any intimate details were to be had, Jenny had to admit, she didn't want to know.

Ignorance truly was bliss, and for a change, she'd take it, and how.

Kathryn kissed Jenny goodbye as she headed off to work the next morning and watched her walk down the street until she was out of sight. She went to the kitchen and deposited the dishes from breakfast into the sink, then grabbed her jacket and a flashlight and headed out the back door.

Curiosity about the greenhouse led her along the shore of the lake to the woods, where she followed the overgrown path to the derelict building and went inside.

She pulled back the corner of the damp, weathered rug and immediately dropped it, yelping, "Shit!" as she jumped out of the way of a circus of subterranean creepy crawlers darting for the safety of the shadows.

She shook her arm, on the off chance one had found the inside of her sleeve inviting, and uttered a heartfelt, "Blugh," as she shuddered and shook off the heebie-jeebies.

She braced herself for the mass exodus of insects, then quickly flipped the rug to the side. She was not surprised, nor disappointed, to find the rug had hidden a wooden trapdoor.

"Yes," she whispered.

The large rectangular door protested with a sorrowful moan as she heaved up on the rusted recessed handle, but it did not resist her efforts. She was energized by the unknown as she peered into the dark hole in the ground, and with a final glance at her sunlit surroundings, she shined her flashlight down the path of the wooden steps and ventured inside.

The boards creaked with every step, and she gave each a test bounce before trusting her weight to it. Halfway down, she ducked her head and scanned the interior with her light. It was a small room, half the size of the greenhouse floor space above, with old brick walls that were mostly obscured by shelving and rusty gardening tools.

A string dangled from a porcelain light fixture to her right, and she tugged on it, only have it break off in her hand. "Swell," she said, as she reached out with the flashlight and eased some spider webs aside.

She crept deeper into the cellar. It was damp and musty but surprisingly warm, considering the chilly temperature above. She swept her light around the confined space and was disappointed to find it nothing more than an underground potter's shed. She looked to the hard-packed dirt floor for signs of footprints or a path leading into a wall and then to the ceiling for electrical conduits doing the same, but found nothing but a self-contained room.

Suddenly, a noise from the far corner spun her around, and she looked accusingly down the beam of her flashlight as she slowly approached the sound. There was a pile of burlap bags in the corner, once filled with mulch, if the debris field of shredded bark was any indication, and Kathryn plucked a long crowbar from the wall to investigate.

She slowly extended the iron bar and gingerly lifted a piece of shredded burlap, only to have it come alive, as a family of rats scattered in every direction, including right at her.

She stumbled backward, dropping the flashlight and the crowbar, and let out a high-pitched scream only a bat could love. She found her back plastered to a shelving unit, with her heart beating wildly, and terracotta pots, old cookie tins, and jars filled with nails raining down on her from the shelves above.

"Damn!" she spat, as she put her hand to her chest.

To add insult to injury, one of the junior rats was boldly sniffing at her flashlight beam, casting a menacing shadow on the wall behind it.

She lunged at it and yelled, "Git!" as more pots fell in her wake.

She grabbed the light and quickly scanned the floor for more of the little beasts, and, satisfied she'd shown them, she focused her light on the wreckage from the shelves. She'd fallen into two shelving units, but, curiously, while one unit's contents had fallen to the floor, its neighbor's contents were wholly intact and sitting just where she had found them. She reached for one of the pots and found it securely attached to its shelf, as was everything else in the unit.

Kathryn grinned and tugged on the shelving, hoping it would give way to some great mystery. Nothing. She knelt and aimed her light underneath the wooden structure and found it wasn't touching the ground at all. She stood and pushed on it.

It popped open, revealing a locked wooden door behind it.

She put her hands on her hips and smiled from ear to ear. "Well, well, well."

Kathryn's smile and self-congratulation had all but disappeared by the time she stood in the study and stared at the wall to ceiling bookcase she had just emerged from behind.

She'd made quick work of the lock on the wooden door in the cellar of the greenhouse, only to be met with an echoing black hole behind it.

Peering into the darkness with her flashlight, she saw it was a tunnel with a row of single light bulbs hanging from porcelain sockets every ten yards or so along the conduit lining the ceiling. There was an electrical box to her right, and when she threw the switch, she was pleased to see the lights illuminate the plastered brick arch of the tunnel.

The straight passageway seemingly had no end, with each bulb measuring the distance in short patches of light, like a steady stream of Morse code for the hearing impaired. From the mineral stains on the plaster walls, it seemed the tunnel had been there for some time, but the hard-packed dirt floor yielded no clues as to how recently it had been used or by whom.

She ventured inside and counted her strides—four hundred twenty in all—until she came to another locked door, this one metal and a lot older than its updated lock suggested. Her skill with a lock pick wasn't severely tested, and soon the door gave way to a room. A quick mash of the light switch beside her elbow revealed a laboratory.

She stood in awe of her discovery, like a crusader in the presence of the Holy Grail. She took a few moments to take in her surroundings and then slowly stepped down the few steps into the room.

Every sound she made was magnified as she cautiously pressed on and found herself enveloped by the deathly silence of a tomb long abandoned. The long black lab counters were gray with dust, and brown bottles that once contained chemicals lay empty and discarded beneath a bare cabinet. Filing cabinet drawers lay open mid-yawn, and remnants of their contents littered the floor, the obvious result of a hasty clean out. It was a stark contrast to the shelves and their rows of perfectly aligned glassware standing at attention for a doctor who would never return.

Kathryn was drawn to the corner of the room where a desk looked as though it had been thoroughly relieved of its secrets. She scanned the bookcase above it, and among the medical text books, found well-worn copies of Daniel Ryan's three-volume medical publication. Perplexed by the obvious frequency of its use, she took the first volume from the shelf and thumbed through it. Each page had a random number written in pencil on the top outside corner, but other than that, she saw nothing out of the ordinary. She pulled down the next volume and the next and found the same thing. She returned them to the shelf and exhaled in exasperation at the lack of information left behind.

She went through the desk, emptying the drawers of their common office clutter, and then she squatted down and shined her flashlight on the underside of the drawers, checking for anything taped beneath them or false bottoms. Nothing.

While she was at eye level with the desk, she directed her light into the mail slots against the wall but again found nothing. She put the office clutter back where she found it and tilted the blank notepads she'd found to the light, to see if any were indented with the former top page's content. Two were brand new and contained nothing, but the third looked promising. She retrieved a pencil and lightly rubbed the side of the lead across the surface of the top page.

Concentration turned to triumph, as a partial bit of a message emerged. It was a series of numbers separated by periods and spaces. Her eyes grew wide, and she knew exactly what she was looking at and why the volumes were so worn.

"Of course!" she muttered aloud. "How could I have been so blind?"

The Ryan papers were book coded, and she had just held the key in her hands. In fact, she'd had the key for nearly a year, but it never once occurred to her. She pulled Daniel Ryan's medical publications from the shelf and spread them on the desk. The OSS had the same books, and she couldn't believe it hadn't occurred to them that they were the key.

She tore a sheet of paper from the bottom of the coded pad and wrote the numbers she'd revealed.

The numbers ran on in sets of four, and it was immediately apparent that the last number in each set referred to the volume, as it never exceeded the number three. As per a typical book code, the first number referred to the page, the second number the line, and the third number the word on that line.

She excitedly transcribed the bit of code she could read and shook her head at how obvious the answer seemed now.

Usually, dictionaries or encyclopedias were used as the key to a book code for their abundant word selection, but it made perfect sense for Daniel Ryan to choose his own books, as the terminology would be built in.

She looked at her transcription and was disappointed; the

random words meant nothing. She frowned, wondering if the numbers were not in typical book code, and then she looked at the number penciled into the top corner of the volume page and, suddenly, they made sense.

She added the corner number to each number referred to by that page, and lo and behold, it made a sentence.

"Smart, Dr. Ryan. Very smart."

Anyone with access to his books and any knowledge of codes could have easily broken the coded documents if they guessed the books were the key. Because of this, Daniel Ryan super encrypted his messages by adding the numbers he'd written in the corners, which meant only someone with the books and the numbers in the corners could accurately decode the message. He could change those numbers at any time if need be. The method was foolproof—unless one discovered these books.

She glanced up at the shelf to see several copies of the three volumes, but after checking, none had the special numbers penciled in. She could only assume those books were reserved for whomever he decided to trust with his secret. For Jenny's sake, she hoped there was only one set that could decipher the code.

My time is short. Reservoir secure. Proceed as planned with, the message said. The rest was too faint to read, but it didn't matter. She'd found it. She'd found the key. Overcome with a profound sense of relief, she sank into the oak office chair and stared at the three volumes. So much blood spilled over three little books.

She would turn them over to the OSS and it would all be over. No more Bouchaule, which meant no more uncomfortable evenings at home with Jenny trying to pretend they both weren't hurting. She could finally honor her promise to Jenny about not using sex as a weapon in her assignments for the OSS. She would train their agents, go overseas if she had to, but she would not surrender her body to the cause again. She had changed. Her life had changed.

She waited for the demons to taunt her with memories of the dead and the burden of her debt, but her head was silent, and she suddenly felt very alone.

She looked around the abandoned lab and thought, *it was all for nothing in the end*. Everything Daniel Ryan had tried so hard to hide was about to be exposed. She would expose it. Suddenly the weight of what she was about to do gave her pause.

She always thought Daniel was concealing something, not giving something to the enemy. If she turned the key over to the OSS, whatever he was hiding would be out there, and if there was something shady going on in the government—and she had her suspicions—the information could wind up in the wrong hands.

She sat back in the creaking chair, torn. It was her job, her duty, to turn in the books. If she turned in the books, she would be free to pursue her life with her family and Jenny. She was an OSS agent, trusted to do the right thing. There really wasn't anything to think about. But she felt uneasy. What if the right thing was to do nothing?

Men had died to get this key. Men had died to protect it.

She exhaled and weighed the books in her hands. Her head told her to do what she was trained to do, required to do—turn them over without delay. Her gut told her to hold off. What were a few more days? Weeks? Maybe Bouchaule could tell her more about what she was about to unleash.

She nodded and stood up, books in hand. What to do with them now? She didn't dare leave them. Someone might be back for them.

That gave her pause. *Might be back for them.*

She looked around at the disheveled lab. Someone had cleaned it out, and she had the feeling it wasn't Daniel Ryan anticipating his demise. There was no way he would dispose of everything else and leave the books where they could be found, secret lab or not.

Papers and journals had disappeared, experiments were terminated and cleaned up, and from the empty cages in the side room, lab animals removed.

Someone cleaned up after Daniel's death, which meant someone else knew about the lab—someone living. Her first thought, though fleeting, was Jenny, but that was absurd. She gave her the books freely from the beginning, and she was too stunned by the classified files she saw, too open emotionally, to hide such a thing. She knew her too well. For a moment, Kathryn was reminded of Juliette and how thoroughly deceived she'd been by her. The notion was quickly dismissed, and she got angry at herself for even thinking the situations, or the women, were even remotely alike.

She turned her attention back to the problem at hand—the books. She couldn't leave them, but she didn't dare take them elsewhere, for fear they would be discovered. She decided she would hide them someplace close by.

She swept her eyes to the ceiling, with its heavy wooden beams and exposed ductwork, and wondered where exactly on the grounds she was. A steel staircase on the far wall rose to a narrow landing, and she followed it up until it emptied into a slender hallway with a dead end. The inner wall of the hallway had a levered handle on it, so she pulled it, only to have a five-foot section of wall release slightly into another room.

She shouldered her way from the darkened hallway into the light and was dumbfounded to find herself in the study, the beautiful Bosendörfer piano her welcoming host.

"Unbelievable," she muttered, stunned that the answer had been so close the whole time. She looked at the books in her hand and knew she had to take care of them immediately. Hiding them in a cookie tin and placing it on a shelf with the other tins in the potter's shed would work. She found a cookie tin the right size in the kitchen and dumped the cookies onto a plate. Garbage can liners would protect the books from dampness, so she securely wrapped the three volumes in the white waxy paper bags and tucked them safely inside the tin.

As she was securing the lid, the doorbell rang, momentarily paralyzing her, as if she were in a glass house and her every move was on display. She quickly recovered and rushed to the study, where she put the cookie tin just inside the door to the lab and leaned on the bookcase until it clicked closed.

She looked around the room to make sure everything was in place and brushed off her slacks before putting on a pleasant face to answer the door.

To her surprise, her smiling niece was standing on the doorstep before her holding the hand of a taxi driver, whose cab was at the curb.

"Steph—"

"Hi!" the little girl chirped and threw her arms open wide.

Kathryn couldn't help but stoop into the hug with a smile, until her eyes drifted up to the cab driver and she saw that he was the cab driver from the nighttime encounter with the FBI. She released her niece and protectively pulled her behind her back as she straightened to her full height.

"Wait inside, Stephanie."

"But—"

"Now!"

The girl scurried into the house, and Kathryn shut the door, using all her patience not to slam it. She got in the face of the cabbie, her voice low and angry. "I don't know what kind of game you people are playing, but I swear, if you—"

The cabbie raised his hands. "Whoa, whoa, whoa. The kid skipped out of the school playground and walked four blocks to a bus stop, where I picked her up."

"Why would she do that?"

He handed her an index card with her name and address on it.

"She handed me this and told me the wildest tale about why she had to get here. I thought it best to play along."

Kathryn exhaled, relieved, but still upset. She looked at the man, then the cab, and wondered why there was still a tail on her family.

The man read her concerned face.

"We're here to keep your family safe, Miss Hammond."

It disturbed her that the FBI thought it necessary to protect her family, but it assured her she was doing the right thing by distancing herself from them. She nodded, no longer displeased with the surveillance. "Thank you."

The cabbie nodded and started back to the cab.

"Hey," Kathryn called after him. "A lot can happen to a little girl in four blocks. Tighten it up."

He smiled and tipped his hat.

Kathryn watched him drive away and took a deep breath to calm her sudden panic before entering the house to deal with her niece. She didn't even want to think of what might have happened had the agent not picked her up.

Stephanie stood in the hallway in her navy blue wool coat and matching hat—the picture of innocence—with her hands behind her back, like a little angel. Kathryn stared at her for a few hesitant moments and decided dealing with the adults would be a little easier.

She picked up the telephone.

Stephanie looked at her with trepidation. "Are you calling Mommy?"

"No, I'll let your dad do that."

The youngster rushed to her side, grasping her pant leg. "Oh, don't call Daddy. He'll be so angry."

"*I'm* angry!" Kathryn snapped, momentarily losing her poise.

She wasn't prepared for the profound hurt in the young girl's eyes, and she looked away, unable to bear it. "Just ... just go sit on the couch." She pointed toward it.

The rattled aunt got an earful from a worried but relieved father, and she then went into the living room, where she found Stephanie sitting on the couch, crying. She gathered herself, ill-equipped for sensitive chats with children, and stood before her niece.

"Here," she said gently, as she held out her hand. "Hand me your coat."

Stephanie sniffled as she stood, wiggled out of her coat, and removed her hat.

Kathryn internally winced at the little girl's misery as she took the items and draped them over the arm of the sofa and then sat beside her.

"Don't cry."

"You're mad at me."

"I'm not mad ... I'm ..."

Stephanie's sad eyes peeked out from below her wrinkled brow, and the tears broke Kathryn's heart. She took her hand.

"I'm not mad, honey, I was scared for you. What you did was wrong. Do you know that?"

Stephanie nodded.

"But you did it anyway. Why?"

"Daddy said you're poison ivy and he didn't want you anywhere near us."

"He said that to you?"

"No, he thought I was sleeping. But that's what he told Mommy, and she didn't fight for you. No one asked me, and I don't think it's fair they keep me from you. So I ran away."

Kathryn squeezed the little girl's hand. "Running away is not the answer."

"You ran away."

Kathryn was stunned that the girl not only knew she had run away but thought it was something to emulate.

"I was wrong to run away, Stephanie. Terribly wrong. I hurt so many people ... your Pop Pop, your dad, myself. I lost all those years with you because of it. It's not the answer, honey, believe me."

"It's not fair that I can't see you."

"That's not your mom and dad's fault. It's mine."

Stephanie lifted her eyes, the edges brimming with hurt. "You don't want to see me?"

"Oh, honey, no." Kathryn pulled her into a hug and then released her. "That's not it at all. I love you madly. You know that."

"Then why, Aunt Kath?"

Kathryn prepared to tread carefully, knowing that no one senses a lie like a child. "Well, it's complicated."

Stephanie tilted her head, daring her to hang on to that as an excuse. "I'm nine, not three."

Kathryn rubbed her forehead and smiled. "Right."

She paused again as she tried to formulate an explanation that the little girl would accept and understand, but the little girl was anything but little, and the stall did not sit well.

"Mommy says you don't have to think about the truth."

Kathryn felt herself being outmaneuvered by a nine-year-old.

"Okay," she drew out, answering the challenge. "My job may take me away for a while, and I've been trying to get used to the idea of not seeing you and your mom and dad, so I stayed away."

"But if you're going away, wouldn't you want to see more of us while you can?"

Kathryn merely blinked at the girl, her logic irreproachable.

"Besides," Stephanie continued, "that sounds an awful lot like running away, and you just told me that wasn't the answer."

"This is different."

"Why?"

Kathryn suddenly understood why *Because I said so* was such a popular parental retort. The child expected nothing less than the truth, and Kathryn supposed she deserved the best she could do in that regard.

"Sometimes the more you love someone, the harder it is to say goodbye. I guess I was trying not to love you so much."

Stephanie frowned, obviously finding her aunt's reasoning confounding. "Did it work?"

Kathryn smiled, as her foolish logic was exposed. "No."

"No wonder Daddy's mad at you." Stephanie folded her hands across her lap in an annoyed gesture very much like her mother's. "I think I'm mad at you too."

Kathryn stared at her for a moment and couldn't really blame her. "I'm sorry."

Without hesitation, Stephanie extended her hand. "I accept your apology."

Her niece forgave her easily and completely, as only a child could, and Kathryn gladly shook her hand and kissed her cheek.

"Thank you."

The girl nodded and stared at her shoes.

"Will I ever see you again?"

The question took Kathryn by surprise. "Well, I should hope so."

Stephanie didn't move.

Kathryn tilted the little girl's chin up "Hey, this is just for a little while, honey."

Stephanie's doubtful stare made her feel like a liar, as if her niece's youthful innocence gave her a preternatural ability to see the future and she knew better.

Kathryn had no assurances that the young girl's doubt was unfounded, and they both stared at each other in silence, lamenting their uncertain future, until Stephanie took pity on her.

"I know you'll do your best to come back to us, Aunt Kathryn."

Defensively, Kathryn answered, "Yes, I will."

Stephanie nodded and regarded her shoes again. "Just in case, I'm glad I met you."

The child's resignation stung, and Kathryn realized the impact her decision to distance herself from her family had on the young girl. Children protect themselves, just like adults, something she should have been acutely aware of, but time and well-worn habits had blinded her to her own defense mechanisms, and she hadn't anticipated Stephanie would employ some of her own.

Kathryn put a comforting hand on her niece's back, but Stephanie got up from under it and walked to the window.

"When will Daddy be here?"

"Soon."

Kathryn watched the young girl clasp her hands behind her back, the way her father does when he thinks, and she imagined the child calmly committing her quirky Aunt Kathryn to memory as she filed her next to boring Aunt Clara, who smells funny, and the myriad other disappointments collected in her very young life.

"Daddy's going to yell a lot."

Kathryn got up and moved to her side. "Daddy's just worried and scared, honey. He's not really angry."

"Why don't adults just say what they mean?"

"Sometimes we don't know how."

Stephanie crossed her arms. "Well, that's silly." She paused. "He's going to yell a lot."

Kathryn knelt beside her.

"He just loves you."

"Then he shouldn't yell."

Kathryn smiled and rubbed the little girl's back.

"You know when you have a bad dream and Mommy and Daddy hold you until you're not scared anymore?"

Stephanie nodded.

"Well, when your Mom and Dad are worried and scared about you, it's like a bad dream, and you just have to hold them until they're not scared anymore. Okay?"

The young girl stared at her for a moment and then nodded enthusiastically and suddenly threw her arms around her neck.

"Tell me when you're not scared anymore, Aunt Kath."

Kathryn smiled and put her arms around her niece. "Promise me you won't ever run away again, and I promise you I won't be scared."

Stephanie held her at arm's length and nodded. "I promise."

Kathryn held out her little finger. "Pinky swear?"

"Pinky swear."

"So we're square?"

Stephanie straightened and raised her chin confidently. "On the level."

Kathryn pulled her into her arms. "That's my girl."

Stephanie squeezed with all her might. "I'm going to miss you."

"I'm going to miss you too, honey."

When they separated, Stephanie was rubbing a tear from her eye with the back of her hand.

Kathryn kissed her cheek. "Now, now ... none of that." She stood up and held out her hand. "Come with me, I have something for you."

She led her niece into the bedroom and took a photo from a silver frame on the vanity.

"I want you to keep this for me."

Stephanie took the photo and her eyes lit up. It was a black and white photo of her birthday celebration at the club. She'd seen a group photo that had since disappeared from her father's desk, but this was a close-up of just her and her smiling aunt behind the candle-topped hot fudge sundae she'd been given for dessert.

She held the picture to her heart. "Are you sure?"

"Absolutely."

Stephanie greedily tucked it into the large bib pocket of her blue and white checkered jumper dress. "I'm not showing this to anyone, and I promise I'll take good care of it."

Kathryn smiled and held out her hand. "I know you will. Come on, how about some cookies?"

"Sure!"

They shared cookies and milk at the kitchen table, and Stephanie seemed to have adjusted well to their impending separation—the resiliency of childhood, Kathryn imagined. The adults, however, were going to be another matter.

Stephanie was standing on a step stool at the kitchen sink drying the dishes passed to her, when a car door slammed. She turned to Kathryn and whispered, "Daddy's here."

Kathryn took the dish from her niece's hand and set it gently on the counter. "I know."

They solemnly walked hand in hand to the living room, where Kathryn helped Stephanie put on her coat and hat, all the while memorizing every detail about her and trying desperately not to cry.

Clay's fervent pounding on the door told her everything she needed to know about his state of mind, and she knew this would be her last chance for a peaceful goodbye.

She knelt and attempted to straighten her niece's coat, but Stephanie dispensed with the emotionally awkward last few moments and hugged her as hard as she could.

"I love you, Aunt Kath."

Kathryn savored it and didn't want to let go. "Oh, sweetie, I love you too."

Clay's incessant knocking loomed menacingly in the background. "Kathryn!"

Stephanie gave a final squeeze and pulled back, where she found tears welling in Kathryn's eyes. "None of that," she scolded with a pointed finger.

Kathryn wiped away a tear, vowing to be brave for just a few more minutes. "Right."

The youngster reached out and arranged Kathryn's hair on her shoulders like she would primp one of her dolls.

"Don't stay away too long, Aunt Kath. Jenny will miss you too."

Kathryn had to swallow the heart in her throat before answering. "I won't."

Clay tried the doorknob. "Kathryn!"

Kathryn blew out a breath. "Ready, pretty girl?"

Her niece imitated her exhale. "Ready."

Kathryn went to the door and opened it, almost getting her brother's fist in her face, as he was caught mid-knock.

The sight of his daughter made him drop to his knees, where he gathered her into his arms. "Stephanie! Oh, thank God you're safe."

She barely had time to utter, "I'm fine, Daddy," before he had her at arm's length and the predicted yelling began.

"What were you thinking? Huh? What were you thinking?"

"I wanted—"

"Your mother was frantic! What were you thinking?"

Kathryn stepped forward. "Clay ..."

"You stay out of this!"

"Answer me! What were—"

"Clay, you're scaring her."

"You need to stay out of this!"

"You need to calm down."

Clay looked at his upset daughter and took a breath. He rubbed her shoulders after he loosened his grasp. "Are you okay?"

Stephanie nodded.

He took her in his arms and rocked her gently. "I'm sorry, baby. Are you okay?"

She nodded again, and as her father picked her up and carried her to the waiting taxi, she threw a helpless glance over her shoulder.

Kathryn reassured her with a wink and a smile, and one was bravely returned.

A few minutes were spent getting Stephanie settled into the backseat, and all appeared fine between father and daughter, but Kathryn bucked up for her brother's ire as he stood and stalked back up to the house.

"What the hell is she doing here?"

Kathryn fished the address card out of her pocket and handed it to her brother.

"She walked out of the playground at school and handed this to a cab driver."

"Why the hell would she do that?"

"She thought you were keeping her away from me."

"That was your decision, Kathryn. Not mine."

"I told her that. I also told her you weren't mad at her, just scared, so don't be too hard on her."

"Don't tell me how to raise my kid. She never would have done this before she met you ... *never!* You're not to see her, or speak to her, or write to her again, do you hear me?"

"Clay—"

"No! I let you into my family, Kathryn, and this is how you repay us?"

"Look, I'm sorry. I didn't mean for this to happen."

"No, you never mean for anything to happen. One day you'll learn family isn't something you throw away because it's inconvenient."

Kathryn ground her teeth on the reason for her actions. "I'm not throwing you away. I can't explain right now, but one day—"

"One day is already too late. I'll not subject Stephanie to your erratic behavior. Love isn't something you just turn on and off."

"I haven't turned anything off. I love you both dearly, please know that."

Her brother snorted, effectively throwing her words back in her face.

"Stay away from us," he spat and turned to leave.

"Clay!"

He reluctantly stopped and looked back.

"Hug me goodbye."

"Nuts to you."

"For Stephanie's sake, don't make this ugly."

Her brother looked at the cab and saw his daughter watching intently through the backseat window. He relented and gave his sister a rigid hug, saying, "I'll never forgive you for hurting her."

He tried to pull back, but Kathryn held fast.

"She's going to be fine, Clayton. Just forgive me for hurting you."

He pushed away with angry tears in his eyes and tore up the address card in his hand, which he then shoved into her midriff.

"I won't be needing this."

He stormed back to the taxi, and Kathryn forced a smile for her departing niece. She blew her a kiss as the cab backed out of the drive and stood on the front step, waving until her family was out of sight.

She closed her eyes and stood motionless for a few gut-kicked moments with the pieces of the address card digging into her tightly closed fist. It was every bit the confrontation she envisioned and ten times harder than she imagined to say goodbye. She understood that her brother was doing what he felt was necessary to protect himself and his family, and she would now do what she had to do to protect herself from the pain of losing them.

The pain was a familiar one that started in the pit of her stomach, like a belly full of acid, and then seeped into her heart, where it felt like a fist plunged through her chest, pulling the life from her. Her body was turning to stone and she had to remind herself to breathe.

She'd played this scene before as a teen, when she watched her brother walk away in anger, knowing she may never see him again. She could no more tell him the truth now than she could then. She filled her lungs with air and teetered on unsteady legs, trying to recall her defenses, trying to save herself.

Breathe, she told herself. *Breathe and forget it. Breathe and pretend you'll see them next week.*

It didn't work as well as she remembered. She was too old to convince herself she'd see them again soon, and she knew the pain she felt was a piece of herself dying as she let them go.

She absorbed the blow and straightened. She had given Stephanie the photograph—the only physical reminder she had of her brief reunion with her family—and she knew in time that her memories of them would fade, the pain would sink into the collective quicksand of her blackened soul, and family would be nothing but a dream she once had in a life that, for a brief time, offered her more than she dared hope for. They were an unexpected gift, however fleeting, and she was grateful for it, no matter how painful the loss now.

She couldn't deny the finality of it all, and she had a tinge of self-pity, until she remembered this was her lot: crime and punishment. Fitting. Jenny was a gift too, and she didn't know why she was allowed it, but a family was pushing it, and she'd been called out. So be it.

Her world was darker now than when she'd awakened that morning but more familiar than it had been in months. This was the world she knew and expected. The demons were setting up lawn chairs. The show was about to begin.

CHAPTER THIRTY-FIVE

athryn's next meeting with Bouchaule was nothing like her previous encounters. She was escorted from the club by a burly man who did not speak even when spoken to. They went to a different upscale hotel in the city—not the one from the night before—and it was obvious he felt the need to stay on the move.

The silent man led Kathryn to Bouchaule's room on an upper floor and knocked twice on the door while Kathryn waited patiently over his shoulder.

An uncharacteristically disheveled Thierry Bouchaule opened the door, and the man stepped aside to allow Kathryn to enter.

"Thank you for coming, Kathryn," the distracted doctor said curtly as he quickly shut the door, leaving the escort outside.

Kathryn smiled as she removed her gloves. "You're going to run out of first-class hotels."

"I will not need them much longer," he replied cryptically, as he lifted the calf-length wool cape from her shoulders and then laid it across the end of the bed. He held out his hand to the nearest armchair. "Please, I will not keep you long."

Kathryn sensed she'd lost whatever intimate connection she'd had with the doctor, and she feared once he had what he wanted—a sample of her blood again, she assumed—he'd be gone and she'd be left in the dark with the burden of Daniel Ryan's code key and no answers.

She'd only seen glimpses of this serious Bouchaule. His face had a pronounced crease splitting his brow and a determined set to his usually carefree lips. She wasn't sure of his emotions toward her, but she had to believe that he may have had genuine feelings for her at one time, because that was her only hope of reigniting their extinguished flame. To that end, she immersed herself in the role of a jilted lover, used and thrown aside—angry, but deceptively tolerant, as only a woman seeking validation can be.

She casually slapped her gloves into her open hand. "I'm not in a hurry."

He didn't respond as he jotted something down in his notes, but he must have sensed her intense stare because he looked up and replied absentmindedly in French. "Pardon?"

She sat in the offered low back chair off to the side and attempted to engage him on a more visceral level, crossing her long legs while casually easing up her dress to expose more skin.

He didn't notice, and she didn't bother repeating herself, as she could tell her agenda was of no interest to him. "You seem a bit undone, Thierry."

He hardly looked up as he sifted through the papers spread before him on the small round table. "Sorry. A very trying day."

Kathryn gazed enviously at the doctor's notes. What she wouldn't give for an up-close look, but she pretended to be politely indifferent.

"Anything I can do?"

He threw a hand up and shook his head. "Imbeciles. The *weltschmerz* makes me weary."

One's ideal and the reality of it rarely ever met, and he wasn't the only one weary of the difference between the two. In her perfect world, Kathryn would give the doctor her blood and be done with him. She would leave the code books to rot in the ground and she would walk away. She would walk away from it all, reclaim her relationship with Jenny, do what she could to help win the war through conventional dedication and sacrifice, like every other citizen, and live happily ever after.

But she had no time to be weary of the evils of the world. No room to pretend she was merely the average citizen entitled to the happy ending. She had to get to the heart of Bouchaule's obsession, discover the root of his particular evil.

Hearing the German word roll off his tongue so easily only served to remind her that, despite his considerable charm, Bouchaule was somehow connected to Daniel Ryan's research and very much the enemy.

It was apparent their intimate relationship was lost and that the only tool left her was the possession of something he needed. If he wanted it, he was going to have to work for it, for he was about to become the victim of a woman's prerogative to change her mind.

"Are you working with the Nazis?"

He looked up at her briefly and smirked, obviously insulted that his use of German disturbed her. "I speak Italian as well ... does that mean I am a fascist?"

She stood and smoothed down her dress, wishing she had a cigarette for a prop so she could take an irritated drag and impatiently blow the smoke to the ceiling before answering.

"I don't know, are you a fascist?"

For the first time since she arrived, Bouchaule gave her his full attention and stepped away from his work.

"You are angry."

"Are you working with the Nazis?"

He moved in like a parent consoling a poor, misguided child, but Kathryn stepped away, demanding an answer.

Bouchaule put his hands in his pockets.

"Not in the way you think I am."

"God—" Kathryn turned away, pretending his association with the party was a shocking revelation.

The doctor reached out for her. "Kathryn ..."

She turned to face him with the appropriate rage in her eyes. "My government is far from innocent, but I will not help the Nazis."

"Nor will I."

Kathryn stared at him doubtfully.

He moved closer, his arms open and inviting.

"Nor will I, darling."

His endearment was embarrassingly transparent, betraying his desperation, and Kathryn knew she'd made the right move.

She grabbed her cape from the end of the bed. "I don't believe you."

"Kathryn," he said, standing between her and the door, hands raised like a horse trainer corralling an unruly filly.

"Get out of my way, Thierry."

"Please. Let me explain."

Kathryn made him suffer her silence for a moment and then tossed her cape back onto the bed and waited, pleased she had gained the upper hand.

Bouchaule gratefully accepted his reprieve with a nod and wandered back to his notes, where he shifted them around with his fingertips before leaning on the table and raising his eyes, his external cool restored.

"Have you any idea what this is all about?"

She crossed her arms. "Senseless slaughter. World domination. The usual."

Bouchaule smiled. "I see you grasp the basic concept."

"One as old as time."

"Unfortunately so, but this time they go too far."

"They?"

"The Nazis. Your government. Insignificant, despicable men like Forrester and those from Chicago, who have no idea what they are toying with."

"And what are they toying with?"

"An uncontrollable weapon. A virus."

He said it so easily, as if he had nothing to hide.

She pretended to be surprised and then concerned.

"That doesn't seem very smart."

"It is not. Nor will they succeed if I can help it."

He looked to his notes again, but Kathryn sensed it was more a distraction than a necessity. When he spoke again, his voice was softer, more intimate, revealing more of the man she knew.

"I am sorry you have been drawn into this ugliness," he said. "You should never know such things."

She returned to the chair again and sat down, crossing her legs. "You'll have to take my word for it when I tell you, I'm far beyond the point of shock at man's inhumanity to man."

This time he noticed her legs but quickly looked away, finding refuge in his notes and an odd, out of the blue defense of the Nazi regime. "Actually, Hitler is vehemently opposed to biological weapons," he said.

"That's very funny, but you'll forgive me if I don't laugh."

"Ironic, but true. The fear of reprisal is strong."

"Sanity among the mad. Imagine."

"Your words are truer than you know."

Kathryn stared blindly at the subtle herringbone pattern material on the raised divider between the front and backseat of the sedan. Thierry Bouchaule now held her hand, his calm confidence a stark contrast to her conflicting emotions.

It was the beginning of the end. In her heart she knew it, but she would do her best to ignore it, because the truth of it was too much to bear. Instead, she would continue playing her part—more of a lifestyle now that everything had changed and paths had been chosen—and she would continue struggling for what was right and good, though right and good had never been more relative than at that moment.

She started the evening determined to get answers and bring down the doctor and his associates. Now she was torn. Her determination was tempered by his honesty, and in turn, her need for conquest was dulled, like her thoughts, which were numbed by the monotonous drone of the highway as they rode in silence away from a night of revelations and hard choices.

This wasn't the way it was supposed to be. It was supposed to be cut and dry. He was the bad guy, the enemy. She was armed with enough anger and skill to easily overcome his charm and any other methods he tried to employ to sway her. She didn't expect to find that they were both victims of their pasts and prisoners of their futures and circumstances.

She had pressed him about his connections, and he gave the information freely. Some she knew—enough to know he told the truth—and the rest would be thoroughly investigated when she turned in her report tomorrow.

Bouchaule dutifully denounced the use of viral research for any reason other than a vaccine to stave off an epidemic and claimed to be part of a group of medical scientists dedicated to stopping anyone tempted to use a constantly mutating pathogen as a weapon.

Common sense should prevent such a thing, of course, but Kathryn knew in war there was no such thing.

"That all sounds lovely and noble," she had said earlier in the evening as they stood in the middle of his hotel room, "but why should I believe you?"

He seemed disappointed when she doubted his sincerity, but he did not hesitate to offer a compelling argument.

It began as a typical tale of blackmail. He was a man forced to do things against his will. He claimed colleagues had been killed for not cooperating with the Nazis after they marched into Paris and took over their research facility and that he had no choice. He was deemed important because of his U.S. connections, and they needed to ensure his cooperation.

"I am not a particularly brave man, Kathryn," he said. "I did not want to die, so I did what they asked of me." He then told of how, for added insurance, they took his sister from her home in the middle of the night, leaving her husband to die from a gunshot wound to the head after a futile attempt to fight off the intruders.

The story sounded suspiciously like Juliette's—forced, she had claimed, into Nazi service in exchange for the lives of her mythical children.

Kathryn looked Bouchaule up and down, trying to size him up, gauge his sincerity. The agent in her applauded his technique. He chose the perfect moment for a well-placed sob story, and she would have viewed it as a convenient contrivance had she not known the Nazis capable of it and worse. She was not, however, wholly convinced it was true, and it irritated her to hear the same excuse employed against her again, especially when she was inclined to believe it—again.

She raised a doubtful brow. "So they're holding your sister?"

"Not anymore." His piercing eyes grew haunted and he looked away, momentarily stripped of his composure. "My sister is dead now." When he spoke again, it was almost to himself. "She was always a fragile thing." He cleared the emotions, and his throat, and turned his attention to the paperwork on the table, which he gathered in an irritated fashion.

"No matter. Her suffering is over."

Kathryn could picture vividly the poor woman's torture and imagined her saying anything, even pleading for death, just to make it stop. If Bouchaule was playing her, he was playing hard and in all the right places. It made her own struggle for normalcy seem futile, as memories of her own interrogations surfaced and momentarily stole her away.

For better or worse, her captors had been more interested in mental torture than physical, and she was spared the fate of many who had succumbed to the Nazi's sick pleasures. From her dingy concrete cell, she'd heard the macabre choir of the tortured, and she shuddered, as the ghostly echoes filled her head again.

She flinched when Bouchaule touched her arm.

"You're trembling," he said.

She dismissed it as a random shiver and quickly returned to the present. This was no place for past demons.

"I'm so sorry."

His eyes accepted her sympathy, but his demeanor remained unchanged as he turned his back on her. He was angry. That was not what she intended.

"The man in the hall is my sister's husband, Bertrand," Bouchaule went on as he continued packing up his papers. "He was brought to me that night. I saved his life, now he protects mine ... hardly the actions of a man who believes me the enemy. The bullet stole his speech, not his life, and not his hatred of the Nazis who destroyed his world." He looked up. "My rage is no less."

Bouchaule snapped his folio shut and leaned on it.

"You may believe what you like about me, Kathryn, but believe I have no love for the Nazis or their evil schemes. They are a means to an end, a way to continue my work. War is nothing more than greed disguised as ideology. I care for none of it. Had your government not expelled me, I would be using them instead, and I promise you, morally they are no better."

As his frustration grew, so did his bitterness along with the staccato of his accent. He tossed his folio on a nearby chair where his coat was draped.

"You are like a foolish child, choosing this side or that, as if it really matters. Either would destroy the world if given the chance, and it saddens me you think me capable of facilitating such madness. I would hope after all we have shared—"

"Don't play the victim with me, Thierry, I'm not buying it."

It was her turn to flash a little anger. If he thought he would bully her into cooperating, he had another thing coming. They had to be on equal footing for her plan to work. There had to be some measure of respect, attraction—something.

"You've made it perfectly clear what I mean to you, and any schoolgirl notions I had to the contrary have certainly been put in their place." She longed for that cigarette prop again. "Any way the wind blows for you, right? Well, apparently, the wind is blowing in my direction, and this little fool knows it."

He clearly expected her to cave in, and the curious lilt of his head as he considered her reaction told her he understood the root of her anger, as she intended. On cue, he resurrected his charming self.

"You are wrong, Kathryn," he said, his voice softer as he moved closer. "I care for you very much."

She laughed. "Let's not kid ourselves. You care only for your work."

"More than that," he readily admitted. "I live for my work. It is more important than my life, and, yes, more important than your life, and I am sorry if that sounds cruel or coldhearted, but it is a fact. I cannot, will not, lose sight of that."

Kathryn tilted her head, unimpressed. "And why should this make me believe you're not working for the Nazis?"

He stared at her for a moment, and she could see him changing course like a sailor hoisting his sails into the prevailing winds.

He sat on the edge of the bed and rested his clasped hands on his knees. "I cannot force you to help me, but I would like to take you somewhere and show you something. Do you trust that I will not harm you?"

Kathryn thought it an odd thing to ask, as if he knew all along their relationship had been nothing more than a mutual ruse. The chess match was on, and both sides had run out of pawns to sacrifice. Now the real moves would begin, with dire consequences for any misstep.

She reached out and touched his shoulder. Time to play nice.

"I trust you."

"Thank you."

He stood up with a relieved grin and then eagerly rolled down his sleeves, buttoned the top button of his white shirt, and smoothed his disorderly hair back with the palms of his hands, quickly becoming the well-coiffed man she knew. After a final look around, he gathered up his leather folio, black doctor's bag, coat and hat, and escorted Kathryn out the door. He whispered something in French to Bertrand in the hall, which elicited a disapproving glance over the shoulder.

Bouchaule responded sternly, "Just do as I ask."

Obviously, against his better judgment, the silent man led them to a sedan parked around the corner.

Once settled in the backseat, Bouchaule pulled out a dark silk handkerchief and fashioned it into a blindfold.

"Firing squad?" Kathryn asked with a smirk.

"I am sorry. This is not for me but for the men I work for."

"Well, the men you work for can pay for what that's going to do to my hair."

Bouchaule laughed.

"You are beautiful, no matter your hair."

Their first personal exchange of the day seemed like a triumph. She closed her eyes as he raised the handkerchief to her face but not before surreptitiously glancing at her watch, so she'd at least know how long it took to get to wherever they were going.

Forty-three minutes later, she found herself standing before an ominously dark estate, the only light coming from the row of lamps lining the twisting gravel drive.

Kathryn gazed up at the two-story gray stone building and was reminded of Forrester and his wealth. "Yours?"

Bouchaule smiled as he stuffed the silk handkerchief into his pocket. "Friends in high places again."

Kathryn smiled too, sensing they'd reached solid footing again.

Bertrand entered the house first and turned on a light. Sheets covered the furniture and the large paintings decorating the walls. The place appeared abandoned.

They lingered in the first spacious room as the bodyguard disappeared, and Kathryn leaned on what could only be a grand piano hidden under a significant shroud of white.

"What is this place?"

"My temporary home, my workplace."

"Doesn't seem very lived in."

"I told you, I live for my work. I have no need for this—" He waved his hand at the neglected opulent surroundings.

Bertrand came back and shook his head.

"Good," said Bouchaule. "We have the place to ourselves."

It occurred to Kathryn she should feel threatened. She was in a strange place with a burly man who could snap her like a twig and another whose intentions were cloudy at best, but her need to know overpowered her reason, and she was left with the comfortable illusion of safety.

"Come with me, please," Bouchaule said.

Bertrand removed his coat and hat and eyed Kathryn suspiciously as she passed.

For the first time, she noticed the scar on his temple, and the possibility that the sister story was true made her nauseous.

Bouchaule led her through the house and out the back door of the spacious kitchen, where a lighted pathway led to a smaller stone building that housed a few rooms and a small laboratory.

He led her into a claustrophobic office teeming with boxes and files. He moved some of the clutter from the green leather loveseat against the wall opposite the antique oak desk and offered her a seat.

"These boxes contain files." He pointed around the room. "Each file represents a patient. Every patient represented here is dead because ambitious men had no regard for the consequences of their actions. This is merely a sampling of their arrogance. This is what I wish to prevent, with your help."

He went to a wood filing cabinet in the corner and pulled out a folder from which he removed a black and white photograph of what looked like a fuzzy spherical amoeba. He held it up like he was showing her a mug shot.

"What do you see?"

He was becoming the serious, intense Bouchaule again, and Kathryn needed him a little closer to Prince Charming.

"Is this one of those tests where I tell you it looks like a pet from my youth and you tell me all my troubles stem from my overbearing mother?"

His grim expression fell away, and he smiled as he sat beside her. "I think we have seen the same psychologist."

They laughed easily, and he seemed more like the man she had come to know. Their eyes remained locked, smiling in spite of the circumstances and the posturing. Confident that things were moving in the right direction, Kathryn was the first to break contact.

"What am I looking at?"

"That is a healthy cell." He showed her another photo, this time an oblong fuzzy blob. "This is a cell infected by the virus. This man died within hours of exposure." He handed her another photo. "This is yours."

Kathryn stared at it in confusion. It looked the same as the first. "It's healthy."

"So it appears."

"But?"

Bouchaule gave her a quick lesson in normal cell biology and reproduction before explaining her abnormality.

"Your cells did not allow the virus to infect them."

"I have a natural immunity?"

"That was what they thought and hoped when you did not become ill. If you carry the antibodies, your blood could provide a vaccine, but you do not, which is why they have no interest in you."

"So, why do you have an interest in me?"

He paused for a moment, and she thought he was going to say something personal, but he turned away and reached for a large manila envelope on the edge of the desk.

"You carry something far more extraordinary."

"Which is?"

He opened the envelope, which Kathryn noted had University of Pennsylvania stamped on the back, and showed her a series of photos. He pointed out subtle nuances in the cells as the series progressed, and using terms that went far beyond her brief education in biology and chemistry, he enthusiastically pronounced her somewhat of a miracle woman.

Bouchaule took pity on her slightly befuddled look and smiled. "Simply put, your cells absorbed the virus, but they did not succumb to it. You see, viruses take over the cells they infect. They change the healthy cell into a host for their own reproduction. The cell bursts, distributing more virus cells, and so it goes. Your cells consumed the foreign invader and transformed it … used its own techniques against it, as it were. They reproduced like an infected cell, only they reproduced your own healthy cells and then some."

"And then some what?"

He moved closer and took her hand, his face beaming. "Your cells, my darling … your beautiful, healthy, reproduced cells … essentially treated the damaged cells in your body as foreign invaders and replaced them."

Kathryn waited, as if he was joking and at any moment would say something that actually made sense and was medically feasible. His silence told her he wasn't joking, and seeing his face, she knew he certainly believed what he said to be true. It didn't sound possible, but she couldn't deny her recovery, and found her heart begin to pick up its pace on the off chance he wasn't insane or wildly off the mark in the blind pursuit of his obsession. She slowly put her hand to her throat, imagining her "beautiful, healthy, reproduced cells" working their magic.

"The miraculous return of my voice."

"Precisely. You should not be able to sing, but …"

He waited for the magnitude of what he had revealed to sink in. Kathryn found it hard to let go of conventional wisdom.

"But I've been sick or injured before and—"

"It is not inherent to your physiology. It was done to you."

"The accident?"

Bouchaule frowned grimly as he put his photographs back into the envelope on his lap. "I think we both know what happened to you was no accident." He looked up again and continued, as if it was now understood they were both on the same side. "What happened to you was done before the incident, or you would not have survived the virus exposure."

Kathryn's theory about being used as bait for his return was beginning to feel like a fact. "How can you be so sure I was infected at all?"

He merely smiled. "Oh, you were infected. Trust me."

She would have to.

He took her hand. "Think, darling. Have you had any vaccinations, given blood, had a transfusion, anything of that nature recently?"

Now she was intrigued and felt a little like a character in a science fiction novel thrust into a strange reality. Her rational brain still told her it couldn't be true.

"No, nothing."

While Bouchaule rubbed his chin at the mystery of her inoculation, Kathryn pondered her "miracle woman" status. Did she believe in the spontaneous rejuvenation of her damaged cells? She was no genius, but she'd had enough biology to know things didn't work that way. Surely, he was mistaken.

"You're a doctor … a man of science. You know it's not possible."

He smiled. "I have learned to remove that phrase from my vocabulary. You should as well, because you are living proof."

"If I'm so special, why would the government just let me go?"

Bouchaule leaned back, his frustration back at the mention of the group.

"Because they are myopic fools who cannot see beyond their desire for destruction. They are looking for antibodies in your blood, which they will not find. It is the proteins, you see?"

"No, I don't see."

He waved away the explanation as if the how and why were irrelevant to her pending cooperation.

This was nothing like the weapon she thought she was chasing. This was so much more, and if it was true, more important in the global scheme of things.

As the medical implications turned her confused expression into awe, Bouchaule's grin grew wider, and he was almost giddy.

"Now you see, my darling?"

She did indeed see, and for the moment, she was drawn into the humbling ramifications. Not only could it be used in place of the dreaded vaccine, but it could also be used to cure countless maladies that had plagued mankind since the dawn of time.

"My God."

Bouchaule squeezed her hand enthusiastically. "I knew you would understand!"

He released her hand quickly and babbled on about his precious proteins and cell behavior and abnormalities as if she were one of his lab buddies and she had the slightest inkling of what he was talking about.

She could easily see how this driven man had made his work his life. There was no cool control to his passion, only excitable chatter, and she had to admit, this bookwormish man-child had taken her by surprise, as if the real Thierry Bouchaule had just made his first appearance.

"Will you help me, Kathryn? Help me make history?"

How could she say no?

"What do you need me to do?"

Bouchaule led Kathryn to the front section of the lab, which was a separate room with a metal-framed hospital bed set up in the corner. A tray of equipment waited on a nightstand beside it, and he donned gloves and took 500 ccs of her blood. He then pressed a small gauze square to the needle entry point in her upper inner forearm and gently lifted her arm by the wrist and held it high.

"Elevate this for a moment."

Kathryn smiled at his serious bedside manner.

He returned the smile, evidently aware of his intensity, and kissed her palm.

"Thank you for this, Kathryn."

"I'm just lying here."

"You put your trust in me. That means more than you know." He kissed her palm again and laid her arm on the bed. "Lie still, just for a little while. I must attend to this." He picked up the bottle of her precious blood and crimped off the rubber tube protruding from the stopper with a twist of a metal band. "You may recline here if you wish, or when you feel able, wait in the office."

Kathryn nodded, and Bouchaule gave her a reassuring pat on the hand before disappearing through the main door of the lab.

She couldn't believe he just offered her free roam of the office that overflowed with files, including the folio he was carrying that night. He didn't need to offer it twice. As soon as he was out of the room, she sat up but immediately regretted it, as the room faded. She felt nauseated.

"Damn," she whispered, putting her hand to her forehead and slowly letting herself back down on the bed. Maybe he knew she'd never recover in time to dig up anything useful.

She didn't intend on waiting. She didn't know how long he'd be gone or what "attending" to blood involved—he could be gone an hour or a few minutes—but in either case, she might not get another opportunity to study those files.

She gave herself a few more minutes out of necessity and then slowly sat up, praying her body would cooperate. Satisfied that she could at least make it to the office couch, she slipped out of the outer lab and into the office next door.

The room had one window with wide wooden blinds that overlooked the main lab. The blinds were open, but Bouchaule was too engrossed in his work in the isolated quarantine room to notice her watching him as he slowly turned the handle on his centrifuge and watched the attached vials spin like he was God, hovering over a carnival ride.

With a watchful eye on the window and her ears focused on the hallway, in case Bertrand approached, Kathryn planned out her route of discovery, starting with Bouchaule's leather folio.

Kathryn peered through the blinds and watched Bouchaule throw his lab coveralls to the ground. He was very agitated. Apparently, all did not go as expected, and she wondered what that meant for her future. The door to the office suddenly opened and Bertrand entered. From the look on his face, he was not happy to see her in there alone.

"Hello," Kathryn said pleasantly, turning to face him.

The imposing man glared at her, the same glare Forrester's lawyer, Floyd Robeson, used to employ.

She leaned back on the windowsill and in French said, "Take it easy. I'm not your enemy."

Bertrand appeared momentarily surprised she knew the language and raised his chin like an animal investigating the scent of a new creature, but in the end, he was obviously not impressed, as his eyes narrowed with disdain and his lips twisted into a sneer.

Kathryn smirked and shook her head as she pushed off the sill and casually sat on the edge of the desk. Despite her cool demeanor, her heart was racing. She was glad he hadn't shown up five minutes earlier, while she was snapping pictures of documents with her small Minox camera, which she carried inside her purse.

There was no conversation to be had, and she couldn't really blame the man for his attitude after what he'd been through. In fact, she felt compelled by a sense of *esprit de corps* to acknowledge his tragedy.

She clasped her hands around one knee and continued speaking his language. "Thierry told me what happened. I'm so sorry for your loss."

The Frenchman looked away, clearly uncomfortable with Kathryn's sincere condolences. He quickly resumed his glare, giving fair warning he was not swayed by her feminine guile like his brother-in-law.

Bouchaule returned from the lab, distracted again and still displeased. He brushed by everyone present without a word and tossed a folder onto his desk before collapsing into his chair and rubbing his eyes.

"I take it we're not making history today?" Kathryn chided.

"Thank you again for your cooperation, Kathryn. Bertrand will take you home now. I will not trouble you again."

Kathryn pushed off the desk and turned in disbelief. "That's it?"

Bouchaule's face was indifferent. "Is there something more?"

Yes, Kathryn thought. *What about the flirting, the obvious attraction, the inevitable sex, the uncovering of secrets, the saving the world from itself?*

It all suddenly seemed moot, which was wholly unexpected. All she could hope for now was that someone could make sense of the documents she'd photographed.

"I guess not," she said, as she picked up her purse from the desk and headed toward the door.

Bertrand blocked her way and snatched the purse from her hand.

"Hey—"

"Bertrand!" Bouchaule yelled.

The man ignored him and dumped the contents on the desk, fishing around inside when he didn't find anything suspicious among the lipstick, face powder, flowered handkerchief, thin wallet, and change purse.

Kathryn crossed her arms and eyed the purse. "It doesn't go with your shoes, but you're welcome to it. Would you like to frisk me?" She held out her arms and then turned to Bouchaule. "Would you?"

"Pick that up," Bouchaule said in French to his bodyguard.

Bertrand made one more pass inside the empty purse before glaring at Kathryn and begrudgingly replacing her belongings. He handed it over and burned *I know you're up to something* into her face with his unflinching glare.

"*Merci*," she said politely, thankful for false bottoms.

"Kathryn, would you wait at the house, please?" Bouchaule said. "You will be taken care of shortly."

Kathryn sat at the piano in the grand entry room of the house and played Beethoven's appropriately moody "Moonlight Sonata" while she waited for Bertrand to carry out his orders, whatever they might be.

You will be taken care of shortly, Bouchaule had said. She wondered if he was upset and misspoke or if it was intended to be as ominous as it sounded. She feared the worst. After all, there was no reason to keep her around, now that she was apparently no longer the *miracle* woman.

As she walked away from the office, she could hear Bouchaule reprimanding poor Bertrand, who was just doing his job. Once she got outside, she thought about running. She had fifty shots in her camera, and she had used them all. She had to get the film to headquarters.

The files stacked in the office belonged to patients. Every one she checked was deceased, just as Bouchaule had said. She photographed a few of the files, but the contents of Bouchaule's leather portfolio made up the bulk of the photos.

Littered with page after page of biochemistry equations, some in perfect order, others scribbled in the margins like afterthoughts or eureka moments, the folio appeared to be the treasure trove she had hoped it would be. There were also photographs, like she had been shown, and coded documents that looked like they were coded with Daniel Ryan's book code. She was tempted to steal a page but feared Bouchaule would miss it and then her cover would be blown.

Her gamble to give him what he wanted in hopes of gaining his favor, had backfired. Not only was her mission a failure, but her life was now in serious jeopardy as well.

She heard footsteps on the polished marble floor and chose not to turn to see her fate. She steeled herself and kept on playing.

Bouchaule slid in beside her on the bench.

She raised her brow, surprised he'd stick around for the execution. He seemed to have a hard time starting the conversation, so she thought she'd get on with it.

"Where's Bertrand?" *Loading his gun?*

"He has retired for the evening."

Kathryn glanced at him sideways but continued playing.

"Don't be angry with him. He was just doing his job."

Bouchaule started playing softly with his left hand, adding another layer to the bass parts.

"He was rude. It was uncalled for." He kept playing. "I was rude as well. It was wrong of me to dismiss you so. I apologize. Please forgive me. I was—" He searched for an explanation, but, in the end, offered none.

"You were disappointed, and I forgive you," Kathryn replied nonchalantly.

"Yes. Terribly disappointed. I thought we had something this time."

Kathryn stopped playing. "This time? You've seen this before?"

Bouchaule continued playing and reached across to fill in Kathryn's abandoned treble part.

"Once," he said, his voice carrying over the warm acoustics of the piano. "The result is the same. The body naturally replenishes its cells, but because the anomaly is not inherent, it loses its potency until it is thoroughly flushed out."

She knew for sure now that she wasn't needed any longer and that Bouchaule had reached a dead end.

"I'm sorry, Thierry."

He smiled and shrugged. "A mere setback. The reservoir is out there somewhere, and I will find it. It is only a matter of time."

Kathryn tried to remain calm as Bouchaule spoke the magic word. She began playing again to mask her interest.

"Reservoir?"

"A host. Someone to whom the anomaly is inherent. They would be like a life spring to my work." He stopped playing and turned, the bookwormish man-child revived. "The effect of their gift, however short-lived, would be invaluable to unlocking our greatest physiological mysteries. Do you see?" He faced forward and let out a dispirited sigh. "There is so much we do not know. So much we cannot see, but it is all right there." He grasped at the air with his fist.

While Bouchaule looked to his scientific castle in the sky, Kathryn looked to her fate. She stopped playing and the room fell into an eerie silence.

"You're not going to let me go, are you?"

Bouchaule seemed offended by the question, but then slowly shifted and bowed his head. He was silent for a moment, and when he finally spoke, it was with the funereal candor of the bearer of bad news.

"I cannot. I think you understand."

She closed her eyes and smiled humorlessly. "Of course."

He took the hand closest to him.

Kathryn stiffened, as her survival instincts awakened, and she mentally took inventory of the objects around her that she could use as a weapon in her attempt to escape. She had learned about the reservoir, so she couldn't regret her earlier decision not to run, but it was all for naught if she didn't survive the night.

She cursed her instincts for being wrong and lulling her into a false sense of security. She didn't take Bouchaule for the murdering kind—not for her murder anyway.

Her first stab at survival would be to reason with him, beg for her life. He had a soft spot for her. She knew he did. He had to. She turned to face him, as vulnerable and desperate as she could manage and still keep her edge, and tried to convince him to spare her life.

"Thierry, please. I promise I won't—"

Her lips were captured in a passionate kiss, and she realized he didn't have murder in mind at all. He pulled away, his eyes hungry and searching, and Kathryn's startled expression was not altogether an act. She finally smiled, signaling her approval and relief, and Bouchaule relaxed, as if he had expected rejection. He tenderly stroked her face, his eyes now filled with adoration and respect.

"I cannot be without you. I have tried."

Validation had never felt so good, and Kathryn bathed in its satisfaction and let Bouchaule caress her face with his repentant eyes.

"I am so sorry for the pain they caused you."

"Thierry ..." She certainly didn't need to be reminded.

He kissed her gently. "I know the pain of your injuries, the burning agony of the antidote injections. I know it all, and it hurts my heart to know it was because of me."

Kathryn tried to block out the memory. She hadn't told anyone of the pain, not even Jenny, simply stating that she didn't remember anything about the first few days, hoping that one day it would be true.

"I want to send you far away from me, from this," Bouchaule went on, "but I cannot, for I can think of nothing else when you are absent from me."

"Then don't send me away."

"It is not safe for you."

"I don't care."

He closed his eyes, as if struggling against his better judgment.

Kathryn saw her opportunity. Certain things trumped better judgment every time. Whether he had found a reason to keep her for his work or he genuinely cared for her was irrelevant. She was in, and she would make sure that wouldn't change. She kissed him long and hard and then pulled back, her half-lidded eyes filled with promises of great things to come.

Predictably, he relented.

"It will not be easy."

"I don't care."

He put his arms around her, his new possession, and smiled contentedly. "You are so brave, my darling." He kissed her gently again and smiled. "Now, tell me of these schoolgirl notions."

CHAPTER THIRTY-SIX

"Where was your camera?" Colonel Holmes asked accusingly, not satisfied with Kathryn's verbal account of what she'd seen in Bouchaule's office and in the folio.

"I didn't have my purse," she lied. "I had nowhere to hide it."

"Surely, there is someplace on your person you could hide a small camera."

"Colonel Holmes, there is no place on my person Thierry does not, or has not, had access to. I couldn't risk it."

That shut him up, as he turned back to Kathryn's report in his hand. Brian, Holmes's mousy aide, quickly ducked his head to hide a grin.

Like with Daniel Ryan's code books, she found herself hesitant to reveal all she learned from Thierry Bouchaule. Intellectually, she knew it was not her place to decide what was and wasn't turned over to her agency. The information could be vital to winning the war, but it also could lead to Armageddon, and she reasoned they'd waited this long to destroy each other, so a few more days or weeks to find out exactly what was going on wasn't going to put too much of a dent in the Committee on Medical Research's quest for a vaccine to make way for their precious biological weapon for the Department of War.

She couldn't shake the feeling there was a mole in her agency, and she couldn't disagree with Bouchaule's assessment of the ethics and morality of her government, though that wasn't new.

Kathryn didn't mind lying to Colonel Holmes about the photos, but she had never lied to Colonel Forsythe before, and she couldn't help but feel her sin magnified under his attentive stare. He had trusted her, stood up for her, and now she was lying to his face. She did her best to remain indifferent and typically agitated at Colonel Holmes. She was playing another part in a place that normally was a purge point for her skills of deception. Now they were her victims, and it was not sitting well. She kept telling herself it was just temporary. She would uncover the truth and then act accordingly.

The world seemed like a safer place with Daniel Ryan's code books hidden away and Thierry Bouchaule's research at a standstill. Neither side was making progress, nor would they until the mysterious reservoir was found. Kathryn felt confident she was doing no harm holding on to her film while she determined the best course of action.

Colonel Holmes was not making her feel bad about that decision, as he was being as evasive as ever when she questioned him about Bouchaule's connection to Daniel Ryan's work.

"It's classified, Miss Hammond," was his dismissive reply.

Bouchaule had practically admitted access to the Ryan research, although he never mentioned the man by name. In fact, the doctor had been more than open with her about everything involving his work, which gave her greater pause about bringing him down. What if his agenda was exactly what he said it was and turning on him would set in motion the very thing she was trying to prevent?

She had told her superiors the basics—that Bouchaule had no interest in "their" war and was obsessed with some "miracle" cure of unknown origin, and the last thing he wanted was a vaccine in the hands of either side.

"And you believe him?" Colonel Holmes asked with the expected skepticism.

"From experience, I know you don't want my opinion, Colonel Holmes, so I'm just recounting my evening."

"I want your opinion," Forsythe said.

"At the moment? Yes, I believe him."

Holmes did not. "A real hero. Who do you think was responsible for the deaths of those patients in the files you saw?"

"Bouchaule was not the doctor of record in those files."

"No?" He turned to a page in his notes. "How about these doctors ..." He read a list of names.

"Yes, they look familiar."

He slid a page containing six wallet-sized headshots with brief biographies from a French laboratory prospectus before her.

"These are those doctors. Note the figure on top, the head of the department."

It was Thierry Bouchaule.

"I can only tell you what I saw, Colonel Holmes. I'll leave the rest to you."

"See that you do."

"And what does that mean?"

"I think you know what that means."

Kathryn leaned in. "Colonel Holmes, anytime you want to replace me on this case, feel free. I'm doing all I can to gather information for you, and all I get in return is, 'It's classified.' I learned more about this case in one evening with Thierry Bouchaule than I've learned from you people in a year, and while I realize it's not in your nature to disseminate information freely, neither is it in my best interest to fly blind here. I'm only going to learn more from him, and you standing there telling me pertinent information is classified is a little silly at this point, don't you think?"

Holmes looked to Forsythe, who didn't disagree. The British colonel sifted through the blue folder in his hand and pulled out a photograph. "Certain things will always be classified, Miss Hammond, but I do see your point." He passed it to her.

It was Bouchaule with a group of scientists, judging from the lab in the background. One of the scientists was Daniel Ryan. The date stamped on the back was January 1940, two months before the Frenchman was deported.

"He wasn't in your country long, but he was here, and they were working together."

What she had already gathered was confirmed, and she pushed the colonels for details, anything she could use to catch Bouchaule in a lie. One lie, she decided, would cost him everything.

All he had told her thus far appeared on the level, including the story of his sister. She was unaccustomed to the truth in her line of work, and his frankness had the strange effect of making her personally comfortable but professionally uneasy. There was no room for such a conflict and no reason to feel anything personally. She felt unbalanced in the one place she'd never doubted her footing. One more unbalancing blow came from Colonel Holmes, when he turned to his aide and said, "Brian, kindly show Miss Hammond to A42 and give her as much time as she needs and any clearance required." He smiled and turned to her. "It wouldn't do to have her flying blind, after all."

Room A42 was in the archives. Surely, he did not grant her access to the Ryan files?

Brian nodded and extended his hand toward the door as he stood. Colonel Holmes wandered to the window, chewing on the end of his unlit pipe, and Colonel Forsythe courteously half-rose as Kathryn got up and was escorted from the room.

The two officers were silent as they gathered their thoughts.

"She's personalized this," Holmes said, staring out the window to the busy streets below.

Forsythe settled back into his seat. "I know."

"How much do you trust your agent, Walter?"

After Kathryn and Brian signed in with the guard, Kathryn left her purse and hat in a locker in the outer room at the entrance to the archives and unbuttoned her jacket to leave it behind too. Brian, seemingly the opposite of his hard-nosed boss, said, "You don't have to do that, Miss Hammond."

Kathryn pointed to the large white sign beside the door that stated clearly, in bold red letters, No Personal Items, Satchels, or Outerwear Beyond This Point.

"Rules, Brian. We wouldn't want to give your boss any more ammunition."

"He really is a good chap," the aide said in his cockney accent as he flipped through the collection of keys at the end of the chain in his hand. "He's quite impressed with you, really. He's a bit of a prat, but he's only got our countries' best interests in mind."

Kathryn smiled weakly. "Don't we all."

Brian opened the door and paused, hesitant, but determined to say what he was thinking. "We're all quite impressed with you, Miss Hammond, and though I don't make a habit of apologizing for Colonel Holmes, I feel I—"

"Skip it, Brian."

She'd never heard the aide speak more than a few words, and he certainly didn't need to waste them on excuses for his boss's behavior. He looked a little hurt at her dismissive interruption, though, so she put her hand on his shoulder to relieve him of the words unspoken. "Thank you."

He smiled and nodded and led her into the room. "Right this way, Miss. I needn't tell you, nothing leaves this room."

"Of course."

There were several rows of metal shelving units filled with file box upon file box that reached almost to the ceiling in the moderately sized room. There was a small table with a lamp, a chair, and a step stool.

"Which section?" she asked.

"All of it."

She looked around. *All of it.* She briefly thought of Jenny. This is the room she was looking for: her family's history. She'd not sensed Jenny's discontent about her heritage lately, but, then again, with their conflicting schedules, they hadn't spent that much quality time together as of late. That wasn't going to get any better, especially now.

"Are you all right?" Brian asked.

She shook off the guilt, and the soft spot for Jenny, and fine-tuned her focus. This was about Bouchaule.

"A bit overwhelming."

Brian smiled. "Quite. Take your time, Miss Hammond. The most recent acquisitions start on the right. The door will lock when you leave. If you need anything, the guard will summon me."

"Thank you, Brian," she said absentmindedly. The door click closed and she blinked, realizing what the man had said. *Summon him?*

She was alone in the room. They left her alone in a room with the entire history of the Ryan case.

It would soon be apparent why they felt safe in doing so. Most of the boxes contained coded documents. They had no way of knowing she had the key. She went to the earliest records first, which, according to the simple date code, went all the way back to 1914. She had a lot of work to do.

Kathryn dropped the first musty file box beside the table and spread the contents of its first folder onto it. She sat in the chair, and with a reassuring glance at the closed door, removed her peep-toed shoe. She pried the sole of the thick high heel away and slid her subminiature camera from it. She removed her other shoe and removed an extra film cartridge from its heel.

There were one hundred shots between the film in the camera and the extra roll, and she would take a sampling of the file contents from each decade. The dates were old but the paper wasn't, so she hoped Daniel Ryan had transcribed them all around the same time period and hadn't changed the code from the one in the books she'd found.

She thought she would feel dirty, essentially spying on her own government, but, lately, it had done nothing to inspire her confidence or her loyalty, and she used that to justify her actions, clearing her conscience about it.

She worked quickly, unsure if "take your time" was literal or said to make her feel trusted, but soon, the patterns of numbers became a meaningless blur, as the monotonous click of her camera shutter and the feeble whir of the advancing film became a rhythmic distraction to her thoughts, which had drifted to Thierry Bouchaule and the consequences of their previous evening.

Passionate kisses and hands in familiar places left no doubt about the outcome. Bouchaule led Kathryn to the grand staircase and dramatically swept her into his arms.

She laughed at his machismo. "Why, Rhett Butler, you put me down this instant," she teased, impersonating Scarlett O'Hara. He laughed, and she kissed him again and felt his hold weaken because of it. He was hers. She slid her hand behind his head and gathered his hair in her fist. "Save your strength. You're going to need it."

His eyes grew dark and his nostrils flared, and with renewed gusto, he repositioned her in his arms and headed up the stairs to the bedroom.

She didn't think of Jenny at all that night—the infidelity, the fallout. No, it was all about Bouchaule, securing her place in his world, her place at his side. To that end, she felt she'd succeeded, and for that moment, it made it all worth it.

"Where have you been?" Kathryn asked breathlessly as she lay across Bouchaule's heaving chest.

He gently guided her hair away from her eyes.

"Too far away."

She put her hand over his pounding heart. "Don't leave me here again, Thierry."

He kissed her forehead.

"I never make the same mistake twice."

Thoughts of Jenny would come later. And come with a vengeance.

CHAPTER THIRTY-SEVEN

"Where have you been?" Jenny asked, pulling Kathryn into Luc's apartment and into her arms.

"Mmm," Kathryn hummed as her answer was momentarily smothered with a kiss. "Sorry, honey. Rehearsal ran long."

Jenny looked at her watch. "Kat—"

"I know. I feel terrible about it." She tightened her embrace. "I've missed you so."

Jenny found it hard to pout with her arms full of beautiful and a mouth about to be occupied with a delicious kiss.

"You're forgiven," she said, and then she received her reward.

They hadn't seen each other in days. Love notes left around the house were the only clue the two cohabitated. Kathryn looked tired and weary, but she sure wasn't kissing that way.

Sometimes her kisses were slow, seductive, and sensual, a combination that exuded playful danger followed by a smoldering look that confirmed it, which always made Jenny grin from ear to ear as she shrank in gleeful submission, knowing she was helpless to do anything but surrender.

Other times, her kisses were strong and purposeful, more desperate than passionate. The gaze that followed those kisses was intense. Her eyes reflected love, yet they were edged with fear, as if she could never express herself fully and it would become her undoing. It always took Jenny's breath away, the depth of this beautiful woman's love for her, and she eagerly accepted her devotion and did everything in her power to let her know it was reciprocated.

This was one of those intense days, and having found her release quickly under Kathryn's touch, she responded in kind. Kathryn reacted to her intimate kisses and caresses with deep throated moans and sensuous writhing, which always drove Jenny wild. That she could have such an effect on another human being, let alone this one, would never cease to amaze and arouse her.

Kathryn slid her hand up Jenny's inner thigh, and Jenny almost gave in to it, but it was her turn to show her love, and she would not be distracted.

"Stop, Kat," she said in between kisses as she tried to work her way down Kathryn's torso.

"Make me," Kathryn replied with an evil grin.

"I'm trying—mmph!" Jenny moaned as a hand found her center. "Kat!" She fought against surrendering. "S-stop!"

Kathryn guided her back into her arms and kissed her. "I'm fine, honey, really. But you ..." She grinned with that smoldering look.

Jenny sat up abruptly. This is the way it had been for the past few weeks. Every time she tried to make love to Kathryn she would say she was fine and then would distract her by making love to her again. They usually came together, and hard, no matter who instigated the lovemaking, so it didn't seem out of the ordinary that she was satisfied, but something wasn't right, and Jenny knew when it started.

Kathryn didn't get in until after dawn a few weeks ago. It was the first night she'd been out all night since her new assignment began, and Jenny had been worried sick, but she didn't let on; she just welcomed her home and went about getting ready for work.

When Kathryn stepped out of the shower, Jenny was there with a clean towel and wrapped it around her shoulders. It was then that she saw the trail of fingernail marks on her back, and she hadn't made them. Kathryn obviously didn't know they were there, and

Jenny tried hard not to react, even though she felt like she'd been kicked in the gut. She used another cup of coffee as an excuse to get out of the room, and no amount of rationalization would ease the pain of the raw truth piercing her heart: Kathryn's assignment had turned sexual.

She had to get out of there. She felt sick. She mustered all the indifference she could and hurried into the bathroom to say goodbye.

"I'm sorry, baby, but I've got to go. Early meeting this morning."

"Okay."

Kathryn looked so … normal. Like nothing had happened. Just another day at the office.

"Love you."

"Love you back. Hey," Kathryn called out to her, "where's my kiss?"

Jenny swallowed her nausea, stuck her head back in the doorway, grinned, and planted a hasty one on her lips.

Their schedules were at opposite ends now, and Jenny was almost thankful for the time to get her head together about what had happened. She feared her reaction to the next time they would make love. How could she overcome the image of Kathryn making love to someone else? She agonized about it for days. Every time she thought about it, she felt sick, but when the time came, when she was in Kathryn's arms like this and her eyes were filled with love and desire for her, all the ugly images faded into oblivion. Someone else may have had her body, but she had her heart and soul, and no one could touch their love. They would do what they had to do.

As promised, she handled it, just as Kathryn handled it, but Jenny wanted to make sure she really was fine—that they were fine—in every way, because she had a feeling Kathryn was struggling with it.

"What?" Kathryn said lazily as she raised herself onto her elbow.

"Let me make love to you."

Kathryn smiled and gently guided Jenny's hair behind her ear. "I told you, I'm fine."

Jenny tried so hard to fight it, but she was hurt, and she couldn't hide it. "They've taken so much from us. You're my lover. Don't let them take that away too."

Kathryn looked as though she was the one kicked in the gut this time.

"They're not. I promise you, they're not."

"Let me make love to you."

Kathryn hesitated, and Jenny got the picture. She got out of bed, but Kathryn was right there with her, corralling her in her arms. "Jenny—"

"It's fine, Kat." She tried to escape before she started to cry.

"Jenny, please ..." She had her back in her arms. "I'm sorry." She kissed her. "I love you." She kissed her again. "I need you." She sought her eyes. "I want you."

Jenny looked away but didn't try to run.

Kathryn took Jenny's hand and slid it up her side until she cupped her breast.

Jenny's raised eyes were filled with hope and healing.

"I want you," Kathryn repeated huskily, as she guided Jenny's other hand between her legs and into her wetness. "Make love to me."

Kathryn sat on the edge of the bed and mindlessly smoothed her nylon from her ankle to her thigh before snapping the garter welt into its belt. For the first time in her relationship with Jenny, she had faked her orgasm.

"Will I see you tonight?" Jenny asked from behind a thinly-veiled mask of expected disappointment as she came out of the bathroom buttoning her blouse.

Kathryn could tell that the waiting, the wondering, and the interrupted sleep because of her unpredictable schedule was taking its toll on her. She couldn't subject Jenny to that way of life any longer, nor herself to the guilt of being the cause of it. She could only think of one solution, and while she knew this day would come, there was no preparing for it and no easy way to impart her decision.

"Listen—" she began.

"You're moving back to your place."

Kathryn raised her eyes. Jenny's intuition was astounding sometimes, much to her great relief.

"You don't sound surprised." *Or upset.*

Jenny shrugged off her disappointment. "I've been expecting it ever since your assignment began."

How well she hid it. "Sorry, honey."

"I'm grateful for the extra time we had together."

Kathryn nodded in silence.

Jenny sat beside her and took her hand. "My house is still your home, Kat."

Kathryn smiled. "I'll be sure to leave a few white shirts and a hat box or two."

"You can leave the shirts, but I'm afraid those hat boxes have got to go. They take up too much room."

The two women laughed wearily, with Kathryn clearly taking it the harder of the two.

Jenny tugged on her hand. "Hey, we still have this place."

Kathryn nodded.

Jenny tugged on her hand again. "This is not the beginning of the end, Kat."

"I didn't say that."

Jenny smiled. "I know you, baby. I know how you think. We're going to be okay. We're going to make it. This war won't last forever, and we're going to be standing together at the end, giving der Führer and his brown clad lads a big up yours." She made the gesture.

Kathryn chuckled and gazed at her with admiration. "You're a saint."

"And don't you forget it."

"I won't." She would never forget. The love and devotion in

Jenny's eyes whenever she looked at her told her so, and she would remember it always.

Jenny kissed her and then slapped her on the knee as she got up. "Come on. Help me make the bed."

Kathryn captured her hand and pulled her back down beside her. "Tell me again we're going to make it."

Jenny must have seen the hopelessness in her eyes.

"What is it?"

Kathryn shook her head, on the verge of tears. Everything seemed held together with the frailest of threads, and she felt the frailest of all. What could she say? She settled on "Long day."

Long day. Long night. Long life.

Jenny enveloped her in her arms, and Kathryn melted into them, safe for the moment. They were the only truth she knew, and she would hang on for dear life, for as long as she could.

"We're going to make it, baby," Jenny whispered. "I promise. Do you hear me? I promise."

Jenny was in an exceptionally good mood as she bounded up the backstage stairs at The Grotto on her way to Kathryn's dressing room. It was early afternoon in the mostly empty club, and she'd switched shifts with a friend down at headquarters, intending to make the most of the extra time with Kathryn. Things had been much better for them emotionally and physically for the past two weeks. It seemed Kathryn finally started to believe things were going to work out for them.

Their time situation hadn't gotten any better though, especially with Kathryn living back at her place, but she would show up at the house often, leaving yellow roses in a vase on the kitchen table or a sweet note on her pillow, to let her know she still considered it home.

Jenny hated to admit it, but the move had made things easier to handle. She still worried, but it was just a general worry and not a specific anxiety about what Kathryn was doing at any particular time when they weren't together. Kathryn knew when the hard choices had to be made, and she had the courage to make them. Jenny had never been prouder of her strength or loved her more for it than now.

She entered Kathryn's dressing room as she always did, with a quick rap and a cheerful, "Knock knock."

What she saw inside threw her back against the doorjamb like a prizefighter's knockout blow. She wanted to run, but she couldn't move. She wanted to close her eyes, but she couldn't believe they were open and burning the image before her into her brain—the image of Kathryn fucking her ex, Satan herself, Marcella.

CHAPTER THIRTY-EIGHT

*J*enny had heard of tunnel vision, and despite its name, never imagined it akin to the sudden burst of distorted motion when a subway car hurls headlong into its dark passageway. Everything around her was rushing toward her in a blur, everything but Kathryn, dead center, moving with all the urgency of a casual stroll through the park on a perfect spring day, as she slowly dismounted the redhead and wrapped herself in the top sheet.

Marcella had no such modesty, as she stretched her naked body out like a comfortable feline, right at home in Kathryn's bed. She lazily threw her arm behind her head and twisted the sword already piercing Jenny's heart.

"Sugar, you have the most uncanny ability to interrupt me when I'm about to come. Why don't you back out of here for just a few more minutes so I—"

"Marcy," Kathryn warned, as she sat in the chair beside the bed.

The redhead acquiesced with a raised hand and a shake of her head as she reached for her cigarettes on the small table beside her.

Jenny didn't need Kathryn's help or pity handling Marcella. It made her sick—Marcella triumphantly smoking her disgusting cigarette and Kathryn pretending she'd merely been interrupted by a stranger asking her companion the time.

She was devastated and infuriated all at the same time, and Jenny would have lashed out or walked out if her body would have cooperated, but her limbs had been reduced to tingling entities, with no corporeal form, and she wasn't sure she was even breathing. *Run!* Every instinct was screaming, but the scene was too surreal, too impossible. There had to be an explanation.

"Please say something, Kat."

"You're early," was her cold, unapologetic reply.

Marcella turned to Kathryn and laughed. It was a hen-like cackle that tore through Jenny's spine like a hawk snatching its prey from above.

"Oh, baby, that was rich!" the redhead said. "I love a woman with a quick tongue ... I mean wit."

She passed her cigarette to Kathryn, who took a drag and exhaled as she leaned back and crossed her legs. "What do you want me to say, Jenny?"

Kathryn's disposition said it all, and everything Jenny knew about their relationship vanished in the face of the obvious. Kathryn hadn't been occupied with an assignment ... she'd been having an affair. How perfect for her. She could have anyone she pleased, whenever she pleased, and she had the perfect alibi throughout. Suddenly, it was all clear. Kathryn *was* the whore she thought she'd met the first day at the club. The months of adoration that had blinded her dissolved, and Kathryn's exquisite beauty was stripped away in an instant, revealing the arrogant posturing of a pathological liar.

The realization filled her with a rage that she would substitute for strength. It coursed through her veins, until she found her footing and pulled the sword from her chest.

"You clever fucking bitch." She struggled to keep her voice steady. "I trusted you. I believed the things you said, and you used it as an excuse to fuck *her*? God, what an idiot I am. What an idiot *you* are for that matter. There are easier ways to get a piece of ass ... but then you would know all about that, wouldn't you, you fucking whore."

Marcella raised her brow and snorted as she turned to Kathryn and took back her cigarette. "Say, sister, you're getting the whole nine yards. All I got was a slamming door."

For Jenny, the image of Marcella fucking the doorman on the night of her father's death was all too clear, and, once again, yielded the same result.

"Here's part two for you, bitch."

Jenny slammed the door as she left and heard a picture fall from the wall, along with Marcella's irritating voice. "Dramatic little minx, isn't she?"

Suppressing the urge for physical violence on one or both of the women behind her, Jenny dashed for the exit before the echoes of the woman's prolonged cackling made her change her mind.

Jenny nearly fell down the stairs from the dressing room. She was losing feeling in her limbs again, and she was definitely going to be sick. The rage that had given her the strength to move was quickly dissolving into hysterics, as devastation forced her to push through it in order to escape. She felt like the oxygen had been sucked from the building, and she gasped for air as she burst through the backstage exit door and promptly threw up in the alley.

She couldn't breathe, she couldn't control her tears, and she couldn't stay there. She stumbled to her car and could barely steady her hand at the dashboard enough to get the key in the ignition. She willed herself to be calm, just calm enough to get out of there. She didn't care where she went, just out of there.

She drove until she could no longer trust herself to drive safely and pulled to the curb moments before breaking down completely.

How could she have been so wrong? Where could she go? Home? Home, where everything reminded her of Kathryn and their life together? She derided herself for being so stupid and believing Kathryn's lies, and to add insult to injury, the words of the redheaded saxophone player from the Mayfly kept injecting their poison: *She'll take what she wants from you, and she'll leave you as quickly as she came.*

It wasn't true. How could it be true? The things they shared, the love they professed, the emotional support they gave each other time and again.

She couldn't stop sobbing. She felt so helpless, so used, so betrayed, but for a moment, anger was there to rescue her.

"You fucking bitch!" She pounded the steering wheel. "You said you loved me! You said—"

The memory of their love, coupled with the sudden solitude and the overwhelming sense of loss, drained whatever strength she had left, and she dissolved into uncontrolled tears again and collapsed across the car's front seat, unable to restrain the pain of Kathryn's betrayal.

When the reality of what she'd seen had left her spent, denial was there to ease the ache. Denial came easier than anger or self-recrimination, because with denial came the hope that, somehow, there was an explanation.

Having cried herself out until she was numb, Jenny stared blindly at the large black and white clock in her car's swirl-patterned metal dashboard. Time was moving on, moving her further and further from the woman she was. The woman who knew one thing for certain—she was loved. She was not ready to concede the loss of that love or the woman she knew and had loved like no other.

She kept replaying the tender moments they'd shared, looking for any hint of a lie. There was none. She remembered Kathryn's confession of love on the beach after Forrester's plane crash and the beautiful day that followed. And then there was the record that she made with the promise that whatever happened, she would love her. Only two weeks ago, she had asked for reassurance that they were going to make it! Nothing, *nothing*, indicated their love was anything but strong and true.

Jenny's eyes grew wide and she sat up. The record.

"Oh, shit."

She promised. Whatever happened, she would remember that

moment, wrapped safely in Kathryn's arms, and know that she loved her always. Whatever happened.

It suddenly occurred to Jenny that Marcella could be Kathryn's new assignment. She had assumed it was a man, but who knew who the OSS was investigating as part of her father's case, and Kathryn certainly couldn't say anything about it.

Jenny put her hand to her mouth and then over her eyes. The hateful things she'd said to Kathryn, the lack of faith, the lack of trust —again. How could she ever make that up to her?

"Shit. Shit, shit, shit, dammit all to hell. Jenny, you are such a fucking idiot!"

Jenny did her best to look presentable, considering, and subconsciously pleading for some kind of karmic rewind, she entered the club through the same door she'd exited. She hadn't realized how long she'd lain on the front seat of her car before she had her epiphany, and by the time she stood in the wings beside the stage, Kathryn was finishing a song in the middle of her last set of the evening.

Their eyes met, and Jenny tried to look as contrite as possible. Kathryn looked away with annoyed indifference and leaned in to say something to Jimmy, the bandleader.

Jenny knew it wasn't going to be easy, and she certainly didn't blame Kathryn for her anger. The woman didn't look her way again as she took her place at the microphone and the bandleader passed on the instructions to the band. It was apparent a message was going to be sent via the next song, and Jenny figured that as long as it wasn't "Praise the Lord and Pass the Ammunition," she could handle it.

The tune was "Just One of Those Things," and it appeared to be an apology from Kathryn, like the scene with Marcella couldn't be helped. It bolstered Jenny's theory about the assignment angle, and while it would take some doing to swallow the idea of Kathryn being assigned to Marcella, at least their relationship hadn't been a lie, and it was certainly preferable to the devastation of her initial impression.

As the song went on, however, it seemed less like an apology and more like notice that their relationship was the one that had run its course and, according to the gist of the lyrics, good riddance.

Jenny's chest tightened again. The air was getting thick, and she despised the song for being so cheerful as it delivered Kathryn's killing blow. The audience was added to her hit list, as they applauded the tune at its finish and became unwitting accomplices in the pain caused by the end of her relationship and her life as she had known it for the past eleven months.

Kathryn came to the edge of the stage, an intimidating figure as she towered over her and looked down from the top step.

Jenny gathered her nerve, unsure she really wanted to have the impending conversation, but pressed on. "I need to talk to you."

"I imagine you do," Kathryn said coolly.

Jenny didn't say anything, confused by her attitude, which conveyed a great deal more than just anger.

Kathryn crossed her arms, waiting.

Jenny looked around, uncomfortable at the public setting, and grew irritated that Kathryn insisted on turning the screw.

"Can we go somewhere a little more private, please?" She looked briefly toward the stairs leading to the dressing room.

Kathryn exhaled in irritation and looked at her wristwatch. She got the attention of the bandleader and flashed five fingers twice. He nodded.

Ten minutes. Jenny frowned as Kathryn stepped from the stage and brushed past her, heading for the stairs. All they had shared, all the promises made, and it would all come down to ten final minutes.

She almost didn't bother. Kathryn's demeanor told her all she needed to know, but she dutifully followed her up the stairs, already regretting that she'd come back.

Kathryn entered her dressing room, waited for Jenny to pass by, and slammed the door behind her.

"Private enough? Talk."

Jenny felt ten again, trying to explain how the dog wound up shaved bare to his haunches and painted blue.

"You're angry."

Kathryn snorted a contemptuous laugh and pushed by. "Let's hear it for Jenny for being so perceptive, but I'm sure you came here to do more than state the obvious." She turned and crossed her arms.

Jenny would go for the apology first. Kathryn sure wasn't acting like someone who had been caught having an affair.

"I once made a promise to you." Jenny sat on the end of the bed, feeling as small as she appeared in the shadow of Kathryn's anger. "That whatever happened, I would remember how much you loved me at that particular moment, and I would never forget. No matter what."

She watched Kathryn's face for any hint of recognition or absolution. There was none.

"I didn't forget that promise, but I did misplace it briefly."

Kathryn may as well have been a marble statue, for all the help she was giving her. Surely, she could understand the shock of the situation.

"Kat," Jenny pleaded in a more familiar tone. "I knew you had an assignment, and I knew it might turn sexual, but I never, in a million years, expected it to be Marcella! You can understand why I went insane, can't you?"

Kathryn broke off her acerbic gaze and seemed to relax as she moved slowly to the comfortable chair beside her vanity and sat down. She smiled a disconcerting smile as she reached for a cigarette pack beside the cold cream jar and removed one as she spoke.

"Marcy wasn't an assignment, Jenny, just a good lay."

She lit the cigarette and exhaled to the ceiling as Jenny stared on in confusion. Who was this woman? The attitude, the smoking— Jenny's mind was working overtime, trying to make sense of it all. She came to the conclusion that the cigarette was a sign. After the incident at the center and the damage to her lungs, Kathryn would never take up the habit again, of that she was sure. Only one explanation made sense. Jenny took out a small notepad from her purse, scribbled a note, and then handed the pad to Kathryn.

First, I'm really sorry! it said, underlined twice, and then, *Can we talk safely? Are we being watched or listened to?*

A slow grin formed on Kathryn's lips as she read it, and Jenny's heart lifted. Kathryn's odd behavior was an act. Just as she thought.

Hope quickly turned to despair, as the grin became a chuckle and then an outright laugh when Kathryn shook her head and handed back the notepad.

"You've seen too many movies, Jenny."

Jenny stared at her, searching those eyes she knew so well. She was devastated to find not just a stranger there but no one. She stared into the glassy blue infinity of a glacier, devoid of life and just as hostile.

She refused to believe it. She knew this woman, perhaps better than the woman knew herself. She was capable of many things, but after what they had shared, this coldhearted betrayal was not one of them.

"You're lying to me."

Kathryn shook her head with a smirk and settled into her chair and her condescending attitude as she took another drag of her cigarette and exhaled it with her bottom line.

"I'm sure this is difficult for you, Jenny, but please don't make a fool of yourself. This wasn't how it was supposed to end, and for that I am truly sorry, but there's no point in going on about it now."

Jenny couldn't believe she was reducing their love to a roadmap of planned acts—the chase, the conquest, the merciful end. The ugly truth was threatening to swallow her whole again, and she could only flail helplessly as it swelled within her.

"And how was it *supposed* to end, Kat?"

Kathryn raised her brow as she flicked the ash from her cigarette into the ashtray on the vanity. Her ensuing shrug was just as casual and infuriating as her answer.

"You'd get assigned somewhere, I'd get assigned somewhere, we'd go our separate ways, drift apart, no one gets hurt."

"No one gets hurt?" Jenny said incredulously.

Kathryn leaned forward. "Look, Jenny, I think you're a swell gal ... honestly, I do. You were there for me when I needed a friend, and the last thing I wanted to do was hurt you ..."

"Too fucking late!"

"Obviously."

It was clear to Jenny from Kathryn's attitude that the fling with Satan wasn't new. "How long has this been going on with Marcella?"

Kathryn took an impatient drag on her cigarette and looked at her wristwatch before answering. "Does it really matter?"

Volatile emotions were pressing on fragile nerves, and it was all Jenny could do to speak in even tones without unleashing her temper that was fueled by pain and a desperate urge to hang on to the truth as she knew it.

"It matters to me!"

Kathryn stood. "Look, I haven't time for this, and it won't help to—"

Jenny was on her feet and in Kathryn's face in an instant, demanding an answer.

"*How long?*"

Kathryn stared at her with those cold, unflinching eyes.

"On and off since we first met in the grocery store."

"Bullshit! You're not that fucking good."

"No, but I am that good at fucking, and, apparently, that's enough to make some people believe anything, especially when they're desperate enough or naïve enough to believe in things like *love* and *forever.*"

Jenny was speechless for a moment. The woman was throwing everything of value back in her face, making a mockery of their life, their love. It wasn't true. It couldn't be true.

"You believed in those things."

Kathryn laughed and took her seat again. "Did I?"

She said it with a smirk, made it a challenge—what do you know, and how can you be so sure?

Jenny was no longer sure. Nothing made sense, least of all the woman before her. It was as if she was seeing her for the first time, rose glasses crushed at her feet. What once was exquisite had become an aberration.

Kathryn's face was suddenly too angular, her lips too thin, and her eyes so unnaturally blue, as to be made by the devil himself as a tool to trap and hypnotize. A modern day Eve with her apple.

"I don't know who you are."

In a blink, Kathryn was serious, her gaze almost menacing as she leaned forward. "You're right, Jenny, you don't know who I am. You never have. The best thing for you to do is to walk out of this room and never look back." She sat back and took a slow drag on her cigarette and then released her poison into the air with a maddening smirk. "But you won't."

Jenny noticed the routine with the cigarette was the same as the night they met: the tilt of her head, the squint on the purposeful inhale, and then the eventual exhale. It cut through her anger that first night and aroused her in spite of herself, but tonight it was repulsive, the mechanics of a disgusting habit by a woman who no longer merited the perverse fascination of the past.

"The hell I won't," Jenny said. As she turned to walk out the door, she was caught by Kathryn's laughter, felling her like a well-placed whip around her neck. It was more than she could take. She faced her torturer. "Stop laughing at me!"

Tears were coming, and she struggled to keep them at bay, because Kathryn Hammond would get no such satisfaction from her. Why was she doing this? If she didn't love her, then just leave. Why go through the motions of a relationship? Was it really worth it to just cruelly taunt her in the end? No, something was very wrong.

Kathryn was doing her best to drive her away, and she knew all the right buttons to push. Jenny's heart was telling her everything about the situation was a lie, but her head and her insecurities were telling her *I told you so.*

She tried to fight it. *It's what she wants,* she told herself. *Don't give in to it.*

Every time she convinced herself it wasn't over, gave herself permission to hope, the relief was overwhelming. She became desperate for it all to be some misguided plot, and she wasn't above begging.

"Kat, please, if this is some kind of crazy guilt thing with you, or some OSS scheme to keep me out of harm's way, just tell me, please. I'll do whatever you ask, I'll go away ... whatever I have to do. Just, please, tell me we weren't a lie."

Kathryn was silent, with no hint of empathy in her indifferent stare.

Jenny felt her last semblance of hope burn out and drift away like the smoke from an extinguished candlewick. "You told me you loved me."

"Nothing comes for free, Jenny. I gave you what you wanted, and I got what I wanted in return. It's what I do."

Jenny couldn't help herself. She had to know. "And what did you want?"

"The chance to live the life everyone raves about. They call it love, and people spend their entire lives trying to find it ... that one person who fills your world and makes you whole."

"You found that person. You found stability for the first time in your life, and you're throwing it all away."

Kathryn chuckled. "Stability is another word for boring, Jenny, and that's not for me."

"Our life was anything but boring, Kat."

"Oh, yes, evenings by the firelight, reading, playing cards, listening to the radio, recounting the minutia of each day, like anyone really cares. Like I said, it's not for me."

Jenny was defeated. Her questions were a reflex, like a twitching corpse with no knowledge of its actions and no care for the results.

"Why did you stay?"

For some reason, Kathryn found the question amusing, and she grinned.

"You're the best sex I've had in years. Seemed like a small price to pay."

Jenny died more and more, as every aspect she loved about their relationship was unmercifully torn down and degraded, until it felt cheap and pathetic—until *she* felt cheap and pathetic. Kathryn kept hurling her daggers, uncaring.

"I should have left long ago," she went on, "but I could have my cake and eat it too, so why not?"

How much cruelty was she expected to bear? Fury found its way back to her, and Jenny refused to be kicked anymore. "How many others were there?"

"None of your business," was Kathryn's flippant reply.

Jenny had enough.

"You disgust me!"

Kathryn responded with another laugh, which sealed it for Jenny. She wasn't the woman she knew and loved. How could it all have fallen apart so quickly, and how could she have been so wrong? The tears finally fell.

"I used to think you were so beautiful. Now, I can honestly say you are the ugliest person I've ever met."

Kathryn smiled. "Now you're getting to know me."

"Fuck you, Kathryn!"

"Jenny," Kathryn said with a consoling tone as she got up, "don't cry. I don't want you to go like this." She moved closer. "The others are just sex. And Marcy ... well, she's like a circus sideshow of sex. You know what I'm talking about. I don't want you to be upset."

Kathryn's tone, the humiliation of being made the fool, and the memory of Marcella's insatiable quest for bizarre sex in the most inappropriate places, all clawed at her broken heart, until she couldn't stand it anymore. She had to get out of there, and this time her body would have no problem following orders.

As she reached for the door, Kathryn was quickly there, blocking her way with her hands on her shoulders. "Come on, Jenny, don't be angry. We were friends, weren't we? The others were just sex. You know that doesn't mean anything to me. If you say what we had was love, then okay, maybe it's worth taking another look."

Kathryn's long fingers were in her hair, like dead tree branches scratching the gray winter sky, and then they were cupping her face.

It made Jenny's skin crawl, as the sociopath made a blatant attempt to worm her way back into her bed. Jenny tried to shrink away, but Kathryn bent her head and kissed her. It was the full-on sensual kiss that always made her knees weak and her heart soar.

Jenny shoved her away and spit the foul taste of cigarettes onto the floor. "Don't touch me! You're sick, and you disgust me."

"So you said. Worth a try though, don't you think? For *love*?"

It was the last time she would be mocked by this despicable creature. It was finally Jenny's turn for a perfectly executed departure. She brushed past the pathetic whore, and before slamming the door in her face, she did her one last favor, for old times' sake.

"Your things will be on the roadside until tomorrow morning. That's garbage day. If you come by when I'm home, I'll have you arrested for trespassing."

Jenny found herself knocking on Smitty's apartment door. It was sometime after midnight, but she had long since lost track of the time. She had spent the entire evening relieving her home of everything Kathryn brought into it, including some things of her own that would forever be linked to the woman and their relationship.

She'd gone through every possible emotion—anger, sorrow, self-pity, hate, even love—and she rode each one until they'd all had their say and left her battered and worn. She couldn't bear to stay at home, and she couldn't stand to be by herself any longer, a prisoner of her thoughts and memories. She'd been sentenced to solitary confinement and was drawn to the only crack in her cell, like a weed trapped beneath a sidewalk, clamoring for the light of the sun. She cringed at how pathetic it was that at that particular moment, her only friend, her only chance for escape, was Smitty, a man who merely tolerated her.

He answered the door wearing only his pants, which he held up with one hand while planting the other on the doorjamb, in an attempt to block the view into his room.

"Hi ya, kid, what brings you down here?"

Jenny had a moment of panic when she looked past his shoulder and saw a tall, dark-haired woman by the bed securing her hose at the thigh. She immediately thought it was Kathryn, and visions of a murderous crime of passion flashed in her mind. Smitty knew she saw the woman and reluctantly removed his hand from the doorjamb and scrubbed his chin, momentarily chagrined.

The tall woman sauntered to the door and held out her hand. Smitty reached into his pocket and counted out some money, almost losing his pants in the process.

"Thanks, angel puss." She stroked his cheek. "Same time next week?"

"I'll let you know."

The prostitute looked Jenny up and down like she was the reason his answer wasn't the usual yes, and she smiled. "I'll be waiting."

Smitty watched her ass as she walked away, and now Jenny was the one who was momentarily embarrassed.

"Sorry, Smitty."

He shrugged it off.

"What's wrong?"

"I caught Kathryn screwing my ex-girlfriend."

Smitty blinked once, then simply said, "Ouch."

"You don't seem surprised."

He stepped aside. "Come on in."

His apartment was a small, poorly lit one-room affair, with the bed taking up most of the space. It was disorganized and cluttered, and thanks to the previous visitor, smelled of sex, booze, and cigarettes.

"You look a little rough," Smitty said. "You want a drink?"

Jenny declined and started slowly pacing around the room. If she started drinking now, she might not find a reason to stop.

"I don't know why I'm surprised," she began, as Smitty fastened his pants and then grabbed an undershirt. "Apparently, it's been going on for some time, but you probably knew that."

He raised an unfazed brow. "She's a very sexual woman."

He pulled on the shirt, and Jenny imagined that from her stricken look, he realized the insensitivity of his comment. "It's just sex to her, Jenny. It doesn't mean anything."

Jenny turned, incredulous. "Why do people keep saying that to me like it's going to make me feel better?"

"Because it means it's not personal."

"Sex couldn't be more personal."

"Not for her."

It was infuriating the way he was making excuses for Kathryn and her disgusting behavior, and she hated the way she was left sounding like the unreasonable one, but, considering her audience, and the fact that he had just paid for sex, it was hardly a surprising defense. Jenny took a deep breath. If she wanted answers, Smitty was her only hope.

She sat on the bed, and he sat beside her.

"I know you don't like me, Smitty."

"That's not true. She was just wrong for you."

"Don't you mean I was wrong for *her*?"

"Most people are wrong for her, Jenny. Good, decent people, strong enough or stupid enough to fall in love with her, are wrong for her. She chews them up and spits them out and never looks back or apologizes."

Jenny was surprised he was being so honest, but she sensed it came from experience.

"Well, I'm feeling pretty stupid all right."

He patted her knee, as if to welcome her to the club.

"Your first instinct is to stick it out," he said, "to be the one who fixes her, but you can't."

"You're wrong, Smitty. My first instinct right now is to run as far away as I can, because loving her will only destroy me." It already had.

"You have good instincts."

It was the answer she expected but not what she wanted to hear. She closed her eyes and shook her head.

He took pity on her and put his arm around her shoulders. "She's damaged goods, kid, and as much as we love her, we can't fix that."

"You should know."

He released his hold and looked at her askance.

"Sorry, Smitty. I didn't mean it that way."

He relented. "You probably should."

He got up and reached for the pack of cigarettes on the dresser. He had one out and in his mouth before he paused with the match on the striker. "Oh, sorry. May I?"

More cigarettes. "Your place."

He smiled and put the cigarette down.

"Who is she? Do you know?"

His sympathetic look turned to one of consternation. "I'm not going to judge her."

"I'm not asking you to."

She didn't blame him for defending her. She just needed to know what to believe, which woman to believe, because each was equally convincing.

"She said she loved me."

Smitty's disparaging snort was far from comforting, but more than that, if one more person laughed at her tonight—

To his credit, he did apologize immediately, and Jenny could see the laugh was more a reflex than a reflection on her naiveté. He threw the box of matches onto the dresser.

"She said she loved you." The laugh snuck out again. "Of course she did."

His comment was bitter, and it took Jenny by surprise. It seemed to take Smitty by surprise too, as he offered a softer, "She doesn't know what love is," to ease the jab.

He sat beside her again, and there didn't seem to be anything to say, as they both contemplated their respective wounds.

"She's not coming back, is she ... the woman I knew?"

"No, kid. She's not coming back."

Jenny leaned back on her hands and looked at the ceiling. "If she ever existed at all."

"It's not her fault, you know."

Jenny smiled and lolled her head in his direction. "You don't have to defend her to me. I don't even know that I'm angry right now. Just numb."

He nodded, and she knew she didn't have to explain. She blew out a weary breath and collapsed onto her back.

"I think I'll take that drink now."

From the chair beside her vanity, Kathryn savored the last taste of Jenny on her lips and stared at the coat hanging from the back of her dressing room door. Despite the promise to the contrary, she had watched Jenny walk away with unflinching defiance. Her parting words no longer hung in the air, and the slamming door no longer echoed in her head.

The cigarette in her hand supported the skeleton of its former self in the form of an arc of ash about to fall onto the floor. Kathryn found it a parallel to her own desolate shell. She slowly brought her hand to the ashtray, daring the ash to maintain its integrity. It tumbled from its precarious perch and soiled her hand, the chair, and the carpet, as it landed in an unrecognizable heap on the floor. Of course it did.

She snuffed out the remaining stub in the ashtray and brushed away the ash like she had brushed away her life. It was her last chance to save Jenny. Not from herself this time, but from Bouchaule and the men he worked for. It was only a matter of time before those men realized what she had known for weeks. Jenny was the key they were looking for. Jenny was the reservoir.

The first clue came to her the night she went to the estate after Bouchaule's return.

"Think, darling," he had said. "Have you had any vaccinations, given blood, had a transfusion, anything of that nature recently?"

She had replied "No," as a matter of course, and to her knowledge, it was the truth. But as she lay beside Bouchaule that night, unable to sleep, his question wouldn't leave her alone. The closest she'd come to any medical procedures before the incident at the center was getting stitches at the hospital the night of her accident with Jenny. And then it hit her—the accident! It seemed inconsequential, but Jenny's blood had mixed with hers as they lay sprawled at the bottom of her overturned car.

She nearly sat straight up in bed. *Could that be it?* It had to be, and, suddenly, everything made sense. Daniel and Paul's actions were all about protecting Jenny from men like Bouchaule and his associates, not out of fear of blackmail, but because she was the key to their precious vaccine.

Kathryn knew she had to get as far away from Jenny as she could, for fear her interest in her would spark their interest as well.

When Jenny begged her to tell her the truth, she nearly broke down and told her. She wanted to. God, how she wanted to. Breaking up with her this way was selfish and cruel, but it had to be. Jenny might have been strong enough to stay away, but she wasn't. She'd tried.

She couldn't tell Jenny the truth. It would destroy her life. She'd always be looking over her shoulder for the next mad scientist who sought to use her. This way, her secret would be safe, even from her, and she could still have a normal life after the war.

Kathryn inhaled and exhaled slowly. The woman Jenny loved no longer existed, and she would teeter on the edge of nothingness until she became someone else—whoever she needed to be to survive. She was familiar with that transition, but for now, she would savor the welcoming oblivion of the void.

She sat motionless as the band played out the rest of the set without her. Dominic wouldn't be happy.

She stood and faced the mirror on the vanity, purposely avoiding her reflection, as she slid the cigarette pack into the garbage pail—the prop no longer needed.

CHAPTER THIRTY-NINE

Kathryn saw Dominic peeking through the blinds in his office with equal parts curiosity and concern in his squinted gaze. She'd skipped the last set, and at her behest, the bandleader was about to stray from the carefully curated set list for the second time this evening. The club owner tolerated the first song because it was upbeat, but he would not tolerate this one.

The first somber notes of "Yesterdays" drifted through the club and, as predicted, Dominic burst out of his office. The languid bass thumped solemnly beneath the song like a broken heart searching for a reason to repeat its wounded beat, and Kathryn's voice rang out strong, serious, and precise, honoring her former life with an appropriate sendoff.

Dominic got halfway down the aisle to the stage when the rapt silence of the audience stopped him in his tracks. All conversation had ceased and glasses were frozen mid-drink. If the recovery of her vocal abilities had ever been in question, the slow anthem to treasured days gone by alleviated any doubt. It wasn't the voice of old but one just as sophisticated—smoky and mature—captivating all within earshot, including the staff. Her emotive rendition brought tears to some and an appreciation for life too often taken for granted to others. She held the last note impossibly long, as if it were the last she would ever sing. It wouldn't be the last note she'd ever sing, but it would be the last note she'd sing for Dominic Vignelli at The Grotto.

The ensuing silence after the song echoed the gravity of the moment, but soon the crowd was on its feet, applauding Kathryn for her raw honesty and for making them feel again.

She acknowledged the standing ovation with a gracious bow and left the stage in the opposite direction of her swiftly approaching boss.

"Make it a stiff one, Bobby," she said as she arrived at the bar.

"Why'd you do it?" he whispered, pouring her vodka rocks.

The last bandleader had been fired for inserting his own arrangement into Dominic's precious playlist, and while Kathryn knew she was special to her boss, the charging Italian didn't look very forgiving at the moment.

Kathryn knocked back the vodka rocks she'd been handed and shuddered as it went down. "I feel free, that's why I did it." She tapped on the bar for another.

"You're gonna be free all right."

He quickly poured her another and backed away, as Dominic loomed menacingly beside his soon to be unemployed singer. Kathryn ignored him and reached for her drink. It never made it to her mouth, as Dominic plucked it from her hand and slammed it onto the counter.

"I will put up with a lot, Kathryn, especially from you. You know that. This, however, *this*—"

She thought the bulging vein in his brow would pop when he was unable to find the words to express his disappointment and anger.

"I quit, Nicky," she said before he could fire her.

He flinched, the notion unacceptable.

"Come into my office."

"I don't want to go into your office. I don't want your expensive gowns, or your fancy nightclub, or your misplaced sense of debt over Luc, and I don't want to sing your happy songs anymore."

He took her words like punches to the face and raised his chin, daring her to knock him another one.

"I'm sorry," she said. "You've been grand to me in every way." She put her hand on his cheek. "More than I deserve. But I need to sing the truth of my heart, and happy songs are not in my heart."

"We are happy here," he said sadly, letting her know he would not change his policy. Not even for her.

"I know."

He reluctantly accepted her decision and tapped on the bar. Bobby stepped forward and poured a second glass. The two toasted as friends, downed their drinks, and embraced before Dominic hastily retreated to his office to hide the tears in his eyes.

Kathryn exhaled after he'd gone, and Bobby held up the vodka bottle. She shook her head and asked him to wrap up a bottle of wine instead.

"Can I call you a cab?"

"I'm a cab." She deadpanned.

It took him a moment to get it, but he finally laughed and handed over the bottle in a brown paper bag, holding on to it as she tried to take it.

"Don't be a stranger."

She smiled and shook his hand. "I know where to come for the best martini in town." She held up the expensive bottle as she walked toward the exit. "Tell Nicky to keep my last paycheck."

Kathryn sauntered up to the bar at the Mayfly and was greeted by the bulky bartender. "Well, well, well. Couldn't stay away, could you?"

Kathryn ignored the comment. "Two glasses, please, Ruby."

Ruby looked at the bottle in Kathryn's hand.

"You can't bring that in off the street, Hammond."

"If you served a decent wine, I wouldn't have to." She drummed her fingers on the counter. "Two glasses?"

Ruby looked enviously across the crowded room toward the

woman on the stage and then smirked as she pulled two glasses from the rack above her head. "You're pretty sure of yourself."

Kathryn smiled. "Shouldn't I be?"

Ruby looked her up and down in her shimmering gold lamé gown and decided the question was rhetorical. She handed over the glasses. "Have fun."

It didn't take Kathryn long to get Lani's attention. Heck, the way she was dressed, the whole bar would have to have been dead or blind not to notice her. She raised the glasses and the bottle and cocked her head toward the hall in the back.

The gesture needed no explanation, and Lani grinned as she quickly abandoned the last verse of her song and exited the stage while the band played on without her. She went to the end of the hall, where Kathryn was perched on the stairs, leaning back on one elbow, legs crossed, and all smiles.

"Busy?" she asked coyly.

Lani grinned. "For you, doll?" Kathryn's very presence was a prelude to sex.

She leaned in and collected her kiss, which was just as intoxicating as she remembered. It brought her back to last year, when Kathryn was a frequent visitor to her bed—a welcome apparition from the past, who appeared as quickly as she had disappeared years ago. Despite the time in between, they effortlessly picked up where they'd left off. They were sexual partners of convenience, with no intent or design, until Kathryn's job at the high-class joint uptown went to her head and she couldn't be bothered to slum with the old gang.

Soon, she was on the front page of this newspaper or that, on the arm of some millionaire, and the natives mourned the loss of another from their ranks, until she restored their faith by showing up again sporting a little blonde.

Lani was undeterred by Kathryn's fickle libido. Kathryn's motto had always been *anything goes*. Today, Lani was just happy the woman had found her way back to her again—thankfully, without the little blonde in tow.

She savored the familiar taste of those sensuous lips, as the passion she reserved only for the woman beneath her ignited. She pulled back, breathless and aroused, checking to make sure she wasn't dreaming.

Kathryn smiled, reassuring her. "Still live around here?"

Those were the last words spoken, as Lani took Kathryn by the hand and led her to her room at the top of the stairs. She wasted no time making sure Kathryn Hammond didn't get away.

Kathryn didn't object to being disrobed. In fact, she stood like a criminal during a shakedown as Lani slid her hands and mouth hungrily along her body, unsure which delight she wished to indulge in first. She would indulge in every delight, some more than once, and would be devoured in return in a way that surprised even her.

"I forgot you like it rough," she said, as she watched Kathryn shimmy into her long dress.

"Sorry."

"Please," Lani said, as she leaned against the headboard, naked and exhausted. "You know I love it that way. It was the best sex I've had since ... well ... since you."

Kathryn was silent as she fastened the hook on the back of her dress and struggled with the zipper at the small of her back.

"Here ..." Lani motioned her over.

As she finished pulling up the zipper, she ran her hand across Kathryn's strong back, and her body hummed again with the sensual rush of the warm skin beneath her palm. She could get used to this.

"Will I see you again?"

Kathryn adjusted the strap on her shoulder and moved to the mirror, where she attended to her hair.

"No."

"We're good together, Kat."

Kathryn looked at her from the mirror. "No, we aren't. We just have great sex."

Lani smirked. "Like I said."

Kathryn finished putting up her hair and then sat on the bed to put on her shoes.

Lani pulled up her knees and wrapped her arms around them, wondering what brought her old flame back.

"What happened to that kid?"

"Didn't work out."

Lani laughed. "Yeah, I didn't think she was your type."

"I wasn't *her* type."

"What, is she crazy?"

Kathryn slipped her foot into her shoe and stood. "Smartest woman I know."

Lani gazed at her curiously as she moved to the dresser and retrieved her watch. She certainly wasn't the woman she remembered. She wasn't even the woman she'd seen only months before. She was sad, and serious, and Lani pitied her. She once wanted to be just like her, a free spirit, willing to try anything and anyone, in search of a thrill, but seeing her today, Lani could see she'd paid for her feckless ways.

"What happened to you, Kat?"

Kathryn exhaled a humorless chuckle as she fastened the catch on her watch.

"Life, Lani. Life."

Lani watched her gather her things. Nothing was said—they never really had much to say—but she sensed it would be the last time she saw the woman, and she realized she'd never know how much she really cared for her.

"Say, Kat. You're welcome here anytime."

Kathryn let out another humorless chuckle.

"No ..." Lani quickly stammered. "I don't mean for sex. Well, I mean, if you want sex."

Both women grinned, but then Lani grew serious.

"Really, if you just need a friend or someplace to go ..."

It seemed silly when she said it out loud, especially since they'd never really been what could be considered friends. She expected her to laugh in her face. The old Kathryn would have, and then she would laugh too, as if it had all been a grand joke. To her surprise, Kathryn didn't laugh.

"You're sweet, Lani. Thank you."

Lani had always been sweet under her brash exterior, and available. Kathryn couldn't help but feel bad that she'd used her to try to exorcise her demons.

"I'm sorry."

Lani could see right through her guilt.

"Don't be. I'm not."

Kathryn nodded and turned to leave.

"Hey," Lani called out, "take that bottle with you. I think you need it more than I do."

Kathryn picked up the unopened bottle of wine and smiled. "You may be right."

Thierry Bouchaule was waiting for her a short cab ride away in another of his first-class hotel room hideaways. It was a short ride to the beginning of the rest of her life, and the bottle couldn't hurt.

"Thanks, Lani. See you around."

"Yeah, see you around, Hammond."

CHAPTER FORTY

Kathryn poured half a glass of wine and swallowed it quickly as Bouchaule washed his face in the bathroom. He arrived late, and she had been left to wait alone with her memories and regrets.

The bliss of oblivion had been replaced by self-loathing and anger. She just wanted some mindless sex from Lani, to feel pleasure again, to come again. She got neither. Sex had become an exercise in futility. If she wasn't faking pleasure with Jenny to hide her guilt, she was faking pleasure with Bouchaule to secure her future.

She fought thoughts of Jenny as she let Lani take her. She couldn't help feeling she was betraying their love, even though there was no love left to betray. It made her angry. She had to move on. She went to Lani for pleasure. To give it was easy—to Jenny, Bouchaule, Lani. All she had to do was show up, but this time she wanted the satisfaction to be hers, and who better to give it than an old fuck buddy who expected nothing less.

It wasn't Lani's fault, she knew, but when the woman failed to move her, she got desperate, and things got rough, which wasn't out of the ordinary for them, but it certainly wasn't intended this time around. She wasn't the prostitute who survived the trick by using anger to feel superior and the intoxication of power to numb her senses.

This time she only wanted to feel, to become aroused, to feel the blood rush to her most sensitive parts until any stimulation drove her to madness and beyond. She wanted to be teased until she begged for release, and she wanted to cry out in relief as her wish was granted and her body exploded with the blinding white heat of her climax.

She felt nothing but guilt and frustration as she tried to wrest the feelings from her partner, who clearly had ecstasy to spare, and as Lani lay exhausted and sated, Kathryn hated her for coming repeatedly and for reminding her how good it should be and what she'd thrown away.

Now she had to deal with Bouchaule. She took the extra shot of wine, hoping it would make her care less, or care more—at that moment, either would do. Oblivion was fine for a respite, but she found herself sinking deeper into nothingness, as the light of who she'd struggled to become was growing dim. She was not yet ready to return to what she was, not yet ready to release the last trace of the woman Jenny found worthy to love, and she started to panic, like a child lost in a crowded store. There were people everywhere, but no direction home.

It took her a moment to remember Thierry Bouchaule was her home now, and she had a job to do. The woman Jenny loved was an illusion, one visible only to her.

She filled two glasses and turned, smiling, as her new home approached.

"Cheers, darling," she said with a grin as she passed him his glass.

"Indeed, my love."

They took a sip, Kathryn taking a large one without being obvious, and then Bouchaule commented favorably on the fine vintage before sealing their toast with a kiss.

If she was going to survive, Kathryn decided she had to become his. She would have to own him, and he, in turn, would have to own her, move her in a way she dared not allow until now, when she had nothing to lose.

Bouchaule crossed the room to the radio and turned on some soft music. Kathryn took the opportunity to swallow as much wine as possible before involuntarily shuddering as the last in her glass slid down her throat. She set her glass down and melted into his waiting arms for a slow dance. The wine was working. Her head cared less about her guilt and more about the man in her arms and the life she would now embrace.

His touch was gentle, his movements sublime. He was a graceful man, and already his magic was stirring something in her, spreading warmth to her extremities and engorging her center with a pent-up yearning to be taken and consumed. Finally, her senses were awakening. If anyone was strong enough to make her feel again, to come again, it was him ... with a little help from the wine.

Bouchaule mindlessly hummed the tune as he rested his cheek against hers and expertly led them in a close dance. Kathryn closed her eyes and held him tighter, as the prospect of his domination over her aroused her alcohol-addled libido.

"Make love to me," she whispered.

Bouchaule stopped dancing and tilted up her chin, where he was drawn in to her submissive gaze. He kissed her gently, then harder, as she insisted, but he soon pulled back, unfamiliar with her desperation.

She wanted him to take her. Hard. This was no time for confused looks or second thoughts. It was time for his suave sophistication to yield to his primal urges. "Fuck me, Thierry."

He was stunned by her vulgarity but was ultimately conquered by her urgent desire. She captured his mouth again and drank from his lips with a fervor she'd never used with him before. Her desperation tapped into his own, and he swept her off her feet and carried her into the bedroom, where he laid her on the bed and groped at her body as he tried to keep up with her insistent kisses. She tore away his tie and blindly fumbled with the buttons on his shirt as he aggressively pulled at her gold lamé gown, confounded by the straps, hooks, and zippers.

"Tear it off," she pleaded between kisses.

He stopped and looked at her.

"Tear it off," she repeated, beyond caring about the cost of the dress and the fact that it was the property of The Grotto.

He tore off his own shirt first and then made one more noble attempt at saving the dress before giving up under her deriding laughter. He snapped the thin straps across the back with an easy swipe of his hand and worshipped her exposed breasts, while she released his belt and pants.

She wanted to be controlled, debased—pleasure through punishment, and oh, how she deserved to be punished.

The sex was rough and sloppy, befitting her primal desperation, but despite Bouchaule's best efforts, pleasure eluded her. Anger and frustration grew exponentially beside his ecstasy, as it became apparent he would not make her come any more than Lani had. She did her best to feign pleasure, but her anger would not be denied, and he was going to pay for letting her down.

She took control of her position astride his hips and kept on him, even as he came, pulling sounds from him she'd never heard before, as the pleasure consumed him and left him humbled and spent as never before.

She didn't bother faking an orgasm for his benefit. She stared at his heaving, sweaty, exhausted body and despised him for letting her down.

She dismounted him without ceremony and went directly into the shower, where she leaned one hand against the tile wall and let the steaming hot water wash her deed away. Rage and disgust—at Bouchaule, and at herself—consumed her. She prepared to unleash a fist to the wall when the shower curtain flew open and startled her.

Bouchaule appeared before her, still breathing unevenly, fully clothed, shirt open, tie haphazardly draped around his neck, and fury in his eyes.

"Have I ever treated you like a whore?" he shouted.

"Of course not."

"Then do not act like one!"

He threw a handful of bills into the shower and stormed out the door.

Kathryn stood stunned, and the ineffectual reflex of calling his name arrived long after the front door had slammed.

She leaned against the shower wall again and watched hundred-dollar bills circle the drain.

The hot water of the shower beat an insistent rhythm on Kathryn's skin as she sat numbly at the bottom of the tub. She stared at the five soggy bills clutched in her hand and didn't know whether to laugh or cry. At least Bouchaule thought her sexual prowess was worth a premium and then some. It was the best payday of her career, and it had cost her everything. She should have been wondering how she could get him back. She should have been wondering how she could have been so stupid as to let her façade slip. Instead, she stared at the bills and wondered why she couldn't come.

She should have been devastated over the loss of Jenny and devastated over her catastrophic misstep with Bouchaule. Instead, she was empty. Her anger was gone like her assignment, and her motivation was stripped from her like her last shred of dignity, when she first spread her legs in the name of survival. She closed her eyes and lifted her face to the falling water. She wanted to be cleansed. She wanted to start her life over. She wanted to dissolve like a pillar of salt in the rain and be reborn as someone else—somewhere else— in a different time, a different place, a different world. She wanted to love without the fear of loss, and she wanted to feel without the cost of her sanity. She wanted to come.

She took control of the only thing in her power and slid her hand between her parted thighs. She felt the pain of her evening's exploits as she slipped her fingers inside. The pain was only fitting, and it did, for the moment, bring pleasure. She massaged her swollen center and brought herself close very quickly. It wasn't about extended pleasure, or self-control; it was an aching need to find release, to find something alive in her desolate shell.

She was so close, but relief wouldn't come. She could find no fantasy to push her over, no memory to pull her home. The only emotion that hadn't abandoned her returned, as anger fueled her working hand. She spread her legs wide and begged for success.

"Come on!" she ground out in frustration as she worked harder. "Come on, come!"

Her body trembled from exhausted muscles, and her center was numb to her efforts, but still she tried harder, plunging her fingers frantically, until cries of desperate encouragement turned to cries of resignation, and finally devastation, as she stopped the madness, unsatisfied.

The hot water had turned to cold, bringing a jolting slap of reality. Kathryn felt. Finally. Tiny stings of ice cold water pierced her brittle shell as she curled into a ball. Naked and raw, money clenched in one hand, the other cradling her useless sex, she finally acknowledged and despised herself for the pathetic creature she had become.

What she thought was an empty vessel, spilled its contents through her tears and cries, and the pain of what she'd lost—her family, Jenny, hope—poured out from deep within and kept coming and coming like an endless spring of sorrow, until her uncontrolled sobs gave way to silent desolation.

She had found release, just not the one she sought. She was small and alone as she accepted her fate, and under the watchful eyes of her concerned demons, she dissolved like a pillar of salt in the rain and washed away.

Kathryn stepped into the early morning darkness of her apartment and closed the door with a heavy sigh. A light suddenly went on and she jumped.

"Jesus!"

"Sorry," Smitty said from the couch, with his hand on the end of the lamp's pull chain.

She didn't see his car outside, which meant he came up through the cellar. The perfect ending to the perfect night. She hadn't seen him in weeks, and tonight, of all nights, there he was. How he always knew when she screwed up was beyond her, but tonight she had no interest in a lecture.

"Did they send you over here to check up on me? Report back on my *mental faculties*? Kat Hammond makes a mess and Smitty's right there to clean it up, right?"

"I'm leaving tomorrow," he said quietly.

Kathryn had her bitter sarcasm kicked back through her teeth, and she swallowed it whole, as she regretted not only her words right then, but also all the unkind words and unkind things she'd ever said or done to him. Her apathetic mind abandoned its self-pity, and she moved to the couch and slowly sat beside him.

"When?"

He looked at his watch. "A few hours. First thing."

"God," she uttered under her breath, as her shoulders slumped and she rubbed her forehead.

"I need to know you're going to be all right, Kat."

"I don't think I'm the one we need to worry about now."

He took her hand, emphatically repeating himself. "I need to know you're going to be all right."

She patted his hand. "I always land on my feet, Smitty."

He stared at her, not accepting her platitudes. "Jenny came to see me tonight. She told me what happened."

Kathryn searched his face for any hint of the scene as it played out. She didn't need to ask how she was. He knew what she wanted to know.

"She was pretty devastated."

His answer tore up what was left of her insides, and she grimaced, as the mantle of tormentor settled around her shoulders.

"What did you tell her?"

"I know you're crazy about the kid, so I figured you had a pretty good reason for what you did, so I backed you up. Said that's just the way you are and you weren't coming back."

"Did she buy it?"

He nodded.

Kathryn was reflexively hurt that Jenny bought it, but she had set up the breakup and acted it out perfectly. She was, after all, a professional. "Thank you, Smitty."

"Promise me you'll be all right."

She squeezed his hand and looked him in the eyes. "I'll be all right. I have to be, or it all will have been for nothing."

She knew that's what he wanted to hear. He knew she would focus all her pain and anguish on her assignment. God help the victim.

"Is there something I have to clean up, Kat?"

"No."

"What happened?"

"What you knew would happen. I did what I had to do. What you knew I would have to do eventually."

"I take no pleasure in that."

She reassured him with a sad smile. "I know that, Smitty."

He cleared his throat, thankfully not wanting to linger on *I told you so*. "Well, anyway, it must mean your assignment's going well."

"Yeah. Very well."

He tugged on her hand, mistaking her lie for guilt.

"Jenny will be fine."

"I know she will. She's a strong woman."

"So are you."

Kathryn smiled. There was no way she could tell him she had lost everything, including her strength, and that she was hanging on by the barest of threads. If Bouchaule didn't contact her again, it was all for nothing, and she couldn't bear the thought of it or what would become of her or her sanity. She was lying to everyone—Jenny, the OSS, Smitty, and to herself—when she convinced herself her debt was reason enough to care what tomorrow might bring.

Smitty did his best to console her, unaware of her precarious position.

"The war will be over before you know it, and—"

"And then what happens to people like us?"

He thought about it seriously for a moment, but she knew the truth was nothing good, and he wouldn't say it. He merely smiled and put his arm around her shoulders.

"No one else will put up with us, so we'll have to marry and have ten kids."

Kathryn laughed and rested her head on his shoulder. There were no answers for them, or the thousands like them, who, by the war's end, would be scarred by the things they'd seen and done in the name of what's good and right, and they would struggle for the rest of their lives to reconcile their right to happiness against the rights of the fallen.

Her entire life felt like a war. Since the age of fourteen, every day seemed like a fight for survival. And then she met Jenny and the world yawned in Technicolor to give her a glimpse of what she supposed was the real world. It just wasn't her real world. Her real world kept getting darker. She couldn't shake the feeling it was the last time she'd ever see Smitty.

"Please be careful. Don't go getting into trouble over some pretty girl."

He smiled. "You're the only pretty girl I stick my neck out for."

She smiled too, but it quickly faded, as their imminent separation weighed on her heart. She raised her head and they both stared into each other's eyes. Both felt lost. Words were insignificant and emotions were too overwhelming to comprehend farewell. She wanted to be a girl again, lying by his side in a tree house, staring up at the stars while they plotted their futures with gleeful innocence only found in youth.

She had been crushed by Jenny's loss, and the only other constant she had ever known was leaving to an uncertain future. She was not yet ready to be stripped bare.

"Stay with me tonight?"

"Sure thing, doll."

Kathryn smiled and rested her head on his shoulder again.

There would be no goodbyes for them. Smitty would lay with his arms wrapped protectively around her until the early morning hour came and then he would slip silently from her presence and leave behind his love and faith in her and the unspoken promise that they would see each other again.

CHAPTER FORTY-ONE

Kathryn leaned into the vanity mirror she shared with another singer and twelve chorus girls and removed her lipstick. Her show was over for the night, and the cramped dressing room had stopped buzzing with the chaotic crush of costume changes and last-minute facial touch-ups.

She found comfort in the madness of the small hive of beings rushing headlong with a purpose, even if it was only to make their cues on stage, and she longed for the activity, now that the theater was still.

The silence in the deserted dressing room magnified her failure and preyed on her fragile state of mind. She knew it wouldn't be long before she had to make a proactive decision about her future, or go mad.

Her life had become a game of sit and wait, a slow torture, with her only lifeline to sanity the hope that Bouchaule would return. As time went on, it seemed less likely. There was no reason for him to return. He no longer needed her for his precious work, and their physical and emotional relationship had obviously been dealt a blow beyond repair.

She hadn't seen or heard from Thierry Bouchaule since her catastrophic misstep three weeks ago, but she went through the motions of having an assignment, initially lying to the OSS about why she hadn't had contact with him, by simply claiming ignorance on the matter and then feigning indifference when the OSS quickly discovered the doctor was in Pennsylvania. After seeing the University of Pennsylvania address on the envelope of photos Bouchaule had showed her, Kathryn could only assume he was utilizing the university's advanced equipment to get a closer look at his obsession and document it for his investors. It wouldn't be long before his business was finished in the U.S. and then he would head home to France and far out of her reach.

Patience was wearing thin at headquarters, and Holmes never failed to display his disappointment in her progress on the case. She sensed she was on the verge of reassignment, and she couldn't say that she wouldn't welcome it. Anything would be welcome now. Anything would be better than withering under the consequences of her arrogance. She had no one to blame but herself, and she played the scene over and over, as it should have ended, with Bouchaule undeniably hers.

It was the night she was to commit herself completely to him, in whatever capacity would ensure the success of her assignment and Jenny's safety. Her ill-advised descent into alcohol and the reckless abandon it inspired made sure that didn't happen, and now she would suffer for her lack of judgment.

She was so sure she could control Bouchaule. He was a man after all, and all men have the same weakness. It was just her luck she would find the one man whose pride trumped his desire.

Arrogance makes you careless, Smitty had said once. He was right, as usual. She had made a mess of everything. She'd hurt every person she loved, betrayed the people with whom she worked and respected, and now she was left with nothing and no one.

She wanted to curse her damn foolish heart for falling in love and then her damn foolish head for giving into it. She knew it was wrong and that no good would come of it. No good would ever come from loving her.

At least she could use that to her advantage with Bouchaule, but as hope waned for his return, she was coming undone. Without love and purpose, she was the sum of her damaging acts, past and present, and she searched desperately for anything to deflect the reoccurring anguish of her sins.

She turned to music as a distraction. The uncertainty of working with new musicians and new arrangements rattled her perfectionist sensibilities, but the challenge was a welcome diversion, as a new musical venue every week provided boundaries into which she could channel her disintegrating psyche.

Music was a living, breathing entity, her only friend. A song was honest, clean emotion on a tide of sound, and it lifted her body and soul like a kite in the wind and swept her away from the troubles of the outside world. She felt alive when she performed, and for those moments, never truer to herself.

Her current schedule was nothing like her gig at The Grotto. She was part of an ensemble cast now, a guest player, with no perks or flexible hours. Her musical numbers were more Vaudeville than sophisticated nightclub this time, but after singing the blues in a few dark, moody clubs to appease her disposition, she grew weary of the bloodletting and was grateful for the light atmosphere of the variety show. Dominic's motto, *we are happy here*, suddenly had its charms.

She chose her latest venue specifically because it was hard work. There were shows in the afternoon, in the evening, and a midnight show on Saturdays. Rehearsals often went on until three or four in the morning, and free time was scarce, which was the point. Kathryn welcomed the structure, but in the end, it always gave way to a maddening silence that ushered in everything she was trying to forget.

She walked away from Jenny to save her, but the pain, devastation, and hatred she saw in her eyes would haunt her forever. The hate meant that Jenny would move on and love again. She could find someone who would cherish her above all else. Oh, that it could have been her.

Tears came when she allowed them. She told herself happiness was not for her, that she didn't deserve it. That's what she always told herself when the good things in her life went the way of all good things in her life. It was a tried and true coping tool that made the tragedies and disappointments bearable, but this time was different.

She almost had it all. That Jenny loved her and accepted her so completely, baggage and all, was nothing short of a miracle. She missed her terribly—her friendship, the no-nonsense way about her, her hairbrained schemes, her laughter, and how her very presence lit up a room and made her heart smile.

When she was alone in bed, surrounded by the unforgiving still-ness of the night, she longed for Jenny's warmth against her. She wanted to lose herself in the scent of her, the taste of her, the lust, the possession, the surrender, the bliss, the calm, the love. God. She had to stop. She no longer had the right to any of those things. Jenny was gone. She'd made sure of that.

Kathryn put her head in her hands. Where was her detachment, her practiced indifference? Guilt and grief kept hitting her in waves, and she was caught in their emotional churn.

She lifted her gaze to the mirror. Apart from her stage persona and the front she put up at her infrequent visits to headquarters, she was lost. She could fool those on the outside and pretend all she liked, but the eyes staring back at her knew her secrets and she had nowhere to hide. Stripped of an act and an audience, she had no identity and couldn't comprehend the broken woman before her. This wasn't her. She made her own opportunities, pressed forward, always, but without Bouchaule to distract her, she had to endure the full-on assault of Jenny's loss; and interest, in the form of guilt, was collecting on her debt to the boys overseas.

Her thoughts were fragmented and conflicted. Doing what was right meant doing some things wrong, and more and more, she was losing her ability to tell the difference. She'd lost the ground beneath her feet, lost herself, and she realized she never really knew who that person was. She moved from situation to situation, letting her goals determine who she needed to be, and now she was alone, grasping for the security and the sanity of purpose.

If only she had Bouchaule. She seriously thought of heading to Philadelphia to get him back, but that couldn't be done. He needed to return to her. He needed to need her, which led her back to despondency. He didn't need her. Her assignment and all she sacrificed for it was gone.

Jenny was gone.

Her heart weighed her down like a stone in her chest, as memories and shattered dreams fell on her like layers of cold earth, until she was suffocating in a grave of her own making. She hadn't seen the light of day in ages, and her face was drawn and pale. Sleep was nothing more than unconsciousness brought on by exhaustion.

If she wasn't performing or rehearsing, she was hidden away in Daniel Ryan's secret lab, using his specially coded books to decode the documents she'd photographed.

It was sweet torment knowing Jenny was on the other side of the wall. Sometimes she could hear her shoes as she crossed the hardwood floors or the radio when she played it loud. It made it easy to pretend walking away had just been a terrible nightmare. Sometimes she expected Jenny to pop her head out from the passageway leading to the study bookcase. "Can I get you anything, baby?" she imagined her saying.

Kathryn would lean back in Daniel Ryan's creaking wooden chair and close her eyes when the ghost of her love echoed in her head. She would savor it for as long as she dared and then quickly discard it. Sentiment was left to the past, where it belonged. She would open her eyes to a cacophony of numbers, notes, and formulae, and she was reminded she'd done the right thing. She was doing the right thing.

The right thing was cold comfort to her now, as her thin veil of composure unraveled, revealing physical manifestations of her deconstruction. Her hand trembled as she reached for the jar of cold cream, and she made a fist, trying to deny her frailty. She had to keep it together, had to regain control.

Breathe, she told herself. *Breathe.*

She regained some equilibrium and shook off the tremors. *One day at a time,* she reminded herself. *One day at a time.* One day at a time for what? She didn't know, but she would drag herself there because she must.

She rubbed the cold cream onto her face, erasing her makeup like she wished she could erase her pain. Bouchaule wasn't here to save her. She had to save herself. While she washed her face, she vowed to take control of what was left of her life. She just needed a stage, any stage, to pretend she was sane until sanity found her again. For now, this theater was her stage, and she would wait patiently for the OSS to decide when her assignment was over.

Her hair fell in long wavy tendrils around her face as she removed the pins holding it up. She looked like Medusa, and just as deadly.

There was relief in accepting her failure. She no longer had to pretend to be strong or proud, for she was neither. She exhaled what little strength she had and bowed her head. Her body was weak and shaky, and she grabbed the sink to steady herself. She wanted to cry, but she resisted.

It was time to be reborn. She raised her chin and waited to become a new person.

Moments went by, and she didn't feel new. She felt exhausted and beaten. Maybe tomorrow she would feel new.

One day at a time.

She opened her eyes, hoping to find herself at least physically transformed in some way, but she was met with bloodshot eyes and a haggard face framed by hair that made her look as mad as she felt. She snorted derisively and shook her head, and then something in the mirror caught her eye. Over her shoulder, from just inside the doorway, someone was watching her.

She blinked the figure into focus. It was a man impeccably dressed in a double-breasted somber gray suit, hat in hand. Thierry Bouchaule had returned. She couldn't move for a moment, as she tried to convince herself it was real and not a product of her shattered mind finally pushed over the edge. She held her breath and turned.

He was real.

"Thierry." It was all she could manage to say as her knees went weak. She trembled again, but this time it was relief, elation, and a frantic scramble to collect herself. She quickly turned away to hide her rapidly forming tears but realized she'd been betrayed by her reflection in the mirror.

She'd practiced this scene over and over, knew the woman to become inside and out, and that woman did not shed hysterical tears. She raked her fingers back through her hair several times, corralling it, as she corralled her emotions, hoping Bouchaule could not see her shaking hands or hear her pounding heart. She pinned her hair back and straightened, shedding her sins and the useless woman they'd bred.

"What are you doing here?" she asked calmly.

"Why did you not tell me you had lost your job at the club?"

Interesting opening, Kathryn thought, as she moved to the vanity, where she capped the cold cream for a distraction while she continued to gather herself.

"It didn't matter. I can get a job anywhere in this town."

Bouchaule looked around the dingy room with disdain. "Evidently."

She slammed the jar down and turned, finding her character easily.

"Did you come here to humiliate me again, Thierry?"

He moved into the room and tossed his hat onto a chair.

"It was I who was humiliated."

Kathryn snorted in disbelief.

"Right, because the whole world revolves around you. You and your precious work."

"That was not an accusation," he said, stepping closer. "I admit my manners may leave something to be desired, but I will never apologize for my dedication to my work."

"Of course you won't." She watched his eyes narrow and realized she was playing it a little too hard. "Nor should you," she relented, almost as an apology.

He smiled, becoming the charming man she knew. They were getting off on the wrong foot, and he apparently didn't want that any more than she did.

"I do not wish to make you angry, Kathryn. As I said, it was I who was humiliated. I left you unsatisfied. I am not accustomed to leaving a woman unsatisfied."

Kathryn couldn't believe his conceit.

"You came here to soothe your ego?"

The charm immediately fell away.

"I came here to apologize."

"You've apologized, now go."

He hesitated, as if considering it, and she prepared to bolt after him. She would do anything to keep him—cry, beg, even have his child, she had decided in her desperation. Anything. Her hard to get routine was what she thought he would find attractive in a woman, vulnerable, but not desperate, and strong when it mattered most, but not emasculating.

Their drama was interrupted when Kathryn's male lead from the show stuck his head in the door.

He eyed Bouchaule suspiciously. "Is everything all right, Kat?"

"Yes, Clem. Thank you."

Kathryn turned back to the mirror, where she observed the two men sizing each other up. The pissing contest was a draw, evidently, and Clem bid Kathryn good night.

"Great show tonight, angel."

"Thanks, Clem. You too."

Bouchaule glared at the man until he was out of sight. "Friend of yours?"

Kathryn smiled internally. Bouchaule's jealousy was a good sign. "Mr. Goddard seems to have mistaken musical chemistry with sexual chemistry, and, no, he is not a friend of mine."

Bouchaule flexed his shoulders and cracked his neck like a prizefighter warming up for the ring when he affected a Brooklyn accent and said, "You want I should punch his lights out?"

Kathryn grinned, genuinely amused at the man's humor and command of the accent, but she did not let him off the hook. "Perhaps I should have him punch *your* lights out."

Bouchaule straightened, his suave sophistication restored. "I should like to see him try."

"That might be amusing."

"Not for him."

Bouchaule's humor was suddenly gone, replaced by a serious scowl, as he looked her up and down.

"You do not look well."

She eyed him in the tall mirror. "Thank you, Thierry. I can always count on you to make me feel good about myself." She leaned over and picked up a lipstick, acknowledging a little makeup couldn't hurt her ragged appearance.

"I speak out of concern."

She turned to face him. "I'm touched."

He moved forward and gently took her elbow. "You are pale. Are you ill, Kathryn?"

His concern was genuine, and Kathryn got lost for a moment in the depth of his worried eyes.

"I'm not ill." She lifted her arm from his grasp and turned back to the mirror. "I'm tired. It's two in the morning, and it's been a long week." She set the lipstick down, unused, and met his eyes in the mirror. It was time for reconciliation. "It's been a long three weeks."

Bouchaule moved to her back and placed his hands tenderly on her shoulders.

"For me as well."

Her look was not one of forgiveness—not yet—and he removed his hands and stepped away.

"I am a vain and prideful man. So, yes, I am here to soothe my ego, but more than that, I lost control. I was embarrassed, and I handled it badly. I am sorry for what I said. Please forgive me."

That was too easy. She eyed him warily. Had something happened in his work? Did he need her blood again?

"If you want your money back, I haven't got it. I've got bills to pay."

In actuality, she deposited the money at the nearest war bond office and signed ownership of the bond over to the young salesgirl.

Bouchaule was incredulous. "I do not want the money. Why are you being so difficult?"

"Why are you here?"

"Because I love you."

Kathryn turned. She was surprised, *and* pleased. It meant she could use the best part of her speech.

"For how long? Until you disappear again? I'm not going to be that woman ... the one who sits at home waiting and wondering when you'll return, *if* you'll return."

He moved closer, and his voice was tender when he said, "I returned that night, but you had gone. You no longer worked at the club, and I did not know where to find you."

She hadn't thought of that.

"Then I was called away. I sought you out as soon as I could."

He moved closer and stroked her cheek.

"Please forgive me."

She hesitated, not for lack of an answer, but out of surprise that she was moved by his words. She moved out from under his hand and walked away.

"I saw your face when I appeared at the door," he said to her back. "You are angry and you are hurt, but you love me."

She turned to face him—and her future.

"So, I love you. What of it? Little good it does me."

Bouchaule looked appropriately contrite.

"I hate with all my heart the words I spoke to you, and I am sorry. I have been going mad these past few weeks without you, wondering what you must think of me." He shook his head, as if his words were insignificant against his transgression. "You can grant me your forgiveness or not. I leave it to you. If you want me to go, I will leave and never bother you again."

She approached him until they stood face to face. His words were confident, but his eyes belied a fear of losing her.

"And what of your promise?" she asked.

He blinked in confusion.

She slowly placed her hands on his chest, thankful they had stopped shaking. "You promised you wouldn't leave me again."

He physically relaxed and took her hands in his. "I will not leave you again." He kissed her hands and then wrapped her in his arms.

She smiled into his dark gray suit and tightened her embrace. Once it would have been a smile of triumph, a fake embrace with a sly smirk behind his back, but this time it was real. She clung to him tightly and almost cried. She was saved. She was someone again, someone with a mission and a purpose. Her demons cheered as they welcomed her home and slapped her on the back for a job well done.

Confidence restored and compass set, it was time to embark on a new path in her life.

"Do you have a room in the city tonight?" she asked.

"No.

"Did Bertrand drive you in?"

"I took a taxi."

"From the estate? How extravagant." *And risky.*

He smiled. "Love makes one do foolish things."

She was counting on it. "Would you care to stay at my place tonight?"

It had taken Kathryn a few minutes to assure the doctor that going to her apartment was safe for them.

"What of your roommate?" he had asked.

"I'm afraid I wore out my welcome with my friend. I've got my own place now, and it's perfectly safe."

He looked skeptical.

She smiled. "You'll see."

Bouchaule was quite pleased and impressed as they parked at a garage on the next block and made their way through the maze of basement passageways and finally up the cellar steps to Kathryn's apartment.

"A relic from Prohibition," Kathryn explained about the building's unusual architecture. "And a coachman's house before that."

Bouchaule wandered through Kathryn's apartment with great interest, exhaling a whistle as he ran his hand along the satin mahogany of the majestic Steinway that filled most of the living room.

"Came with the apartment," Kathryn lied. "Some gangster in the thirties bought it for his starlet girlfriend, and when baby went Hollywood, well ... there it sits."

Bouchaule laughed and shook his head. "Very extravagant."

"Ah, *l'amore*." Kathryn smiled.

Bouchaule continued his walkabout and ducked his head into the bedroom, where Kathryn blushed when he saw a picture of them together tucked into the frame of her vanity mirror. It was there to remind her of who she was to become, but discovered by the man himself, the picture served an even better purpose.

He smiled and placed a loving hand on the small of her back. "Thank you, darling, for not giving up on me."

"I didn't have a choice," she replied honestly.

"That is good, I think."

On the way to the kitchen, he raised a curious brow at the closed door leading to her painting studio, which she had passed without comment.

In response, Kathryn claimed it contained the personal belongings of the owner of the apartment and had been locked since she moved in.

He chuckled. "This place suits you. Deceptively uncomplicated but harboring secrets as deep as the sea."

"I think that's a compliment."

He kissed her cheek. "It means I shall never tire of you."

He pulled back and looked deeply into her eyes. She thought he was about to kiss her mouth for the first time since their reunion, but he didn't. He merely smiled, so she filled the awkward moment with small talk.

"Can I get you something?" she asked, as she moved into the kitchen. "I don't have much, I'm afraid. Coffee, tea, milk?" She opened the barren refrigerator, removed the paper cap from the milk bottle, and winced as the sour smell hit her. "Okay, no milk."

He laughed, holding out his hand to her. "Nothing, thank you." He cupped her cheek when she came to him. "You are tired. You need not entertain me."

She relaxed. It was odd having him in her home, and she admitted to some nerves. This first night was important. She had to get it right.

"I'm going to bathe. There's some liquor in the bar, if you'd like. Make yourself at home."

She expected him to join her in the tub, but he didn't, which told her things were not quite square with them. When she came out of the bathroom, she heard music. He was playing her piano. The tune was "Clair De Lune."

She stared at him from the hallway, a little stunned, as she tied her bathrobe around her waist.

"Why are you playing that?"

He removed his hands from the keys and closed the fallboard. "Sorry, I did not mean to—"

"No, no, it's okay. It was beautiful, I just ..." She sat beside him on the bench. "It was the song."

He smiled. "My favorite."

She had a disturbing case of déjà vu, as she thought back to when she sat beside Jenny in her study and played her father's favorite song. Perhaps in some spy manual somewhere there was an entry about preying on your victim's soft spot for a treasured memory. If there wasn't, there should be. It works.

"Mine too."

She lifted the fallboard and let him play. She stared at

Bouchaule's graceful hands as he caressed the keys and then closed her eyes and got lost in the melody and memories of her lost family and her lost life.

Bouchaule's foot released the sustain pedal at song's end, and Kathryn could feel his stare on her cheek.

"What does it mean to you?" he asked.

She smiled, debating on the truth or an elaborate lie. Her answer fell somewhere in between.

"Pleasant childhood memories."

He smiled. "Simpler days."

"To be sure." She paused. "You?"

"Reminds me of Adele. My sister. She used to attempt it."

"Attempt it?"

He smiled again. "Oh, she was horrid. No talent for the instrument whatsoever. I think she did it just to irritate me into playing it for her." His smile slowly vanished and he stared at the ivory keys.

Kathryn took his hand. "I'm sorry, Thierry."

He covered her hand with his and squeezed it but didn't look her way. She could see tears forming in his eyes, but he held them off.

"May I use your bath?"

"Of course."

As he stood, she held fast to his hand until he looked at her. He tugged on her hand and smiled his assurance that he was all right.

"They are happy memories."

She nodded and let him go.

Kathryn exhaled when she heard the water running. That the man moved her could not be denied. If he was using her for something, he was good—too good in her current overtired state. As it was, her heart went out to him anyway. She couldn't help it. The story about his sister was true in any case, and for that alone, she felt compassion for him.

She was sitting on the edge of her bed when he entered the bedroom with one towel slung low around his hips and another in his hands, scrubbing at his wet hair.

"Better?" she asked.

"Much. Thank you."

She stood and pulled the corner of the bedspread and top sheet back. Bouchaule understood he was being invited into her bed, but he hung the towel in his hands around his neck and hesitated.

"I will sleep on the couch."

She didn't know why he was so hesitant. Maybe he hadn't gotten over his embarrassment or hadn't forgiven her for causing it.

"Thierry ..." She reached out and bade him sit beside her on the bed to hear her explanation.

He sat with her and gave her his undivided attention.

"I'd lost a friend that day," she began.

His face immediately registered sympathy. "To the war?"

In a way. "Yes ... to the war. I was upset and angry, and I took it out on you. I'm sorry, you didn't deserve it. I just—" She swallowed down the memory of that terrible night.

"Wanted the pain to stop," he finished for her.

His voice was full of understanding and his eyes were soft and compassionate. It seemed he could see right to her core.

"Yes. I wanted the pain to stop."

"It does not stop, does it?"

She knew he spoke from experience, and she felt closer to him just then.

"No, it doesn't."

He entwined his fingers with hers. "You can confide in me. You did not have to go through that alone."

She squeezed his hand. "You have enough problems. You certainly don't need mine."

"I would be honored if you would share your problems with me."

"Like you share yours?"

"Hardly the same, I am afraid."

She stared at him until he softened his position.

"You cannot help me with my problems."

"And you may not be able to help me with mine, but it's nice to know there's someone who cares, don't you think?"

He couldn't disagree. "I see your point."

They sat in silence for a few moments, and she sensed a lingering awkwardness from their last encounter. The longer she let that go, the larger an obstacle it would become.

"I'm sorry about that night. It won't happen again."

"Well," he said with a rakish grin as he scratched his cheek, "I would not go that far."

Kathryn smiled internally. He was a man after all.

"But the next time," he went on seriously, "it will be because you seek pleasure, not a distraction."

How well he understood.

He was dirty—dirty and damaged like her. They were a perfect match. Game or not, they deserved each other, and if it was a game on his part, it would be the best game of his life. She would make sure of it.

"Well," he said dismissively, patting her hand and then standing.

It appeared she had not convinced him to share her bed.

"Stay," she said with longing in her eyes.

He returned to her side and searched her face.

"Stay," she repeated, her intentions perfectly clear.

He leaned in and softly kissed her expectant mouth.

This was what she had waited for, when she would welcome him back into her body and mind and accept him as her home and her future. She parted her lips and invited him in. He was her savior, her new religion, and everything she had done was for this moment.

Bouchaule gladly accepted his role and took her in his arms.

His gentle probing kiss was sensual and thoughtful, befitting her rebirth, and ever mindful of his pride, she was submissive to his advances as he eased her onto her back and parted her robe. She soon realized it wasn't merely consideration for his pride or her assignment that inspired her surrender. He would absolve her of her guilt, if not her sins, and with absolution, would come freedom, and with freedom, pleasure.

This is how it must feel for her victims, she thought—men in power who know better, yet they cannot resist. They'll be strong and wily tomorrow, they must think, because that's what she was thinking. Tonight, she and Bouchaule would be together, two broken creatures seeking shelter in each other.

Bouchaule's eyes were filled with the kind of temporary devotion arousal brings, and as he slid his body between her open thighs, she knew her eyes reflected the same. This encounter was nothing like their previous encounters. It was nothing like any they'd ever had.

His movements were slow and attentive and his eyes never left hers. She found it disconcerting and intoxicating. His gaze was open and she saw his desire, his admiration, and she swore, his love. Whatever Thierry Bouchaule's intentions in the long run, tonight was no game for either of them.

It felt good to feel pleasure without guilt and good to have sex without the anger so often accompanying it. She closed her eyes, waiting for Bouchaule's hips to begin the slow, rhythmic thrusting that would finally bring her back to life. That's how she imagined it would be tonight.

It was something to look forward to, as he was better than most, but she hoped he would just stay where he was and let her enjoy the sensation of his presence bearing down on a particularly erogenous spot deep inside her.

As if he could read her mind, he didn't move, and she opened her eyes to find him still staring at her, his gaze now boring into her, demanding the truth. She hid nothing from him—she was pure now —and this was the beginning of her new life.

"I love you."

She wanted to cry when she said it. How far she'd fallen from the last time she'd said it and meant it, but it was true, in a way, this time too—nothing like the love she shared with Jenny—but true in that she loved him for saving her.

"*Je t'aime aussi*," he whispered and took her in earnest.

Her surrender was mindless, the act itself like so many before it, but this one was for her pleasure, not her partner's. When she came, she clutched at his back, unleashing a guttural cry that rode unfettered beside the waves of her spasms, as she dug her fingers into his flesh.

In the throes of the euphoric moment after, she began to laugh uncontrollably. She'd come. Finally. But the laughter turned into sobbing, as she lost all control of her emotions. So much hit her at once: release, Bouchaule's return, Jenny's loss. God, Jenny's loss. She'd only ever lost control like this with Jenny, and that was a pure expression of love like she'd never experienced before. This was the exact opposite.

She had just reached the pinnacle of pleasure with someone other than the woman she loved, and it accentuated the grief of the wasted last weeks, as guilt sabotaged their sex life. These tears were a bloodletting. Every sob leeched a little more of Jenny from her soul, until it was raw, and bleeding, and begging for the pain to stop. Bouchaule would make it stop. He had to or she would die. She had no guilt with him now, and it ushered in the beginning of Jenny's complete erasure from her mind and body. It was as painful as it was liberating.

Bouchaule cradled her in his arms and rocked her gently, almost as if he expected her breakdown, and she buried her face in her hands, sobbing apologies into his chest.

He kissed her head and whispered soft words of comfort. He didn't discourage her from crying, and he didn't shy away from her display of emotion. When she calmed, he went to the bathroom and brought back a cold washcloth for her face.

"Here," he said, as he gently wiped the tears from her cheeks.

She gladly took it from his hand and hid her eyes with it, afraid she'd revealed too much of herself.

"I'm sorry, Thierry."

He guided her hair from her downturned face. "Why?"

She looked at him. "I'm sure a hysterical woman is not exactly what you had in mind tonight."

"You are tired. The day was too much for you. Here ..." He climbed into bed behind her and leaned against the headboard, easing her head to his chest.

He held her wordlessly for a few moments, and the tears stopped as quickly as they began. Kathryn sat up and offered a few more ignored apologies as she dabbed her eyes and wiped her nose.

Bouchaule ran his hand across her slumped shoulders, proffering his silent support until she was ready to talk about it. Opening up wasn't the norm. Usually, one would guard their weaknesses against possible exploitation, but the truth in this case could work toward her advantage, and she knew she had to give to get.

She lifted her tear-ravaged eyes to him in regret. "I hate that I need you so." She dropped her gaze. "I suppose it's foolish of me to admit that to you."

He was silent, and she sought his eyes to gauge his reaction. A single tear stained his cheek.

She wiped it away, unsure of his emotions. "Thierry ..."

He took her hand and kissed it. "I love that I need you so."

That was not what she expected to hear.

"Oh, I do not wish to," he assured her. "I have neither the time nor the temperament for love, believe me. I should be more sorry for you than glad, but I love that I need you so."

Kathryn couldn't tell if he was lying, and she didn't like being on the other side of the game, wondering if the heartfelt words threatening to breach her defenses were merely a Trojan horse, planted for her eventual destruction, or genuine words of love, spoken from an enchanted heart.

"You don't have to say that. Just because I—"

"It is the truth," he interrupted. "I have never cared so deeply for another. I do not wish to be without you, and for me, that is, at the very least, disconcerting."

Kathryn chuckled. "The reluctant lovers. Sounds like a sordid dime store romance novel."

"There is nothing sordid about what I feel for you."

"No," she said softly. "Nor I for you."

Silence surrounded them as they contemplated their respective positions. Bouchaule took her in his arms and leaned back against the headboard again.

"We are very much alike, Kathryn. I know you feel it too."

"Yes," she agreed honestly and rested her head on his chest.

"They are looking for me, so it will not be easy for us to be together."

"I know."

"I'm willing to risk it. Are you?"

She closed her eyes and tightened her embrace on his torso. Tonight, she was home and would feed on his strength. Tomorrow she would be strong and wily. Tomorrow.

"Yes. I'm willing."

CHAPTER FORTY-TWO

Ripples went through the local music scene last month when velvety voiced chanteuse Kathryn Hammond parted company with the swanky uptown club The Grotto. Any loyal reader of my column knows I've never been a fan of Miss Hammond's. She blew onto the scene a few years ago, brimming with promise and rave reviews, possessing the looks and the pipes to take this town by storm, but despite her undisputed vocal talent, she never rose above outward appearances to accomplish anything of substance. Saddled with a maddening by-the-book approach to her material, her performances neither inspire nor incite one to take the flight of fancy with her, as any musician worth their licks must. That being said, it is rare that I am mistaken and even rarer that I admit it, so hold on to your hats, folks—I was wrong about Kathryn Hammond.

You may recall, Miss Hammond made the news recently for her miraculous comeback after an automobile accident late last year nearly ended her career. Appreciate her musically or not, you couldn't help but pull for the gal after that. Her voice was a little different (not better or worse, just different), but, sadly, her ho-hum interpretations were the same, so it was out of the mere curiosity of my sentimental heart that I went to see her perform at her first gig post-Grotto at Back Alley Blues last month. As you know, I've a soft spot for the blues, and I fully expected Miss Hammond to underwhelm me with her pedestrian approach once again, but a curious thing happened: Kathryn Hammond has been reborn and has bewitched me utterly. Not only did she take me on her flight of fancy, she ripped my heart out and left me in tears—literally. And I wasn't the only one.

The blues were her genre, I thought, confirmed when she moved on to Essence the following week and wowed that crowd. Imagine my surprise when she hit the Footlight Theater last week and performed lighthearted musical comedy with equal aplomb! I can only guess it was the short-sighted vision of The Grotto's owner that held the reins on the lovely Miss Hammond and nothing to do with the lady's devotion to her craft—but that's for another column!

Absent a distracted dinner crowd and an overbearing boss, Kathryn Hammond has found her heart and soul, and aren't we the lucky ones!

I caught a rehearsal for this week's stint at the Savoy-Plaza's Café Lounge, and look out! Could it be that all those reviewers fawning over Miss Hammond from the beginning were right? I've admitted I was wrong; don't make me admit I've been blind as well. It's bad for business.

Starting tomorrow, Kathryn Hammond is appearing at the Savoy-Plaza's Café Lounge for one week only. Don't miss it!

Kathryn watched the drummer fold up his newspaper and nudge the saxophone player, who whistled to get the rest of the band's attention.

"Here she is."

Everyone stood and applauded as she arrived for rehearsal.

She shook her head and raised her hand. "Stop."

"You melted the iceberg, baby," the drummer said. He retrieved the paper from under his arm and handed her the article. "You can write your own ticket in this town now."

Kathryn smirked as she folded the article to the inside. "I don't need Lionel Sinclair's approval to write my own ticket in this town."

"Get her," the saxophone player joked.

Kathryn smiled kindly at their enthusiasm. "Thanks, fellas. Now let's kick this set, hm?"

Kathryn's plan was backfiring. She was trying for a low profile, and finally appealing to the toughest critic in town wasn't helping. She tossed the paper in the garbage on her way out of rehearsal and headed across town to a meeting at headquarters, where she'd have to suffer Holmes's self-righteous gloating over Bouchaule's return.

Saddled with a maddening by-the-book approach to her material, her performances neither inspire nor incite one to take the flight of fancy with her, as any musician worth their licks must.

"Sinclair, you're an ass," Jenny spat, as she sat on her couch and read the *Entertainment* section from a rival newspaper. She was tempted to toss out the entire section when she saw Kathryn's picture staring back at her, but knowing Sinclair's opinion of Kathryn, she was ready to agree with him, just out of spite. Unfortunately, when she read his intro, he just made her mad, as he always did. That in itself was infuriating. Try as she might to put Kathryn behind her, she was in constant flux between love and hate. The article prompted both, and she crumpled it up and threw it to the floor when a tendril of pride snuck around her hardened heart. She hated Kathryn Hammond. Now, if only her sentimental heart would remember that.

She finished her morning coffee and kicked the paper out of her path on her way to the rest of her day.

Kathryn sat at Daniel Ryan's lab desk and rubbed her tired eyes after staring at the results of hours of decoding. The notes were all science and medicine now. Earlier pages were half confession, half science, as Dr. Ryan felt the need to explain the sins of desperate doctors from decades ago who were willing to do anything, morals and ethics be damned, to stop a runaway virus that was devastating populations worldwide—the Spanish Influenza of 1918.

Kathryn was too young to remember the hysteria, but she had heard the stories. One in particular was the the tale of an uncle on her mother's side, whose entire family had succumbed to it within a week. It wasn't her place to judge Daniel Ryan or his colleagues. Her self-appointed task was uncovering Thierry Bouchaule's true intentions and keeping everyone involved as far away from Jenny as possible.

Kathryn offered a thought to Jenny in the house above her. She heard her arrive home from work, turn on her favorite nightly radio show, and imagined her making dinner for one.

It was quiet now, and she pictured her reading while curled up on one end of the large russet colored leather couch in the living room, with a fire in the fireplace. She liked to think of Jenny as content, with her life back to normal.

It would never be normal again if the truth was revealed, and Kathryn had all but decided that some things should remain buried.

She shook off thoughts of Jenny—more of a fading habit now than a need—and she turned back to her coded numbers. She was coming to the end of her stolen photographed documents. Soon, she would have no reason to return to Daniel Ryan's lab, or any opportunity to find comfort in Jenny's routine. Just as well. Bouchaule was her life now, something Colonel Holmes was all too willing to reiterate in their afternoon meeting.

"I don't have to remind you, Miss Hammond, your singing career is a cover, and your first obligation is to this agency."

Kathryn noted the newspaper on Colonel Holmes's desk turned open to Sinclair's article.

"No, Colonel Holmes, you needn't remind me."

Colonel Forsythe's smile at her response spoke of both an apology for his colleague and his enduring confidence in her abilities. She appreciated both, though she hated to imagine what he would think of her if he knew of her deception.

"Things are back on track with Bouchaule?" Forsythe asked.

"Yes, sir."

"How on track?"

"He asked me to move to the estate with him."

Holmes raised his brow. "And?"

"Not very practical, given my cover, but we worked out a compromise."

"I'm not sure I like the sound of that. It smacks of putting your career first."

"Colonel Holmes, any singer with any self-respect is not going to throw away the opportunities that are coming her way because a man snaps his fingers and says, 'Here, girl.' That's not the kind of woman Bouchaule wants, and it's not the kind of woman I am. He knows this and understands completely."

Holmes grunted his reluctant approval.

"What have you learned, Kathryn?" Forsythe asked.

Kathryn went on to explain that Bouchaule had freely given the location of his recent trip to Pennsylvania, and the reason, just as she thought, was that the university had the latest in microscope technology: an electron microscope that enabled him to observe his work like never before. Holmes seemed less than impressed, pointing out that the OSS already had that information.

The point he was missing was that Bouchaule had given the information without prompting. Kathryn stifled a glare and refrained from asking if it was a mere coincidence that the government's Office for Scientific Research and Development had their Committee on Medical Research chaired by a University of Pennsylvania pharmacologist. It wouldn't do to suggest a connection between Bouchaule's "friends in high places" and the U.S. government, but it was in the back of her mind, and it did nothing to dissuade her from her deceptive path. *Status quo at headquarters and another point to Bouchaule for his honesty*, she thought.

Kathryn shook her head at the irony as she returned to the present and blinked the coded document on the desk into focus. She noted the numbers on the page and thumbed to the proper page in Daniel Ryan's medical journal. She then ran her index finger to the corresponding line and over to the correct word, which she wrote in her composition notebook. She glanced at her watch and saw she had three more hours before she would meet Bouchaule at the estate. Such was their arrangement when she had no reason to be close to the city. He no longer kept the location a secret from her. Bertrand would pick her up at her apartment and chauffeur her to the estate, no blindfold required, though she did note he kept a watchful eye for a tail and often took a roundabout route if he had the slightest reservation about the car in the rearview mirror. Kathryn and Bertrand had reached a truce. He had been cordial, friendly even, since their initial confrontation.

She absently smiled at how well things were going. Content in her task and steadfast in her purpose, she moved on to the next set of numbers before her. Her concentration was broken when she heard music drifting down from above. She froze with her finger on the page when she recognized the tune and then slowly looked up when the voice she heard was her own. Jenny was playing her record.

Her first instinct was to scream, "Don't do that!" No good could come of it. Jenny was supposed to be moving forward, not backward. Kathryn was surprised the record still existed. She was sure Jenny would have put it in the roadside trash with the rest of her belongings.

Kathryn climbed the stairs to the passageway leading to the back of the study bookcase and carefully put her ear to the door. Oddly, she had no emotion for the song or the occasion of its giving. Her love for Jenny was such a disconnected memory that she may as well have dreamed it one night.

The music stopped abruptly mid-song, and like an obsessive voyeur, Kathryn listened intently for Jenny's next move. She was met with silence for several long minutes, but just when she was about to head back into the lab, random notes drifted to her ears from the piano on the other side of the wall. The sound was so close that she backed away from the door for fear her presence could be felt in the next room.

A meager attempt at a song turned into a fistful of sour notes, as Jenny pounded the keyboard and shouted, "I fucking hate you!" to the empty study.

The next thing Kathryn heard was sobbing, and she closed her eyes and put her hand to the door.

No, Jenny, she silently pleaded.

For a moment, Kathryn became the woman Jenny loved, the woman who wanted to burst through the bookcase and take her in her arms and tell her it had all been a mistake. She loved her and she was trying to protect her. Jenny may never forgive her, but the pain of self-doubt would dissolve, and at least she would know their love was real.

The transformation was fleeting, and as Jenny poured out her grief on the other side of the door, Kathryn turned her back to it and slid down to the floor. Intellectually, she knew she was the cause of it, but emotionally, she refused to take responsibility.

She was almost overpowered by the anguishing guilt swelling inside her, but she willed it down. She was through with guilt. She had a new life now, and the guilt was replaced by resentment. How dare Jenny wallow in their defunct love affair and force those feelings up in her.

Just because Jenny was weak was no reason she should suffer. She convinced herself Jenny's pain was her own doing. She had tried to warn the woman off before their affair started, but Jenny wouldn't hear of it, and now she was paying the price. Kathryn sat motionless until the wailing in the next room became the unfortunate result of some abstract tragedy and nothing to do with her.

She picked herself up off the floor and walked away from her former life. She systematically packed up the books and notes and left the lab, looking forward to a guilt-free evening in the arms of Thierry Bouchaule.

Jenny sat at the disharmoniously ringing Bösendorfer and buried her face in her hands as she cursed herself for still loving Kathryn Hammond. She hoped the more she tried to hate the woman, the more she would, but it wasn't working yet. Kathryn had been on her mind all day, ever since the article in the morning paper. Jenny had the urge to catch a show at the Savoy-Plaza's Café Lounge in the upcoming week, curious to see what changed the mind of the critic she loved to hate, but she was afraid Kathryn would see her in the audience, and the last thing she wanted to do was let Kathryn Hammond think she was giving her a second thought.

Her empty home did nothing to purge the woman from her mind, and she gave in to her relentless memories by playing the record Kathryn had made for her.

Jenny knew it was a mistake immediately. A dagger laced with their tainted love pierced her heart when she heard Kathryn's voice. She quickly pulled the needle from the grooves, unable to stand the emotions it stirred.

Her sense of loss was overwhelming, no less than the pain she felt the day their relationship ended, over a month ago. She was melancholy in love this day, and she'd wandered aimlessly from the living room to the study and to the piano Kathryn admired so much. She tried to play something, to coax some enjoyment from the instrument, but she was met with nothing but pain, and she broke down, tired of being tortured by grief and taunted by memories that would surely last a lifetime.

When would she stop loving her? Not today, apparently, as she wiped her tear-stained face on her sleeve and left the study. She picked up the crumpled newspaper from the floor where she'd kicked it that morning and smoothed the *Entertainment* section out on the coffee table. She cut out Kathryn's article and lovingly placed it in the scrapbook Kathryn's father had kept. It was only fitting to add it to the book that represented unconditional love for a woman who turned her back on love.

Jenny leafed through the book and imagined the bittersweet pride felt by Kathryn's father as he added to the book. She could almost see him searching the newspaper every day for a glimpse of the daughter he loved and lost, guilt pulling at him constantly, knowing her loss was his fault. Jenny didn't feel guilty, but she did feel the pain of loss and a masochistic urge to remain connected to Kathryn. She couldn't help feeling the tragedy of her life. It muted her hate. The woman was broken after all.

She's damaged goods, kid, Smitty had said. *And as much as we love her, we can't fix that.*

But Jenny wanted to fix that, and in her moments of residual love, she thought she had come so close, and that led her back to wondering what went wrong, which led to a vicious circle of what ifs and more tears.

She closed Jackson Hammond's last gift to his daughter and vowed not to open it again. It contained someone else's pain, someone else's regret, and she had enough of her own. She returned the book to the box of Kathryn's belongings that now resided on the floor at the back of her closet, having rescued it from the roadside garbage in a moment of weakness, when Kathryn never showed to retrieve it.

She thought about sealing the record in there, but she couldn't. She made it her ultimate test instead. When she could listen to the record and feel nothing for Kathryn Hammond, she would be over her, and then she would celebrate by purging these last few remnants of her existence from her life.

Until then, Jenny did what she had done every night since their breakup; she pulled a leather-bound journal from the shelf above her writing desk, uncapped the black heirloom Wirt fountain pen with the inlaid mother of pearl barrel, and poured out her feelings, be them love or hate, to the woman who haunted her still.

CHAPTER FORTY-THREE

Kathryn returned an affectionate smile to Thierry Bouchaule over her wine glass. They were sitting opposite across a long table in the large dining room at the estate, lording over a dinner party for a handful of Bouchaule's connections in the U.S. There were seven in all—businessmen, doctors, scientists —and no new faces for Kathryn. Most she'd already met from her association with Marcus Forrester, and the others she'd seen on the periphery as part of Bouchaule's contingent, none of whom were strangers to the government's surveillance.

The leader of the group, Colin Donnelly, was a businessman from Chicago who had a slight Irish accent and an urgent need for results. He had a long-standing distrust of anyone present not vital to his goal, which, for the past few days, put Kathryn directly under his disapproving glare.

Donnelly had never liked Kathryn constantly on Forrester's arm, and he liked even less finding her cohabitating with the head of his research team.

Bouchaule finally put an end to the man's sour disposition during a private heated argument, when he defended Kathryn's honor and her right to be at his side.

"She is vital to my work in ways you could not even begin to understand, Donnelly," she heard Bouchaule say with her ear hovering over the heat register grate in the library above his study. A satisfied grin pulled at her lips as he continued with his emotional defense.

"I see," was Donnelly's unconvincing reply to Bouchaule's lie about the unique properties of her blood.

In truth, the doctor had periodically tested her and found no trace of the anomaly that saved her life and restored her voice. Kathryn didn't know what Bouchaule and his associates were poring over the last few days in the lab behind the main house, but it wasn't her blood, of that she was certain. In fact, Bouchaule had instructed her to stay away from the estate as much as possible while they had visitors, for fear someone might ask for a fresh sample and find nothing of value.

As per his request, she was leaving directly after dinner, under the guise of a late rehearsal.

Bouchaule walked her to the front door and took her hands as he kissed her on the cheek.

"Thank you, darling," he whispered.

She smiled for their audience as she embraced him and whispered, "Be careful, Thierry, I don't trust them."

"Nor do I, but do not worry. They need me."

She reiterated her concern with her eyes as she backed off and then casually put her hand on his cheek and tenderly kissed his lips. "See you later then." She turned. "Gentlemen."

The milling group in the main hall lifted their heads in surprise, as if they hadn't been straining to eavesdrop on her goodbye. She received smiles and nods as she slipped out the door, and she cursed them all as she got into her car—Bouchaule included.

"You're sure it's the reservoir?" she had heard Donnelly say in his meeting with Bouchaule.

Kathryn's eyes grew wide and she stopped breathing as she waited, ear against the grate, for Bouchaule's reply.

"The sample is too degraded now to show you, but from the original test results, yes, I am sure."

"Under their noses the whole time. How was this missed?"

"I told you ... they do not know what they are looking for."

"How did you know where to look?"

"This is my life's work. I followed the science and the records. It all led me here."

"Then I'm glad we have you, Doctor."

She heard Bouchaule making a drink, a mundane task used to deflect the importance of the next question—a technique she'd used many times herself.

"We are the only two who know?" Bouchaule asked casually.

"Of course."

"And a new sample is on the way?"

"A blood drive has been set up at the paper. You'll have your sample by tomorrow afternoon, and then we shall proceed."

"Excellent."

Kathryn closed her eyes. The thing she feared most had happened. Somehow, they discovered that Jenny was the reservoir.

She listened in panic as they discussed ways to make her disappear without a trace, and when their conversation was over, Kathryn had to endure dinner as if nothing had happened. Now she was in her car, driving at breakneck speed to do what she could to foil their plans.

Her white-knuckled grasp on the steering wheel tightened as she berated herself for not sending Jenny away sooner, for not telling her how she fit into the events swirling about her when she first discovered it.

Looking back, it seemed like it would have been so simple then. Explain to her why she had to go away while there was still love between them, while Jenny would listen and believe with an open heart and know it was out of love that she let her go. But no, Kathryn had decided, not while there was a chance Jenny could have a normal life, a happy life, free from paranoia and fear of discovery. The truth had destroyed her life. She didn't want that to happen to Jenny if she could help it. Now it was too late.

She gambled on Jenny's future and lost, and now, with her back against the wall, hindsight was rewriting history and assailing her with doubt, even though she knew deep in her heart that she wouldn't, couldn't, change a thing.

Kathryn's suspicions were confirmed when she decoded the early documents she'd photographed in the archive room at the center. One dated 1918—the height of the Spanish Influenza pandemic—told of a program that started as a study involving infected pregnant women and turned into an ethically bankrupt attempt to create a child with a natural immunity to the virus, which then could be used to create a vaccine.

Kathryn could only assume Jenny's mother was part of the program, which was how she met Daniel, and, eventually, from the photo Jenny had shown her, they had fallen in love. The child wasn't his, but Daniel would protect it as such, out of love for the mother.

According to the records, while pregnant, Patient 46, as she was known, survived her bout with the flu at the height of the pandemic in the early fall of 1918, only to die in childbirth in March 1919, the month and year of Jenny's birth.

The official documents reported the child as stillborn, but the timeline made it clear why Daniel Ryan singled out that particular patient in his notes.

The pieces were all falling into place, and it made her current task —sending Jenny under—imperative.

Kathryn parked her car in Paul Ryan's drive and rushed up the walk to his front door.

An earlier call to Jenny's house revealed no one was home—odd for half past nine on a Sunday night—and fearing the worst, Kathryn drove out there and ventured inside through the secret lab entrance in the study. She found the house empty and intact except for various clothing items strewn about Jenny's bed and a suitcase missing from the hall closet. Jenny had obviously gone away, but Kathryn wondered whether she was lured away or warned to get away?

All the terrible things that could have happened to her went through Kathryn's paranoid mind, and she feared that she was too late.

By the time she got to Paul's door, desperation was gnawing at her edges. Her time was short. She had to get to Jenny before tomorrow, and she still had to drop in on a nightly jam session to secure her cover for the evening, in case one of Bouchaule's associates decided to check on her whereabouts. She would need an alibi, especially if their precious reservoir mysteriously disappeared on the verge of its long-awaited acquisition.

She rang the bell and waited and then finally resorted to furious pounding when Paul seemed to take forever to answer.

"What do you want?" was his charming greeting when he finally opened the door.

"Where's Jenny?"

"Do you know what time it is?"

"*Where's Jenny?*"

"None of your business."

Paul began to close the door, but Kathryn threw her shoulder into it.

"They're coming for her, Paul!"

The flash of fear in his eyes told her he understood what was happening, but he tried to downplay it.

"What on earth are you talking about?"

"I haven't time for this. Where is she?"

"Get off my property or I'm calling the police."

He tried to close the door again, but Kathryn fought it off.

"I know about the lab," she said, forcing her way into his foyer, "and the books, and the coded documents that you were passing through your newspaper. Number puzzles that were more than just brainteasers at the end of the *Funnies* page ... sound familiar?"

Paul stared at her and then looked back into the house to make sure his wife hadn't heard. He led Kathryn into his study, just off the foyer, and leaned in closely, his voice low and menacing. "I don't know who you think you are or what you think you know, but—"

"Stop it, Paul! They know about her and they're coming for her. I've got to get to her before they do."

"And then what?"

"And then she's got to go away."

Paul straightened slowly, as the reality of Kathryn's words sunk in. "Why should I trust you?"

She didn't have a good reason for him, but she could see that he had already begun to accept the inevitable. "We both want the same thing ... Jenny safe, once and for all. I've arranged everything through Dominic. You trust him, don't you?"

Paul nodded reluctantly.

"Where is she?" she asked again, this time softer, sympathetic to his impending loss.

"I had no choice."

Kathryn had no interest in his guilt. "I'm sure you had your reasons, but, frankly, I don't care what they are. We're running out of time."

He deliberated, despite her urgency, but finally said, "She went upstate to visit her photographer friend. He's at his parents', on leave ... an injury or something."

"When is she due back?"

He looked at his watch.

"Her train arrived forty minutes ago. She should be on her way home from the station now."

"Shit," Kathryn spat, as she turned and hurried to her car.

"Wait!" Paul yelled, as he ran after her and closed his front door behind him. "I'm coming with you."

"No," she said in an urgent whisper. "I need you to call Dominic. He'll tell you what you need to do."

With that, Kathryn was off. She had just careened around the first corner when, from the backseat, a woman's voice said, "Stop the car."

Kathryn glanced in the rearview mirror as she pulled over. Usually a pointing gun accompanied such an ominous request, but this time, the stern but nervous voice belonged to Jenny's Aunt Betsy, who rose into view, with no threatening instruments in hand.

Kathryn set the brake and turned around. "I'm sorry, I haven't time for—"

"I know. Here." The woman passed her a small leather book.

"What's this?"

"For Jenny. The truth. Everything. Danny wanted her to have it when the time was right. This seems like the time. I'd give it to her myself, but there are too many questions I don't have answers to."

"I'm afraid I don't have many answers for her either, and I'm not sure she'd listen to me if I did, but I've got to try."

"I know she's upset with you, but she'll listen."

Kathryn looked hopefully at the book in her hand. She would need all the help she could get to make Jenny understand she had to go away. "Upset isn't the word I'm afraid."

"She can't see past the hurt and anger right now, but one day she will, and she'll realize you did it for her own good."

Kathryn was surprised she understood. Part of her hoped Jenny would forgive her someday, just to preserve some fondness of their time together, but the other part hoped Jenny would move on and never give their relationship another thought. Better not to have the bittersweet memory of what might have been, she reasoned.

"I don't pretend to know what's going on here, Kathryn, but I know you love her, and I can see everything you've done is to protect her."

Kathryn was struck by how much Betsy's understanding of the situation meant to her. "Thank you."

"No, thank you. Thank you for being stronger than the rest of us. We all knew it might come to this one day. Truth be told, Danny never should have kept her, but he loved her mother so. He couldn't bear to lose the child too. We should have sent her away after we lost him, but she was so devastated about her father, and we just hoped ... well, we hoped that this would never come to our door. We weren't strong enough to let her go."

Kathryn swallowed the bitter taste of what she'd done and what was to come. She wasn't strong. She had let go of Jenny in the most cowardly way, and now, at the end, after everything she'd done, and even knowing there was no other option, her defenses were crumbling, and her decision to let Jenny go and the reality that she would never see her again was making her sick. She could only nod in silence in the face of Betsy's candor and thumbed through the book for a distraction. She stopped in the middle and moved the pages into the light of the dim street lamp. "Coded."

"Danny said she'd know what to do with it."

Kathryn looked closer. It wasn't the book code of the medical documents. It appeared to be a transposition code, the plaintext inscription on the first page obviously leading Jenny to a key that only she would understand.

My dearest Jenny, the inscription began. *Behind your mother's smile hides the yellow rose of my love for you.*

She held up the book. "How do you know about this?"

"I heard them ... Danny and Paul."

"I gather Paul doesn't know you're here."

"I'll handle Paul. He's not always reasonable in a crisis, but he'll see it was the right thing to do."

Kathryn nodded.

Betsy squeezed Kathryn's shoulder, and with tears forming in her eyes, left the car without another word.

Kathryn's hurried footsteps echoed through the long tunnel to Daniel Ryan's secret lab, and it sounded like an army rushing with her. She almost wished it so, because it might take an army to convince Jenny to go with her.

She'd gone over what she'd say a hundred times, but it all sounded disingenuous, considering. Given the urgency of her task, and the inevitable confrontation, she knew it was going to be an uphill battle, and she feared she hadn't the skills to earn Jenny's trust again.

She finally gave up trying to predict how Jenny would react to every tact she chose and decided she'd know what to say when the moment arrived. The closer she got to the lab, the worse her nerves became. Coming face to face with the wreckage of one's treacherous acts is never an easy thing, and to win over the victim once you've betrayed them is almost impossible, but she couldn't fail at this.

From a look through her binoculars as she idled at the crossroad on the hill overlooking the long road to the house, she knew Jenny wasn't home yet. The house was dark, just as she'd left it earlier in the evening. Memories of happy times there were a threat suddenly, and she wasn't sure she'd welcome the wait once inside the house.

She shook off the useless insecurities and picked up her pace. She made her way to the bookcase entry into the study and released the door, expecting it to yawn open as usual. It didn't move, so she gave it an extra push, which didn't move it either. She braced one foot against the wall behind her and pressed her shoulder to the door and gave a mighty shove.

The door gave way slowly and then suddenly burst open, propelling her forward, with her arms outstretched. She found herself sprawled on the study floor, having fallen over a body that had been crumpled against the base of the bookcase.

The light from the lab passageway revealed a man who had been shot several times in the chest, his vacant, glassy stare fixed on the far wall. She stared at his face. It looked familiar, and then it came to her. She'd seen him on the night of the accident with Jenny, when someone shot at them and ran them off the road. He was the man who had peered at her through the windshield of her overturned car.

She pulled back, as if he were a threat, and it took her a few moments to realize the room had been ransacked.

"Jesus," she muttered, as she slowly became aware of her surroundings. She felt alone, but she scrambled to her feet and closed the bookcase to extinguish the light, just in case. She pulled her gun and her flashlight from her coat pocket and checked the body for identification. There was none. She swept her light around the room and into the living room beyond and found both had been thoroughly gone over. She had no doubt the rest of the house had gotten the same treatment. Some welcome home for Jenny. The body was still warm, so whatever happened, happened recently, and since they didn't get what they came for, Kathryn was confident they would be back, and soon.

She checked each room, ending up in the art studio above the study. She had a fondness for the room, remembering many moonlight picnics under the protective canopy of the massive skylight. She closed her eyes and tried to fight the memories of lovemaking bathed in moonlight on the very spot where she stood.

A car door slammed and she cursed herself for getting distracted. She ran to the window and saw Jenny paying a cabbie after he set her suitcase on the curb beside her. Kathryn gave a quick glance up the road to make sure they didn't have company, and safe for the moment, she rushed down the spiral staircase and into the study, hoping she could head Jenny off before she entered the house. She was too late.

"What the hell?" Jenny said, as she dropped her suitcase where she stood in the foyer and slapped at the light switch at the entrance to the living room. A toppled lamp in the living room illuminated tables turned on end, bookcases and drawers emptied, and magazines and books strewn about in a debris field befitting a violent storm.

"Turn off that light," Kathryn called out, as she emerged from the study with gun in hand.

"*You?*" Jenny said angrily at the sight of her.

Kathryn turned off the light from the wall switch on her side of the room and held out her hand. All plans for a gentle introduction to current events went out the window. "Jenny, you have to come with me ... right now."

She looked at the gun. "Or what? You'll shoot me? Look at this place! What the hell have you done?"

"I didn't do this. Please, come with me. I'll explain everything."

Jenny let out a humorless chuckle and shook her head. "I'm not going anywhere with you."

Kathryn moved into the room as she put her gun in her coat pocket. "Jenny, some people are coming for you. They've already been here, and they'll be back shortly. We have to go."

Jenny stubbornly put her hands on her hips. "You've destroyed my life, you've destroyed my home, and now you're pretending to be my best friend and savior? You'll pardon me, Kat, if I don't believe a word that comes out of your lying mouth."

Kathryn moved forward and reached for her. "Jenny—"

"Don't fucking touch me!"

"Jenny, please. Just come with me right now, and I'll explain everything."

"I told you, I'm not going anywhere with you."

"Look, I know you're angry and you don't trust me, and I don't blame you, but you were right ... what I did, I did to protect you. The people I'm involved with are dangerous. I had to keep you as far away from me and them as possible."

Jenny looked around at her violated home. "Good job."

Kathryn absorbed the sarcasm and focused on getting her to cooperate. She turned to the phonograph cabinet beside her and was pleased to find her record still there.

She lifted it from the turntable and held it out. "Do you remember what I asked of you? Whatever happened. You promised. Do you remember?"

Jenny looked at the record in the dim light cast into the room from the foyer and gingerly took it from Kathryn's hand. "I promised I would always remember how much you loved me at that moment. No matter what."

Kathryn smiled in relief, as Jenny's demeanor was becoming more hospitable. "Yes, that's it. I meant every word of it, then and now. I know that's hard to grasp after all that's happened, and I'm not asking for forgiveness, but for the sake of what we had, come with me now. Give me five minutes, that's all I ask."

Jenny stared at the disc in her hands. "This was the most beautiful thing anyone had ever done for me." She ran her hand reverently across the record. "It meant so much to me, I can't even tell you. It meant so much I couldn't bear to part with it, even after everything." She smiled. "You knew something like this would happen, and you prepared for it by giving me this ... so I would trust you when the time came."

"Yes."

Jenny nodded. "Smart."

Kathryn offered her hand. "Come on, let's get out of here."

Jenny didn't move. "I'm smart too, Kathryn. Smart enough to see right through you, and to see that this"—she held up the record—"is just another manipulation in a long line of manipulations, beginning the day we met."

"Jenny—"

"Fuck you, Kathryn, and fuck this!" She threw the fragile shellac disc to the floor.

Kathryn watched helplessly as her declaration of love, and the only recording of her pristine voice, shattered into pieces at her feet. She was unable to move for a moment, as she physically felt the loss of both. She closed her eyes for a beat, absorbing the loss, and then pushed it aside. Her pain was irrelevant.

"Don't even try the waterworks, sister," Jenny said bitterly. "I'm wise to you. Now get out of my house."

Kathryn had one more tact before resorting to force. She removed the small leather journal from the back of her waistband and held it out.

"Your father wanted you to have this."

Jenny laughed in her face. "You'll try anything, won't you? You're despicable."

Kathryn opened it to the inscription and held it to the light so Jenny could see.

Jenny snatched it from her hand and moved toward the foyer to examine the book. She read the inscription and hurriedly turned the pages. Recognizing the coded section as a transposition code, she looked up. "Where's the key?"

"I was told you'd know what to do with it."

Jenny reread the inscription for clues and absently looked around as she put her mind to it. *Behind your mother's smile, yellow rose.* It seemed familiar, but she didn't know why. So many questions swirled in her head, it was hard to focus.

"By whom? Where did you get this?"

"Come with me, and I'll tell you what I know."

"Bullshit! You'll tell me now or I'm not going anywhere with you."

There was no easy way to break the news, and Kathryn didn't have time to hold her hand. "You're in danger, Jenny, and you have to go under. Remember when we talked about that?"

Jenny was stunned for a moment but then nodded, as her father's book finally convinced her she should listen. "What's happening, Kathryn?"

Kathryn exhaled in relief. Jenny's anger was subsiding. Her relief was short-lived, however, as headlights passed the living room windows and a car pulled up to the curb in front.

From Jenny's wide, searching eyes, Kathryn could see she barely had time to register that she would never see her home again, but the urgency of the situation propelled her into action.

"Out the back!" she said, as she prepared to sprint down the hall to the kitchen.

Kathryn held out her hand. "No, here!"

Jenny hesitated.

Kathryn ran to her and grabbed her coat sleeve. "Trust me."

"What are you doing?" Jenny protested as she was dragged into the study. "We're trapped in here!" She looked at the path of destruction illuminated by the ambient light of the foyer and then stopped dead in her tracks as she got to the piano. "Is that a body?"

Kathryn tilted the wall sconce beside the bookcase, releasing the secret lab door. "Come on!"

Jenny was too stunned to move, as a new room opened up to her. "What the—"

"Jenny!" Kathryn grabbed her arm and pulled her inside.

"Wait!" Jenny wriggled free at the last second. She picked up her mother's picture from beside the body on the floor and quickly opened the gun rack in the bookcase to retrieve her Browning High Power and a box of rounds. She ducked inside the lab entrance, and Kathryn shut the bookcase behind them just as one of the men from the car kicked open the front door.

Neither woman dared breathe as they stood motionless in the passageway, their hearts beating wildly. They listened to two men do a quick search of the first floor and then looked at each other when the searchers paused at the body on the other side of the door.

"Anything?" one man asked.

"Not out back."

"She's here somewhere."

"We've got to get rid of this."

"Find the girl first."

Kathryn silently motioned Jenny down the passageway and into the lab. "We're safe here," she said softly, as she descended the metal staircase.

Jenny was speechless as she followed slowly and gazed around the space in wonder.

Kathryn let her move at her own pace now that they were out of immediate danger. Jenny moved methodically through the lab while tightly clutching her few worldly possessions to her chest.

"How long have you known about this place?"

"Since I found you at the greenhouse. There's an underground passage that leads to the cellar beneath it." She pointed at the back door.

Jenny stared at Kathryn in disbelief and then finally shook her head, obviously wondering why she was so surprised. "You lied to me for months."

"I was protecting you."

"From what? The truth? Don't you think after everything that I deserve the truth?"

"Yes, I do."

Jenny threw her possessions on her father's desk and put her hands on her hips. "Well?"

Kathryn handed over Daniel Ryan's coded medical books and proceeded to tell her what she knew. Jenny absorbed it all in silence and stared at the books Kathryn had handed her.

"These are what all the fuss was about? Why didn't you turn these in?"

"Because they belong to you, and I don't trust anyone else."

Jenny seemed touched by the words, but Kathryn could see trust wasn't a two-way street yet. "No more manipulation or lies. I'm giving you your life. Take it, before they do ... and they will."

Jenny considered Kathryn's words and set the volumes beside her other possessions. She put her hand on the leather journal. "Do you know what's in here?"

"Everything, according to your aunt, but I haven't a clue about the key, so I don't know where to begin to decode it."

Jenny did. She looked at the photograph of her smiling mother with her father under the large oak tree, which concealed the poem inscribed on the back that mentioned the yellow rose. She knew this was the key, and given her training, she wouldn't have any trouble decoding the journal. Without her training, it would have been a challenge, but her father had taught her simple codes and word puzzles for fun growing up, and she smiled internally at his faith in her ability to figure it out.

"Now what?" she asked.

"My car is parked on the access road at the edge of the woods. Go to the club. I've arranged everything with Dominic. He'll make sure you get away safely. Your aunt and uncle will be there to say goodbye."

Reality was a cold, hard slap in the face, and Kathryn watched with regret as Jenny's world crumbled around her.

Jenny took in the lab she never knew existed, looked up toward the home she would never see again, and then closed her eyes and put her hand to her forehead. "This isn't happening."

"I'm so sorry, Jenny."

Despair quickly turned to anger, as Jenny opened her eyes and spewed her frustration. "I hate you. There were so many ways you could have done this, and you picked the shittiest one!"

"I know," Kathryn said, as she straightened and put her hands in her coat pockets. No explanation would change that now. "Don't worry ... this is the last you'll see of me."

"Good."

"Yes, very good."

Their emotions settled around them like the dust on the countertops and blended seamlessly with the lab's desolate silence. Jenny dropped her acerbic glare and opened the Browning's wooden gun case on the desk so she could load rounds into the pistol's magazine. Once full, Jenny eased the magazine into the semi-automatic's grip until it clicked, pulled back the slide to load a round into the chamber, and then flicked the safety on with her thumb, as an automatic part of the routine.

Kathryn took her car keys from her pocket and set them beside Jenny's belongings. "Your keys in the foyer?"

"Bowl on the side table, as always. What are you going to do?"

"I'm going to lead those goons away from here. They know you're home, and they won't stop searching until they find you. I can't have them searching the woods. Here ..." She handed Jenny the flashlight. "Wait at the greenhouse until you hear them follow me down the street, then get to my car and go."

"Will you be able to shake them?"

Kathryn was struck by the concern in Jenny's voice. Her whole demeanor had changed in an instant. Suddenly, she was the Jenny she once knew. Her eyes looked worried, and all traces of anger and disillusionment were gone.

Kathryn was glad to see her again and barely suppressed a grin. "Do you have a fast car?"

"Damn fast."

"Then I'll be able to shake them."

They exchanged affectionate glances, and Kathryn felt her heart open up to a connection she thought she'd never experience again. The sensation was like a drug, morphine to the ache of her life without the woman before her, an ache hidden until love's return revealed the true torture of its loss.

Jenny reached for her hand, but Kathryn stepped back, knowing Jenny's touch at that moment would be fatal to her plans. This couldn't happen. Not now. Jenny's about-face had pierced her hardened heart like a pickax to a fragile dam, and the love she'd so skillfully locked away was bleeding into her hungry soul, turning courage to let Jenny go into courage to throw away everything she'd worked for.

"Go on, Jenny," she said quickly, before it was too late. "Follow the access road around the lake to the Hanson's property and pick up the highway from there. Okay?"

Jenny nodded.

"Be careful."

Jenny nodded again, and Kathryn turned for the stairs, thankful Jenny wasn't acting on what they'd just experienced. She had just reached the bottom step when Jenny found her voice.

"Where will you go?"

The only place she could go. "Back to the fight. Where I belong."

She saw Jenny swallow the reality of what that meant. "Be careful."

Kathryn pressed her lips together, more in determination for the task ahead than a smile, and said farewell with a curt nod before traveling the remaining steps to the landing above. *A few more seconds and it would be over*, she told herself. *Just keep walking.* The back door to the lab below clicked shut, and the sound pulled at her like a beggar for her last dime. She couldn't help but look down at the place where Jenny last stood. She'd given her professional integrity, her hopes and dreams, and her last ounce of strength to make this happen, and she regretted none of it. She had saved Jenny's life and put her father's work out of the reach of those who would misuse it. She would forever carry that success with her, and should she ever long for what might have been, it would give her the strength to go on.

She lingered a moment more on the ghost of that part of her life and then pulled her gun from her coat pocket and set her chin toward the passageway door—and the future. Jenny wasn't safe yet. It was time to finish what she'd started.

CHAPTER FORTY-FOUR

"Hey, hey, what a pleasant surprise!" the trombone player said as he hopped from his seat in front of the small stage and extended his hand. "To what do we owe this grand treat?"

Kathryn greeted him with a firm handshake and as easy a smile as she could muster. "On the level, fellas?" she addressed the group. "I need a favor. I've been here all night, okay?"

Without a beat, nods and mumbles of concerned sures went around the room. Kathryn knew she could count on the boys. They were a nonjudgmental lot, each with their own secrets and demons. Music bound them together, and they were a family. Family looks after their own.

The bass player put his hand on her shoulder. "Are you in trouble, honey?"

She grinned. "Not if I've been here all night."

"All night it is then. Drink?"

"Make it a double."

She'd made quick work of losing the men searching Jenny's house after she got them to follow her. She entered the house from the study and crept toward the foyer, and when she was sure both men were upstairs, she carefully lifted Jenny's car keys from the blue and white porcelain bowl on the side table and she was off and running.

She slammed Jenny's car door loud enough to get the intruders' attention, and then cursed the exotic Cord when it hesitated to start and she had to crank open the car's retractable headlights to hopefully blind the men to the driver as they leaped from the front porch without touching the steps on the way to their car.

Her annoyance with the quirky car quickly fell away when the Cord's supercharged V8 roared to life and easily outpaced her pursuers' Chrysler sedan. She left Jenny's car at the train station and took a taxi to the jam session, where she did her best to put her evening behind her. She'd done all she could, and there was nothing to do now but wait.

She felt at home with the musicians. They met at Charlie's Tavern every Sunday after hours for the sheer joy of their craft. A variety of players attended whenever their schedules allowed, and you never knew who you'd meet there. The music was always first rate and exciting, and tonight it was a pleasant distraction that eased the tension while she waited for events to play out.

She added her voice to the magic and kept one distracted eye on the door for the signal that Jenny had gotten away safely. She was enjoying the band's rousing rendition of "Swing Without Words" when a delivery boy from The Grotto dropped off her car keys. It meant Jenny was safe in Dominic's hands. Kathryn breathed a sigh of relief. It was over.

She made a mental note to send her thanks to Dominic. She had gone to him the day after she quit to square things with him, but he wouldn't hear of it, already sensing her actions had something to do with her work for the government. His only concern was for her safety, and, unfortunately, she did nothing to ease his mind when she asked him to use his contacts to make arrangements for Jenny's disappearance at a moment's notice. He offered to do the same for her, but she declined, knowing she had to follow her particular path to the very end.

What happened now with Bouchaule was merely maintenance.

Whatever he could have learned from Jenny or her father's documents was lost to him, and Kathryn couldn't help the superior smirk that crossed her lips. She had won.

She settled in and thoroughly enjoyed the rest of the jam session, even forgetting for a while that she had to return to Bouchaule and deal with the fallout from her evening's activities. She was listening to the trumpeter blow a sizzling solo in the middle of "Like the Moon Above You" when she had a sudden wave of nostalgia for the old days. She missed Tommy Wallace at that moment and knew he would have loved the arrangement. She had a brief notion of trying out for one of the big bands when everything was over—touring, radio, the works—and she smiled, imagining Tommy's enthusiasm for such a thought, but a thought was all it was, and she was reminded why as she sang the final verse and caught sight of Bertrand lurking in the shadows by the entrance. She pretended not to notice and joined in the self-congratulatory celebration of a song well done, her jubilation all the better to contrast with her somber act coming up.

Bertrand stepped into the light, hat in hand, and Kathryn winked at her concerned bandmates. She went to him immediately, grasping his arm upon her arrival. "*Qu'est-ce que c'est?*" she whispered.

He covered her hand and shook his head to alleviate her concern, and then he handed her a note in French that read *He let you go without protection. Not smart.*

"Did he send you here?" She continued in his native language.

Bertrand shook his head, and Kathryn didn't know whether to be touched by his concern or offended by his distrust.

"Thierry is the one who needs your protection, Bertrand. I can take care of myself."

The mute man took the note back and scribbled *Not against these men* on the back.

"What is it?" she repeated. "What's happened?"

He shook his head, as if nothing were wrong.

She squeezed his arm tighter. "Thierry!"

He smiled and covered her hand with his as he shook his head again.

"Don't lie to me Bertrand."

The man scribbled *Thierry is fine, but we should go.*

Kathryn nodded and returned to the stage to retrieve her coat. "Sorry, fellas, gotta run."

"Say, Kat, about next week," the bass player called out as a ploy to get her back to him and out of earshot of the stranger. When she arrived, he whispered, "Is this Joe on the up and up?"

She smiled her thanks and nodded she'd be all right. "Great, I'll see you then," she said loudly for Bertrand's sake. "Thanks, gang, it was swell."

As they reached the street, Kathryn removed her keys from her coat pocket. "I'll follow you."

Bertrand stilled her hand and pointed to his chest, indicating he would take her to the estate. Kathryn smiled internally. The man was worried. Things were definitely coming to a head.

When they got to the estate, Bertrand went directly to Bouchaule's study after halting Kathryn in the main hall with a raised hand.

"Well?" was Bouchaule's anxious reply when he answered Bertrand's knock at his study door.

The mute man slipped inside, and a few minutes later, Bouchaule emerged issuing orders. He rushed across the main hall and took Kathryn's hands with controlled urgency. "We have got to leave, darling, quickly. Pack a few things and meet me at the car."

"I don't need anything."

Bouchaule smiled and kissed her. "We have a long journey ahead."

"Where are we going?"

"Home. Are you with me?"

France. "Of course."

He squeezed her hands. "Thank you, darling. Go quickly."

Kathryn climbed the stairs and heard Bouchaule order Bertrand to secure the study and wait for him at the car. He had to take care of the lab.

Kathryn didn't know what had become of their houseguests, but she noticed the estate was empty as she made her way to the front door. She assumed Bertrand had gone to the lab to help dispose of things, because he was nowhere to be found when she loaded the small suitcase into the trunk of Bouchaule's sedan. She went around to the driver's side door and paused with her hand on the cold chrome of the handle when she saw the shoe of a prone man on the ground in front of the car. She slowly leaned around the DeSoto's large fenders to see it was Bertrand, with a gunshot wound to his stomach, covered by bloody hands, and his light blue shirt stained with an ever-expanding island of red.

She went to him instinctively but barely had his name out of her mouth when she knew it was a mistake. She felt the presence at her back too late, and as she turned, she never saw the punch that leveled her to the gravel drive.

CHAPTER FORTY-FIVE

Kathryn regained consciousness to the sound of angry voices. She recognized Bouchaule defending her value to the project, followed by the sickening crack of skin against skin, which reminded her why her jaw felt like it had been struck by a two-by-four.

She tried to get up but found her arms strapped by the wrists to the cot in the small outer room of Bouchaule's lab. She saw that the sleeve of her burgundy blouse had been torn from its stitching at the shoulder and now gathered in folds at the twisted belt holding her wrist. Blood oozed from a puncture wound in the crook of her elbow, and she knew they had taken her blood. She looked toward the lab as the loud voices continued.

"You are fools!" she heard Bouchaule shout, followed by another punch, this time, from the dull sound of it, a blow to his body.

"Now would be a good time to cooperate, Dr. Bouchaule," Kathryn heard Colin Donnelly say. "It is you who are the fool for trying to betray us. Give us the girl, and we may let you live."

"Go to hell!" Bouchaule shouted in French.

"As you wish. Gentleman?"

Kathryn struggled against her restraints, cursing in frustration when she was unable to free herself. A man ducked his head around the screen at the end of the bed when he heard her stir, and he knocked on the lab window to get his boss's attention.

Donnelly delayed his order to beat Bouchaule into submission and signaled the man to bring Kathryn into the lab.

"No funny business, doll, get me?" the man said as he came to her side and showed her the gun under his jacket. She agreed, with contempt in her eyes, and was a good girl when he set her free. She stood, rubbing her wrists, and then feigned annoyance at her ruined blouse.

"Unbutton and roll up," she complained, as she tugged at the limp sleeve, the cuff still buttoned at her wrist. "How hard is that?"

The man exhaled an amused chuckle and casually reached for his gun. "Dames."

Kathryn waited until the gun cleared his shoulder holster before unloading an elbow to his face. She caught him square on the nose and he fell onto his backside, sending his gun skittering across the floor. She lunged for the weapon, but the prone man had the where-withal to kick her legs out from under her, hurling her head first across the polished linoleum tiled floor. She scrambled for the gun, only to have it kicked out of her reach at the last second by another man entering from the lab.

She found herself looking up into the barrel of the second man's revolver. She slowly raised herself to her knees and noticed that his knuckles were bloodied with what she assumed was Bouchaule's blood.

"Familiar position for you, isn't it, sweetheart?" the man said with a smirk. "Up." He motioned with his gun.

He ordered Kathryn into the lab, keeping well out of the reach of flying elbows, as his partner followed behind, muttering curses as he held a handkerchief to his bloodied nose.

Donnelly had brought in four thugs and retained one of the scientist houseguests for his little coup, and he seemed pleased with the results.

"Do not harm her," Bouchaule pleaded, as he struggled to escape the two men holding his arms.

"Right, because her blood is special," Donnelly said sarcastically.

"Yes, we need her!"

"You know, Dr. Bouchaule, I know you're not stupid, so you must be delusional to hold the line when we have her blood right here and we know there is nothing extraordinary about it."

"You do not know what to look for."

"So you keep saying."

Donnelly nodded to his scientist, who removed a small green case from his lab coat pocket and unzipped it. It contained two glass syringes. He removed one and started toward Kathryn.

Kathryn backed into the man with the gun, who quickly had her arm wrenched behind her back and his forearm across her neck in a stranglehold. She pulled at her human noose with her free hand to no avail, and soon, the man with the bloody nose had a hold of her sleeveless arm, extending it for the man with the syringe.

"What are you doing?" Bouchaule shouted. "You are making a terrible mistake!"

Donnelly ignored him and addressed Kathryn.

"I'm sure this is cold comfort to you, Miss Hammond, but believe me when I say, this is not personal. You are an unfortunate loose end."

Kathryn couldn't have answered even if she wanted to, as the arm around her neck choked her voice from her. In her panic, she could only think of Smitty. This is where he should burst in and save her life, but Smitty was thousands of miles away. He would not save her life this day.

"Stop!" Bouchaule shouted. "I will give you what you want."

"I'm afraid the time for negotiation ended when you sent your men to steal my reservoir, Dr. Bouchaule. You can't be trusted, you see." He nodded to the scientist to proceed.

"No! Wait! My briefcase, the papers in my briefcase. Behind a hidden panel in the back, they contain all the information you need. Please, do not harm her."

Donnelly approached the restrained doctor. "You are a curious man, Bouchaule. If she is immune, as you claim, there should be no fear of this." He held up the case containing the remaining syringe. "But she is not immune, is she?"

Bouchaule was suddenly calm and surprisingly menacing, considering his position. "Let her go and I will help you. Kill her, and you are all dead men. My people will see to it."

Donnelly laughed and nodded again to the man with the syringe.

Kathryn's strangled attempts at protest were drowned out by Bouchaule's desperate pleading for her life, but both were useless, as the needle went into her arm and its contents were emptied.

Bouchaule's final *No!* died on his lips when Kathryn stopped struggling and slowly went limp in her captor's arms.

Donnelly gave his scientist the other syringe and then tilted Kathryn's lolling head in his direction. "As I said, Miss Hammond, nothing personal. I don't wish you to suffer. The first injection was merely a sedative. No need for you to be conscious for what's to come."

Bouchaule had one more burst of protest, but his struggle was futile. He could only watch as the second syringe was injected into Kathryn's listless arm.

Kathryn could barely comprehend Donnelly's words as she felt her body shutting down. The big ape behind her had an arm around her waist, and she knew she no longer stood of her own accord. She wanted to pull her arm away from the man with the needle, but her muscles wouldn't obey. She was helpless as she watched the second needle disappear into her flesh. The injection burned, and her body convulsed as the fire spread through her veins.

"You may want to step away," she heard Donnelly say to the man holding her. "It's going to get messy."

Bouchaule was still screaming protests when Kathryn swore she heard a gunshot. The man behind her released her, and she crumpled to the floor, as the burning and spasms subsided and her body

succumbed to the darkness. Her last vision before she lost consciousness was Bouchaule collapsing to the ground before her. If she could
have smiled, she would have. She was dead, Bouchaule was dead, and
Jenny was safe—all in all, a good day.

CHAPTER FORTY-SIX

Kathryn was falling. She wasn't afraid, nor did she struggle against it. She didn't remember hitting the ground, but she knew she lay among the ruins of a great stone stairway. Just moments before, it had wound around a thick-walled tower that it seemed she'd been climbing forever, struggling to conquer monotonous step after monotonous step, ever moving upward. Her eyes were always fixed toward the sky, drawn to the top of the enormous tower by a bright shimmering light that beckoned her like a moth to a flame.

Suddenly, a fierce wind swirled about her, forcing her to shield her eyes and cower against the wall for safety. She peered up at her guiding light and, for the first time, was blinded by its radiance. The wind grew stronger and the tower swayed, then crumbled, and soon she was falling, with fellow humans and great chunks of stone tumbling alongside.

She was content to plunge without hope of survival. Her struggle was over. The light to which she had devoted such effort grew dim through the debris and distance, until darkness consumed everything around her.

She woke up surrounded by rubble, unable to move. Her fellow humans seemed as perplexed as she, as they chattered on in anxious foreign whispers around her, their confusion compounded by the darkness. The voices got louder, the language more familiar, and she frowned, recognizing a distinct Creole patois. She felt a hand on her shoulder and inhaled sharply as she opened her eyes.

There were men huddled around her, with straw hats clutched in their hands. They were dressed for hard labor and had machetes slung low on their hips. For a moment, she thought they were the devil's minions come to escort her to the gates of hell.

When she lifted her head and blinked them into focus, they backed up, as if they'd seen a ghost. A quick look around at the dirt floor and shoddy wood structure told her this wasn't hell, but the warm temperature led her to believe it might be nearby. The room smelled sickly sweet, and though wholly out of context to her last known location, she realized that what looked like burnt bamboo stacked in the corner was actually sugarcane and the hovering minions plantation workers.

"*Monsieur!*" one of the men called out the door, and soon, Thierry Bouchaule burst in, bringing with him the bright early morning sun. He looked haggard. His face was beaten, shirt bloodied, and hair unkempt, but he was alive and overjoyed to see her awake. He put a concerned hand to her forehead and then to her cheek.

"How do you feel?"

"Sore," she said, as she rubbed her bruised jaw and raised herself on one elbow. "Weak." She was also surprised they were both alive. "Thierry, I heard the gunshot. I saw you fall."

He nodded and patted her hand and then got up and shooed the loitering men out the door. "*S'il vous plait ... merci, merci.*"

Every muscle in Kathryn's body complained as she swung her legs off the makeshift bed of hay bales draped with a green canvas tarp. Bouchaule's jacket surrounded her, and she was thankful for it, because, despite the warm room, she suddenly felt cold.

"Lie down, darling," Bouchaule said as he returned to her.

Kathryn refused, wanting answers. "I saw you fall."

He kneeled at her feet. "The gunshot came from Bertrand."

"But he was—"

"Wounded but able to make his way to us. He saved our lives."

"Donnelly and his men?"

"Dead."

Kathryn hesitated a beat as she quickly scanned the room. "Bertrand?"

Bouchaule bowed his head. "I could do nothing for him."

Kathryn exhaled, genuinely saddened. She barely knew the man, but he had gone out of his way to protect her and, in the end, had saved her life. Convention said she should comfort Bouchaule for his loss, but his cold, calculating plan to make Jenny disappear still burned in her memory. Intellectually, she knew Jenny was safe now, which made the doctor just a man with an unobtainable goal, like he was before, and no longer a threat. Emotionally, out of respect for Bertrand, she decided Bouchaule was worthy of pity and ran her hand through his disheveled hair. "I'm so sorry, Thierry. He was a good man."

Bouchaule was quiet, but it was a silence born of guilt, something Kathryn recognized immediately.

"They are both dead now because of me," he finally said.

Kathryn found Bouchaule's remorse over the loss of his sister and brother-in-law perfectly natural and predictable, but she had no words of comfort, as the guilt of her own dead made a surprise appearance.

Bouchaule looked up, questioning her silence, and mistook her pained lost look for one of compassion. He took her hand. "You know such feelings."

She offered a grim half-smile, to which the doctor nodded and then rested his head on her knee. "That comforts me."

Kathryn closed her eyes and found it comforted her too. She was reminded they were both broken, dirty, and alone in the world. If he was going to be her companion for the time being, she had to know where things stood.

"What happened? Donnelly said something about the reservoir."

He lifted his head and then shifted to the side as he leaned back against a hay bale, his hands in his lap and his shoulders slumped in defeat. "It is gone. I wanted to protect it, but it is in their hands now."

Bouchaule went on to explain how Donnelly had brought him the blood sample to verify as the reservoir's. He knew the Irishman needed him for their work, so he felt safe in confirming the sample as genuine. He planned on spiriting the reservoir away before Donnelly could get a hold of it, thus protecting it from people like Donnelly's group, who had nothing but dollar signs in their eyes.

Bouchaule seemed appropriately distressed for one who had just lost his Holy Grail, but he also seemed sincere in his desire to shelter the reservoir from harm and spare the world the inevitable weapon made possible from its eventual vaccine.

Kathryn took pleasure in the doctor's mistaken assumption that Donnelly's group had Jenny. It meant one more wild goose chase for him as he plotted to get her back.

"What will you do now?"

Bouchaule smiled and pushed himself up from the ground to sit beside her, his swagger returning. He leaned forward, resting his elbows on his knees as he clasped his hands together. "I wait. Someone will contact me."

She raised a doubtful brow.

"I have been giving them false data," he said. "In my absence, they will soon realize this and they will be back. Without Donnelly, and without my research, they are lost, the reservoir a mere medical curiosity." He smiled confidently. "They will be back."

It occurred to her that Daniel Ryan, hoping to protect his daughter, must have employed the same tactic. "Clever man," she said, as she leaned her head on his shoulder and put her arm through his, wondering if the outcome would be the same.

As Bouchaule took her hand, Kathryn looked around the room, noticing the details of the long storage shack for the first time. It was filled with harvesting tools and discarded cane mill parts. Large cast iron sugar kettles sat empty, longing for their sweet brew. An odd piece of equipment on the far wall had her perplexed. "Is that a still?"

Bouchaule laughed. "Rum."

"Where are we?"

"Martinique."

"Martinique? That's almost two thousand miles away. How long have I been out?"

Bouchaule squeezed her hand. "Long enough. You did not miss a thing. Horrid flight."

Kathryn mindlessly rubbed her sore forearm.

"Are you all right?" Bouchaule asked.

Kathryn nodded as she exposed her arm to inspect Donnelly's handiwork. She was bruised from his needles, but his weren't the only ones. When she looked closer, she saw a new needle mark.

She raised her eyes accusingly at Bouchaule, her anger building. "And what did you find?"

He raised his hands in defense. "Please understand—"

"What did you find?"

"Nothing. As before, I found nothing."

"Don't tell me *nothing*! I saw the virus injection myself. I felt it invade my body."

"And your body has been fighting it all night. Your fever broke this morning."

Kathryn ran her hand through her hair and found the truth in its dampness. She had survived another encounter with the virus, cheated death again, and wondered when she would run out of lives.

"That doesn't make sense. There's no fighting this. The cells that saved me before have long since left my body. You told me that's how it works." She pointed at her abused arm. "This should have killed me."

Bouchaule looked vaguely aside.

"What does this mean?"

"I do not know."

"What do you mean, *you don't know*?"

"You are immune, obviously, but it is not in your blood. The original infection has ... it remains, but it is part of you now."

"Part of me? What does that mean?"

"I cannot explain it."

"Well, you'd better try."

"I cannot. It has changed you ... your physiology ... yet I can find no abnormality." His frustration sharpened his accent and movements. "We do not have the means to see it," he explained. "It must be in your organs, your tissue, somewhere ... I do not know! You are alive. That is all I know, and the answer is not in your blood."

"It's not possible, though, is it?"

Bouchaule offered no further explanation. "Yet here you are, proving it to be so."

If there was any doubt before, it was clear now why the doctor had taken her with him. It would have been so much easier for him to travel without her, but she was the next best thing to his precious reservoir, and there was no way he would leave her behind now.

"I see," she said with disdain, strangely disappointed that his heroic flight with her at his side was inspired by his head and not his heart.

Kathryn could see her scorn reflected in his wounded eyes, and she saw him absorb her distrust like a knife to his heart. He vaguely shook his head and exhaled in disbelief as he stood. His decision was swift and without reservation.

"We part ways here. I will make arrangements for your journey home, or you may stay here if you wish."

As she watched Bouchaule walk away, she didn't think for one moment he was serious. This was part of their game. He would expect her to protest, do anything to stay close to him, and he would react to her protest with indignant objection, but in the end, he would give in, satisfied he had proven himself a noble creature, capable of thinking of someone other than himself and his work.

Not one to disappoint, Kathryn sprang to her feet. "Don't you dare leave me, Thierry. You promised!" She should have been more careful, considering what she'd been through, but she stood without thinking and found the world spinning, as she collapsed back onto the canvassed hay bales, placing her hand on her suddenly perspiring forehead.

Bouchaule was there instantly to catch her, and he sat down beside her. "Here, lie down."

She felt nauseated. "Shit."

"Lie down. Please."

"I'm fine. Just give me a minute." She closed her eyes and cursed her human frailties for interfering with her scene.

"Kathryn—"

"I'm fine!"

He lifted his hands from her in surrender and gave her the minute, but no more, before addressing her anger.

"What would you have me do? We had love and trust, and you have disregarded both. My trust cannot stand alone, and I will not have my love thrown in my face."

Brother, he's pouring it on, Kathryn thought through her swimming head, and she dismissed his self-serving declaration with a withering glance. After the events of the last twenty-four hours, she was weary of their game and had no interest in massaging his wounded pride, real or manufactured. She had no patience left, and the truth rose easily to the surface.

"Please, Thierry," she said, as she put her head in her hands and prayed for her equilibrium to return. "It's obvious why I'm here. We both know you only care for your work."

Bouchaule stood but didn't say anything, causing Kathryn to look up into his decidedly disgusted glare.

"There is nothing I can say if you do not already know my feelings," he said, as if their breakup was all her fault. He walked away, pausing only to reiterate, "I will make arrangements for your passage home."

Kathryn let him go this time. The look in his eyes held a sadness that comes with the final disappointment at the end of an affair. She stared at the closed door as her mind entertained the possibility he was sincere. A man that obsessed with his work would never just let her go, not when he needed what he perceived as her unique physiology more than ever, but he had let her go, and she was left wondering what his game was now.

She didn't believe he was actually in love, but explanations were scarce, and that one rang truest.

Perhaps they were indeed alike, more than she ever imagined. She had fallen for Jenny and walked away to save her. Could the same be true for Bouchaule?

She got a chill when she remembered his desperate cries to spare her life as Donnelly's man moved in with his needle. He even revealed the location of his hidden papers, compromising his precious work, the very thing he had said meant more to him than her life. That was no game.

He loved her. He was letting her go. She had a moment of panic when she feared she might actually lose him. She scrubbed her face with her hand, wishing her mind were clearer. She had a disconcerting realization that part of her needed to be with him. Unable to face her life without Jenny, or a purpose, he had been her savior. It was a moment of weakness ... a crisis of identity she knew would pass.

She raised her chin. Bouchaule was still her assignment, and it was her duty to follow where that assignment led. That's what she told herself. In truth, hiding Daniel Ryan's work from the government was treasonous. It made her a fallen agent, drowning in her own legend. But her body was a part of this medical mystery now, and she was still in position to determine the progress and scope of his project.

She took a calming breath and put her mind to the next move.

She pulled the yellow silk display handkerchief from the breast pocket of Bouchaule's jacket, and a slow smile formed as she ran it through her fingers. She used the handkerchief to corral her unruly hair, just like she would now use Bouchaule to corral her unruly emotions.

She prepared her surrender speech, stood as quickly as she dared, and then followed his path outside. She found him standing beside a large sedan ready to take him to the gleaming silver DC-3 waiting on the private airstrip in the valley below.

Bouchaule conveniently finished with the driver when he saw her approach and met her at the passenger door.

"Go back inside, Kathryn. I do not want you with me."

Her brow knit in confusion as Bouchaule became a man she didn't recognize. She'd seen glimpses of him in his moments of anger or discontent, but now the transformation was complete. She reached out to him.

"Thierry—"

"Go back, Kathryn," he repeated, his voice cold. "I do not want you with me."

She pulled back, searching his eyes. There was no love, no hate, no distrust, no future. Nothing.

"You need me."

He chuckled humorlessly. "There are more with your particular affliction where I am going, so, sorry to say, I no longer need you for my work. But thank you for showing me there is something there to find."

Kathryn raised a brow at his obvious lie. "So, I've an affliction now, is it? I see. Tell me, if you no longer need me, why did you bring me this far?"

"I could hardly leave you to wake among the bodies."

His words came with a tidal wave of memories of waking up in a cold, dirty cell with the bodies of her executed friends at her feet.

"How very thoughtful of you," she managed evenly before stepping away to hide her cracking façade. She moved awkwardly, her heels sinking into the damp, soft earth. Her vision was replaced by atrocities too easily accessed, and she couldn't see where she was going. As she stumbled away, she pleaded with herself to hold it together. *Breathe.*

Suddenly, Bouchaule was at her back with steadying hands on her shoulders, and she found his touch a grounding reminder that she was far from the horrors of her past. She felt lightheaded again and allowed him to carry her to the car and into the sedan's roomy backseat.

"Sorry," she said, as she put a hand to her forehead. Pride gave way to purpose, and she was no longer angry at her human frailties.

"You need to rest, Kathryn. I will send someone to look after you. You will be fine here, and when you have recovered, you may go where you like."

His words were gentle, but his eyes were still those of a stranger. She turned to face him and put her hand on his thigh, redoubling her efforts to bring him back to her.

"I know what you're doing. What happened last night scared the hell out of you and you're trying to protect me. Well, it scared the hell out of me too, but separating is not the answer. We're stronger together than we are apart. Don't you remember what it was like? The constant worry, the sleepless nights?"

He was unresponsive, and she straightened with a disbelieving tilt of her head.

"Or was that just me?"

Bouchaule ignored her questions and brushed some dirt from his trousers.

"Look, if you want me to apologize—"

"I want you to go, Kathryn," he said sternly. "That is all I want."

He was leaving no room for negotiation, and it only made her more determined.

"I know you need me for your work, and I'd like to think you need me for more than that."

"Well, I do not. For either."

She knew he was lying, but she also knew his mind was set on leaving her. She had nothing left to lose, so she went all in.

"I haven't the strength to play the game any longer."

He seemed offended by the suggestion. "It was never a game."

"It was always a game. It started the moment you asked me to Tango so you could get close to Marc Forrester."

That got his attention, and Kathryn smiled at his narrowing glare. "I didn't mind," she went on. "You were an attractive man, and I despised Marc Forrester. When that game was over, another began when someone decided to use me as bait to lure you back, and here we are, with you running away again but, this time, for a different reason."

"I do not know what—"

She silenced him with a raised hand. "Don't. Not now. We've been through too much."

It was time to draw him out, expose what he thought he had concealed so well.

"You didn't trust me, and I didn't trust you, so we tested each other constantly. How far would the other go to get what they wanted? We both gave as good as we got, but underneath it all, there was something else, something between us that you can't deny. I understand what you're doing, because we're alike, just as you said ... but much more than you know."

Bouchaule laughed. "While I find a confident woman quite attractive, I find an arrogant one a fool and a desperate one rather revolting."

A nerve had been struck. Kathryn smiled and leaned back. His insult was merely the table onto which she would play her final hand. "Continue playing your game. Maybe that's all you know. All you trust. I know that feeling too. But I'm free of that now. I'm offering you the same."

Bouchaule was silent, and Kathryn ducked her head slightly to catch his downturned eyes.

"When was the last time you felt free?"

He tried to remain still and nonchalant, but the flex of his tense jaw gave him away.

Kathryn smiled. "I couldn't remember either, but it feels so good." She held out her hand. "Let me show you how it feels."

He wasn't giving in, and, for a moment, Kathryn was surprised at his resolve, but they were alike after all, and she thought back to her stoic breakup with Jenny, when she had given up everything to ensure her safety.

Perhaps it was the same with Bouchaule. Perhaps he loved her too much to carry her into the pit of vipers that was Paris under Nazi rule. She had a strange affection for his conviction. It warmed her battered heart that there was love like that in the world for their kind.

She looked at Bouchaule's indifferent figure and withdrew her hand. He'd made up his mind. She leaned in to kiss his cheek in farewell, but he pulled away. That brought a smile to her lips, because she had done the same to Jenny when she reached for her at the end, avoiding the straw that would have broken her back.

That was it then. She had lost Bouchaule.

Failure was a new consideration, but gone was her anxiety of being alone. The world was waiting, and there was much to do. Returning to the OSS would require more lies, she supposed. The murders at the estate afforded her ample material for any story she wished to make up about her disappearance and whereabouts. She could say she awoke alone and Bouchaule was gone. Assignment closed.

With Bouchaule out of her reach, and a mole in her government likely, she would remain silent about Daniel Ryan's books. They belonged to Jenny now, along with all the decoded documents she'd stashed in a safe deposit box. Dominic would have given Jenny the key the night she went under.

She could hope the OSS would assign her overseas, but with her recent history, and now the dramatics with Bouchaule, a post in the war zone was doubtful. The OSS was keeping her out of the fight, and it was time to part ways. It would be easy to claim mental instability and leave the agency. No one would doubt it had all been too much for her. She would make her way overseas on her own.

On the home front, she had standing instructions to dispose of the contents of her apartment should she miss her rent payment, save the photograph of her as a child with her mother, the piano, and the painting above it, which she requested go to her brother. She hoped Clayton would retrieve the items—the piano especially, for Stephanie.

Martinique was as good a starting point as any other. She would work, singing preferably, until she had enough money for passage to

Lisbon. From there, she would join some resistance organization and do her part. She opened the car door and stepped into her new life.

"*Adieu*, Thierry."

She had barely straightened to her full height when he called to her through the open door.

"I think we both know what I wanted. What did you want?"

Kathryn looked out across the roof of the car, excusing herself from her future for a moment, and exhaled before ducking her head inside. Bouchaule's penchant for games was a hard habit for him to break, apparently. She was through with the game though, so she told him the truth.

"I wanted my loved ones safe from Forrester, from you, from the government, and from madmen like Donnelly."

Kathryn saw the slight lift of his brow and wondered if he was surprised she had spoken the truth or offended that he was on the list of threats. If he was offended, he got over it quickly.

"And are they safe?"

"Yes, they are."

He gave her a sympathetic smile, as if he appreciated everything she wasn't saying.

"That must have cost you a lot."

"It cost me everything, but now I'm free."

Bouchaule balked at the notion with a derisive chuckle, and Kathryn decided to leave him with all he was giving up.

"Deny it all you like, but it's not as hard as you think to let go." She shut the door and shed his jacket, folding it over the open window to prove her point. He pulled the jacket inside, accepting her point and her silent goodbye.

As she walked away, Kathryn loosened the yellow silk scarf from her hair and let it flutter away in the early morning breeze, taking Bouchaule along with it. She welcomed her first breath of freedom and was only moderately disturbed by how easily she dismissed her responsibility to the OSS and her assignment. She felt lighter, absolved, cleansed. She would begin again. Become someone new. Make the world safer for Stephanie. For Jenny.

Jenny.

Love and longing threatened to well up in her. She tamped it down but gave one last thought to their parting. Did Jenny still hate her? She hoped not. Or maybe she hoped she did. Their separation would be easier that way. Jenny would make a new start too. The truth was hers now, and her life was her own. She nodded, satisfied she had done the right thing.

The Frenchman called out for his driver, and shortly after, the car drove away. She smiled—another chapter closed, but this one felt good. She lifted her face to the awakening day and closed her eyes, drinking in its promise of new horizons and new hope, when she heard a voice from behind.

"Freedom is an illusion treasured by those who do not realize it is defined by its boundaries." It was Bouchaule.

Kathryn opened her eyes. The morning no longer offered the future she imagined. She gazed into the never-ending blanket of blue sky before her and felt she was gazing through a window into a world beyond her station. She wasn't upset. In fact, it made her smile. It was only right.

Bouchaule's return left her pleased she hadn't lost her touch. She turned to face him, chin held high and ready to meet the challenge. "I'm well aware of the boundaries of my freedom. Are you?"

The doctor, a macabre dandy, with his bloodstained shirt, bruised face, and expensive jacket slung casually over his shoulder, approached until they were standing toe to toe. His eyes swept over her face, and he reached out and caressed her cheek with his hand, once again the gentle lover. "My freedom begins and ends in your eyes."

Kathryn laughed out loud at the corny line, sincere though it was in its delivery. She quickly apologized for her outburst.

To her surprise, Bouchaule was grinning from ear to ear. "Too much?"

Kathryn laughed again. "For that moment? Perfect."

He smiled and swung his jacket around her back, settling it onto her shoulders, as if that was where it belonged. She smiled her thank you and tucked her hair behind her ear, fighting the breeze at her back. Bouchaule produced the discarded yellow silk handkerchief from his pocket, a flag of truce. She took it—tethered once more—and while she tied back her hair with it, Bouchaule put his hands on his hips.

"I do not know what to do with you, Kathryn."

Kathryn was going to make sure he knew exactly what to do with her. "Since when?"

Bouchaule smirked but hesitated a beat before answering. "I do care about you, and because of that, I cannot take you with me. It is too dangerous. I will not risk you. I've lost too many to them."

Well, that wouldn't do. She stepped forward and took his hand. "It's dangerous everywhere."

"You do not know, Kathryn. The things—"

"You think I don't know what I'm in for? Men have died over your work, and I'm not so naïve as to think you didn't have something to do with some of that." He glared at her, obviously offended by the accusation, and then tried to pull away, but she wouldn't let him. "I don't say this to upset you. I only want you to see I know the score. I mean, my God, look what's happened to me over these past months. Do you think what's left of Donnelly's operation, or my government, or whoever else has a stake in this, is just going to forget about me because you disappear?"

Bouchaule closed his eyes, his conflict exposed. "What they did to you ... I wanted to kill them with my bare hands. Instead, I could do nothing. I am powerless to protect you."

She grasped his tense arms. "We're here, we're together. We should stay that way."

"I cannot show up with an American in tow. It would cause undue attention, and I cannot afford—"

Kathryn pulled his hands around her back and situated herself in his arms, addressing his concerns by responding in his native tongue. "No one would have to know I was American unless you told them."

He smiled, giving in to her close proximity and her flawless language skills. "You are a wicked temptress."

Kathryn grinned and raised an expectant brow. "On to Paris then?"

He deliberated, but only for a moment. "To *Paris*."

She kissed him again. It didn't matter if he truly loved her or was just using her for his work—she suspected a little of both. She had regained perspective, found her purpose. She was in the spy business again, only this time, she was a free agent, and she had a ride to Paris, where she would charm the occupying devils until it was time to strike and repay her debt.

Colonel Holmes sat alone in his office with the phone to his ear and moved the receiver aside to exhale in frustration as he crushed his cigarette into the full ashtray under his hand. He'd been there all night, and every report was worse than the last.

"I understand that," he said into the receiver, "but we may have to face the ugly possibility that Miss Hammond has gone astray. Someone warned Jenny Ryan, who has disappeared without—"

He was interrupted by a knock at the door.

"I'm on the line," he barked.

The secretary bravely entered anyway.

Holmes impatiently pressed his hand over the mouthpiece and shouted, "Didn't you hear what I—"

His jaw clamped shut as his secretary stepped aside and Jenny Ryan entered the room.

"Good morning, Colonel Holmes," she said with a pleasant smile. "I think I have something you've been looking for."

Rendering the British colonel speechless was a crowning achievement in a week that featured Jenny making the biggest mistake of her life—and that was saying something, considering her track record. It took ten minutes of arguing with Holmes's secretary to gain access to him, but it was worth every minute to see his usually smug expression slide off his face when he lifted his eyes to her mid-shout.

He eyed the leather briefcase she hugged to her chest, and his smirk was back. She allowed it this time without disdain. She would need every ounce of indifference in the days ahead.

She knew Kathryn would think *this* was the biggest mistake of her life, but for Jenny, that was the moment she let Kathryn walk up the stairs of her father's secret lab and out of her life.

It didn't take long to realize what Kathryn had done for her. The anger over her perceived affair with Marcella paled to the anger over Kathryn's lack of trust in her ability to handle the truth. But even that anger had dissipated by the time she emerged from the tunnel under the greenhouse and heard Kathryn gunning the Cord's engine down her street.

After the second car followed and disappeared, she was left cradled in the nocturnal sounds of the surrounding woods. It was in this soothing thrum that the weight of the last hour took her legs out from under her.

Kathryn had sacrificed herself—sacrificed their love—to save her. Tears should have come, as everything she'd lost filled her with regret, but regret was drowned by Kathryn's love for her, and determination straightened her spine instead.

She'd once asked Kathryn if she was sorry she'd learned the truth about her mother's death. Kathryn said yes, she was sorry she'd learned the truth. She could now see that Kathryn was trying to spare her from the same fate. She loved her for trying, but she knew the truth now, and she would use whatever she could of it to win the war. Then she would find Kathryn and prove to her that, once and for all, they belong together. Forever.

Kathryn and Jenny's story continues with *In the Shadow of Victory* (Shadow Series Book 4), available for preorder now at your retailer of choice. Scan the QR code with your phone's camera app. Projected release date, late 2023.

If you enjoyed this book, please leave a review so that other readers can discover Kathryn and Jenny as well. Thank you so much!

Visit jeleak.com to sign up for my newsletter and receive updates on new releases, works in progress, blog posts, giveaways, and more!

AUTHOR NOTES

My characters are not based on any particular real-life individuals; however, the Office of Strategic Services (OSS), for whom Kat and Jenny work, was a real wartime organization established in July 1942 by President Franklin D. Roosevelt, based on the British intelligence Special Operations Executive (SOE).

The New York City offices of the OSS were headquartered in the International Building at Rockefeller Center. For expediency in my story, I housed several divisions there, but, in reality, the OSS had offices scattered throughout the city, in various buildings. Morale Operations, where Jenny works, was indeed housed in a building off Times Square. The British Security Coordination (BSC), part of the British Secret Intelligence Service, was also housed in the International Building at Rockefeller Center.

OSS Director William Donovan called his recruits "Glorious Amateurs," but the contributions of these brave men and women of the intelligence services are immeasurable, and without them, the war could have had a very different outcome.

Historical fiction propels the reader into a story set in the past. Today, that time period's values and morals might be considered old-fashioned or uptight, but this was the reality for our characters. In some ways, the core of their struggle is still our struggle today. Science progresses, attitudes change, even maps and boundaries change, but the human heart still loves who it loves. Some things are timeless.

ABOUT THE AUTHOR

J.E. Leak was born in Washington, DC, and grew up on the beautiful South Jersey shores of Long Beach Island. An antiques conservator by trade, she has always been fascinated by history and the stories objects could tell if they could speak. When she isn't bingeing 1940s noir films, she's writing or photographing nature on the spring-fed azure rivers of Central Florida. She has an Associate of Science degree in graphic design and is a devoted night owl.

In the Shadow of Truth is the third novel in the Shadow series.

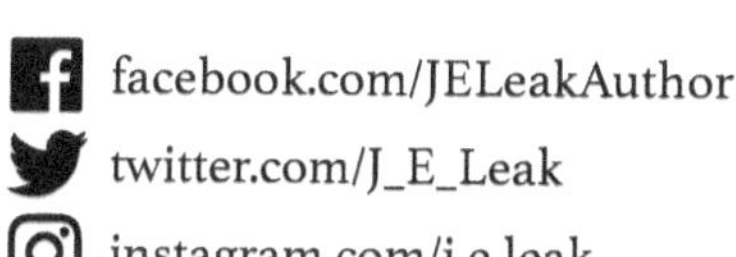

facebook.com/JELeakAuthor

twitter.com/J_E_Leak

instagram.com/j.e.leak

9 781955 294065